JONATHAN SWIFT was born in Dublin, Ireland, on November 30, 1667. He attended Kilkenny Grammar School and graduated from Trinity College. From 1689 to 1699, he worked as secretary to Sir William Temple in Moor Park, Surrey, England, returning for a short period to Ireland in 1694, where he was ordained an Anglican priest. It was during his stay in Moor Park that Swift became involved in contemporary history and discovered his talent for writing intense, almost murderous satire. From 1708 to 1714, much of his time was spent on ecclesiastic missions in London, where the brilliance of his political pamphleteering earned him the respect of the leading governmental figures of his day. For the remaining thirty-odd years of his life, he served as Dean of St. Patrick's Cathedral in Dublin. During this period he wrote *Gulliver's Travels* (published in 1726) and went on to become a national hero for defending Ireland against the inequities of the English Whigs. Jonathan Swift died at the age of seventy-seven, on October 19, 1745. His body was interred in St. Patrick's Cathedral.

LEO DAMROSCH was educated at Yale, Cambridge, and Princeton universities, and has taught at the universities of Virginia and Maryland and at Harvard University, where he is presently Ernest Bernbaum Professor of Literature. He has published nine books on such subjects as Samuel Johnson, Alexander Pope, William Blake, and the eighteenth-century novel.

Gulliver's Travels

BY *Jonathan Swift*

WITH A NEW INTRODUCTION
BY LEO DAMROSCH

Revised and Updated Bibliography

A SIGNET CLASSIC

SIGNET CLASSIC
Published by New American Library, a division of
Penguin Putnam Inc., 375 Hudson Street,
New York, New York 10014, U.S.A.
Penguin Books Ltd, 27 Wrights Lane,
London W8 5TZ, England
Penguin Books Australia Ltd, Ringwood,
Victoria, Australia
Penguin Books Canada Ltd, 10 Alcorn Avenue,
Toronto, Ontario, Canada M4V 3B2
Penguin Books (N.Z.) Ltd, 182–190 Wairau Road,
Auckland 10, New Zealand

Penguin Books Ltd, Registered Offices:
Harmondsworth, Middlesex, England

Published by Signet Classic, an imprint of New American Library,
a division of Penguin Putnam Inc.

First Signet Classic Printing, February 1960
First printing (Damrosch Introduction), June 1999
10 9 8 7 6 5 4 3 2

 REGISTERED TRADEMARK—MARCA REGISTRADA

Printed in the United States of America

INTRODUCTION

In 1726 a book was published in London entitled *Travels into Several Remote Nations of the World,* ostensibly written "by Lemuel Gulliver, First a Surgeon, and then a Captain of several Ships." Only a few intimate friends knew that the real author was Dr. Jonathan Swift, the distinguished Dean of the Anglican St. Patrick's Cathedral in Dublin. Readers appreciated its novel mixture of corrosive satire and tongue-in-cheek mimicry of conventional travel writing, and it sold well, but no one knew quite what to make of it. Samuel Johnson remembered fifty years later that *Gulliver's Travels*, as it came to be known, was then "a production so new and strange that it filled the reader with a mingled emotion of merriment and amazement." Swift was amused to hear of a bishop who said he hardly believed a word of it, which implies that he did believe some of it.

Swift's critique of the weaknesses of human nature is as piercing today as it ever was, and the term "Swiftian" has come to mean a special kind of biting ironic wit. At many points Gulliver is (as his name implies) a gullible vehicle of the satire, a mere mouthpiece for the author's views. But in its most memorable passages *Gulliver's Travels* is a masterpiece of fantasy, with its unforgettable little people, giant people, flying islands, and talking horses. Swift was a profoundly skeptical person who had little patience with the pretence, in the newly popular genre of the realistic novel, to present plausible details as if they were literally true. In 1719 Daniel Defoe had published an immensely popular novel, *The Life and Strange Surprising Adventures of Robinson Crusoe of York, Mariner . . . Written by Himself*, that claimed not to be a novel at all. One of Swift's goals in *Gulliver's*

Travels was to show that truth and fiction are more closely intertwined than we normally acknowledge: "facts" can never be established with certainty, and every story (certainly including *Robinson Crusoe*) is suffused with imagination.

In the First Voyage of *Gulliver's Travels*, the shipwrecked narrator awakens to find himself pricked by tiny arrows and immobilized by tiny ropes, an image that has been imitated by countless cartoonists ever since. In Lilliput human follies are made ridiculous by being miniaturized. In the early years of the eighteenth century Swift was deeply engaged in London political controversy, a passionate partisan of the governing Tory party, but when his associates fell from power in 1714, he retreated to his native Ireland in what he regarded as a humiliating exile, since he had hoped to be appointed a bishop in England, and all further advancement in his profession was now at an end. He felt nothing but contempt thereafter for the self-serving pettiness of politicians. In the First Voyage of *Gulliver's Travels*, advancement in the Lilliputian court is accomplished by skill at "leaping and creeping," and Sir Robert Walpole, the powerful Whig prime minister of Britain, is transformed into Flimnap, who dances on a rope an inch higher than his rivals. In the little world of Lilliput, Gulliver literally looks down at the inhabitants, who think they would be doing him a favor if they put out his eyes instead of killing him, and who use him as a super-weapon to defeat their enemy Blefuscu (a parodic reenactment of the ongoing rivalry between Britain and France).

Swift had a deeply conservative temperament, and believed that the modern world was controlled by an unholy alliance between commercial speculators and hired politicians who had no compunction about pillaging their country for personal gain. He was completely unsympathetic to the vast imperial expansion on which Britain's wealth was increasingly based. Ireland had long been exploited as a virtual colony of England, and a few years before he began writing *Gulliver's Travels* Swift became an Irish hero for leading the fight against English imposition of a debased coinage that would have profited only a few insiders. But although he hated oppression, he had little sympathy for its acquiescent victims, and he was no conventional patriot. As his savage satire *A Modest Proposal* reveals, Swift thought the Irish were to blame for their own failure to stand up to oppression, and in a late poem, a defense of his career entitled *Verses on the Death of Dr. Swift*, he referred bitterly to Ireland as "the land of fens and slaves."

In the Second Voyage, in Brobdingnag, the tables are turned. Now it is Gulliver who is tiny, and the King of Brobdingnag "could not forbear taking me up in his right hand, and stroking me gently with the other, after an hearty fit of laughing, asked me whether I were a Whig or a Tory," marveling that human grandeur "could be mimicked by such diminutive insects as I." The more Gulliver proudly describes the European way of life, the more the king is appalled by the selfishness and cruelty he inadvertently reveals: "I cannot but conclude the bulk of your natives to be the most pernicious race of little odious vermin that nature ever suffered to crawl upon the surface of the earth." Gulliver totally misunderstands what the king is saying; soon afterwards he tries to persuade the king to make gunpowder, while the king expresses a philosophy very close to Swift's own—that a person who could make two ears of corn grow where only one had grown before would be more valuable "than the whole race of politicians put together."

The idea of big and little people no doubt began as a simple authorial device of alienating perspective: we look down on the Lilliputians, the Brobdingnagians look down on us. But once the story begins it is difficult not to enter into the fantasy in a more immediate way. The Lilliputians are captivatingly tiny, but they are also dangerously vulnerable; it would be all too easy to crush them, and at times Gulliver is tempted to do so. Conversely, in Brobdingnag, it is Gulliver who could be crushed by people who do not even realize he is there. The bafflement with which the Lilliputians regard his belongings—he consults his watch so often that they think it must be his god—is defamiliarizing in the same way that the changes in scale in *Alice in Wonderland* are, making us see the world, as children do, in all its strangeness. Swift himself probably found writing fantastic tales to be liberating from the constraints of decorum and professional routine. When Gulliver is chained inside a church like a dog in a doghouse, one suspects that Swift sometimes felt painfully tied down to St. Patrick's Cathedral and even to the ecclesiastical profession in general. Writing satires, fantasies, and comic poems—all of which he published anonymously and enjoyed denying that he had written—must have been an indispensable relief for him.

Unlike Swift, Gulliver has no sense of humor, and he never suspects that anything that happens during his travels could possibly be funny. Moreover, he has a chameleonlike tendency to absorb the values of his hosts. When he is accused of impropriety with the Lilliputian Treasurer's wife he responds indignantly that he was never once alone with her, and adds proudly that "I then had the honour to be a *Nardac*, which the Treasurer himself is not; for all the world knows he is only a *Clumglum*, a title inferior by one degree, as that of a Marquis is to a Duke in England." Swift has transposed the British fascination with aristocracy to the island of tiny people, and he has Gulliver overlook the biggest incongruity of all, that he is defending himself against the charge of sexual misconduct with a woman who is only six inches high. But if differences of scale are comic here, at other times they produce more disturbing effects, just as they do in *Alice*. In the Second Voyage, when the enormous maids of honor are disturbing Gulliver with their massive physicality, one senses a deep anxiety about the body that Swift did in fact harbor throughout his life. (In particular, he was tormented by an incurable condition of the inner ear, Ménière's syndrome, that caused nauseating vertigo and sometimes made ordinary conversation impossible.) When Gulliver attends the public execution of a criminal, as was still a common pastime in eighteenth-century Europe, the vast size of the victim

makes it seem like something in a fairy tale or a night-
mare: when the axe falls, blood spurts like a fountain
into the air, "and the head, when it fell on the scaffold
floor, gave such a bounce, as made me start, although I
were at least half an English mile distant."

The Third Voyage of *Gulliver's Travels* has less narrative drive than the first two, and it may seem like a
miscellaneous attack on various attitudes and practices
that Swift happened to dislike. But its central point has
lost nothing in relevance. The eighteenth century was a
great age of scientific and technological advancement,
and the Academy of Lagado—a parody of the then-new
Royal Academy of London—sponsors a whole range of
futile and often destructive experiments. The rulers,
meanwhile, seem far away, hovering above in the flying
island of Laputa (the Spanish word for "prostitute").
They literally live with their heads in the clouds, hopelessly out of touch with practical realities and needing a
servant to slap them on the face when it is their turn to
speak. But the satire has a sinister side, since whenever
the people below attempt to resist arbitrary rule, the
island is maneuvered into position to crush them. Swift
was profoundly prophetic, foreseeing how easily science
and technology could be coopted as tools of political
power.

Still more disillusioned is the Fourth Voyage: Gulliver's stay in the land of the Houyhnhnms produces a
grim picture of human nature that has struck many people as shockingly misanthropic. Swift would not have
objected to this view. He wrote to the poet Alexander
Pope in 1725, "I hate and detest that animal called man,
although I heartily love John, Peter, Thomas, and so
forth. . . . I have got materials toward a treatise proving
the falsity of that definition *animal rationale*, and to show
it would be only *rationis capax*. Upon this great foundation of misanthropy the whole building of my *Travels* is
erected." Ever since ancient times man had been defined
by philosophers such as Aristotle as *animal rationale*, the
rational animal. Swift's point in his remark to Pope is
that man is really an irrational animal, potentially capa-

ble of reason (*rationis capax*) but rarely using it. In his view, one can and should love individuals ("John, Peter, Thomas, and so forth"), but it remains true that the human race as a whole is disastrously corrupt. In this he was simply reiterating a long-established strain of religious thought. One admirer of the Fourth Voyage was the Methodist founder Charles Wesley.

Much satire—Pope's, for example—invites the reader to join with the author in comfortable superiority to fools and knaves. Swift's satire is altogether different, and far more challenging. To be sure, he once ruefully observed, "Satire is a sort of glass, wherein beholders do generally discover everybody's face but their own." Throughout *Gulliver's Travels*, however, the shifts in perspective and the sharp-edged ironies work to unsettle our self-esteem and to make it difficult for us to judge others complacently. Gulliver adores the Houyhnhnms, but they are so coolly rational and so blankly humorless that few readers will be tempted to identify with them as he does. The name of these rational horses is probably meant to be pronounced "whinnims," and scholars have discovered that in the logic textbook Swift studied in college, man is defined as the rational animal and the horse is playfully defined as the whinnying animal, *animal hinniendi.* Horses in ordinary experience are not especially bright, but Swift turns the conventional distinction upside down, as the whinnying animal disconcertingly becomes the rational one.

A truly rational animal would not only be very different from us, it would despise our irrationality, and Gulliver is forced to admit that he is much more like the quarrelsome, excrement-flinging Yahoos—who certainly mistake him for one of their own kind—than he is like the passionless horses who treat the Yahoos as slaves. The land of the Houyhnhnms is a utopia, which means "nowhere" in Greek, a world where lying has no meaning and governments are unnecessary. It thus represents an imaginary standard by which to judge the world we actually know, which is hopelessly remote from the rational ideal. "I am not in the least provoked," Gulliver writes at the very end of the book, "at the sight of a lawyer, a pickpocket, a colonel, a fool, a lord, a gamester, a politician, a whore-master, a physician, an evidence [giver of false evidence in court], a suborner [briber], an attorney, a traitor, or the like." Swift was a master of this kind of deadpan catalogue, implying that there is no significant difference between a gambler and a politician or between an attorney and a traitor. But even if Gulliver is able to accept the inevitability of vice and crime, he is taught by the Houyhnhnms to hate the outrageous presumptuousness with which human beings assert their self-importance: ". . . when I behold a lump of deformity and diseases both in body and mind, smitten with *pride*, it immediately breaks all the measures of my patience. . . . The wise and virtuous Houyhnhnms, who abound in all excellencies that can adorn a rational creature, have no name for this vice in their language." A central tenet of Christian doctrine is that pride is the fundamental sin, the one that motivated Satan's rebellion, and it follows that a being consumed by pride has no right at all to define itself as the rational animal.

Gulliver's long gaze into the abyss of moral failure proves too unsettling to bear, and he becomes almost hysterical at the end of the book. He fails to appreciate that some people (like the captain Don Pedro de Mendez who rescues him) can be generous, he loathes the very smell of human beings, and he deserts his family to live in a stable. But perhaps a direct confrontation with the less attractive elements of human nature would indeed be intolerable for most people. Swift never exempted himself from his own corrosive irony. *Gulliver's Travels* is prefaced by "A Letter from Capt. Gulliver to his Cousin Sympson," in which Gulliver complains that six months after publication his book has produced no reforms, and concludes that "I have now done with all such visionary schemes for ever." Swift himself, misanthrope or not, dedicated his life to improve the world in practical ways, but he had an increasing sense of the hopelessness of the task, and in

Gulliver's ingenuous disappointment he may well be laughing sardonically at his own folly.

Whether or not Swift would have liked to live like an impassive Houyhnhnm, that was never possible for him. As the Irish poet William Butler Yeats wrote, "The heart in his blood-sodden breast had dragged him down into mankind." One of the most disturbing episodes in *Gulliver's Travels* is the account of the Struldbruggs in the Third Voyage, who cannot die but exist in a perpetual senility. Swift's contemporaries believed that he had gone mad in his last years, but in fact he succumbed to a condition which then had no name, but which we know today as Alzheimer's Disease. He may even have foreseen his fate, for when he was walking with a friend one day he unexpectedly remarked, "I shall be like that tree, dead at the top first." In 1743 his housekeeper told him that bonfires were being prepared to celebrate his birthday, and he replied bleakly, "It is all folly; they had better let it alone." In the next year he tried to speak to a visitor, and when he could not find the words he made his last recorded utterance, "I am a fool." A year later the great writer was dead. But he had already left us his true last words, the epitaph he wrote for himself that quoted the Roman satirist Juvenal: "He has gone where savage indignation can lacerate his heart no more."

—Leo Damrosch
Harvard University

I HOPE you will be ready to own publicly, whenever you shall be called to it, that by your great and frequent urgency you prevailed on me to publish a very loose and uncorrect account of my travels; with direction to hire some young gentlemen of either university to put them in order, and correct the style, as my cousin Dampier did by my advice, in his book called *A Voyage round the World*. But I do not remember I gave you power to consent that any thing should be omitted, and much less that any thing should be inserted: therefore, as to the latter, I do here renounce every thing of that kind; particularly a paragraph about her Majesty the late Queen Anne, of most pious and glorious memory; although I did reverence and esteem her more than any of human species. But you, or your interpolator, ought to have considered, that as it was not my inclination, so was it not decent to praise any animal of our composition before my master Houyhnhnm: and besides the fact was altogether false; for to my knowledge, being in England during some part of her Majesty's reign, she did govern by a chief minister; nay, even by two successively; the first whereof was the Lord of Godolphin, and the second the Lord of Oxford; so that you have made me *say the thing that was not*. Likewise, in the account of the Academy of Projectors, and several passages of my discourse to my master Houyhnhnm, you have either omitted some material circumstances, or minced or changed them in such a manner, that I do hardly know my own work. When I formerly hinted to you something of this in a letter, you were pleased to answer that you were afraid of giving offence; that people in power were very watchful over the press, and apt not only to interpret, but to punish every thing which looked like an *innuendo* (as I think you called it). But pray, how could that which I spoke so many years ago, and at about five thousand

leagues distance, in another reign, be applied to any of
the Yahoos who now are said to govern the herd; especially at a time when I little thought on or feared the
unhappiness of living under them? Have not I the most
reason to complain, when I see these very Yahoos carried by Houyhnhnms in a vehicle, as if these were brutes,
and those the rational creatures? And indeed, to avoid
so monstrous and detestable a sight was one principal
motive of my retirement hither.

Thus much I thought proper to tell you in relation to
yourself, and to the trust I reposed in you.

I do in the next place complain of my own great want
of judgement, in being prevailed upon by the entreaties
and false reasonings of you and some others, very much
against my own opinion, to suffer my travels to be published. Pray bring to your mind how often I desired you
to consider, when you insisted on the motive of public
good; that the Yahoos were a species of animals utterly
incapable of amendment by precepts or examples: and
so it hath proved; for instead of seeing a full stop put
to all abuses and corruptions, at least in this little island,
as I had reason to expect: behold, after above six months
warning, I cannot learn that my book hath produced one
single effect according to my intentions: I desired you
would let me know by a letter, when party and faction
were extinguished; judges learned and upright; pleaders
honest and modest, with some tincture of common sense;
and Smithfield blazing with pyramids of law-books; the
young nobility's education entirely changed; the physicians banished; the female Yahoos abounding in virtue,
honour, truth and good sense; courts and levees of great
ministers thoroughly weeded and swept; wit, merit and
learning rewarded; all disgracers of the press in prose
and verse condemned to eat nothing but their own cotton, and quench their thirst with their own ink. These
and a thousand other reformations, I firmly counted
upon by your encouragement; as indeed they were
plainly deducible from the precepts delivered in my
book. And it must be owned that seven months were a
sufficient time to correct every vice and folly to which

Yahoos are subject, if their natures had been capable of the least disposition to virtue or wisdom: yet so far have you been from answering my expectation in any of your letters, that on the contrary you are loading our carrier every week with libels, and keys, and reflections, and memoirs, and second parts; wherein I see myself accused of reflecting upon great states-folk, of degrading human nature (for so they have still the confidence to style it), and of abusing the female sex. I find likewise that the writers of those bundles are not agreed among themselves; for some of them will not allow me to be author of my own travels; and others make me author of books to which I am wholly a stranger.

I find likewise that your printer hath been so careless as to confound the times, and mistake the dates of my several voyages and returns; neither assigning the true year, or the true month, or day of the month: and I hear the original manuscript is all destroyed since the publication of my book. Neither have I any copy left: however I have sent you some corrections, which you may insert, if ever there should be a second edition: and yet I cannot stand to them, but shall leave that matter to my judicious and candid readers, to adjust it as they please.

I hear some of our sea-Yahoos find fault with my sea-language, as not proper in many parts, nor now in use. I cannot help it. In my first voyages, while I was young, I was instructed by the oldest mariners, and learned to speak as they did. But I have since found that the sea-Yahoos are apt, like the land ones, to become newfangled in their words, which the latter change every year, insomuch as I remember upon each return to my own country their old dialect was so altered that I could hardly understand the new. And I observe, when any Yahoo comes from London out of curiosity to visit me at my own house, we neither of us are able to deliver our conceptions in a manner intelligible to the other.

If the censure of Yahoos could any way affect me, I should have great reason to complain that some of them are so bold as to think my book of travels a mere fiction out of my own brain, and have gone so far as to drop hints that the Houyhnhnms and Yahoos have no more existence than the inhabitants of Utopia.

Indeed I must confess, that as to the people of Lilliput, Brobdingrag (for so the word should have been spelt, and not erroneously Brobdingnag), and Laputa, I have never yet heard of any Yahoos so presumptuous as to dispute their being, or the facts I have related concerning them; because the truth immediately strikes every reader with conviction. And is there less probability in my account of the Houyhnhnms or Yahoos, when it is manifest as to the latter, there are so many thousands even in this city, who only differ from their brother brutes in Houyhnhnm-land, because they use a sort of a jabber, and do not go naked? I wrote for their amendment, and not their approbation. The united praise of the whole race would be of less consequence to me than the neighing of those two degenerate Houyhnhnms I keep in my stable; because from these, degenerate as they are, I still improve in some virtues, without any mixture of vice.

Do these miserable animals presume to think that I am so far degenerated as to defend my veracity? Yahoo as I am, it is well known through all Houyhnhnm-land, that by the instructions and example of my illustrious master I was able in the compass of two years (although I confess with the utmost difficulty) to remove that infernal habit of lying, shuffling, deceiving, and equivocating, so deeply rooted in the very souls of all my species, especially the Europeans.

I have other complaints to make upon this vexatious occasion; but I forbear troubling myself or you any further. I must freely confess, that since my last return some corruptions of my Yahoo nature have revived in me by conversing with a few of your species, and particularly those of my own family, by an unavoidable necessity; else I should never have attempted so absurd a project as that of reforming the Yahoo race in this kingdom; but I have now done with all such visionary schemes for ever.

April 2, 1727.

The PUBLISHER *to the* READER

THE author of these Travels, Mr. Lemuel Gulliver, is my ancient and intimate friend; there is likewise some relation between us by the mother's side. About three years ago Mr. Gulliver, growing weary of the concourse of curious people coming to him at his house in Redriff, made a small purchase of land, with a convenient house, near Newark in Nottinghamshire, his native country; where he now lives retired, yet in good esteem among his neighbors.

Although Mr. Gulliver was born in Nottinghamshire, where his father dwelt, yet I have heard him say his family came from Oxfordshire; to confirm which, I have observed in the churchyard at Banbury, in that county, several tombs and monuments of the Gullivers.

Before he quitted Redriff, he left the custody of the following papers in my hands, with the liberty to dispose of them as I should think fit. I have carefully perused them three times: the style is very plain and simple; and the only fault I find is, that the author, after the manner of travellers, is a little too circumstantial. There is an air of truth apparent through the whole; and indeed the author was so distinguished for his veracity, that it became a sort of proverb among his neighbors at Redriff, when any one affirmed a thing, to say it was as true as if Mr. Gulliver had spoke it.

By the advice of several worthy persons, to whom, with the author's permission, I communicated these papers, I now venture to send them into the world, hoping they may be at least, for some time, a better entertainment to our young noblemen than the common scribbles of politics and party.

This volume would have been at least twice as large, if I had not made bold to strike out innumerable passages relating to the winds and tides, as well as to the variations and bearings in the several voyages; together with the minute descriptions of the management of the ship in storms, in the style of sailors: likewise the account of the longitudes and latitudes; wherein I have reason to apprehend that Mr. Gulliver may be a little dissatisfied: but I was resolved to fit the work as much as possible to the general capacity of readers. However, if my own ignorance in sea-affairs shall have led me to commit some mistakes, I alone am answerable for them: and if any traveller hath a curiosity to see the whole work at large, as it came from the hand of the author, I shall be ready to gratify him.

As for any further particulars relating to the author, the reader will receive satisfaction from the first pages of the book.

Richard Sympson

CONTENTS

Part I
A VOYAGE TO LILLIPUT

Part II
A Voyage to Brobdingnag

Part III
A VOYAGE TO LAPUTA, BALNIBARBI, LUGGNAGG, GLUBBDUBDRIB, AND JAPAN

Part IV
A Voyage to the Country of
the Houyhnhnms

TRAVELS

INTO SEVERAL

Remote Nations

OF THE

WORLD

By Captain LEMUEL GULLIVER

Part I. A VOYAGE TO *LILLIPUT*

Part II. A VOYAGE TO *BROBDINGNAG*

Part III. A VOYAGE TO *LAPUTA* &c

Part IV. A VOYAGE TO THE

HOUYHNHNMS

LONDON:

Printed in the Year MDCCXXVI

LILLIPUT
and
Blefuscu

Hogs I
P. Mintaon
I. Good Fortune
I Nassow
Sunda
Sillabar
Straits of Sunda

SUMATRA

Blefuscu

Blefuscu
Mildendo LILLIPUT
Discovered, A.D. 1699

Dimens Land

Chapter I *The Author gives some account of himself and family. His first inducements to travel.
He is shipwrecked, and swims for his life, gets
safe on shore in the country of Lilliput, is
made a prisoner, and carried up the country.*

M Y FATHER had a small state in Nottinghamshire; I
was the third of five sons. He sent me to Emanuel
College in Cambridge at fourteen years old, where I resided three years, and applied myself close to my studies:
but the charge of maintaining me (although I had a very
scanty allowance) being too great for a narrow fortune,
I was bound apprentice to Mr. James Bates, an eminent
surgeon in London, with whom I continued four years;
and my father now and then sending me small sums of
money, I laid them out in learning navigation, and other
parts of the mathematics, useful to those who intend to
travel, as I always believed it would be some time or
other my fortune to do. When I left Mr. Bates, I went
down to my father; where, by the assistance of him and
my uncle John, and some other relations, I got forty
pounds, and a promise of thirty pounds a year to main
tain me at Leyden: there I studied physic two years and
seven months, knowing it would be useful in long
voyages.

Soon after my return from Leyden, I was recommended, by my good master Mr. Bates, to be surgeon
to the *Swallow*, Captain Abraham Pannell commander;
with whom I continued three years and a half, making
a voyage or two into the Levant, and some other parts.
When I came back, I resolved to settle in London, to
which Mr. Bates, my master, encouraged me, and by him
I was recommended to several patients. I took part of a
small house in the Old Jury; and being advised to alter

my condition, I married Mrs. Mary Burton, second daughter to Mr. Edmund Burton, hosier in Newgatestreet, with whom I received four hundred pounds for a portion.

But, my good master Bates dying in two years after, and I having few friends, my business began to fail; for my conscience would not suffer me to imitate the bad practice of too many among my brethren. Having therefore consulted with my wife, and some of my acquaintance, I determined to go again to sea. I was surgeon successively in two ships, and made several voyages, for six years, to the East and West-Indies, by which I got some addition to my fortune. My hours of leisure I spent in reading the best authors, ancient and modern, being always provided with a good number of books; and when I was ashore, in observing the manners and dispositions of the people, as well as learning their language, wherein I had a great facility by the strength of my memory.

The last of these voyages not proving very fortunate, I grew weary of the sea, and intended to stay at home with my wife and family. I removed from the Old Jury to Fetter-Lane, and from thence to Wapping, hoping to get business among the sailors, but it would not turn to account. After three years expectation that things would mend, I accepted an advantageous offer from Captain William Prichard, master of the *Antelope*, who was making a voyage to the South-Sea. We set sail from Bristol May 4, 1699, and our voyage at first was very prosperous.

It would not be proper, for some reasons, to trouble the reader with the particulars of our adventures in those seas: let it suffice to inform him, that in our passage from thence to the East-Indies, we were driven by a violent storm to the north-west of Van Diemen's Land. By an observation, we found ourselves in the latitude of 30 degrees 2 minutes south. Twelve of our crew were dead by immoderate labour and ill food, the rest were in a very weak condition. On the fifth of November, which was the beginning of summer in those parts, the weather being very hazy, the seamen spied a rock, within half a cable's length of the ship; but the wind was so strong, that we were driven directly upon it, and immediately split. Six of the crew, of whom I was one, having let down the boat into the sea, made a shift to get clear of the ship, and the rock. We rowed by my computation about three leagues, till we were able to work no longer, being already spent with labour while we were in the ship. We therefore trusted ourselves to the mercy of the waves, and in about half an hour the boat was overset by a sudden flurry from the north. What became of my companions in the boat, as well as of those who escaped on the rock, or were left in the vessel, I cannot tell; but conclude they were all lost. For my own part, I swam as fortune directed me, and was pushed forward by wind and tide. I often let my legs drop, and could feel no bottom; but when I was almost gone, and able to struggle no longer, I found myself within my depth; and by this time the storm was much abated. The declivity was so small, that I walked near a mile before I got to the shore, which I conjectured was about eight o'clock in the evening. I then advanced forward near half a mile, but could not discover any sign of houses or inhabitants; at least I was in so weak a condition, that I did not observe them. I was extremely tired, and with that, and the heat of the weather, and about half a pint of brandy that I drank as I left the ship, I found myself much inclined to sleep. I lay down on the grass, which was very short and soft, where I slept sounder than ever I remember to have done in my life, and, as I reckoned, above nine hours; for when I awaked, it was just daylight. I attempted to rise, but was not able to stir: for, as I happened to lie on my back, I found my arms and legs were strongly fastened on each side to the ground; and my hair, which was long and thick, tied down in the same manner. I likewise felt several slender ligatures across my body, from my armpits to my thighs. I could only look upwards; the sun began to grow hot, and the light offended my eyes. I heard a confused noise about me, but in the posture I lay, could see nothing except the sky. In a little time I felt something alive moving on my left leg, which advancing gently forward over my

breast, came almost up to my chin; when bending my
eyes downwards as much as I could, I perceived it to be
a human creature not six inches high, with a bow and
arrow in his hands, and a quiver at his back. In the mean
time, I felt at least forty more of the same kind (as
I conjectured) following the first. I was in the utmost
astonishment, and roared so loud, that they all ran back
in a fright; and some of them, as I was afterwards told,
were hurt with the falls they got by leaping from my
sides upon the ground. However, they soon returned,
and one of them, who ventured so far as to get a full
sight of my face, lifting up his hands and eyes by way
of admiration, cried out in a shrill but distinct voice,
Hekinah degul: the others repeated the same words several times, but I then knew not what they meant. I lay
all this while, as the reader may believe, in great uneasiness: at length, struggling to get loose, I had the fortune
to break the strings, and wrench out the pegs that fastened my left arm to the ground; for, by lifting it up to
my face, I discovered the methods they had taken to
bind me, and at the same time, with a violent pull, which
gave me excessive pain, I a little loosened the strings
that tied down my hair on the left side, so that I was
just able to turn my head about two inches. But the
creatures ran off a second time, before I could seize
them; whereupon there was a great shout in a very shrill
accent, and after it ceased, I heard one of them cry
aloud, *Tolgo phonac*; when in an instant I felt above an
hundred arrows discharged on my left hand, which
pricked me like so many needles; and besides they shot
another flight into the air, as we do bombs in Europe,
whereof many, I suppose, fell on my body (though I felt
them not) and some on my face, which I immediately
covered with my left hand. When this shower of arrows
was over, I fell a groaning with grief and pain, and then
striving again to get loose, they discharged another vol-
ley larger than the first, and some of them attempted
with spears to stick me in the sides; but, my good luck,
I had on me a buff jerkin, which they could not pierce.
I thought it the most prudent method to lie still, and my

design was to continue so till night, when, my left hand
being already loose, I could easily free myself: and as
for the inhabitants, I had reason to believe I might be a
match for the greatest armies they could bring against
me, if they were all of the same size with him that I saw.
But fortune disposed otherwise of me. When the people
observed I was quiet, they discharged no more arrows;

but, by the noise I heard, I knew their numbers increased; and about four yards from me, over against my
right ear, I heard a knocking for above an hour, like
that of people at work; when turning my head that way,
as well as the pegs and strings would permit me, I saw
a stage erected, about a foot and a half from the ground,
capable of holding four of the inhabitants, with two or
three ladders to mount it: from whence one of them,
who seemed to be a person of quality, made me a long
speech, whereof I understood not one syllable. But I
should have mentioned, that before the principal person
began his oration, he cried out three times, *Langro dehul
san* (these words and the former were afterwards repeated and explained to me). Whereupon immediately
about fifty of the inhabitants came, and cut the strings
that fastened the left side of my head, which gave me
the liberty of turning it to the right, and of observing
the person and gesture of him that was to speak. He
appeared to be of a middle age, and taller than any of
the other three who attended him, whereof one was a
page that held up his train, and seemed to be somewhat
longer than my middle finger; the other two stood one
on each side to support him. He acted every part of an
orator, and I could observe many periods of threatenings, and others of promises, pity, and kindness. I answered in a few words, but in the most submissive
manner, lifting up my left hand and both my eyes to the
sun, as calling him for a witness; and being almost fam-
ished with hunger, having not eaten a morsel for some
hours before I left the ship, I found the demands of
nature so strong upon me, that I could not forbear showing my impatience (perhaps against the strict rules of
decency) by putting my finger frequently on my mouth,
to signify that I wanted food. The *Hurgo* (for so they
call a great lord, as I afterwards learnt) understood me
very well. He descended from the stage, and commanded
that several ladders should be applied to my sides, on
which above an hundred of the inhabitants mounted,
and walked towards my mouth, laden with baskets full
of meat, which had been provided, and sent thither by

the King's orders, upon the first intelligence he received
of me. I observed there was the flesh of several animals,
but could not distinguish them by the taste. There were
shoulders, legs, and loins, shaped like the wings of a
lark. I ate them by two or three at a mouthful, and took
three loaves at a time, about the bigness of musket bullets. They supplied me as they could, showing a thousand
marks of wonder and astonishment at my bulk and appetite. I then made another sign that I wanted drink. They
found by my eating that a small quantity would not suffice me, and being a most ingenious people, they slung
up with great dexterity one of their largest hogsheads,
then rolled it towards my hand, and beat out the top; I
drank it off at a draught, which I might well do, for it
did not hold half a pint, and tasted like a small wine of
Burgundy, but much more delicious. They brought me a
second hogshead, which I drank in the same manner,
and made signs for more, but they had none to give me.
When I had performed these wonders, they shouted for
joy, and danced upon my breast, repeating several times
as they did at first, *Hekinah degul*. They made me a sign
that I should throw down the two hogsheads, but first
warning the people below to stand out of the way, crying
aloud, *Borach mivola*, and when they saw the vessels in
the air, there was an universal shout of *Hekinah degul*.
I confess I was often tempted, while they were passing
backwards and forwards on my body, to seize forty or
fifty of the first that came in my reach, and dash them
against the ground. But the remembrance of what I had
felt, which probably might not be the worst they could
do, and the promise of honour I made them, for so I
interpreted my submissive behaviour, soon drove out
these imaginations. Besides, I now considered myself as
bound by the laws of hospitality to a people who had
treated me with so much expense and magnificence.
However, in my thoughts I could not sufficiently wonder
at the intrepidity of these diminutive mortals who durst
venture to mount and walk upon my body, while one of
my hands was at liberty, without trembling at the very
sight of so prodigious a creature as I must appear to

them. After some time, when they observed that I made
no more demands for meat, there appeared before me
a person of high rank from his Imperial Majesty. His
Excellency, having mounted on the small of my right leg,
advanced forwards up to my face, with about a dozen of
his retinue. And producing his credentials under the Signet Royal, which he applied close to my eyes, spoke ten
minutes, without any signs of anger, but with a kind of
determinate resolution; often pointing forwards, which,
as I afterwards found, was towards the capital city, about
half a mile distant, whither it was agreed by his Majesty
in council that I must be conveyed. I answered in few
words, but to no purpose, and made a sign with my
hand that was loose, putting it to the other (but over his
Excellency's head, for fear of hurting him or his train)
and then to my own head and body, to signify that I
desired my liberty. It appeared that he understood me
well enough, for he shook his head by way of disappro-
bation, and held his hand in a posture to show that I
must be carried as a prisoner. However, he made other
signs to let me understand that I should have meat and
drink enough, and very good treatment. Whereupon I
once more thought of attempting to break my bonds,
but again, when I felt the smart of their arrows upon
my face and hands, which were all in blisters, and many
of the darts still sticking in them, and observing likewise
that the number of my enemies increased, I gave tokens
to let them know that they might do with me what they
pleased. Upon this the *Hurgo* and his train withdrew
with much civility and cheerful countenances. Soon after
I heard a general shout, with frequent repetitions of the
words, *Peplom selan*, and I felt great numbers of the
people on my left side relaxing the cords to such a degree, that I was able to turn upon my right, and to ease
myself with making water; which I very plentifully did,
to the great astonishment of the people, who conjectur-
ing by my motions what I was going to do, immediately
opened to the right and left on that side, to avoid the
torrent which fell with such noise and violence from me.
But before this, they had daubed my face and both my

hands with a sort of ointment very pleasant to the smell, which in a few minutes removed all the smart of their arrows. These circumstances, added to the refreshment I had received by their victuals and drink, which were very nourishing, disposed me to sleep. I slept about eight hours, as I was afterwards assured; and it was no wonder, for the physicians, by the Emperor's order, had mingled a sleepy potion in the hogsheads of wine.

It seems that upon the first moment I was discovered sleeping on the ground after my landing, the Emperor had early notice of it by an express; and determined in council that I should be tied in the manner I have related (which was done in the night while I slept), that plenty of meat and drink should be sent me, and a machine prepared to carry me to the capital city.

This resolution perhaps may appear very bold and dangerous, and I am confident would not be imitated by any prince in Europe on the like occasion; however, in my opinion, it was extremely prudent, as well as generous. For supposing these people had endeavoured to kill me with their spars and arrows while I was asleep, I should certainly have awaked with the first sense of smart, which might so far have roused my rage and strength, as to have enabled me to break the strings wherewith I was tied; after which, as they were not able to make resistance, so they could expect no mercy.

These people are most excellent mathematicians, and arrived to a great perfection in mechanics by the countenance and encouragement of the Emperor, who is a renowned patron of learning. This prince hath several machines fixed on wheels for the carriage of trees and other great weights. He often builds his largest men-of-war, whereof some are nine foot long, in the woods where the timber grows, and has them carried on these engines three or four hundred yards to the sea. Five hundred carpenters and engineers were immediately set at work to prepare the greatest engine they had. It was a frame of wood raised three inches from the ground, about seven foot long and four wide, moving upon twenty-two wheels. The shout I heard was upon the arrival of this engine, which it seems set out in four hours after my landing. It was brought parallel to me as I lay. But the principal difficulty was to raise and place me in this vehicle. Eighty poles, each of one foot high, were erected for this purpose, and very strong cords of the bigness of packthread were fastened by hooks to many bandages, which the workmen had girt round my neck, my hands, my body, and my legs. Nine hundred of the strongest men were employed to draw up these cords by many pulleys fastened on the poles, and thus, in less than three hours, I was raised and slung into the engine, and there tied fast. All this I was told, for while the whole operation was performing, I lay in a profound sleep, by the force of that soporiferous medicine infused into my liquor. Fifteen hundred of the Emperor's largest horses, each about four inches and a half high, were employed to draw me towards the metropolis, which, as I said, was half a mile distant.

About four hours after we began our journey, I awaked by a very ridiculous accident; for the carriage being stopped a while to adjust something that was out of order, two or three of the young natives had the curiosity to see how I looked when I was asleep; they climbed up into the engine, and advancing very softly to my face, one of them, an officer in the Guards, put the sharp end of his half-pike a good way up my left nostril, which tickled my nose like a straw, and made me sneeze violently: whereupon they stole off unperceived, and it was three weeks before I knew the cause of my awaking so suddenly. We made a long march the remaining part of that day, and rested at night with five hundred guards on each side of me, half with torches, and half with bows and arrows, ready to shoot me if I should offer to stir. The next morning at sunrise we continued our march, and arrived within two hundred yards of the city gates about noon. The Emperor, and all his court, came out to meet us; but his great officers would by no means suffer his Majesty to endanger his person by mounting on my body.

C E Brock
Th 1894

At the place where the carriage stopped, there stood
an ancient temple, esteemed to be the largest in the
whole kingdom, which having been polluted some years
before by an unnatural murder, was, according to the
zeal of those people, looked on as profane, and therefore
had been applied to common uses, and all the ornaments
and furniture carried away. In this edifice it was determined I should lodge. The great gate fronting to the
north was about four foot high, and almost two foot

wide, through which I could easily creep. On each side
of the gate was a small window not above six inches
from the ground: into that on the left side, the King's
smiths conveyed fourscore and eleven chains, like those
that hang to a lady's watch in Europe, and almost as
large, which were locked to my left leg with six and
thirty padlocks. Over against this temple, on t'other side
of the great highway, at twenty foot distance, there was
a turret at least five foot high. Here the Emperor as-
cended with many principal lords of his court, to have
an opportunity of viewing me, as I was told, for I could
not see them. It was reckoned that above an hundred
thousand inhabitants came out of the town upon the
same errand; and in spite of my guards, I believe there
could not be fewer than ten thousand, at several times,
who mounted upon my body by the help of ladders. But
a proclamation was soon issued to forbid it upon pain
of death. When the workmen found it was impossible
for me to break loose, they cut all the strings that bound
me; whereupon I rose up with as melancholy a disposition as ever I had in my life. But the noise and astonishment of the people at seeing me rise and walk, are not
to be expressed. The chains that held my left leg were
about two yards long, and gave me not only the liberty
of walking backwards and forwards in a semicircle; but,
being fixed within four inches of the gate, allowed me
to creep in, and lie at my full length in the temple.

CO

Chapter II *The Emperor of Lilliput, attended by several of the nobility, come to see the Author in his confinement. The Emperor's person and habit described. Learned men appointed to teach the Author their language. He gains favour by his mild disposition. His pockets are searched, and his sword and pistols taken from him.*

WHEN I FOUND myself on my feet, I looked about me, and must confess I never beheld a more entertaining prospect. The country round appeared like a continued garden, and the inclosed fields, which were generally forty foot square, resembled so many beds of flowers. These fields were intermingled with woods of half a stang, and the tallest trees, as I could judge, appeared to be seven foot high. I viewed the town on my left hand, which looked like the painted scene of a city in a theatre.

I had been for some hours extremely pressed by the necessities of nature; which was no wonder, it being almost two days since I had last disburthened myself. I was under great difficulties between urgency and shame. The best expedient I could think on, was to creep into my house, which I accordingly did; and shutting the gate after me, I went as far as the length of my chain would suffer, and discharged my body of that uneasy load. But this was the only time I was ever guilty of so uncleanly an action; for which I cannot but hope the candid reader will give some allowance, after he hath maturely and impartially considered my case, and the distress I was in. From this time my constant practice was, as soon as I rose, to perform that business in open air, at the full extent of my chain, and due care was taken every morn-

ing before company came, that the offensive matter
should be carried off in wheel-barrows, by two servants
appointed for that purpose. I would not have dwelt so
long upon a circumstance, that perhaps at first sight may
appear not very momentous, if I had not thought it necessary to justify my character in point of cleanliness to
the world; which I am told some of my maligners have
been pleased, upon this and other occasions, to call in
question.

When this adventure was at an end, I came back out
of my house, having occasion for fresh air. The Emperor
was already descended from the tower, and advancing
on horseback towards me, which had like to have cost
him dear; for the beast, though very well trained, yet
wholly unused to such a sight, which appeared as if a
mountain moved before him, reared up on his hinder
feet: but that prince, who is an excellent horseman, kept
his seat, till his attendants ran in, and held the bridle,
while his master had time to dismount. When he
alighted, he surveyed me round with great admiration,
but kept without the length of my chain. He ordered his
cooks and butlers, who were already prepared, to give
me victuals and drink, which they pushed forward in a
sort of vehicles upon wheels till I could reach them. I
took these vehicles, and soon emptied them all; twenty
of them were filled with meat, and ten with liquor; each
of the former afforded me two or three good mouthfuls,
and I emptied the liquor of ten vessels, which was contained in earthen vials, into one vehicle, drinking it off
at a draught; and so I did with the rest. The Empress,
and young Princes of the blood, of both sexes, attended
by many ladies, sat at some distance in their chairs; but
upon the accident that happened to the Emperor's horse,
they alighted, and came near his person, which I am now
going to describe. He is taller by almost the breadth of
my nail than any of his court, which alone is enough to
strike an awe into the beholders. His features are strong
and masculine with an Austrian lip and arched nose, his
complexion olive, his countenance erect, his body and
limbs well proportioned, all his motions graceful, and his

deportment majestic. He was then past his prime, being twenty-eight years and three quarters old, of which he had reigned about seven, in great felicity, and generally victorious. For the better convenience of beholding him, I lay on my side, so that my face was parallel to his, and he stood but three yards off: however, I have had him since many times in my hand, and therefore cannot be deceived in the description. His dress was very plain and simple, and the fashion of it between the Asiatic and the European; but he had on his head a light helmet of gold, adorned with jewels, and a plume on the crest. He held his sword drawn in his hand, to defend himself, if I should happen to break loose; it was almost three inches long, the hilt and scabbard were gold enriched with diamonds. His voice was shrill, but very clear and articulate, and I could distinctly hear it when I stood up. The ladies and courtiers were all most magnificently clad, so that the spot they stood upon seemed to resemble a petticoat spread on the ground, embroidered with figures of gold and silver. His Imperial Majesty spoke often to me, and I returned answers, but neither of us could understand a syllable. There were several of his priests and lawyers present (as I conjectured by their habits) who were commanded to address themselves to me, and I spoke to them in as many languages as I had the least smattering of, which were High and Low Dutch, Latin, French, Spanish, Italian, and Lingua Franca; but all to no purpose. After about two hours the court retired, and I was left with a strong guard, to prevent the impertinence, and probably the malice of the rabble, who were very impatient to crowd about me as near as they durst, and some of them had the impudence to shoot their arrows at me as I sat on the ground by the door of my house, whereof one very narrowly missed my left eye. But the colonel ordered six of the ringleaders to be seized, and thought no punishment so proper as to deliver them bound into my hands, which some of his soldiers accordingly did, pushing them forwards with the butt-ends of their pikes into my reach; I took them all in my right hand, put five of them into my coat-pocket, and as to the sixth, I made a countenance as if I would eat him alive. The poor man squalled terribly, and the colonel and his officers were in much pain, especially when they saw me take out my penknife: but I soon put them out of fear; for, looking mildly, and immediately cutting the strings he was bound with, I set him gently on the ground, and away he ran. I treated the rest in the same manner, taking them one by one out of my pocket, and I observed both the soldiers and people were highly obliged at this mark of my clemency, which was represented very much to my advantage at court.

Towards night I got with some difficulty into my house, where I lay on the ground, and continued to do so about a fortnight; during which time the Emperor gave orders to have a bed prepared for me. Six hundred beds of the common measure were brought in carriages, and worked up in my house; an hundred and fifty of their beds sewn together made up the breadth and length, and these were four double, which however kept me but very indifferently from the hardness of the floor, that was of smooth stone. By the same computation they provided me with sheets, blankets, and coverlets, tolerable enough for one who had been so long inured to hardships as I.

As the news of my arrival spread through the kingdom, it brought prodigious numbers of rich, idle, and curious people to see me; so that the villages were almost emptied, and great neglect of tillage and household affairs must have ensued, if his Imperial Majesty had not provided, by several proclamations and orders of state, against this inconveniency. He directed that those who had already beheld me should return home, and not presume to come within fifty yards of my house without licence from court; whereby the secretaries of state got considerable fees.

In the mean time, the Emperor held frequent councils to debate what course should be taken with me; and I was afterwards assured by a particular friend, a person of great quality, who was looked upon to be as much in the secret as any, that the court was under many difficulties concerning me. They apprehended my breaking loose, that my diet would be very expensive, and might cause a famine. Sometimes they determined to starve me, or at least to shoot me in the face and hands with poisoned arrows, which would soon dispatch me: but again they considered, that the stench of so large a carcass might produce a plague in the metropolis, and probably spread through the whole kingdom. In the midst of these consultations, several officers of the army went to the door of the great council-chamber; and two of them being admitted, gave an account of my behaviour to the six criminals above-mentioned, which made so favourable an impression in the breast of his Majesty and the whole board in my behalf, that an Imperial Commission was issued out, obliging all the villages nine hundred yards round the city, to deliver in every morning six beeves, forty sheep, and other victuals for my sustenance; together with a proportionable quantity of bread, and wine, and other liquors; for the due payment of which his Majesty gave assignments upon his treasury. For this prince lives chiefly upon his own demesnes, seldom, except upon great occasions, raising any subsidies upon his subjects, who are bound to attend him in his wars at their own expense. An establishment was also made of six hundred persons to be my domestics, who had board-wages allowed for their maintenance, and tents built for them very conveniently on each side of my door. It was likewise ordered, that three hundred tailors should make me a suit of clothes after the fashion of the country: that six of his Majesty's greatest scholars should be employed to instruct me in their language: and, lastly, that the Emperor's horses, and those of the nobility, and troops of guards, should be frequently exercised in my sight, to accustom themselves to me. All these orders were duly put in execution, and in about three weeks I made a great progress in learning their language; during which time the Emperor frequently honoured me with his visits, and was pleased to assist my masters in teaching me. We began already to converse together in some sort; and the first words I learnt were to express my desire that he would please to give me my liberty, which I every day repeated on my knees. His answer, as I could apprehend it, was, that this must be a work of time, not to be thought on without the advice of his council, and that first I must *Lumos kelmin pesso desmar lon emposo*; that is, swear a peace with him and his kingdom. However, that I should be used with all kindness; and he advised me to acquire, by my patience and discreet behaviour, the good opinion of himself and his subjects. He desired I would not take it ill, if he gave orders to certain proper officers to search me; for probably I might carry about me several weapons, which must needs be dangerous things, if they answered the bulk of so prodigious a person. I said, his Majesty should be satisfied, for I was ready to strip myself, and turn up my pockets before him. This I delivered part in words, and part in signs. He replied, that by the laws of the kingdom I must be searched by two of his officers; that

he knew this could not be done without my consent and
assistance; that he had so good an opinion of my generosity and justice, as to trust their persons in my hands:
that whatever they took from me should be returned
when I left the country, or paid for at the rate which I
would set upon them. I took up the two officers in my
hands, put them first into my coat-pockets, and then into
every other pocket about me, except my two fobs, and
another secret pocket I had no mind should be searched,
wherein I had some little necessaries that were of no
consequence to any but myself. In one of my fobs there
was a silver watch, and in the other a small quantity of
gold in a purse. These gentlemen, having pen, ink, and
paper about them, made an exact inventory of every
thing they saw; and when they had done, desired I would
set them down, that they might deliver it to the Emperor. This inventory I afterwards translated into En
glish, and is word for word as follows.

Imprimis. In the right coat-pocket of the Great Man-
Mountain (for so I interpret the words *Quinbus Flestrin*)
after the strictest search, we found only one great piece
of coarse cloth, large enough to be a foot-cloth for your
Majesty's chief room of state. In the left pocket we saw
a huge silver chest, with a cover of the same metal,
which we the searchers were not able to lift. We desired
it should be opened, and one of us stepping into it, found
himself up to the mid leg in a sort of dust, some part
whereof flying up to our faces, set us both a sneezing
for several times together. In his right waistcoat-pocket
we found a prodigious bundle of white thin substances,
folded one over another, about the bigness of three men,
tied with a strong cable, and marked with black figures;
which we humbly conceive to be writings, every letter
almost half as large as the palm of our hands. In the left
there was a sort of engine, from the back of which were
extended twenty long poles, resembling the palisados before your Majesty's court; wherewith we conjecture the
Man-Mountain combs his head, for we did not always
trouble him with questions, because we found it a great

difficulty to make him understand us. In the large pocket on the right side of his middle cover (so I translate the word *ranfu-lo*, by which they meant my breeches) we saw a hollow pillar of iron, about the length of a man, fastened to a strong piece of timber, larger than the pillar; and upon one side of the pillar were huge pieces of iron sticking out, cut into strange figures, which we know not what to make of. In the left pocket, another engine of the same kind. In the smaller pocket on the right side, were several round flat pieces of white and red metal, of different bulk; some of the white, which seemed to be silver, were so large and heavy, that my comrade and I could hardly lift them. In the left pocket were two black pillars irregularly shaped: we could not, without difficulty, reach the top of them as we stood at the bottom of his pocket. One of them was covered, and seemed all of a piece: but at the upper end of the other, there appeared a white round substance, about twice the bigness of our heads. Within each of these was enclosed a prodigious plate of steel; which, by our orders, we obliged him to show us, because we apprehended they might be dangerous engines. He took them out of their cases, and told us, that in his own country his practice was to shave his beard with one of these, and to cut his meat with the other. There were two pockets which we could not enter: these he called his fobs; they were two large slits cut into the top of his middle cover, but squeezed close by the pressure of his belly. Out of the right fob hung a great silver chain, with a wonderful kind of engine at the bottom. We directed him to draw out whatever was fastened to that chain; which appeared to be a globe, half silver, and half of some transparent metal: for on the transparent side we saw certain strange figures circularly drawn, and thought we could touch them, till we found our fingers stopped by that lucid substance. He put this engine to our ears, which made an incessant noise like that of a watermill: and we conjecture it is either some unknown animal, or the god that he worships; but we are more inclined to the latter opinion, because he assures us (if we understood him right, for he expressed himself very imperfectly) that he seldom did any thing without consulting it: he called it his oracle, and said it pointed out the time for every action of his life. From the left fob he took out a net almost large enough for a fisherman, but contrived to open and shut like a purse, and served him for the same use: we found therein several massy pieces of yellow metal, which, if they be real gold, must be of immense value.

Having thus, in obedience to your Majesty's commands, diligently searched all his pockets, we observed a girdle about his waist made of the hide of some prodigious animal; from which, on the left side, hung a sword of the length of five men; and on the right, a bag or pouch divided into two cells, each cell capable of holding three of your Majesty's subjects. In one of these cells were several globes or balls of a most ponderous metal, about the bigness of our heads, and requiring a strong hand to lift them: the other cell contained a heap of certain black grains, but of no great bulk or weight, for we could hold above fifty of them in the palms of our hands.

This is an exact inventory of what we found about the body of the Man-Mountain, who used us with great civility, and due respect to your Majesty's commission. Signed and sealed on the fourth day of the eighty-ninth moon of your Majesty's auspicious reign.

CLEFREN FRELOCK, MARSI FRELOCK

When this inventory was read over to the Emperor, he directed me, although in very gentle terms, to deliver up the several particulars. He first called for my scimitar, which I took out, scabbard and all. In the mean time he ordered three thousand of his choicest troops (who then attended him) to surround me at a distance, with their bows and arrows just ready to discharge: but I did not observe it, for my eyes were wholly fixed upon his Majesty. He then desired me to draw my scimitar, which, although it had got some rust by the sea-water, was in most parts exceeding bright. I did so, and immediately all the troops gave a shout between terror and surprise; for the sun shone clear, and the reflection dazzled their eyes as I waved the scimitar to and fro in my hand. His Majesty, who is a most magnanimous prince, was less daunted than I could expect; he ordered me to return it into the scabbard, and cast it on the ground as gently as I could, about six foot from the end of my chain. The next thing he demanded was one of the hollow iron pillars, by which he meant my pocket-pistols. I drew it out, and at his desire, as well as I could, expressed to him the use of it; and charging it only with powder, which by the closeness of my pouch happened to escape wetting in the sea (an inconvenience against which all prudent mariners take special care to provide) I first cautioned the Emperor not to be afraid, and then I let it off in the air. The astonishment here was much greater than at the sight of my scimitar. Hundreds fell down as if they had been struck dead; and even the Emperor, although he stood his ground, could not recover himself in some time. I delivered up both my pistols in the same manner as I had done my scimitar, and then my pouch of powder and bullets; begging him that the former might be kept from the fire, for it would kindle with the smallest spark, and blow up his imperial palace into the air. I likewise delivered up my watch, which the Emperor was very curious to see, and commanded two of his tallest yeomen of the guards to bear it on a pole upon their shoulders, as draymen in England do a barrel of ale. He was amazed at the continual noise it made, and the motion of the minute-hand, which he could easily discern; for their sight is much more acute than ours; and asked the opinions of his learned men about him, which were various and remote, as the reader may well imagine without my repeating; although indeed I could not very perfectly understand them. I then gave up my silver and copper money, my purse with nine large pieces of gold, and some smaller ones; my knife and razor, my comb and silver snuff-box, my handkerchief and journal-book. My scimitar, pistols, and pouch, were conveyed in carriages to his Majesty's stores; but the rest of my goods were returned me.

I had, as I before observed, one private pocket which escaped their search, wherein there was a pair of spectacles (which I sometimes use for the weakness of my eyes), a pocket perspective, and several other little conveniences; which, being of no consequence to the Emperor, I did not think myself bound in honour to discover, and I apprehended they might be lost or spoiled if I ventured them out of my possession.

Chapter III *The Author diverts the Emperor and his nobility of both sexes, in a very uncommon manner. The diversions of the court of Lilliput described. The Author hath his liberty granted him upon certain conditions.*

MY GENTLENESS and good behaviour had gained so far on the Emperor and his court, and indeed upon the army and people in general, that I began to conceive hopes of getting my liberty in a short time. I took all possible methods to cultivate this favourable disposition. The natives came by degrees to be less apprehensive of any danger from me. I would sometimes lie down, and let five or six of them dance on my hand. And at last the boys and girls would venture to come and play at hide and seek in my hair. I had now made a good progress in understanding and speaking their language. The Emperor had a mind one day to entertain me with several of the country shows, wherein they exceed all nations I have known, both for dexterity and magnificence. I was diverted with none so much as that of the rope-dances, performed upon a slender white thread, extended about two foot, and twelve inches from the ground. Upon which I shall desire liberty, with the reader's patience, to enlarge a little.

This diversion is only practised by those persons who are candidates for great employments and high favour at court. They are trained in this art from their youth, and are not always of noble birth, or liberal education. When a great office is vacant either by death or disgrace (which often happens) five or six of those candidates petition the Emperor to entertain his Majesty and the court with a dance on the rope, and whoever jumps the highest without falling, succeeds in the office. Very often the chief ministers themselves are commanded to show their skill, and to convince the Emperor that they have not lost their faculty. Flimnap, the Treasurer, is allowed to cut a caper on the straight rope, at least an inch higher than any other lord in the whole empire. I have seen him do the summerset several times together upon a trencher fixed on the rope, which is no thicker than a common pack-thread in England. My friend Reldresal, principal Secretary for Private Affairs, is, in my opinion, if I am not partial, the second after the Treasurer; the rest of the great officers are much upon a par.

These diversions are often attended with fatal accidents, whereof great numbers are on record. I myself have seen two or three candidates break a limb. But the danger is much greater when the ministers themselves are commanded to show their dexterity; for by contending to excel themselves and their fellows, they strain so far, that there is hardly one of them who hath not received a fall, and some of them two or three. I was assured that a year or two before my arrival, Flimnap would have infallibly broke his neck, if one of the King's cushions, that accidentally lay on the ground, had not weakened the force of his fall.

There is likewise another diversion, which is only shown before the Emperor and Empress, and first minister, upon particular occasions. The Emperor lays on the table three fine silken threads of six inches long. One is blue, the other red, and the third green. These threads are proposed as prizes for those persons whom the Em-

peror hath a mind to distinguish by a peculiar mark of
his favour. The ceremony is performed in his Majesty's
great chamber of state, where the candidates are to undergo a trial of dexterity very different from the former,
and such as I have not observed the least resemblance
of in any other country of the old or the new world. The
Emperor holds a stick in his hands, both ends parallel
to the horizon, while the candidates, advancing one by
one, sometimes leap over the stick, sometimes creep
under it backwards and forwards several times, according as the stick is advanced or depressed. Sometimes
the Emperor holds one end of the stick, and his first
minister the other; sometimes the minister has it entirely
to himself. Whoever performs his part with most agility,
and holds out the longest in leaping and creeping, is
rewarded with the blue-coloured silk; the red is given to
the next, and the green to the third, which they all wear
girt twice round about the middle; and you see few great
persons about this court who are not adorned with one
of these girdles.

The horses of the army, and those of the royal stables,
having been daily led before me, were no longer shy,
but would come up to my very feet without starting. The
riders would leap them over my hand as I held it on the
ground, and one of the Emperor's huntsmen, upon a
large courser, took my foot, shoe and all; which was
indeed a prodigious leap. I had the good fortune to divert the Emperor one day after a very extraordinary
manner. I desired he would order several sticks of two
foot high, and the thickness of an ordinary cane, to be
brought me; whereupon his Majesty commanded the
master of his woods to give directions accordingly; and
the next morning six woodmen arrived with as many
carriages, drawn by eight horses to each. I took nine of
these sticks, and fixing them firmly in the ground in a
quadrangular figure, two foot and a half square, I took
four other sticks, and tied them parallel at each corner,
about two foot from the ground; then I fastened my
handkerchief to the nine sticks that stood erect, and extended it on all sides till it was as tight as the top of a

drum; and the four parallel sticks rising about five inches
higher than the handkerchief served as ledges on each
side. When I had finished my work, I desired the Emperor to let a troop of his best horse, twenty-four in
number, come and exercise upon this plain. His Majesty
approved of the proposal, and I took them up one by
one in my hands, ready mounted and armed, with the
proper officers to exercise them. As soon as they got into
order, they divided into two parties, performed mock
skirmishes, discharged blunt arrows, drew their swords,
fled and pursued, attacked and retired, and in short discovered the best military discipline I ever beheld. The
parallel sticks secured them and their horses from falling
over the stage; and the Emperor was so much delighted,
that he ordered this entertainment to be repeated several days, and once was pleased to be lifted up and give
the word of command; and, with great difficulty, persuaded even the Empress herself to let me hold her in
her close chair within two yards of the stage, from
whence she was able to take a full view of the whole
performance. It was my good fortune that no ill accident
happened in these entertainments, only once a fiery
horse that belonged to one of the captains pawing with
his hoof struck a hole in my handkerchief, and his foot
slipping, he overthrew his rider and himself; but I immediately relieved them both, and covering the hole with
one hand, I set down the troop with the other, in the
same manner as I took them up. The horse that fell was
strained in the left shoulder, but the rider got no hurt,
and I repaired my handkerchief as well as I could: however, I would not trust to the strength of it any more in
such dangerous enterprises.

About two or three days before I was set at liberty,
as I was entertaining the court with these kind of feats,
there arrived an express to inform his Majesty that some
of his subjects riding near the place where I was first
taken up, had seen a great black substance lying on the
ground, very oddly shaped, extending its edges round as
wide as his Majesty's bedchamber, and rising up in the
middle as high as a man; that it was no living creature,

as they at first apprehended, for it lay on the grass without motion, and some of them had walked round it several times: that by mounting upon each other's shoulders, they had got to the top, which was flat and even, and stamping upon it they found it was hollow within; that

they humbly conceived it might be something belonging
to the Man-Mountain, and if his Majesty pleased, they
would undertake to bring it with only five horses. I presently knew what they meant, and was glad at heart to
receive this intelligence. It seems upon my first reaching
the shore after our shipwreck, I was in such confusion,
that before I came to the place where I went to sleep,
my hat, which I had fastened with a string to my head
while I was rowing, and had stuck on all the time I was
swimming, fell off after I came to land; the string as
I conjecture, breaking by some accident which I never
observed, but thought my hat had been lost at sea. I
entreated his Imperial Majesty to give orders it might
be brought to me as soon as possible, describing to him
the use and the nature of it: and the next day the wag-
goners arrived with it, but not in a very good condition;
they had bored two holes in the brim, within an inch
and an half of the edge, and fastened two hooks in the
holes; these hooks were tied by a long cord to the harness, and thus my hat was dragged along for above half
an English mile: but the ground in that country being
extremely smooth and level, it received less damage than
I expected.

Two days after this adventure, the Emperor having
ordered that part of his army which quarters in and
about his metropolis to be in a readiness, took a fancy of
diverting himself in a very singular manner. He desired I
would stand like a Colossus, with my legs as far asunder
as I conveniently could. He then commanded his General (who was an old experienced leader, and a great
patron of mine) to draw up the troops in close order,
and march them under me, the foot by twenty-four in a
breast, and the horse by sixteen, with drums beating,
colours flying, and pikes advanced. This body consisted
of three thousand foot, and a thousand horse. His Majesty gave orders, upon pain of death, that every soldier
in his march should observe the strictest decency with
regard to my person; which, however, could not prevent
some of the younger officers from turning up their eyes
as they passed under me. And, to confess the truth, my

breeches were at that time in so ill a condition, that they afforded some opportunities for laughter and admiration.

I had sent so many memorials and petitions for my liberty, that his Majesty at length mentioned the matter, first in the cabinet, and then in a full council; where it was opposed by none, except Skyresh Bolgolam, who was pleased, without any provocation, to be my mortal enemy. But it was carried against him by the whole board, and confirmed by the Emperor. That minister was *Galbet*, or Admiral of the Realm, very much in his master's confidence, and a person well versed in affairs, but of a morose and sour complexion. However, he was at length persuaded to comply; but prevailed that the articles and conditions upon which I should be set free, and to which I must swear, should be drawn up by himself. These articles were brought to me by Skyresh Bolgolam in person, attended by two under-secretaries, and several persons of distinction. After they were read, I was demanded to swear to the performance of them; first in the manner of my own country, and afterwards in the method prescribed by their laws; which was to hold my right foot in my left hand, to place the middle finger of my right hand on the crown of my head, and my thumb on the tip of my right ear. But because the reader may perhaps be curious to have some idea of the style and manner of expression peculiar to that people, as well as to know the articles upon which I recovered my liberty, I have made a translation of the whole instrument word for word, as near as I was able, which I here offer to the public.

GOLBASTO MOMAREN EVLAME GURDILO SHEFIN MULLY ULLY GUE, most mighty Emperor of Lilliput, delight and terror of the universe, whose dominions extend five thousand *blustrugs* (about twelve miles in circumference) to the extremities of the globe; monarch of all monarchs, taller than the sons of men; whose feet press down to the centre, and whose head strikes against the sun; at whose nod the princes of the earth shake their knees; pleasant as the spring, comfortable as the summer, fruitful as autumn, dreadful as winter. His most sublime Majesty proposeth to the Man-Mountain, lately arrived to our celestial dominions, the following articles, which by a solemn oath he shall be obliged to perform.

First, The Man-Mountain shall not depart from our dominions, without our licence under our great seal.

2nd, He shall not presume to come into our metropolis, without our express order; at which time the inhabitants shall have two hours warning to keep within their doors.

3rd, The said Man-Mountain shall confine his walks to our principal high roads, and not offer to walk or lie down in a meadow or field of corn.

4th, As he walks the said roads, he shall take the utmost care not to trample upon the bodies of any of our loving subjects, their horses, or carriages, not take any of our said subjects into his hands, without their own consent.

5th, If an express requires extraordinary dispatch, the Man-Mountain shall be obliged to carry in his pocket the messenger and horse a six days journey once in every moon, and return the said messenger back (if so required) safe to our Imperial Presence.

6th, He shall be our ally against our enemies in the Island of Blefuscu, and do his utmost to destroy their fleet, which is now preparing to invade us.

7th, That the said Man-Mountain shall, at his times of leisure, be aiding and assisting to our workmen, in helping to raise certain great stones, towards covering the wall of the principal park, and other our royal buildings.

8th, That the said Man-Mountain shall, in two moons' time, deliver in an exact survey of the circumference of our dominions by a computation of his own paces round the coast.

Lastly, That upon his solemn oath to observe all the above articles, the said Man-Mountain shall have a daily allowance of meat and drink sufficient for the support of 1728 of our subjects, with free access to our Royal Person, and other marks of our favour. Given at our Palace at Belfaborac the twelfth day of the ninety-first moon of our reign.

I swore and subscribed to these articles with great cheerfulness and content, although some of them were not so honourable as I could have wished; which proceeded wholly from the malice of Skyresh Bolgolam the High Admiral: whereupon my chains were immediately unlocked, and I was at full liberty; the Emperor himself in person did me the honour to be by at the whole ceremony. I made my acknowledgements by prostrating myself at his Majesty's feet: but he commanded me to rise; and after many gracious expressions, which, to avoid the censure of vanity, I shall not repeat, he added, that he hoped I should prove a useful servant, and well deserve all the favours he had already conferred upon me, or might do for the future.

The reader may please to observe, that in the last article for the recovery of my liberty the Emperor stipulates to allow me a quantity of meat and drink sufficient for the support of 1728 Lilliputians. Some time after, asking a friend at court how they came to fix on that determinate number, he told me that his Majesty's mathematicians, having taken the height of my body by the help of a quadrant, and finding it to exceed theirs in the proportion of twelve to one, they concluded from the similarity of their bodies, that mine must contain at least 1728 of theirs, and consequently would require as much food as was necessary to support that number of Lilliputians. By which the reader may conceive an idea of the ingenuity of that people, as well as the prudent and exact economy of so great a prince.

Chapter IV *Mildendo the metropolis of Lilliput described, together with the Emperor's palace. A
conversation between the Author and a principal Secretary, concerning the affairs of that
empire. The Author's offers to serve the Emperor in his wars.*

THE FIRST request I made after I had obtained my
liberty, was, that I might have licence to see Mildendo, the metropolis; which the Emperor easily granted
me, but with a special charge to do no hurt either to the
inhabitants or their houses. The people had notice by
proclamation of my design to visit the town. The wall
which encompassed it is two foot and an half high, and
at least eleven inches broad, so that a coach and horses
may be driven very safely round it; and it is flanked with
strong towers at ten foot distance. I stept over the great
Western Gate, and passed very gently, and sideling
through the two principal streets, only in my short waistcoat, for fear of damaging the roofs and eaves of the
houses with the skirts of my coat. I walked with the
utmost circumspection, to avoid treading on any strag-
glers, that might remain in the streets, although the orders were very strict, that all people should keep in their
houses at their own peril. The garret windows and tops
of houses were so crowded with spectators, that I
thought in all my travels I had not seen a more populous
place. The city is an exact square, each side of the wall
being five hundred foot long. The two great streets,
which run cross and divide it into four quarters, are five
foot wide. The lanes and alleys, which I could not enter,
but only viewed them as I passed, are from twelve to
eighteen inches. The town is capable of holding five hun-

36

C E Brock
1894.

dred thousand souls. The houses are from three to five stories. The shops and markets well provided.

The Emperor's palace is in the centre of the city, where the two great streets meet. It is enclosed by a wall of two foot high, and twenty foot distant from the buildings. I had his Majesty's permission to step over this wall; and the space being so wide between that and the palace, I could easily view it on every side. The outward court is a square of forty foot, and includes two other courts: in the inmost are the royal apartments, which I was very desirous to see, but found it extremely difficult; for the great gates, from one square into another, were but eighteen inches high and seven inches wide. Now the buildings of the outer court were at least five foot high, and it was impossible for me to stride over them without infinite damage to the pile, though the walls were strongly built of hewn stone, and four inches thick. At the same time the Emperor had a great desire that I should see the magnificence of his palace; but this I was not able to do till three days after, which I spent in cutting down with my knife some of the largest trees in the royal park, about an hundred yards distant from the city. Of these trees I made two stools, each about three foot high, and strong enough to bear my weight. The people having received notice a second time, I went again through the city to the palace, with my two stools in my hands. When I came to the side of the outer court, I stood upon one stool, and took the other in my hand: this I lifted over the roof, and gently set it down in the space between the first and second court, which was eight foot wide. I then stept over the buildings very conveniently from one stool to the other, and drew up the first after me with a hooked stick. By this contrivance I got into the inmost court; and lying down upon my side, I applied my face to the windows of the middle stories, which were left open on purpose, and discovered the most splendid apartments that can be imagined. There I saw the Empress and the young Princes, in their several lodgings, with their chief attendants about them. Her Imperial Majesty was pleased to smile very gra-

ciously upon me, and gave me out of the window her
hand to kiss.

But I shall not anticipate the reader with farther descriptions of this kind, because I reserve them for a
greater work, which is now almost ready for the press,
containing a general description of this empire, from its
first erection, through a long series of princes, with a
particular account of their wars and politics, laws, learning, and religion: their plants and animals, their peculiar
manners and customs, with other matters very curious
and useful; my chief design at present being only to relate such events and transactions as happened to the
public, or to myself, during a residence of about nine
months in that empire.

One morning, about a fortnight after I had obtained
my liberty, Reldresal, principal Secretary (as they style
him) of Private Affairs, came to my house attended only
by one servant. He ordered his coach to wait at a distance, and desired I would give him an hour's audience;
which I readily consented to, on account of his quality
and personal merits, as well as the many good offices he
had done me during my solicitations at court. I offered
to lie down, that he might the more conveniently reach
my ear; but he chose rather to let me hold him in my
hand during our conversation. He began with compliments on my liberty; said he might pretend to some
merit in it: but, however, added, that if it had not been
for the present situation of things at court, perhaps I
might not have obtained it so soon. For, said he, as
flourishing a condition as we may appear to be in to
foreigners, we labour under two mighty evils; a violent
faction at home, and the danger of an invasion by a most
potent enemy from abroad. As to the first, you are to
understand, that for above seventy moons past there
have been two struggling parties in this empire, under
the names of *Tramecksan* and *Slamecksan*, from the high
and low heels on their shoes, by which they distinguish
themselves. It is alleged indeed, that the high heels are
most agreeable to our ancient constitution: but however
this be, his Majesty hath determined to make use of only

low heels in the administration of the government, and
all offices in the gift of the Crown, as you cannot but
observe; and particularly, that his Majesty's Imperial
heels are lower at least by a *drurr* than any of his court
(*drurr* is a measure about the fourteenth part of an
inch). The animosities between these two parties run so
high, that they will neither eat nor drink, nor talk with
each other. We compute the *Tramecksan*, or High-Heels,
to exceed us in number; but the power is wholly on our
side. We apprehend his Imperial Highness, the Heir to
the Crown, to have some tendency towards the High-
Heels; at least we can plainly discover one of his heels
higher than the other, which gives him a hobble in his
gait. Now, in the midst of these intestine disquiets, we
are threatened with an invasion from the Island of Blefuscu, which is the other great empire of the universe,
almost as large and powerful as this of his Majesty. For
as to what we have heard you affirm, that there are other
kingdoms and states in the world inhabited by human
creatures as large as yourself, our philosophers are in
much doubt, and would rather conjecture that you
dropped from the moon, or one of the stars; because it
is certain, that an hundred mortals of your bulk would,
in a short time, destroy all the fruits and cattle of his
Majesty's dominions. Besides, our histories of six thousand moons make no mention of any other regions, than
the two great empires of Lilliput and Blefuscu. Which
two mighty powers have, as I was going to tell you, been
engaged in a most obstinate war for six and thirty moons
past. It began upon the following occasion. It is allowed
on all hands, that the primitive way of breaking eggs
before we eat them, was upon the larger end: but his
present Majesty's grandfather, while he was a boy, going
to eat an egg, and breaking it according to the ancient
practice, happened to cut one of his fingers. Whereupon
the Emperor his father published an edict, commanding
all his subjects, upon great penalties, to break the
smaller end of their eggs. The people so highly resented
this law, that our histories tell us there have been six
rebellions raised on that account; wherein one Emperor

lost his life, and another his crown. These civil commotions were constantly fomented by the monarch of Blefuscu; and when they were quelled, the exiles always fled for refuge to that empire. It is computed, that eleven thousand persons have, at several times, suffered death, rather than submit to break their eggs at the smaller end. Many hundred large volumes have been published upon this controversy: but the books of the Big-Endians have been long forbidden, and the whole party rendered incapable by law of holding employments. During the course of these troubles, the Emperors of Blefuscu did frequently expostulate by their ambassadors, accusing us of making a schism in religion, by offending against a fundamental doctrine of our great prophet Lustrog, in the fifty-fourth chapter of the *Brundecral* (which is their Alcoran). This, however, is thought to be a mere strain upon the text: for the words are these: *That all true believers shall break their eggs at the convenient end*: and which is the convenient end, seems, in my humble opinion, to be left to every man's conscience, or at least in the power of the chief magistrate to determine. Now the Big-Endian exiles have found so much credit in the Emperor of Blefuscu's court, and so much private assistance and encouragement from their party here at home, that a bloody war hath been carried on between the two empires for six and thirty moons with various success; during which time we have lost forty capital ships, and a much greater number of smaller vessels, together with thirty thousand of our best seamen and soldiers; and the damage received by the enemy is reckoned to be somewhat greater than ours. However, they have now equipped a numerous fleet, and are just preparing to make a descent upon us; and his Imperial Majesty, placing great confidence in your valour and strength, hath commanded me to lay this account of his affairs before you.

I desired the Secretary to present my humble duty to the Emperor, and to let him know, that I thought it would not become me, who was a foreigner, to interfere with parties; but I was ready, with the hazard of my life, to defend his person and state against all invaders.

Chapter V *The Author, by an extraordinary strata-
gem, prevents an invasion. A high title of honour is conferred upon him. Ambassadors
arrive from the Emperor of Blefuscu, and sue
for peace. The Empress's apartment on fire by
an accident. The Author instrumental in saving the rest of the palace.*

THE EMPIRE of Blefuscu is an island situated to the
north-north-east side of Lilliput, from whence it is
parted only by a channel of eight hundred yards wide. I
had not yet seen it, and upon this notice of an intended
invasion, I avoided appearing on that side of the coast,
for fear of being discovered by some of the enemy's
ships, who had received no intelligence of me, all intercourse between the two empires having been strictly forbidden during the war, upon pain of death, and an
embargo laid by our Emperor upon all vessels whatsoever. I communicated to his Majesty a project I had
formed of seizing the enemy's whole fleet: which, as our
scouts assured us, lay at anchor in the harbour ready to
sail with the first fair wind. I consulted the most experienced seamen, upon the depth of the channel, which
they had often plumbed, who told me, that in the middle
at high-water it was seventy *glumgluffs* deep, which is
about six foot of European measure; and the rest of it
fifty *glumgluffs* at most. I walked towards the north-east
coast over against Blefuscu; and lying down behind a
hillock, took out my small pocket perspective-glass, and
viewed the enemy's fleet at anchor, consisting of about
fifty men-of-war, and a great number of transports: I
then came back to my house, and gave order (for which
I had a warrant) for a great quantity of the strongest
cable and bars of iron. The cable was about as thick as

packthread, and the bars of the length and size of a knitting-needle. I trebled the cable to make it stronger, and for the same reason I twisted three of the iron bars together, binding the extremities into a hook. Having thus fixed fifty hooks to as many cables, I went back to the north-east coast, and putting off my coat, shoes, and stockings, walked into the sea in my leathern jerkin, about half an hour before high water. I waded with what haste I could, and swam in the middle about thirty yards till I felt ground; I arrived at the fleet in less than half an hour. The enemy was so frightened when they saw me, that they leaped out of their ships, and swam to shore, where there would not be fewer than thirty thousand souls. I then took my tackling, and fastening a hook to the hole at the prow of each, I tied all the cords together at the end. While I was thus employed, the enemy discharged several thousand arrows, many of which stuck in my hands and face; and besides the excessive smart, gave me much disturbance in my work. My greatest apprehension was for my eyes, which I should have infallibly lost, if I had not suddenly thought of an expedient. I kept among other little necessaries a pair of spectacles in a private pocket, which, as I observed before, had scaped the Emperor's searchers. These I took out and fastened as strongly as I could upon my nose, and thus armed went on boldly with my work in spite of the enemy's arrows, many of which struck against the glasses of my spectacles, but without any other effect, further than a little to discompose them. I had now fastened all the hooks, and taking the knot in my hand, began to pull; but not a ship would stir, for they were all too fast held by their anchors, so that the boldest part of my enterprise remained. I therefore let go the cord, and leaving the hooks fixed to the ships, I resolutely cut with my knife the cables that fastened the anchors, receiving above two hundred shots in my face and hands; then I took up the knotted end of the cables to which my hooks were tied, and with great ease drew fifty of the enemy's largest men-of-war after me.

The Blefuscudians, who had not the least imagination of what I intended, were at first confounded with astonishment. They had not seen me cut the cables, and thought my design was only to let the ships run a-drift, or fall foul on each other: but when they perceived the whole fleet moving in order, and saw me pulling at the end, they set up such a scream of grief and despair, that it is almost impossible to describe or conceive. When I had got out of danger, I stopt awhile to pick out the arrows that stuck in my hands and face, and rubbed on some of the same ointment that was given me at my first arrival, as I have formerly mentioned. I then took off my spectacles, and waiting about an hour, till the tide was a little fallen, I waded through the middle with my cargo, and arrived safe at the royal port of Lilliput.

The Emperor and his whole court stood on the shore expecting the issue of this great adventure. They saw the ships move forward in a large half-moon, but could not discern me, who was up to my breast in water. When I advanced to the middle of the channel, they were yet in more pain, because I was under water to my neck. The Emperor concluded me to be drowned, and that the enemy's fleet was approaching in a hostile manner: but he was soon eased of his fears, for the channel growing shallower every step I made, I came in a short time within hearing, and holding up the end of the cable by which the fleet was fastened, I cried in a loud voice, *Long live the most puissant Emperor of Lilliput!* This great prince received me at my landing with all possible encomiums, and created me a *Nardac* upon the spot, which is the highest title of honour among them.

His Majesty desired I would take some other opportunity of bringing all the rest of his enemy's ships into his ports. And so unmeasureable is the ambition of princes, that he seemed to think of nothing less than reducing the whole empire of Blefuscu into a province, and governing it by a Viceroy; of destroying the Big-Endian exiles, and compelling that people to break the smaller end of their eggs, by which he would remain the sole monarch of the whole world. But I endeavoured to divert him from this design, by many arguments drawn from the topics of policy as well as justice; and I plainly protested, that I would never be an instrument of bringing a free and brave people into slavery. And when the matter was debated in council, the wisest part of the ministry were of my opinion.

This open bold declaration of mine was so opposite to the schemes and politics of his Imperial Majesty, that he would never forgive it; he mentioned it in a very artful manner at council, where I was told that some of the wisest appeared, at least by their silence, to be of my opinion; but others, who were my secret enemies, could not forbear some expressions, which by a side-wind reflected on me. And from this time began an intrigue between his Majesty and a junto of ministers maliciously bent against me, which broke out in less than two months, and had like to have ended in my utter destruction. Of so little weight are the greatest services to princes, when put into the balance with a refusal to gratify their passions.

About three weeks after this exploit, there arrived a solemn embassy from Blefuscu, with humble offers of a peace; which was soon concluded upon conditions very advantageous to our Emperor, wherewith I shall not trouble the reader. There were six ambassadors, with a train of about five hundred persons, and their entry was very magnificent, suitable to the grandeur of their master, and the importance of their business. When their treaty was finished, wherein I did them several good offices by the credit I now had, or at least appeared to have at court, their Excellencies, who were privately told how much I had been their friend, made me a visit in form. They began with many compliments upon my valour and generosity, invited me to that kingdom in the Emperor their master's name, and desired me to show them some proofs of my prodigious strength, of which they had heard so many wonders; wherein I readily obliged them, but shall not trouble the reader with particulars.

When I had for some time entertained their Excellencies, to their infinite satisfaction and surprise, I desired they would do me the honour to present my most humble respects to the Emperor their master, the renown of whose virtues had so justly filled the whole world with admiration, and whose royal person I resolved to attend before I returned to my own country: accordingly, the next time I had the honour to see our Emperor, I desired his general licence to wait on the Blefuscudian monarch, which he was pleased to grant me, as I could plainly perceive, in a very cold manner; but could not guess the reason, till I had a whisper from a certain person, that Flimnap and Bolgolam had represented my intercourse with those ambassadors as a mark of disaffection, from which I am sure my heart was wholly free. And this was the first time I began to conceive some imperfect idea of courts and ministers.

It is to be observed, that these ambassadors spoke to me by an interpreter, the languages of both empires differing as much from each other as any two in Europe, and each nation priding itself upon the antiquity, beauty, and energy of their own tongues, with an avowed contempt for that of their neighbour; yet our Emperor, standing upon the advantage he had got by the seizure of their fleet, obliged them to deliver their credentials, and make their speech in the Lilliputian tongue. And it must be confessed, that from the great intercourse of trade and commerce between both realms, from the continual reception of exiles, which is mutual among them, and from the custom in each empire to send their young nobility and richer gentry to the other, in order to polish themselves by seeing the world and understanding men and manners; there are few persons of distinction, or merchants, or seamen, who dwell in the maritime parts, but what can hold conversation in both tongues; as I found some weeks after, when I went to pay my respects to the Emperor of Blefuscu, which in the midst of great misfortunes, through the malice of my enemies, proved a very happy adventure to me, as I shall relate in its proper place.

The reader may remember, that when I signed those articles upon which I recovered my liberty, there were some which I disliked upon account of their being too servile, neither could anything but an extreme necessity have forced me to submit. But being now a *Nardac*, of the highest rank in that empire, such offices were looked upon as below my dignity, and the Emperor (to do him justice) never once mentioned them to me. However, it was not long before I had an opportunity of doing his Majesty, at least, as I then thought, a most signal service. I was alarmed at midnight with the cries of many hundred people at my door; by which being suddenly awaked, I was in some kind of terror. I heard the word *burglum* repeated incessantly: several of the Emperor's court, making their way through the crowd, entreated me to come immediately to the palace, where her Imperial Majesty's apartment was on fire, by the carelessness of a maid of honour, who fell asleep while she was reading a romance. I got up in an instant; and orders being given to clear the way before me, and it being likewise a moonshine night, I made a shift to get to the Palace without trampling on any of the people. I found they had already applied ladders to the walls of the apartment, and were well provided with buckets, but the water was at some distance. These buckets were about the size of a large thimble, and the poor people supplied me with them as fast as they could; but the flame was so violent that they did little good. I might easily have stifled it with my coat, which I unfortunately left behind me for haste, and came away only in my leathern jerkin. The case seemed wholly desperate and deplorable; and this magnificent palace would have infallibly been burnt down to the ground, if, by a presence of mind, unusual to me, I had not suddenly thought of an expedient. I had the evening before drunk plentifully of a most delicious wine, called *glimigrim* (the Blefuscudians call it *flunec*, but ours is esteemed the better sort) which is very diuretic. By the luckiest chance in the world, I had not discharged myself of any part of it. The heat I had contracted by coming very near the flames, and by la-

bouring to quench them, made the white wine begin to
operate by urine; which I voided in such a quantity, and
applied so well to the proper places, that in three minutes the fire was wholly extinguished, and the rest of
that noble pile, which had cost so many ages in erecting,
preserved from destruction.

It was now day-light, and I returned to my house without waiting to congratulate with the Emperor: because,
although I had done a very eminent piece of service, yet
I could not tell how his Majesty might resent the manner
by which I had performed it: for, by the fundamental
laws of the realm, it is capital in any person, of what
quality soever, to make water within the precincts of the
palace. But I was a little comforted by a message from
his Majesty, that he would give orders to the Grand
Justiciary for passing my pardon in form; which, however, I could not obtain. And I was privately assured,
that the Empress, conceiving the greatest abhorrence of
what I had done, removed to the most distant side of
the court, firmly resolved that those buildings should
never be repaired for her use: and in the presence of
her chief confidents would not forebear vowing revenge.

Chapter VI *Of the Inhabitants of Lilliput; their
learning, laws, and customs, the manner of educating their children. The Author's way of
living in that country. His vindication of a
great lady.*

ALTHOUGH I intend to leave the description of this
empire to a particular treatise, yet in the mean time
I am content to gratify the curious reader with some
general ideas. As the common size of the natives is
somewhat under six inches high, so there is an exact
proportion in all other animals, as well as plants and

trees: for instance, the tallest horses and oxen are between four and five inches in height, the sheep an inch
and a half, more or less: their geese about the bigness
of a sparrow, and so the several gradations downwards
till you come to the smallest, which, to my sight, were
almost invisible; but nature hath adapted the eyes of the
Lilliputians to all objects proper for their view: they see
with great exactness, but at no great distance. And to
show the sharpness of their sight towards objects that
are near, I have been much pleased with observing a
cook pulling a lark, which was not so large as a common
fly; and a young girl threading an invisible needle with
invisible silk. Their tallest trees are about seven foot
high; I mean some of those in the great royal park, the
tops whereof I could but just reach with my fist clenched.
The other vegetables are in the same proportion; but
this I leave to the reader's imagination.

I shall say but little at present of their learning, which
for many ages hath flourished in all its branches among
them: but their manner of writing is very peculiar, being
neither from the left to the right, like the Europeans;
nor from right to the left, like the Arabians; nor from
up to down, like the Chinese; nor from down to up, like
the Cascagians; but aslant from one corner of the paper
to the other, like ladies in England.

They bury their dead with their heads directly downwards, because they hold an opinion, that in eleven thousand moons they are all to rise again, in which period
the earth (which they conceive to be flat) will turn upside down, and by this means they shall, at their resur-
rection, be found ready standing on their feet. The
learned among them confess the absurdity of this doctrine, but the practice still continues, in compliance to
the vulgar.

There are some laws and customs in this empire very
peculiar; and if they were not so directly contrary to
those of my own dear country, I should be tempted to
say a little in their justification. It is only to be wished
that they were as well executed. The first I shall mention
relates to informers. All crimes against the state are pun-

ished here with the utmost severity; but if the person
accused maketh his innocence plainly to appear upon his
trial, the accuser is immediately put to an ignominious
death; and out of his goods or lands, the innocent person
is quadruply recompensed for the loss of his time, for
the danger he underwent, for the hardship of his impris-
onment, and for all the charges he hath been at in making his defence. Or, if that fund be deficient, it is largely
supplied by the Crown. The Emperor does also confer
on him some public mark of his favour, and proclamation is made of his innocence through the whole city.

They look upon fraud as a greater crime than theft,
and therefore seldom fail to punish it with death; for
they allege, that care and vigilance, with a very common
understanding, may preserve a man's goods from
thieves, but honesty has no fence against superior cunning; and since it is necessary that there should be a
perpetual intercourse of buying and selling, and dealing
upon credit, where fraud is permitted and connived at,
or hath no law to punish it, the honest dealer is always
undone, and the knave gets the advantage. I remember
when I was once interceding with the King for a criminal
who had wronged his master of a great sum of money,
which he had received by order, and ran away with; and
happening to tell his Majesty, by way of extenuation,
that it was only a breach of trust; the Emperor thought
it monstrous in me to offer, as a defence, the greatest
aggravation of the crime: and truly I had little to say in
return, farther than the common answer, that different
nations had different customs; for, I confess, I was heartily ashamed.

Although we usually call reward and punishment the
two hinges upon which all government turns, yet I could
never observe this maxim to be put in practice by any
nation except that of Lilliput. Whoever can there bring
sufficient proof that he hath strictly observed the laws
of his country for seventy three moons, hath a claim to
certain privileges, according to his quality and condition
of life, with a proportionable sum of money out of a
fund appropriated for that use: he likewise acquires the

title of *Snilpall*, or Legal, which is added to his name, but does not descend to his posterity. And these people thought it a prodigious defect of policy among us, when I told them that our laws were enforced only by penalties without any mention of reward. It is upon this account that the image of Justice in their courts of judicature, is formed with six eyes, two before, as many behind, and on each side one, to signify circumspection; with a bag of gold open in her right hand, and a sword sheathed in her left, to show she is more disposed to reward than to punish.

In choosing persons for all employments, they have more regard to good morals than to great abilities; for, since government is necessary to mankind, they believe that the common size of human understandings is fitted to some station or other, and that Providence never intended to make the management of public affairs a mystery, to be comprehended only by a few persons of sublime genius, of which there seldom are three born in an age: but they suppose truth, justice, temperance, and the like, to be in every man's power; the practice of which virtues, assisted by experience and a good intention, would qualify any man for the service of his country, except where a course of study is required. But they thought the want of moral virtues was so far from being supplied by superior endowments of the mind, that employments could never be put into such dangerous hands as those of persons so qualified; and at least, that the mistakes committed by ignorance in a virtuous disposition, would never be of such fatal consequence to the public weal, as the practices of a man whose inclinations led him to be corrupt, and had great abilities to manage, and multiply, and defend his corruptions.

In like manner, the disbelief of a Divine Providence renders a man uncapable of holding any public station; for, since kings avow themselves to be the deputies of Providence, the Lilliputians think nothing can be more absurd than for a prince to employ such men as disown the authority under which he acts.

In relating these and the following laws, I would only be understood to mean the original institutions, and not the most scandalous corruptions into which these people are fallen by the degenerate nature of man. For as to that infamous practice of acquiring great employments by dancing on the ropes, or badges of favour and distinction by leaping over sticks and creeping under them, the reader is to observe, that they were first introduced by the grandfather of the Emperor now reigning, and grew to the present height by the gradual increase of party and faction.

Ingratitude is among them a capital crime, as we read it to have been in some other countries; for they reason thus, that whoever makes ill returns to his benefactor, must needs be a common enemy to the rest of mankind, from whom he hath received no obligation, and therefore such a man is not fit to live.

Their notions relating to the duties of parents and children differ extremely from ours. For since the conjunction of male and female is founded upon the great law of nature, in order to propagate and continue the species, the Lilliputians will needs have it, that men and women are joined together like other animals, by the motives of concupiscence; and that their tenderness towards their young proceeds from the like natural principle: for which reason they will never allow, that a child is under any obligation to his father for begetting him, or his mother for bringing him into the world; which, considering the miseries of human life, was neither a benefit in itself, nor intended so by his parents, whose thoughts in their love-encounters were otherwise employed. Upon these, and the like reasonings, their opinion is, that parents are the last of all others to be trusted with the education of their own children: and therefore they have in every town public nurseries, where all parents, except cottagers and labourers, are obliged to send their infants of both sexes to be reared and educated when they come to the age of twenty moons, at which time they are supposed to have some rudiments of docility. These schools are of several kinds, suited to different qualities, and to both sexes. They have certain professors well skilled in preparing children for such a condition of life as befits the rank of their parents, and their own capacities as well as inclinations. I shall first say something of the male nurseries, and then of the female.

The nurseries for males of noble or eminent birth are provided with grave and learned professors, and their several deputies. The clothes and food of the children are plain and simple. They are bred up in the principles of honour, justice, courage, modesty, clemency, religion, and love of their country; they are always employed in some business, except in the times of eating and sleeping, which are very short, and two hours for diversions, consisting of bodily exercises. They are dressed by men till four years of age, and then are obliged to dress themselves, although their quality be ever so great; and the women attendants, who are aged proportionably to ours at fifty, perform only the most menial offices. They are never suffered to converse with servants, but go together in small or greater numbers to take their diversions, and always in the presence of a professor, or one of his deputies; whereby they avoid those early bad impressions of folly and vice to which our children are subject. Their parents are suffered to see them only twice a year; the visit is to last but an hour. They are allowed to kiss the child at meeting and parting; but a professor, who always stands by on these occasions, will not suffer them to whisper, or use any fondling expressions, or bring any presents of toys, sweetmeats, and the like.

The pension from each family for the education and entertainment of a child, upon failure of due payment, is levied by the Emperor's officers.

The nurseries for children of ordinary gentlemen, merchants, traders, and handicrafts, are managed proportionably after the same manner; only those designed for trades are put out apprentices at eleven years old, whereas those of persons of quality continue in their exercises till fifteen, which answers to one and twenty with us: but the confinement is gradually lessened for the last three years.

In the female nurseries, the young girls of quality are educated much like the males, only they are dressed by orderly servants of their own sex; but always in the presence of a professor or deputy, till they come to dress themselves, which is at five years old. And if it be found that these nurses ever presume to entertain the girls with frightful or foolish stories, or the common follies practised by chambermaids among us, they are publicly whipped thrice about the city, imprisoned for a year, and banished for life to the most desolate part of the country. Thus the young ladies there are as much ashamed of being cowards and fools as the men, and despise all personal ornaments beyond decency and cleanliness: neither did I perceive any difference in their education, made by their difference of sex, only that the exercises of the females were not altogether so robust; and that some rules were given them relating to domestic life, and a smaller compass of learning was enjoined them: for their maxim is, that among people of quality a wife should be always a reasonable and agreeable companion, because she cannot always be young. When the girls are twelve years old, which among them is the marriageable age, their parents or guardians take them home, with great expressions of gratitude to the professors, and seldom without tears of the young lady and her companions.

In the nurseries of females of the meaner sort, the children are instructed in all kinds of works proper for their sex, and their several degrees: those intended for apprentices are dismissed at nine years old, the rest are kept to thirteen.

The meaner families who have children at these nurseries are obliged, besides their annual pension, which is as low as possible, to return to the steward of the nursery a small monthly share of their gettings, to be a portion for the child; and therefore all parents are limited in their expenses by the law. For the Lilliputians think nothing can be more unjust, than for people, in subservience to their own appetites, to bring children into the world and leave the burthen of supporting them on the public. As to persons of quality, they give security to appropriate a certain sum for each child, suitable to their condition; and these funds are always managed with good husbandry, and the most exact justice.

The cottagers and labourers keep their children at home, their business being only to till and cultivate the earth, and therefore their education is of little consequence to the public; but the old and diseased among them are supported by hospitals: for begging is a trade unknown in this kingdom.

And here it may perhaps divert the curious reader, to give some account of my domestics, and my manner of

living in this country, during a residence of nine months
and thirteen days. Having a head mechanically turned,
and being likewise forced by necessity, I had made for
myself a table and chair convenient enough, out of the
largest trees in the royal park. Two hundred sempstresses were employed to make me shirts, and linen for
my bed and table, all of the strongest and coarsest kind
they could get; which, however, they were forced to quilt
together in several folds, for the thickest was some degrees finer than lawn. Their linen is usually three inches
wide, and three foot make a piece. The sempstresses
took my measure as I lay on the ground, one standing
at my neck, and another at my mid-leg, with a strong
cord extended, that each held by the end, while the third
measured the length of the cord with a rule of an inch
long. Then they measured my right thumb, and desired
no more; for by a mathematical computation, that twice
round the thumb is once round the wrist, and so on to
the neck and the waist, and by the help of my old shirt,
which I displayed on the ground before them for a pat-
tern, they fitted me exactly. Three hundred tailors were
employed in the same manner to make me clothes; but
they had another contrivance for taking my measure. I
kneeled down, and they raised a ladder from the ground
to my neck; upon this ladder one of them mounted, and
let fall a plumb-line from my collar to the floor, which
just answered the length of my coat; but my waist and
arms I measured myself. When my clothes were finished,
which was done in my house (for the largest of theirs
would not have been able to hold them) they looked
like the patch-work made by the ladies in England, only
that mine were all of a colour.

I had three hundred cooks to dress my victuals, in
little convenient huts built about my house, where they
and their families lived, and prepared me two dishes a-
piece. I took up twenty waiters in my hand, and placed
them on the table; an hundred more attended below on
the ground, some with dishes of meat, and some with
barrels of wine, and other liquors, slung on their shoulders; all which the waiters above drew up as I wanted,

in a very ingenious manner, by certain cords, as we draw the bucket up a well in Europe. A dish of their meat was a good mouthful, and a barrel of their liquor a reasonable draught. Their mutton yields to ours, but their beef is excellent. I have had a sirloin so large, that I have been forced to make three bits of it; but this is rare. My servants were astonished to see me eat it bones and all, as in our country we do the leg of a lark. Their geese and turkeys I usually ate at a mouthful, and I must confess they far exceed ours. Of their smaller fowl I could take up twenty or thirty at the end of my knife.

One day his Imperial Majesty, being informed of my way of living, desired that himself and his Royal Consort, with the young Princes of the blood of both sexes, might have the happiness (as he was pleased to call it) of dining with me. They came accordingly, and I placed 'em upon chairs of state on my table, just over against me, with their guards about them. Flimnap, the Lord High Treasurer, attended there likewise with his white staff; and I observed he often looked on me with a sour countenance, which I would not seem to regard, but ate more than usual, in honour to my dear country, as well as to fill the court with admiration. I have some private reasons to believe, that this visit from his Majesty gave Flimnap an opportunity of doing me ill offices to his master. That minister had always been my secret enemy, though he outwardly caressed me more than was usual to the moroseness of his nature. He represented to the Emperor the low condition of his treasury; that he was forced to take up money at great discount; that exchequer bills would not circulate under nine per cent, below par; that in short I had cost his Majesty above a million and a half of *sprugs* (their greatest gold coin, about the bigness of a spangle); and upon the whole that it would be advisable in the Emperor to take the first fair occasion of dismissing me.

I am here obliged to vindicate the reputation of an excellent lady, who was an innocent sufferer upon my account. The Treasurer took a fancy to be jealous of his wife, from the malice of some evil tongues, who in-

formed him that her Grace had taken a violent affection
for my person; and the court-scandal ran for some time,
that she once came privately to my lodging. This I sol-
emnly declare to be a most infamous falsehood, without
any grounds, farther than that her Grace was pleased to
treat me with all innocent marks of freedom and friendship. I own she came often to my house, but always
publicly, nor ever without three more in the coach, who
were usually her sister and young daughter, and some
particular acquaintance; but this was common to many
other ladies of the court. And I still appeal to my servants round, whether they at any time saw a coach at
my door without knowing what persons were in it. On
those occasions, when a servant had given me notice, my
custom was to go immediately to the door; and, after
paying my respects, to take up the coach and two horses
very carefully in my hands (for if there were six horses,
the postillion always unharnessed four) and place them
on a table, where I had fixed a moveable rim quite
round, of five inches high, to prevent accidents. And I
have often had four coaches and horses at once on my
table full of company, while I sat in my chair leaning
my face towards them; and when I was engaged with
one set, the coachmen would gently drive the others
round my table. I have passed many an afternoon very
agreeably in these conversations. But I defy the Treasurer, or his two informers (I will name them, and let
'em make their best of it) Clustril and Drunlo, to prove
that any person ever came to me *incognito*, except the
secretary Reldresal, who was sent by express command
of his Imperial Majesty, as I have before related. I
should not have dwelt so long upon this particular, if it
had not been a point wherein the reputation of a great
lady is so nearly concerned, to say nothing of my own;
though I then had the honour to be a *Nardac*, which the
Treasurer himself is not; for all the world knows he is
only a *Clumglum*, a title inferior by one degree, as that
of a Marquis is to a Duke in England, although I allow
he preceded me in right of his post. These false informa-
tions, which I afterwards came to the knowledge of, by

an accident not proper to mention, made Flimnap the
Treasurer show his lady for some time an ill countenance, and me a worse; and although he were at last
undeceived and reconciled to her, yet I lost all credit
with him, and found my interest decline very fast with
the Emperor himself, who was indeed too much governed by that favourite.

∞

Chapter VII *The Author, being informed of a design to accuse him of high treason, makes his
escape to Blefuscu. His reception there.*

BEFORE I PROCEED to give an account of my leaving
this kingdom, it may be proper to inform the reader
of a private intrigue which had been for two months
forming against me.

I had been hitherto all my life a stranger to courts,
for which I was unqualified by the meanness of my condition. I had indeed heard and read enough of the dispositions of great princes and ministers; but never expected
to have found such terrible effects of them in so remote
a country, governed, as I thought, by very different maxims from those in Europe.

When I was just preparing to pay my attendance on
the Emperor of Blefuscu, a considerable person at court
(to whom I had been very serviceable at a time when
he lay under the highest displeasure of his Imperial Majesty) came to my house very privately at night in a close
chair, and without sending his name, desired admittance.
The chairmen were dismissed; I put the chair, with his
Lordship in it, into my coat-pocket: and giving orders to
a trusty servant to say I was indisposed and gone to
sleep, I fastened the door of my house, placed the chair
on the table, according to my usual custom, and sat
down by it. After the common salutations were over,

observing his Lordship's countenance full of concern, and enquiring into the reason, he desired I would hear him with patience in a matter that highly concerned my honour and my life. His speech was to the following effect, for I took notes of it as soon as he left me.

You are to know, said he, that several Committees of Council have been lately called in the most private manner on your account; and it is but two days since his Majesty came to a full resolution.

You are very sensible that Skyresh Bolgolam (*Galbet*, or High Admiral) hath been your mortal enemy almost ever since your arrival. His original reasons I know not, but his hatred is much increased since your great success against Blefuscu, by which his glory as Admiral is obscured. This Lord, in conjunction with Flimnap the High Treasurer, whose enmity against you is notorious on account of his lady, Limtoc the General, Lalcon the Chamberlain, and Balmuff the Grand Justiciary, have prepared articles of impeachment against you, for treason, and other capital crimes.

This preface made me so impatient, being conscious of my own merits and innocence, that I was going to interrupt; when he entreated me to be silent, and thus proceeded.

Articles of Impeachment
against Quinbus Flestrin (the Man-Mountain)

ARTICLE I

WHEREAS, by a statute made in the reign of his Imperial Majesty Calin Deffar Plune, it is enacted, that whoever shall make water within the precincts of the royal palace, shall be liable to the pains and penalties of high treason; notwithstanding, the said Quinbus Flestrin, in open breach of the said law, under colour of extinguishing the fire kindled in the apartment of his Majesty's most dear Imperial Consort, did maliciously, traitorously, and devilishly, by discharge of his urine, put out the said fire kindled in the said apartment, lying and being within the precincts of the said royal palace, against the statute in that case provided, *etc.,* against the duty, *etc.*

ARTICLE II

THAT the said Quinbus Flestrin having brought the imperial fleet of Blefuscu into the royal port, and being afterwards commanded by his Imperial Majesty to seize all the other ships of the said empire of Blefuscu, and reduce that empire to a province, to be governed by a Viceroy from hence, and to destroy and put to death not only all the Big-Endian exiles, but likewise all the people of that empire, who would not immediately forsake the Big-Endian heresy: He, the said Flestrin, like a false traitor against his most Auspicious, Serene, Imperial Majesty, did petition to be excused from the said service, upon pretence of unwillingness to force the consciences, or destroy the liberties and lives of an innocent people.

ARTICLE III

THAT, whereas certain ambassadors arrived from the court of Blefuscu, to sue for peace in his Majesty's court: He, the said Flestrin, did, like a false traitor, aid, abet, comfort, and divert the said ambassadors, although he knew them to be servants to a Prince who was lately an open enemy to his Imperial Majesty, and in open war against his said Majesty.

ARTICLE IV

THAT the said Quinbus Flestrin, contrary to the duty of a faithful subject, is now preparing to make a voyage to the court and empire of Blefuscu, for which he hath received only verbal licence from his Imperial Majesty; and under colour of the said licence, doth falsely and traitorously intend to take the said voyage, and thereby to aid, comfort, and abet the Emperor of Blefuscu, so late an enemy, and in open war with his Imperial Majesty aforesaid.

There are some other articles, but these are the most important, of which I have read you an abstract.

In the several debates upon this impeachment, it must be confessed that his Majesty gave many marks of his great lenity, often urging the services you had done him, and endeavouring to extenuate your crimes. The Treasurer and Admiral insisted that you should be put to the most painful and ignominious death, by setting fire on your house at night, and the General was to attend with twenty thousand men armed with poisoned arrows to shoot you on the face and hands. Some of your servants were to have private orders to strew a poisonous juice

on your shirts, which would soon make you tear your
own flesh, and die in the utmost torture. The General
came into the same opinion, so that for a long time there
was a majority against you. But his Majesty resolving, if
possible, to spare your life, at last brought off the
Chamberlain.

Upon this incident, Reldresal, principal Secretary for
Private Affairs, who always approved himself your true
friend, was commanded by the Emperor to deliver his
opinion, which he accordingly did; and therein justified
the good thoughts you have of him. He allowed your
crimes to be great, but that still there was room for
mercy, the most commendable virtue in a prince, and
for which his Majesty was so justly celebrated. He said,
the friendship between you and him was so well known
to the world, that perhaps the most honourable board
might think him partial: however, in obedience to the
command he had received, he would freely offer his sentiments. That if his Majesty, in consideration of your
services, and pursuant to his own merciful disposition,
would please to spare your life, and only give order to
put out both your eyes, he humbly conceived that by
this expedient justice might in some measure be satisfied,
and all the world would applaud the lenity of the Emperor, as well as the fair and generous proceedings of
those who have the honour to be his counsellors. That
the loss of your eyes would be no impediment to your
bodily strength, by which you might still be useful to his
Majesty. That blindness is an addition to courage, by
concealing dangers from us; that the fear you had for
your eyes was the greatest difficulty in bringing over the
enemy's fleet, and it would be sufficient for you to see
by the eyes of the ministers, since the greatest princes
do no more.

This proposal was received with the utmost disappro-
bation by the whole board. Bolgolam, the Admiral,
could not preserve his temper, but rising up in fury said
he wondered how the Secretary durst presume to give
his opinion for preserving the life of a traitor: that the
services you had performed, were, by all true reasons of

state, the great aggravation of your crimes; that you, who were able to extinguish the fire, by discharge of urine in her Majesty's apartment (which he mentioned with horror), might, at another time, raise an inundation by the same means, to drown the whole palace; and the same strength which enabled you to bring over the enemy's fleet, might serve, upon the first discontent, to carry it back: that he had good reasons to think you were a Big-Endian in your heart; and as treason begins in the heart, before it appears in overt acts, so he accused you as a traitor on that account, and therefore insisted you should be put to death.

The Treasurer was of the same opinion; he showed to what straits his Majesty's revenue was reduced by the charge of maintaining you, which would soon grow insupportable: that the Secretary's expedient of putting out your eyes was so far from being a remedy against this evil, it would probably increase it, as it is manifest from the common practice of blinding some kind of fowl, after which they fed the faster, and grew sooner fat: that his sacred Majesty and the Council, who are your judges, were in their own consciences fully convinced of your guilt, which was a sufficient argument to condemn you to death, without the formal proofs required by the strict letter of the law.

But his Imperial Majesty, fully determined against capital punishment, was graciously pleased to say, that since the Council thought the loss of your eyes too easy a censure, some other may be inflicted hereafter. And your friend the Secretary humbly desiring to be heard again, in answer to what the Treasurer had objected concerning the great charge his Majesty was at in maintaining you, said that his Excellency, who had the sole disposal of the Emperor's revenue, might easily provide against that evil, by gradually lessening your establishment; by which, for want of sufficient food, you would grow weak and faint, and lose your appetite, and consequently decay and consume in a few months; neither would the stench of your carcass be then so dangerous, when it should become more than half diminished; and

immediately upon your death, five or six thousand of his
Majesty's subjects might, in two or three days, cut your
flesh from your bones, take it away by cartloads, and
bury it in distant parts to prevent infection, leaving the
skeleton as a monument of admiration to posterity.

Thus by the great friendship of the Secretary, the
whole affair was compromised. It was strictly enjoined,
that the project of starving you by degrees should be
kept a secret, but the sentence of putting out your eyes
was entered on the books; none dissenting except Bolgolam the Admiral, who, being a creature of the Empress,
was perpetually instigated by her Majesty to insist upon
your death, she having borne perpetual malice against
you, on account of that infamous and illegal method you
took to extinguish the fire in her apartment.

In three days your friend the Secretary will be directed
to come to your house, and read before you the articles
of impeachment; and then to signify the great lenity and
favour of his Majesty and Council, whereby you are only
condemned to the loss of your eyes, which his Majesty
doth not question you will gratefully and humbly submit
to; and twenty of his Majesty's surgeons will attend, in
order to see the operation well performed, by discharg-
ing very sharp-pointed arrows into the balls of your eyes,
as you lie on the ground.

I leave to your prudence what measures you will take;
and to avoid suspicion, I must immediately return in as
private a manner as I came.

His Lordship did so, and I remained alone, under
many doubts and perplexities of mind.

It was a custom introduced by this prince and his ministry (very different, as I have been assured, from the
practices of former time) that after the court had decreed any cruel execution, either to gratify the monarch's
resentment, or the malice of a favourite, the Emperor
always made a speech to his whole Council, expressing
his great lenity and tenderness, as qualities known and
confessed by all the world. This speech was immediately
published through the kingdom; nor did any thing terrify
the people so much as those ecomiums on his Majesty's

mercy; because it was observed, that the more these praises were enlarged and insisted on, the more inhuman was the punishment, and the sufferer more innocent. And as to myself, I must confess, having never been designed for a courtier either by my birth or education, I was so ill a judge of things, that I could not discover the lenity and favour of this sentence, but conceived it (perhaps erroneously) rather to be rigorous than gentle. I sometimes thought of standing my trial, for although I could not deny the facts alleged in the several articles, yet I hoped they would admit of some extenuations. But having in my life perused many state trials, which I ever observed to terminate as the judges thought fit to direct, I durst not rely on so dangerous a decision, in so critical a juncture, and against such powerful enemies. Once I was strongly bent upon resistance, for while I had liberty, the whole strength of that empire could hardly subdue me, and I might easily with stones pelt the metropolis to pieces; but I soon rejected that project with horror, by remembering the oath I had made to the Emperor, the favours I received from him, and the high title of *Nardac* he conferred upon me. Neither had I so soon learned the gratitude of courtiers, to persuade myself that his Majesty's present severities quitted me of all past obligations.

At last I fixed upon a resolution, for which it is probable I may incur some censure, and not unjustly; for I confess I owe the preserving my eyes, and consequently my liberty, to my own great rashness and want of experience: because if I had then known the nature of princes and ministers, which I have since observed in many other courts, and their methods of treating criminals less obnoxious than myself, I should with great alacrity and readiness have submitted to so easy a punishment. But hurried on by the precipitancy of youth, and having his Imperial Majesty's licence to pay my attendance upon the Emperor of Blefuscu, I took this opportunity, before the three days were elapsed, to send a letter to my friend the Secretary, signifying my resolution of setting out that morning for Blefuscu pursuant to the leave I had got;

and without waiting for an answer, I went to that side
of the island where our fleet lay. I seized a large man-
of-war, tied a cable to the prow, and, lifting up the anchors, I stripped myself, put my clothes (together with
my coverlet, which I brought under my arm) into the
vessel, and drawing it after me between wading and
swimming, arrived at the royal port of Blefuscu, where
the people had long expected me; they lent me two
guides to direct me to the capital city, which is of the
same name. I held them in my hands till I came within
two hundred yards of the gate, and desired them to signify my arrival to one of the secretaries, and let him
know, I there waited his Majesty's commands. I had an
answer in about an hour, that his Majesty, attended by
the Royal Family, and great officers of the court, was
coming out to receive me. I advanced an hundred yards.
The Emperor and his train alighted from their horses,
the Empress and ladies from their coaches, and I did
not perceive they were in any fright or concern. I lay on
the ground to kiss his Majesty's and the Empress's hand.
I told his Majesty that I was come according to my
promise, and with the licence of the Emperor my master,
to have the honour of seeing so mighty a monarch, and
to offer him any service in my power, consistent with
my duty to my own prince; not mentioning a word of
my disgrace, because I had hitherto no regular information of it, and might suppose myself wholly ignorant of
any such design; neither could I reasonably conceive that
the Emperor would discover the secret while I was out
of his power: wherein, however, it soon appeared I
was deceived.

I shall not trouble the reader with the particular account of my reception at this court, which was suitable
to the generosity of so great a prince; nor of the difficulties I was in for want of a house and bed, being forced
to lie on the ground, wrapped up in my coverlet.

Chapter VIII *The Author, by a lucky accident, finds means to leave Blefuscu; and, after some difficulties, returns safe to his native country.*

THREE DAYS AFTER my arrival, walking out of curiosity to the north-east coast of the island, I observed, about half a league off, in the sea, somewhat that looked like a boat overturned. I pulled off my shoes and stockings, and wading two or three hundred yards, I found the object to approach nearer by force of the tide; and then plainly saw it to be a real boat, which I supposed might, by some tempest, have been driven from a ship; whereupon I returned immediately towards the city, and desired his Imperial Majesty to lend me twenty of the tallest vessels he had left after the loss of his fleet, and three thousand seamen under the command of his Vice-Admiral. This fleet sailed round, while I went back the shortest way to the coast where I first discovered the boat; I found the tide had driven it still nearer. The seamen were all provided with cordage, which I had beforehand twisted to a sufficient strength. When the ships came up, I stripped myself, and waded till I came within an hundred yards of the boat, after which I was forced to swim till I got up to it. The seamen threw me the end of the cord, which I fastened to a hole in the fore-part of the boat, and the other end to a man-of-war; but I found all my labour to little purpose; for being out of my depth, I was not able to work. In this necessity, I was forced to swim behind, and push the boat forwards as often as I could, with one of my hands; and the tide favouring me, I advanced so far, that I could just hold up my chin and feel the ground. I rested two or three minutes, and then gave the boat another shove, and so on till the sea was no higher than my arm-pits; and now the most laborious part being over, I took out my other cables, which were stowed in one of the ships, and fastening them first to the boat, and then to nine of the vessels which attended me; the wind being favourable, the seamen towed, and I shoved till we arrived within forty yards of the shore; and waiting till the tide was out, I got dry to the boat, and by the assistance of two thousand men, with ropes and engines, I made a shift to turn it on its bottom, and found it was but little damaged.

I shall not trouble the reader with the difficulties I was under by the help of certain paddles, which cost me ten days making, to get my boat to the royal port of Blefuscu, where a mighty concourse of people appeared upon my arrival, full of wonder at the sight of so prodigious a vessel. I told the Emperor that my good fortune had thrown this boat in my way, to carry me to some place from whence I might return to my native country, and begged his Majesty's orders for getting materials to fit it up, together with his licence to depart; which, after some kind expostulations, he was pleased to grant.

I did very much wonder, in all this time, not to have heard of any express relating to me from our Emperor to the court of Blefuscu. But I was afterwards given privately to understand, that his Imperial Majesty, never imagining I had the least notice of his designs, believed I was only gone to Blefuscu in performance of my promise, according to the licence he had given me, which was well known at our court, and would return in a few days when that ceremony was ended. But he was at last in pain at my long absence; and after consulting with the Treasurer, and the rest of that cabal, a person of quality was dispatched with the copy of the articles against me. This envoy had instructions to represent to the monarch of Blefuscu the great lenity of his master, who was content to punish me no farther than with the loss of my eyes; that I had fled from justice, and if I did not return in two hours, I should be deprived of my title of *Nardac*, and declared a traitor. The envoy further added, that in order to maintain the peace and amity between both empires, his master expected, that his brother of Blefuscu would give orders to have me sent back to Lilliput, bound hand and foot, to be punished as a traitor.

The Emperor of Blefuscu having taken three days to consult, returned an answer consisting of many civilities and excuses. He said, that as for sending me bound, his brother knew it was impossible; that although I had deprived him of his fleet, yet he owed great obligations to me for many good offices I had done him in making the peace. That however both their Majesties would soon be made easy; for I had found a prodigious vessel on the shore, able to carry me on the sea, which he had given order to fit up with my own assistance and direction; and he hoped in a few weeks both empires would be freed from so insupportable an incumbrance.

With this answer the envoy returned to Lilliput, and the monarch of Blefuscu related to me all that had passed, offering me at the same time (but under the strictest confidence) his gracious protection, if I would continue in his service; wherein although I believed him sincere, yet I resolved never more to put any confidence in princes or ministers, where I could possibly avoid it; and therefore, with all due acknowledgements for his favourable intentions, I humbly begged to be excused. I told him that since fortune, whether good or evil, had thrown a vessel in my way, I was resolved to venture myself in the ocean, rather than be an occasion of difference between two such mighty monarchs. Neither did I find the Emperor at all displeased; and I discovered by a certain accident, that he was very glad of my resolution, and so were most of his ministers.

These considerations moved me to hasten my departure somewhat sooner than I intended; to which the court, impatient to have me gone, very readily contributed. Five hundred workmen were employed to make two sails to my boat, according to my directions, by quilting thirteen fold of their strongest linen together. I was at the pains of making ropes and cables, by twisting ten, twenty or thirty of the thickest and strongest of theirs. A great stone that I happened to find, after a long search, by the sea-shore, served me for an anchor.

I had the tallow of three hundred cows for greasing my boat, and other uses. I was at incredible pains in cutting down some of the largest timber-trees for oars and masts, wherein I was, however, much assisted by his Majesty's ship-carpenters, who helped me in smoothing them, after I had done the rough work.

In about a month, when all was prepared, I sent to receive his Majesty's commands, and to take my leave. The Emperor and Royal Family came out of the palace; I lay down on my face to kiss his hand, which he very graciously gave me: so did the Empress and young Princes of the blood. His Majesty presented me with fifty purses of two hundred *sprugs* a-piece, together with his picture at full length, which I put immediately into one of my gloves, to keep it from being hurt. The ceremonies at my departure were too many to trouble the reader with at this time.

I stored the boat with the carcases of an hundred oxen, and three hundred sheep, with bread and drink proportionable, and as much meat ready dressed as four hundred cooks could provide. I took with me six cows and two bulls alive, with as many ewes and rams, intending to carry them into my own country, and propagate the breed. And to feed them on board, I had a good bundle of hay, and a bag of corn. I would gladly have taken a dozen of the natives, but this was a thing the Emperor would by no means permit; and besides a diligent search into my pockets, his Majesty engaged my honour not to carry away any of his subjects, although with their own consent and desire.

Having thus prepared all things as well as I was able, I set sail on the twenty-fourth day of September 1701, at six in the morning; and when I had gone about four leagues to the northward, the wind being at south-east, at six in the evening I descried a small island about half a league to the north-west. I advanced forward, and cast anchor on the lee-side of the island, which seemed to be uninhabited. I then took some refreshment, and went to my rest. I slept well, and I conjecture at least six hours, for I found the day broke in two hours after I awaked. It was a clear night. I ate my breakfast before the sun was up; and heaving anchor, the wind being favourable, I steered the same course that I had done the day before, wherein I was directed by my pocket-compass. My intention was to reach, if possible, one of those islands, which I had reason to believe lay to the north-east of Van Diemen's Land. I discovered nothing all that day; but upon the next, about three in the afternoon, when I had by my computation made twenty-four leagues from Blefuscu, I descried a sail steering to the south-east; my course was due east. I hailed her, but could get no answer; yet I found I gained upon her, for the wind slackened. I made all the sail I could, and in half an hour she spied me, then hung out her ancient, and discharged a gun. It is not easy to express the joy I was in upon the unexpected hope of once more seeing my beloved country, and the dear pledges I had left in it. The ship slackened her sails, and I came up with her between five and six in the evening, September 26; but my heart leapt within me to see her English colours. I put my cows and sheep into my coat-pockets, and got on board with all my little cargo of provisions. The vessel was an English merchantman, returning from Japan by the North and South Seas; the Captain, Mr. John Biddle of Deptford, a very civil man, and an excellent sailor. We were now in the latitude of 30 degrees south; there were about fifty men in the ship; and here I met an old comrade of mine, one Peter Williams, who gave me a good character to the Captain. This gentleman treated me with kindness, and desired I would let him know what place I came from last, and whither I was bound; which I did in few words, but he thought I was raving, and that the dangers I underwent had disturbed my head; whereupon I took my black cattle and sheep out of my pocket, which, after great astonishment, clearly convinced him of my veracity. I then showed him the gold given me by the Emperor of Blefuscu, together with his Majesty's picture at full length, and some other rarities of that country. I gave him two purses of two hundred *sprugs* each, and promised, when we arrived in England, to make him a present of a cow and a sheep big with young.

I shall not trouble the reader with a particular account of this voyage, which was very prosperous for the most part. We arrived in the Downs on the 13th of April, 1702. I had only one misfortune, that the rats on board carried away one of my sheep; I found her bones in a hole, picked clean from the flesh. The rest of my cattle I got safe on shore, and set them a grazing in a bowling-green at Greenwich, where the fineness of the grass made them feed very heartily, though I had always feared the contrary: neither could I possibly have preserved them in so long a voyage, if the Captain had not allowed me some of his best biscuit, which, rubbed to powder, and mingled with water, was their constant food. The short time I continued in England, I made a considerable profit by showing my cattle to many persons of quality, and others: and before I began my second voyage, I sold them for six hundred pounds. Since my last return, I find the breed is considerably increased, especially the sheep; which I hope will prove much to the advantage of the woollen manufacture, by the fineness of the fleeces.

I stayed but two months with my wife and family; for my insatiable desire of seeing foreign countries would suffer me to continue no longer. I left fifteen hundred pounds with my wife, and fixed her in a good house at Redriff. My remaining stock I carried with me, part in money, and part in goods, in hopes to improve my fortunes. My eldest uncle John had left me an estate in land, near Epping, of about thirty pounds a year; and I had a long lease of the Black Bull in Fetter Lane, which yielded me as much more; so that I was not in any danger of leaving my family upon the parish. My son Johnny, named so after his uncle, was at the Grammar School, and a towardly child. My daughter Betty (who is now well married, and has children) was then at her needlework. I took leave of my wife, and boy and girl, with tears on both sides, and went on board the *Adventure*, a merchant-ship of three hundred tons, bound for Surat, Captain John Nicholas of Liverpool Commander. But my account of this voyage must be referred to the second part of my Travels.

PART II

A Voyage to Brobdingnag

Flanflasnic

Lorbrulgrud

BROBDINGNAG
Discovered, A.D. 1703.

NORTH AMERICA

Streights of Annian

C. Blanco

St Sebastian

NEW ALBION

C. Mendocino

County St Martin

Pto St Francis Drake

P. Monterey

BROBDINGNAG

Chapter I *A great storm described; the long-boat sent to fetch water; the Author goes with it to discover the country. He is left on shore, is seized by one of the natives, and carried to a farmer's house. His reception there, with several accidents that happened there. A description of the inhabitants.*

HAVING BEEN condemned by nature and fortune to an active and restless life, in two months after my return I again left my native country, and took shipping in the Downs on the 20th day of June, 1702, in the *Adventure,* Captain John Nicholas, a Cornish man, Commander, bound for Surat. We had a very prosperous gale till we arrived at the Cape of Good Hope, where we landed for fresh water, but discovering a leak we unshipped our goods and wintered there; for the Captain falling sick of an ague, we could not leave the Cape till the end of March. We then set sail, and had a good voyage till we passed the Straits of Madagascar; but having got northward of that island, and to about five degrees south latitude, the winds, which in those seas are observed to blow a constant equal gale between the north and west from the beginning of December to the beginning of May, on the 19th of April began to blow with much greater violence, and more westerly than usual, continuing so for twenty days together, during which time we were driven a little to the east of the Molucca Islands, and about three degrees northward of the Line, as our Captain found by an observation he took the 2nd of May, at which time the wind ceased, and it was a perfect calm, whereat I was not a little rejoiced. But he, being a man well experienced in the navigation of those seas, bid us all prepare against a storm, which accordingly happened the day following: for a southern wind, called the southern monsoon, began to set in.

Finding it was likely to overblow, we took in our sprit-sail, and stood by to hand the fore-sail; but making foul weather, we looked the guns were all fast, and handed the mizen. The ship lay very broad off, so we thought it better spooning before the sea, than trying or hulling. We reefed the fore-sail and set him, we hauled aft the fore-sheet; the helm was hard a weather. The ship wore bravely. We belayed the fore-down haul; but the sail was split, and we hauled down the yard, and got the sail into the ship, and unbound all the things clear of it. It was a very fierce storm; the sea broke strange and dangerous. We hauled off upon the lanyard of the whipstaff, and helped the man at helm. We would not get down our top-mast, but let all stand, because she scudded before the sea very well, and we knew that the top-mast being aloft, the ship was the wholesomer, and made better way through the sea, seeing we had sea-room. When the storm was over, we set fore-sail and main-sail, and brought the ship to: then we set the mizen, main-top-sail, and the fore-top-sail. Our course was east-north-east, the wind was at south-west. We got the starboard tacks aboard, we cast off our weather-braces and lifts; we set in the lee-braces, and hauled forward by the weather-bowlings, and hauled them tight, and belayed them, and hauled over the mizen tack to windward, and kept her full and by as near as she would lie.

During this storm, which was followed by a strong wind west-south-west, we were carried by my computation about five hundred leagues to the east, so that the oldest sailor on board could not tell in what part of the world we were. Our provisions held out well, our ship was staunch, and our crew all in good health; but we lay in the utmost distress for water. We thought it best to hold on the same course, rather than turn more northerly, which might have brought us to the north-west parts of Great Tartary, and into the frozen sea.

On the 16th day of June, 1703, a boy on the top-mast discovered land. On the 17th we came in full view of a great island or continent (for we knew not whether) on the south side whereof was a small neck of land jutting out into the sea, and a creek too shallow to hold a ship of above one hundred tons. We cast anchor within a league on this creek, and our Captain sent a dozen of his men well armed in the long-boat, with vessels for water if any could be found. I desired his leave to go with them, that I might see the country, and make what discoveries I could. When we came to land we saw no river or spring, nor any sign of inhabitants. Our men therefore wandered on the shore to find out some fresh water near the sea, and I walked alone about a mile on the other side, where I observed the country all barren and rocky. I now began to be weary, and seeing nothing to entertain my curiosity, I returned gently down towards the creek; and the sea being full in my view, I saw our men already got into the boat, and rowing for life to the ship. I was going to hallow after them, although it had been to little purpose, when I observed a huge creature walking after them in the sea, as fast as he could: he waded not much deeper than his knees, and took prodigious strides: but our men had the start of him half a league, and the sea thereabouts being full of sharp-pointed rocks, the monster was not able to overtake the boat. This I was afterwards told, for I durst not stay to see the issue of that adventure; but ran as fast as I could the way I first went, and then climbed up a steep hill, which gave me some prospect of the country. I found it fully cultivated; but that which first surprised me was the length of the grass, which in those grounds that seemed to be kept for hay, was about twenty foot high.

I fell into a high road, for so I took it to be, though it served to the inhabitants only as a footpath through a field of barley. Here I walked on for some time, but could see little on either side, it being now near harvest, and the corn rising at least forty foot. I was an hour walking to the end of this field, which was fenced in with a hedge of at least one hundred and twenty foot high, and the trees so lofty that I could make no computation of their altitude. There was a stile to pass from this field into the next. It had four steps, and a stone to cross over when you came to the uppermost. It was impossible for me to climb this stile, because every step was six foot high, and the upper stone above twenty. I was endeavouring to find some gap in the hedge, when I discovered one of the inhabitants in the next field, advancing towards the stile, of the same size with him whom I saw in the sea pursuing our boat. He appeared as tall as an ordinary spire-steeple, and took about ten yards at every stride, as near as I could guess. I was struck with the utmost fear and astonishment, and ran to hide myself in the corn, from whence I saw him at the top of the stile, looking back into the next field on the right hand, and heard him call in a voice many degrees louder than a speaking-trumpet: but the noise was so high in the air, that at first I certainly thought it was thunder. Whereupon seven monsters like himself came towards him with reaping-hooks in their hands, each hook about the largeness of six scythes. These people were not so well clad as the first, whose servants or labourers they seemed to be. For upon some words he spoke, they went to reap the corn in the field where I lay. I kept from them at as great a distance as I could, but was forced to move with extreme difficulty, for the stalks of the corn were sometimes not above a foot distant, so that I could hardly squeeze my body betwixt them. However, I made a shift to go forward till I came to a part of the field where the corn had been laid by the rain and wind. Here it was impossible for me to advance a step; for the stalks were so interwoven that I could not creep through, and the beards of the fallen ears so strong and pointed that they pierced through my clothes into my flesh. At the same time I heard the reapers not above an hundred yards behind me. Being quite dispirited with toil, and wholly overcome by grief and despair, I lay down between two ridges, and heartily wished I might there end my days. I bemoaned my desolate widow, and fatherless children.

I lamented my own folly and wilfulness in attempting a second voyage against the advice of all my friends and relations. In this terrible agitation of mind I could not forbear thinking of Lilliput, whose inhabitants looked upon me as the greatest prodigy that ever appeared in the world; where I was able to draw an Imperial Fleet in my hand, and perform those other actions which will be recorded for ever in the chronicles of that empire, while posterity shall hardly believe them, although attested by millions. I reflected what a mortification it must prove to me to appear as inconsiderable in this nation as one single Lilliputian would be among us. But this I conceived was to be the least of my misfortunes: for as human creatures are observed to be more savage and cruel in proportion to their bulk, what could I expect but to be a morsel in the mouth of the first among these enormous barbarians that should happen to seize me? Undoubtedly philosophers are in the right when they tell us, that nothing is great or little otherwise than by comparison. It might have pleased fortune to let the Lilliputians find some nation, where the people were as diminutive with respect to them, as they were to me. And who knows but that even this prodigious race of mortals might be equally overmatched in some distant part of the world, whereof we have yet no discovery?

Scared and confounded as I was, I could not forbear going on with these reflections, when one of the reapers approaching within ten yards of the ridge were I lay, made me apprehend that with the next step I should be squashed to death under his foot, or cut in two with his reaping-hook. And therefore when he was again about to move, I screamed as loud as fear could make me. Whereupon the huge creature trod short, and looking round about under him for some time, at last espied me as I lay on the ground. He considered a while with the caution of one who endeavours to lay hold on a small dangerous animal in such a manner that it shall not be able either to scratch or to bite him, as I myself have sometimes done with a weasel in England. At length he ventured to take me up behind by the middle between

his forefinger and thumb, and brought me within three
yards of his eyes, that he might behold my shape more
perfectly. I guessed his meaning, and my good fortune
gave me so much presence of mind, that I resolved not
to struggle in the least as he held me in the air about
sixty foot from the ground, although he grievously
pinched my sides for fear I should slip through his fingers. All I ventured was to raise my eyes towards the

sun, and place my hands together in a supplicating posture, and to speak some words in an humble melancholy
tone, suitable to the condition I then was in. For I appre-

hended every moment that he would dash me against the ground, as we usually do any little hateful animal which we have a mind to destroy. But my good star would have it, that he appeared pleased with my voice and gestures, and began to look upon me as a curiosity, much wondering to hear me pronounce articulate words, although he could not understand them. In the mean time I was not able to forbear groaning and shedding tears, and turning my head towards my sides; letting him know, as well as I could, how cruelly I was hurt by the pressure of his thumb and finger. He seemed to apprehend my meaning; for, lifting up the lappet of his coat, he put me gently into it, and immediately ran along with me to his master, who was a substantial farmer, and the same person I had first seen in the field.

The farmer having (as I supposed by their talk) received such an account of me as his servant could give him, took a piece of a small straw, about the size of a walking staff, and therewith lifted up the lappets of my coat; which it seems he thought to be some kind of covering that nature had given me. He blew my hairs aside to take a better view of my face. He called his hinds about him, and asked them (as I afterwards learned) whether they had ever seen in the fields any little creature that resembled me. He then placed me softly on the ground upon all four, but I got immediately up, and walked slowly backwards and forwards, so let those people see I had no intent to run away. They all sat down in a circle about me, the better to observe my motions. I pulled off my hat, and made a low bow towards the farmer. I fell on my knees, and lifted up my hands and eyes, and spoke several words as loud as I could: I took a purse of gold out of my pocket, and humbly presented it to him. He received it on the palm of his hand, then applied it close to his eye, to see what it was, and afterwards turned it several times with the point of a pin (which he took out of his sleeve), but could make nothing of it. Whereupon I made a sign that he should place his hand on the ground. I took the purse, and opening it, poured all the gold into his palm. There were six

Spanish pieces of four pistoles each, beside twenty or
thirty smaller coins. I saw him wet the tip of his little
finger upon his tongue, and take up one of my largest
pieces, and then another, but he seemed to be wholly
ignorant what they were. He made me a sign to put
them again into my purse, and the purse again into my
pocket, which after offering to him several times, I
thought it best to do.

The farmer by this time was convinced I must be a
rational creature. He spoke often to me, but the sound
of his voice pierced my ears like that of a water-mill,
yet his words were articulate enough. I answered as loud
as I could, in several languages, and he often laid his
ear within two yards of me, but all in vain, for we were
wholly unintelligible to each other. He then sent his servants to their work, and taking his handkerchief out of
his pocket, he doubled and spread it on his left hand,
which he placed flat on the ground, with the palm upwards, making me a sign to step into it, as I could easily
do, for it was not above a foot in thickness. I thought it
my part to obey, and for fear of falling, laid myself at
length upon the handkerchief, with the remainder of
which he lapped me up to the head for further security,
and in this manner carried me home to his house. There
he called his wife, and showed me to her; but she
screamed and ran back, as women in England do at the
sight of a toad or a spider. However, when she had a
while seen my behaviour, and how well I observed the
signs her husband made, she was soon reconciled, and
by degrees grew extremely tender of me.

It was about twelve at noon, and a servant brought in
dinner. It was only one substantial dish of meat (fit for
the plain condition of an husbandman), a dish of about
four-and-twenty foot diameter. The company were the
farmer and his wife, three children, and an old grand-
mother. When they were sat down, the farmer placed me
at some distance from him on the table, which was thirty
foot high from the floor. I was in a terrible fright, and kept
as far as I could from the edge for fear of falling. The wife
minced a bit of meat, then crumbled some bread on a

trencher, and placed it before me. I made her a low bow, took out my knife and fork, and fell to eat, which gave them exceeding delight. The mistress sent her maid for a small dram cup, which held about three gallons, and filled it with drink; I took up the vessel with much difficulty in both hands, and in a most respectful manner drank to her ladyship's health, expressing the words as loud as I could in English, which made the company laugh so heartily, that I was almost deafened with the noise. This liquor tasted like a small cyder, and was not unpleasant. Then the master made me a sign to come to his trencher side; but as I walked on the table, being in great surprise all the time, as the indulgent reader will easily conceive and excuse, I happened to stumble against a crust, and fell flat on my face, but received no hurt. I got up immediately, and observing the good people to be in much concern, I took my hat (which I held under my arm out of good manners) and waving it over my head, made three huzzas, to show I had got no mischief by my fall. But advancing forwards toward my master (as I shall henceforth call him) his youngest son who sat next him, an arch boy of about ten years old, took me up by the legs, and held me so high in the air, that I trembled every limb; but his father snatched me from him, and at the same time gave him such a box on the left ear, as would have felled an European troop of horse to the earth, ordering him to be taken from the table. But being afraid the boy might owe me a spite, and well remembering how mischievous all children among us naturally are to sparrows, rabbits, young kittens, and puppy dogs, I fell on my knees, and pointing to the boy, made my master to understand, as well as I could, that I desired his son might be pardoned. The father complied, and the lad took his seat again; whereupon I went to him and kissed his hand, which my master took, and made him stroke me gently with it.

In the midst of dinner, my mistress's favourite cat leapt into her lap. I heard a noise behind me like that of a dozen stocking-weavers at work; and turning my head, I found it proceeded from the purring of this animal, who seemed to be three times larger than an ox, as I computed by the view of her head, and one of her paws, while her mistress was feeding and stroking her. The fierceness of this creature's countenance altogether discomposed me; though I stood at the farther end of the table, above fifty foot off; and although my mistress held her fast for fear she might give a spring, and seize me in her talons. But it happened there was no danger; for the cat took not the least notice of me when my master placed me within three yards of her. And as I have been always told, and found true by experience in my travels, that flying, or discovering fear before a fierce animal, is a certain way to make it pursue or attack you, so I resolved in this dangerous juncture to show no manner of concern. I walked with intrepidity five or six times before the very head of the cat, and came within half a yard of her; whereupon she drew herself back, as if she were more afraid of me: I had less apprehension concerning the dogs, whereof three or four came into the room, as it is usual in farmers' houses; one of which was a mastiff, equal in bulk to four elephants, and a greyhound, somewhat taller than the mastiff, but not so large.

When dinner was almost done, the nurse came in with a child a year old in her arms, who immediately spied me, and began a squall that you might have heard from London Bridge to Chelsea, after the usual oratory of infants, to get me for a plaything. The mother out of pure indulgence took me up, and put me towards the child, who presently seized me by the middle, and got my head in his mouth, where I roared so loud that the urchin was frighted, and let me drop; and I should infallibly have broke my neck if the mother had not held her apron under me. The nurse to quiet her babe made use of a rattle, which was a kind of hollow vessel filled with great stones, and fastened by a cable to the child's waist: but all in vain, so that she was forced to apply the last remedy by giving it suck. I must confess no object ever disgusted me so much as the sight of her monstrous breast, which I cannot tell what to compare with, so as to give the curious reader an idea of its bulk, shape and colour. It stood prominent six foot, and could not be less than sixteen in circumference. The nipple was about half the bigness of my head, and the hue both of that and the dug so varified with spots, pimples and freckles, that nothing could appear more nauseous: for I had a near sight of her, she sitting down the more conveniently

to give suck, and I standing on the table. This made me reflect upon the fair skins of our English ladies, who appear so beautiful to us, only because they are of our own size, and their defects not to be seen but through a magnifying glass, where we find by experiment that the smoothest and whitest skins look rough and coarse, and ill coloured.

I remember when I was at Lilliput, the complexion of those diminutive people appeared to me the fairest in the world; and talking upon this subject with a person of learning there, who was an intimate friend of mine, he said that my face appeared much fairer and smoother when he looked on me from the ground, than it did upon a nearer view when I took him up in my hand and brought him close, which he confessed was at first a very

shocking sight. He said he could discover great holes in
my skin; that the stumps of my beard were ten times
stronger than the bristles of a boar, and my complexion
made up of several colours altogether disagreeable: although I must beg leave to say for myself, that I am as
fair as most of my sex and country, and very little sun-
burnt by all my travels. On the other side, discoursing
of the ladies in that Emperor's court, he used to tell me,
one had freckles, another too wide a mouth, a third too
large a nose, nothing of which I was able to distinguish.
I confess this reflection was obvious enough; which however I could not forbear, lest the reader might think
those vast creatures were actually deformed: for I must
do them justice to say they are a comely race of people;
and particularly the features of my master's countenance, although he were but a farmer, when I beheld
him from the height of sixty foot, appeared very well
proportioned.

When dinner was done, my master went out to his
labourers, and as I could discover by his voice and gesture, gave his wife a strict charge to take care of me. I
was very much tired, and disposed to sleep, which my
mistress perceiving, she put me on her own bed, and
covered me with a clean white handkerchief, but larger
and coarser than the mainsail of a man-of-war.

I slept about two hours, and dreamed I was at home
with my wife and children, which aggravated my sorrows
when I awaked and found myself alone in a vast room,
between two and three hundred foot wide, and above
two hundred high, lying in a bed twenty yards wide. My
mistress was gone about her household affairs, and had
locked me in. The bed was eight yards from the floor.
Some natural necessities required me to get down; I
durst not presume to call, and if I had, it would have
been in vain, with such a voice as mine, at so great a
distance from the room where I lay to the kitchen where
the family kept. While I was under these circumstances,
two rats crept up the curtains, and ran smelling backwards and forwards on the bed. One of them came up
almost to my face, whereupon I rose in a fright, and

drew out my hanger to defend myself. These horrible animals had the boldness to attack me on both sides, and one of them held his fore-feet at my collar; but I had the good fortune to rip up his belly before he could do me any mischief. He fell down at my feet, and the other seeing the fate of his comrade, made his escape, but not without one good wound on the back, which I gave him as he fled, and made the blood run trickling from him. After this exploit, I walked gently to and fro on the bed, to recover my breath and loss of spirits. These creatures were of the size of a large mastiff, but infinitely more nimble and fierce, so that if I had taken off my belt before I went to sleep, I must have infallibly been torn to pieces and devoured. I measured the tail of the dead rat, and found it to be two yards long, wanting an inch; but it went against my stomach to drag the carcass off the bed, where it lay still bleeding; I observed it had yet some life, but with a strong slash across the neck, I thoroughly dispatched it.

Soon after my mistress came into the room, who seeing me all bloody, ran and took me up in her hand. I pointed to the dead rat, smiling and making other signs to show I was not hurt, whereat she was extremely rejoiced, calling the maid to take up the dead rat with a pair of tongs, and throw it out of the window. Then she set me on a table, where I showed her my hanger all bloody, and wiping it on the lappet of my coat, returned it to the scabbard. I was pressed to do more than one thing, which another could not do for me, and therefore endeavoured to make my mistress understand that I desired to be set down on the floor; which after she had done, my bashfulness would not suffer me to express myself farther than by pointing to the door, and bowing several times. The good woman with much difficulty at last perceived what I would be at, and taking me up again in her hand, walked into the garden, where she set me down. I went on one side about two hundred yards, and beckoning to her not to look or to follow me, I hid myself between two leaves of sorrel and there discharged the necessities of nature.

I hope the gentle reader will excuse me for dwelling on these and the like particulars, which however insignificant they may appear to grovelling vulgar minds, yet will certainly help a philosopher to enlarge his thoughts and imagination, and apply them to the benefit of public as well as private life, which was my sole design in presenting this and other accounts of my travels to the world; wherein I have been chiefly studious of truth, without affecting any ornaments of learning or of style. But the whole scene of this voyage made so strong an impression on my mind, and is so deeply fixed in my memory, that in committing it to paper I did not omit one material circumstance: however, upon a strict review, I blotted out several passages of less moment which were in my first copy, for fear of being censured as tedious and trifling, whereof travellers are often, perhaps not without justice, accused.

Chapter II *A description of the farmer's daughter. The Author carried to a market-town, and then to the metropolis. The particulars of his journey.*

MY MISTRESS had a daughter of nine years old, a child of forward parts for her age, very dexterous at her needle, and skilful in dressing her baby. Her mother and she contrived to fit up the baby's cradle for me against night: the cradle was put into a small drawer of a cabinet, and the drawer placed upon a hanging shelf for fear of the rats. This was my bed all the time I stayed with those people, though made more convenient by degrees, as I began to learn their language, and make my wants known. This young girl was so handy, that after I had once or twice pulled off my clothes before her, she was able to dress and undress me, though I never gave her

that trouble when she would let me do either myself.
She made me seven shirts, and some other linen, of as
fine cloth as could be got, which indeed was coarser than
sackcloth; and these she constantly washed for me with
her own hands. She was likewise my school-mistress to
teach me the language: when I pointed to any thing, she
told me the name of it in her own tongue, so that in a
few days I was able to call for whatever I had a mind
to. She was very good-natured, and not above forty foot
high, being little for her age. She gave me the name of
Grildrig, which the family took up, and afterwards the
whole kingdom. The word imports what the Latins call
nanunculus, the Italians *homunceletino*, and the English
mannikin. To her I chiefly owe my preservation in that
country: we never parted while I was there; I called her
my *Glumdalclitch*, or little nurse: and I should be guilty
of great ingratitude if I omitted this honourable mention
of her care and affection towards me, which I heartily
wish it lay in my power to requite as she deserves, instead of being the innocent but unhappy instrument of
her disgrace, as I have too much reason to fear.

It now began to be known and talked of in the neighbourhood, that my master had found a strange animal
in the field, about the bigness of a *splacknuck*, but exactly shaped in every part like a human creature; which
it likewise imitated in all its actions; seemed to speak in
a little language of its own, had already learned several
words of theirs, went erect upon two legs, was tame and
gentle, would come when it was called, do whatever it
was bid, had the finest limbs in the world, and a complexion fairer than a nobleman's daughter of three years
old. Another farmer who lived hard by, and was a particular friend of my master, came on a visit on purpose to
enquire into the truth of this story. I was immediately
produced, and placed upon a table, where I walked as I
was commanded, drew my hanger, put it up again, made
my reverence to my master's guest, asked him in his own
language how he did, and told him he was welcome, just
as my little nurse had instructed me. This man, who was
old and dim-sighted, put on his spectacles to behold me

better, at which I could not forbear laughing very heartily, for his eyes appeared like the full moon shining into
a chamber at two windows. Our people, who discovered
the cause of my mirth, bore me company in laughing, at
which the odd fellow was fool enough to be angry and

out of countenance. He had the character of a great
miser, and to my misfortune he well deserved it, by the
cursed advice he gave my master to show me as a sight
upon a market-day in the next town, which was half an
hour's riding, about two and twenty miles from our
house. I guessed there was some mischief contriving,
when I observed my master and his friend whispering
long together, sometimes pointing at me; and my fears
made me fancy I overheard and understood some of
their words. But the next morning Glumdalclitch my lit-

tle nurse told me the whole matter, which she had cunningly picked out from her mother. The poor girl laid me on her bosom, and fell a weeping with shame and grief. She apprehended some mischief would happen to me from rude vulgar folks, who might squeeze me to death, or break one of my limbs by taking me in their hands. She had also observed how modest I was in my nature, how nicely I regarded my honour, and what an indignity I should conceive it to be exposed for money as a public spectacle to the meanest of the people. She said, her papa and mamma had promised that Grildrig should be hers, but how she found they meant to serve her as they did last year, when they pretended to give her a lamb, and yet, as soon as it was fat, sold it to a butcher. For my own part, I may truly affirm that I was less concerned than my nurse. I had a strong hope which never left me, that I should one day recover my liberty; and as to the ignominy of being carried about for a monster, I considered myself to be a perfect stranger in the country, and that such a misfortune could never be charged upon me as a reproach, if ever I should return to England; since the King of Great Britain himself, in my condition, must have undergone the same distress.

My master, pursuant to the advice of his friend, carried me in a box the next market-day to the neighbouring town, and took along with him his little daughter my nurse upon a pillion behind him. The box was close on every side, with a little door for me to go in and out, and a few gimlet-holes to let in air. The girl had been so careful to put the quilt of her baby's bed into it, for me to lie down on. However, I was terribly shaken and discomposed in this journey, though it were but of half an hour. For the horse went about forty foot at every step, and trotted so high, that the agitation was equal to the rising and falling of a ship in a great storm, but much more frequent. Our journey was somewhat further than from London to St. Albans. My master alighted at an inn which he used to frequent; and after consulting a while with the inn-keeper, and making some necessary preparation, he hired the *Grultrud*, or crier, to give notice through the town of a strange creature to be seen at the Sign of the Green Eagle, not so big as a *splack-nuck* (an animal in that country very finely shaped, about six foot long) and in every part of the body resembling an human creature, could speak several words, and perform an hundred diverting tricks.

I was placed upon a table in the largest room of the inn, which might be near three hundred foot square. My little nurse stood on a low stool close to the table, to take care of me, and direct what I should do. My master, to avoid a crowd, would suffer only thirty people at a time to see me. I walked about on the table as the girl commanded: she asked me questions as far as she knew my understanding of the language reached, and I answered them as loud as I could. I turned about several times to the company, paid my humble respects, said they were welcome, and used some other speeches I had been taught. I took up a thimble filled with liquor, which Glumdalclitch had given me for a cup, and drank their health. I drew out my hanger, and flourished with it after the manner of fencers in England. My nurse gave me part of a straw, which I exercised as a pike, having learned the art in my youth. I was that day shown to twelve sets of company, and as often forced to go over again with the same fopperies, till I was half dead with weariness and vexation. For those who had seen me made such wonderful reports, that the people were ready to break down the doors to come in. My master for his own interest would not suffer any one to touch me except my nurse; and, to prevent danger, benches were set round the table at such a distance as put me out of every body's reach. However, an unlucky school-boy aimed a hazel nut directly at my head, which very narrowly missed me; otherwise, it came with so much violence, that it would have infallibly knocked out my brains, for it was almost as large as a small pumpkin: but I had the satisfaction to see the young rogue well beaten, and turned out of the room.

My master gave public notice that he would show me again the next market-day, and in the meantime he prepared a more convenient vehicle for me, which he had reason enough to do; for I was so tired with my first journey, and with entertaining company for eight hours together, that I could hardly stand upon my legs or speak a word. It was at least three days before I recovered my strength; and that I might have no rest at home, all the neighbouring gentlemen from an hundred miles round, hearing of my fame, came to see me at my master's own house. There could not be fewer than thirty persons with their wives and children (for the country is very populous); and my master demanded the rate of a full room whenever he showed me at home, although it were only to a single family; or that for some time I had but little ease every day of the week (except Wednesday, which is their Sabbath) although I were not carried to the town.

My master finding how profitable I was likely to be, resolved to carry me to the most considerable cities of the kingdom. Having therefore provided himself with all things necessary for a long journey, and settled his affairs at home, he took leave of his wife, and upon the 17th of August, 1703, about two months after my arrival, we set out for the metropolis, situated near the middle of that empire, and about three thousand miles distance from our house. My master made his daughter Glumdalclitch ride behind him. She carried me on her lap in a box tied about her waist. The girl had lined it on all sides with the softest cloth she could get, well quilted underneath, furnished it with her baby's bed, provided me with linen and other necessaries, and made every thing as convenient as she could. We had no other company but a boy of the house, who rode after us with the luggage.

My master's design was to show me in all the towns by the way, and to step out of the road for fifty or an hundred miles, to any village or person of quality's house where he might expect custom. We made easy journeys of not above seven or eight score miles a day: for Glumdalclitch, on purpose to spare me, complained she was tired with the trotting of the horse. She often took me out of my box at my own desire, to give me air and show me the country, but always held me fast by a leading-string. We passed over five or six rivers many degrees broader and deeper than the Nile or the Ganges; and there was hardly a rivulet so small as the Thames at London Bridge. We were ten weeks in our journey, and I was shown in eighteen large towns besides many villages and private families.

On the 26th day of October, we arrived at the metropolis, called in their language *Lorbrulgrud*, or Pride of the Universe. My master took a lodging in the principal street of the city, not far from the royal palace, and put out bills in the usual form, containing an exact description of my person and parts. He hired a large room between three and four hundred foot wide. He provided a table sixty foot in diameter, upon which I was to act my part, and palisadoed it round three foot from the edge, and as many high, to prevent my falling over. I was shown ten times a day to the wonder and satisfaction of all people. I could now speak the language tolerably well, and perfectly understood every word that was spoken to me. Besides, I had learnt their alphabet, and could make a shift to explain a sentence here and there; for Glumdalclitch had been my instructor while we were at home, and at leisure hours during our journey. She carried a little book in her pocket, not much larger than a Sanson's Atlas; it was a common treatise for the use of young girls, giving a short account of their religion: out of this she taught me my letters, and interpreted the words.

Chapter III *The Author sent for to Court. The*
Queen buys him of his master the farmer, and
presents him to the King. He disputes with
his Majesty's great scholars. An apartment at
Court provided for the Author. He is in high
favour with the Queen. He stands up for the
honour of his own country. His quarrels with
the Queen's dwarf.

THE FREQUENT LABOURS I underwent every day made
in a few weeks a very considerable change in my
health: the more my master got by me, the more unsatia-
ble he grew. I had quite lost my stomach, and was almost
reduced to a skeleton. The farmer observed it, and con-
cluding I soon must die, resolved to make as good a
hand of me as he could. While he was thus reasoning
and resolving with himself, a *Slardral*, or Gentleman
Usher, came from court, commanding my master to
carry me immediately thither for the diversion of the
Queen and her ladies. Some of the latter had already
been to see me, and reported strange things of my
beauty, behaviour, and good sense. Her Majesty and
those who attended her were beyond measure delighted
with my demeanour. I fell on my knees, and begged the
honour of kissing her Imperial foot; but this gracious
princess held out her little finger towards me (after I
was set on a table) which I embraced in both my arms,
and put the tip of it with the utmost respect to my lip.
She made me some general questions about my country
and my travels, which I answered as distinctly and in as
few words as I could. She asked whether I would be
content to live at court. I bowed down to the board of
the table, and humbly answered, that I was my master's
slave, but if I were at my own disposal, I should be

proud to devote my life to her Majesty's service. She
then asked my master whether he were willing to sell
me at a good price. He, who apprehended I could not
live a month, was ready enough to part with me, and
demanded a thousand pieces of gold, which were ordered him on the spot, each piece being about the bigness of eight hundred moidores; but, allowing for the
proportion of all things between that country and Europe, and the high price of gold among them, was hardly
so great a sum as a thousand guineas would be in England. I then said to the Queen, since I was now her
Majesty's most humble creature and vassal, I must beg
the favour, that Glumdalclitch, who had always tended
me with so much care and kindness, and understood to
do it so well, might be admitted into her service, and
continue to be my nurse and instructor. Her Majesty
agreed to my petition, and easily got the farmer's consent, who was glad enough to have his daughter preferred at court: and the poor girl herself was not able to
hide her joy. My late master withdrew, bidding me farewell, and saying he had left me in a good service; to
which I replied not a word, only making him a slight
bow.

The Queen observed my coldness, and when the
farmer was gone out of the apartment, asked me the reason. I made bold to tell her Majesty that I owed no other
obligation to my late master, than his not dashing out the
brains of a poor harmless creature found by chance in his
field; which obligation was amply recompensed by the gain
he had made in showing me through half the kingdom,
and the price he had now sold me for. That the life I
had since led was laborious enough to kill an animal of
ten times my strength. That my health was much impaired by the continual drudgery of entertaining the rabble every hour of the day, and that if my master had
not thought my life in danger, her Majesty perhaps
would not have got so cheap a bargain. But as I was out
of all fear of being ill treated under the protection of so
great and good an Empress, the Ornament of Nature,
the Darling of the World, the Delight of her Subjects,

the Phoenix of the Creation; so I hoped my late master's apprehensions would appear to be groundless, for I already found my spirits to revive by the influence of her most august presence.

This was the sum of my speech, delivered with great improprieties and hesitation; the latter part was altogether framed in the style peculiar to that people, whereof I learned some phrases from Glumdalclitch, while she was carrying me to court.

The Queen, giving great allowance for my defectiveness in speaking, was however surprised at so much wit and good sense in so diminutive an animal. She took me in her own hand, and carried me to the King, who was then retired to his cabinet. His Majesty, a prince of much gravity, and austere countenance, not well observing my shape at first view, asked the Queen after a cold manner, how long it was since she grew fond of a *splacknuck*; for such it seems he took me to be, as I lay upon my breast in her Majesty's right hand. But this princess, who hath an infinite deal of wit and humour, set me gently on my feet upon the scrutore, and commanded me to give his Majesty an account of myself, which I did in a very few words; and Glumdalclitch, who attended at the cabinet door, and could not endure I should be out of her sight, being admitted, confirmed all that had passed from my arrival at her father's house.

The King, although he be as learned a person as any in his dominions, and had been educated in the study of philosophy, and particularly mathematics; yet when he observed my shape exactly, and saw me walk erect, before I began to speak, conceived I might be a piece of clockwork (which is in that country arrived to a very great perfection) contrived by some ingenious artist. But when he heard my voice, and found what I delivered to be regular and rational, he could not conceal his astonishment. He was by no means satisfied with the relation I gave him of the manner I came into his kingdom, but thought it a story concerted between Glumdalclitch and her father, who had taught me a set of words to make me sell at a higher price. Upon this imagination he put several other questions to me, and still received rational answers, no otherwise defective than by a foreign accent, and an imperfect knowledge in the language, with some rustic phrases which I had learned at the farmer's house, and did not suit the polite style of a court.

His Majesty sent for three great scholars who were then in their weekly waiting, according to the custom in that country. These gentlemen, after they had a while examined my shape with much nicety, were of different opinions concerning me. They all agreed that I could not be produced according to the regular laws of nature, because I was not framed with a capacity of preserving my life, either by swiftness, or climbing of trees, or digging holes in the earth. They observed by my teeth, which they viewed with great exactness, that I was a carnivorous animal; yet most quadrupeds being an overmatch for me, and field mice, with some others, too nimble, they could not imagine how I should be able to support myself, unless I fed upon snails and other insects, which they offered, by many learned arguments, to evince that I could not possibly do. One of these virtuosi seemed to think that I might be an embryo, or abortive birth. But this opinion was rejected by the other two, who observed my limbs to be perfect and finished, and that I had lived several years, as it was manifested from my beard, the stumps whereof they plainly discovered through a magnifying-glass. They would not allow me to be a dwarf, because my littleness was beyond all degrees of comparison; for the Queen's favourite dwarf, the smallest ever known in that kingdom, was nearly thirty foot high. After much debate, they concluded unanimously that I was only *relplum scalcath*, which is interpreted literally, *lusus naturoe*; a determination exactly agreeable to the modern philosophy of Europe, whose professors, disdaining the old evasion of *occult causes*, whereby the followers of Aristotle endeavour in vain to disguise their ignorance, have invented this wonderful solution of all difficulties, to the unspeakable advancement of human knowledge.

C.E. Brock
Apl. 1894.

After this decisive conclusion, I entreated to be heard
a word or two. I applied myself to the King, and assured
his Majesty, that I came from a country which abounded
with several millions of both sexes, and of my own stature; where the animals, trees, and houses were all in
proportion, and where by consequence I might be as
able to defend myself, and to find sustenance, as any of
his Majesty's subjects could do here; which I took for a
full answer to those gentlemen's arguments. To this they
only replied with a smile of contempt, saying that the
farmer had instructed me very well in my lesson. The
King, who had a much better understanding, dismissing
his learned men, sent for the farmer, who by good fortune was not yet gone out of town. Having therefore
first examined him privately, and then confronted him
with me and the young girl, his Majesty began to think
that what we told him might possibly be true. He desired
the Queen to order that a particular care should be
taken of me, and was of opinion that Glumdalclitch
should still continue in her office of tending me, because
he observed we had a great affection for each other. A
convenient apartment was provided for her at court; she
had a sort of governess appointed to take care of her
education, a maid to dress her, and two other servants
for menial offices; but the care of me was wholly appropriated to herself. The Queen commanded her own
cabinet-maker to contrive a box that might serve me for
a bed-chamber, after the model that Glumdalclitch and
I should agree upon. This man was a most ingenious
artist, and according to my directions, in three weeks
finished for me a wooden chamber of sixteen foot
square, and twelve high, with sash-windows, a door, and
two closets, like a London bed-chamber. The board that
made the ceiling was to be lifted up and down by two
hinges, to put in a bed ready furnished by her Majesty's
upholsterer, which Glumdalclitch took out every day to
air, made it with her own hands, and letting it down at
night, locked up the roof over me. A nice workman, who
was famous for little curiosities, undertook to make me
two chairs, with backs and frames, of a substance not

unlike ivory, and two tables, with a cabinet to put my things in. The room was quilted on all sides, as well as the floor and the ceiling, to prevent any accident from the carelessness of those who carried me, and to break the force of a jolt when I went in a coach. I desired a lock for my door, to prevent rats and mice from coming in: the smith, after several attempts, made the smallest that ever was seen among them, for I have known a larger at the gate of a gentleman's house in England. I made a shift to keep the key in a pocket of my own, fearing Glumdalclitch might lose it. The Queen likewise ordered the thinnest silks that could be gotten, to make me clothes, not much thicker than an English blanket, very cumbersome till I was accustomed to them. They were after the fashion of the kingdom, partly resembling the Persian, and partly the Chinese, and are a very grave and decent habit.

The Queen became so fond of my company, that she could not dine without me. I had a table placed upon the same at which her Majesty ate, just at her left elbow, and a chair to sit on. Glumdalclitch stood upon a stool on the floor, near my table, to assist and take care of me. I had an entire set of silver dishes and plates, and other necessaries, which, in proportion to those of the Queen, were not much larger than what I have seen of the same kind in a London toy-shop, for the furniture of a baby-house: these my little nurse kept in her pocket in a silver box, and gave me at meals as I wanted them, always cleaning them herself. No person dined with the Queen but the two Princesses Royal, the elder sixteen years old, and the younger at that time thirteen and a month. Her Majesty used to put a bit of meat upon one of my dishes, out of which I carved for myself, and her diversion was to see me eat in miniature. For the Queen (who had indeed but a weak stomach) took up at one mouthful as much as a dozen English farmers could eat at a meal, which to me was for some time a very nauseous sight. She would craunch the wing of a lark, bones and all, between her teeth, although it were nine times as large as that of a full-grown turkey; and put a bit of bread into her mouth, as big as two twelve-penny loaves. She drank out of a golden cup, above a hogshead at a draught. Her knives were twice as long as a scythe set straight upon the handle. The spoons, forks, and other instruments were all in the same proportion. I remember when Glumdalclitch carried me out of curiosity to see some of the tables at court, where ten or a dozen of these enormous knives and forks were lifted up together, I thought I had never till then beheld so terrible a sight.

It was the custom that every Wednesday (which, as I have before observed, was their Sabbath) the King and Queen, with the royal issue of both sexes, dine together in the apartment of his Majesty, to whom I was now become a great favourite; and at these times my little chair and table were placed at his left hand, before one of the salt-cellars. This prince took a pleasure in conversing with me, enquiring into the manners, religion, laws, government, and learning of Europe; wherein I gave him the best account I was able. His apprehension was so clear, and his judgment so exact, that he made very wise reflections and observations upon all I said. But, I confess, that after I had been a little too copious in talking of my own beloved country, of our trade, and wars by sea and land, of our schisms in religion, and parties in the state, the prejudices of his education prevailed so far, that he could not forbear taking me up in his right hand, and stroking me gently with the other, after an hearty fit of laughing, asked me whether I were a Whig or a Tory. Then turning to his first minister, who waited behind him with a white staff, near as tall as the mainmast of the *Royal Sovereign*, he observed how contemptible a thing was human grandeur, which could be mimicked by such diminutive insects as I: and yet, said he, I dare engage, these creatures have their titles and distinctions of honour, they contrive little nests and burrows, that they call houses and cities; they make a figure in dress and equipage; they love, they fight, they dispute, they cheat, they betray. And thus he continued on, while my colour came and went several times with indignation to hear our noble country, the mistress of arts and arms,

the scourge of France, the arbitress of Europe, the seat
of virtue, piety, honour and truth, the pride and envy of
the world, so contemptuously treated.

But as I was not in a condition to resent injuries, so,
upon mature thoughts, I began to doubt whether I were
injured or no. For, after having been accustomed several
months to the sight and converse of this people, and
observed every object upon which I cast my eyes to be
of proportionable magnitude, the horror I had first conceived from their bulk and aspect was so far worn off,
that if I had then beheld a company of English lords
and ladies in their finery and birth-day clothes, acting
their several parts in the most courtly manner, of strut-
ting, and bowing, and prating, to say the truth, I should
have been strongly tempted to laugh as much at them
as the King and his grandees did at me. Neither indeed
could I forbear smiling at myself, when the Queen used
to place me upon her hand towards a looking-glass, by
which both our persons appeared before me in full view
together; and there could be nothing more ridiculous
than the comparison; so that I really began to imagine
myself dwindled many degrees below my usual size.

Nothing angered and mortified me so much as the
Queen's dwarf, who being of the lowest stature that was
ever in that country (for I verily think he was not full
thirty foot high) became insolent at seeing a creature so
much beneath him, that he would always affect to swag-
ger and look big as he passed by me in the Queen's
antechamber, while I was standing on some table talking
with the lords or ladies of the court, and he seldom
failed of a smart word or two upon my littleness; against
which I could only revenge myself by calling him
brother, challenging him to wrestle, and such repartees
as are usual in the mouths of court pages. One day at
dinner this malicious little cub was so nettled with something I had said to him, that raising himself upon the
frame of her Majesty's chair, he took me up by the middle, as I was sitting down, not thinking any harm, and
let me drop into a large silver bowl of cream, and then
ran away as fast as he could. I fell over head and ears,

and if I had not been a good swimmer, it might have gone very hard with me; for Glumdalclitch in that instant happened to be at the other end of the room, and the Queen was in such a fright that she wanted presence of mind to assist me. But my little nurse ran to my relief, and took me out, after I had swallowed above a quart of cream. I was put to bed; however I received no other damage than the loss of a suit of clothes, which was utterly spoiled. The dwarf was soundly whipped, and as a farther punishment, forced to drink up the bowl of cream, into which he had thrown me; neither was he ever restored to favour: for soon after the Queen bestowed him to a lady of high quality, so that I saw him no more, to my very great satisfaction; for I could not tell to what extremity such a malicious urchin might have carried his resentment.

He had before served me a scurvy trick, which set the Queen a laughing, although at the same time she were heartily vexed, and would have immediately cashiered him, if I had not been so generous as to intercede. Her Majesty had taken a marrow-bone upon her plate, and after knocking out the marrow, placed the bone again in the dish erect as it stood before; the dwarf watching his opportunity, while Glumdalclitch was gone to the sideboard, mounted upon the stool she stood on to take care of me at meals, took me up in both hands, and squeezing my legs together, wedged them into the marrow-bone above my waist, where I stuck for some time, and made a very ridiculous figure. I believe it was near a minute before any one knew what was become of me, for I thought it below me to cry out. But, as princes seldom get their meat hot, my legs were not scalded, only my stockings and breeches in a sad condition. The dwarf at my entreaty had no other punishment than a sound whipping.

I was frequently rallied by the Queen upon account of my fearfulness, and she used to ask me whether the people of my country were as great cowards as myself. The occasion was this. The kingdom is much pestered with flies in summer; and these odious insects, each of them as big as a Dunstable lark, hardly gave me any rest while I sat at dinner, with their continual humming and buzzing about my ears. They would sometimes alight upon my victuals; and leave their loathsome excrement or spawn behind, which to me was very visible, though not to the natives of that country, whose large optics were not so acute as mine in viewing smaller objects. Sometimes they would fix upon my nose or forehead, where they stung me to the quick, smelling very offensively, and I could easily trace that viscous matter, which our naturalists tell us enables those creatures to walk with their feet upwards upon a ceiling. I had much ado to defend myself against these detestable animals, and could not forbear starting when they came on my face. It was the common practice of the dwarf to catch a number of these insects in his hand, as school-boys do among us, and let them out suddenly under my nose, on purpose to frighten me, and divert the Queen. My remedy was to cut them in pieces with my knife as they flew in the air, wherein my dexterity was much admired.

I remember one morning when Glumdalclitch had set me in my box upon a window, as she usually did in fair days to give me air (for I durst not venture to let the box be hung on a nail out of the window, as we do with cages in England) after I had lifted up one of my sashes, and sat down at my table to eat a piece of sweet cake for my breakfast, above twenty wasps, allured by the smell, came flying into the room, humming louder than the drones of as many bagpipes. Some of them seized my cake, and carried it piecemeal away, others flew about my head and face, confounding me with the noise, and putting me in the utmost terror of their stings. However, I had the courage to rise and draw my hanger, and attack them in the air. I dispatched four of them, but the rest got away, and I presently shut my window. These insects were as large as partridges: I took out their stings, found them an inch and a half long, and as sharp as needles. I carefully preserved them all, and having since shown them with some other curiosities in several parts of Europe, upon my return to England I gave three of them to Gresham College, and kept the fourth for myself.

Chapter IV *The country described. A proposal for correcting modern maps. The King's palace, and some account of the metropolis. The Author's way of travelling. The chief temple described.*

I NOW INTEND TO give the reader a short description of this country, as far as I travelled in it, which was not above two thousand miles round Lorbrulgrud the metropolis. For the Queen, whom I always attended, never went further when she accompanied the King in his progresses, and there stayed till his Majesty returned from viewing his frontiers. The whole extent of this prince's dominions reacheth about six thousand miles in length, and from three to five in breadth. From whence I cannot but conclude that our geographers of Europe are in a great error, by supposing nothing but sea between Japan and California; for it was ever my opinion, that there must be a balance of earth to counterpoise the great continent of Tartary; and therefore they ought to correct their maps and charts, by joining this vast tract of land to the north-west parts of America, wherein I shall be ready to lend them my assistance.

The kingdom is a peninsula, terminated to the north-east by a ridge of mountains thirty miles high, which are altogether impassable by reason of the volcanoes upon the tops. Neither do the most learned know what sort of mortals inhabit beyond those mountains, or whether they be inhabited at all. On the three other sides it is bounded by the ocean. There is not one sea-port in the whole kingdom, and those parts of the coasts into which the rivers issue are so full of pointed rocks, and the sea generally so rough, that there is no venturing with the smallest of their boats, so that these people are wholly excluded from any commerce with the rest of the world. But the large rivers are full of vessels, and abound with excellent fish, for they seldom get any from the sea, because the sea-fish are of the same size with those in Europe, and consequently not worth catching; whereby it is manifest, that nature, in the production of plants and animals of so extraordinary a bulk, is wholly confined to this continent, of which I leave the reasons to be determined by philosophers. However, now and then they take a whale that happens to be dashed against the rocks, which the common people feed on heartily. These whales I have known so large that a man could hardly carry one upon his shoulders; and sometimes for curiosity they are brought in hampers to Lorbrulgrud: I saw one of them in a dish at the King's table, which passed for a rarity, but I did not observe he was fond of it; for I think the bigness disgusted him, although I have seen one somewhat larger in Greenland.

The country is well inhabited for it contains fifty-one cities, near an hundred walled towns, and a great number of villages. To satisfy my curious reader, it may be sufficient to describe Lorbrulgrud. This city stands upon almost two equal parts on each side of the river that passes through. It contains above eighty thousand houses, and about six hundred thousand inhabitants. It is in length three *glongluns* (which make about fifty-four English miles) and two and a half in breadth, as I measured it myself in the royal map made by the King's order, which was laid on the ground on purpose for me, and extended an hundred feet: I paced the diameter and circumference several times barefoot, and computing by the scale, measured it pretty exactly.

The King's palace is no regular edifice, but an heap of buildings about seven miles round: the chief rooms are generally two hundred and forty foot high, and broad and long in proportion. A coach was allowed to Glumdalclitch and me, wherein her governess frequently took her out to see the town, or go among the shops; and I was always of the party, carried in my box; although the girl at my own desire would often take me out, and hold me in her hand, that I might more conveniently view the houses and the people, as we passed along the streets. I reckoned our coach to be about a square of Westminster Hall, but not altogether so high; however, I cannot be very exact. One day the governess ordered our coachman to stop at several shops, where the beggars, watching their opportunity, crowded to the sides of the coach, and gave me the most horrible spectacles that ever an English eye beheld. There was a woman with a cancer in her breast, swelled to a monstrous size, full of holes, in two or three of which I could have easily crept, and covered my whole body. There was a fellow with a wen in his neck, larger than five wool-packs, and another with a couple of wooden legs, each about twenty foot high. But the most hateful sight of all was the lice crawling on their clothes. I could see distinctly the limbs of these vermin with my naked eye, much better than those of an European louse through a microscope, and their snouts with which they rooted like swine. They were the first I had ever beheld, and I should have been curious enough to dissect one of them, if I had proper instruments (which I unluckily left behind me in the ship) although indeed the sight was so nauseous, that it perfectly turned my stomach.

Besides the large box in which I was usually carried, the Queen ordered a smaller one to be made for me, of about twelve foot square, and ten high, for the convenience of travelling, because the other was somewhat too large for Glumdalclitch's lap, and cumbersome in the coach; it was made by the same artist, whom I directed in the whole contrivance. This travelling closet was an exact square with a window in the middle of three of the squares, and each window was latticed with iron wire on the outside, to prevent accidents in long journeys. On the fourth side, which had no window, two strong staples were fixed, through which the person that carried me, when I had a mind to be on horseback, put in a leathern belt, and buckled it about his waist. This was always the office of some grave trusty servant in whom I could confide, whether I attended the King and

Queen in their progresses, or were disposed to see the gardens, or pay a visit to some great lady or minister of state in the court, when Glumdalclitch happened to be out of order: for I soon began to be known and esteemed among the greatest officers, I suppose more upon account of their Majesties' favour, than any merit of my own. In journeys, when I was weary of the coach, a servant on horseback would buckle my box, and place it on a cushion before him; and there I had a full prospect of the country on three sides from my three windows. I had in this closet a field-bed and a hammock hung from the ceiling, two chairs and a table, neatly screwed to the floor, to prevent being tossed about by the agitation of the horse or the coach. And having been long used to sea-voyages, those motions, although sometimes very violent, did not much discompose me.

Whenever I had a mind to see the town, it was always in my travelling-closet, which Glumdalclitch held in her lap in a kind of open sedan, after the fashion of the country, borne by four men, and attended by two others in the Queen's livery. The people who had often heard of me, were very curious to crowd about the sedan, and the girl was complaisant enough to make the bearers stop, and to take me in her hand that I might be more conveniently seen.

I was very desirous to see the chief temple, and particularly the tower belonging to it, which is reckoned the highest in the kingdom. Accordingly one day my nurse carried me thither, but I may truly say I came back disappointed; for the height is not above three thousand foot, reckoning from the ground to the highest pinnacle top; which allowing for the difference between the size of those people and us in Europe, is no great matter for admiration, nor at all equal in proportion (if I rightly remember) to Salisbury steeple. But, not to detract from a nation to which during my life I shall acknowledge myself extremely obliged, it must be allowed that whatever this famous tower wants in height is amply made up in beauty and strength. For the walls are near an hundred foot thick, built of hewn stone, whereof each is about forty foot square, and adorned on all sides with statues of gods and emperors cut in marble larger than the life, placed in their several niches. I measured a little finger which had fallen down from one of these statues, and lay unperceived among some rubbish, and found it exactly four foot and an inch in length. Glumdalclitch wrapped it up in a handkerchief, and carried it home in her pocket to keep among other trinkets, of which the girl was very fond, as children at her age usually are.

The King's kitchen is indeed a noble building, vaulted at top, and about six hundred foot high. The great oven is not so wide by ten paces as the cupola at St. Paul's: for I measured the latter on purpose after my return. But if I should describe the kitchen-grate, the prodigious pots and kettles, the joints of meat turning on the spits, with many other particulars, perhaps I should be hardly believed; at least a severe critic would be apt to think I enlarged a little, as travellers are often suspected to do. To avoid such censure, I fear I have run too much into the other extreme; and that if this treatise should happen to be translated into the language of Brobdingnag (which is the general name of that kingdom) and transmitted thither, the King and his people would have reason to complain that I had done them an injury by a false and diminutive representation.

His Majesty seldom keeps above six hundred horses in his stables: they are generally from fifty-four to sixty foot high. But when he goes abroad on solemn days, he is attended for state by a militia guard of five hundred horse, which indeed I thought was the most splendid sight that could be ever beheld, till I saw part of his army in battalia, whereof I shall find another occasion to speak.

Chapter V *Several adventures that happened to the Author. The execution of a criminal. The Author shows his skill in navigation.*

I SHOULD HAVE lived happy enough in that country, if my littleness had not exposed me to several ridiculous and troublesome accidents, some of which I shall venture to relate. Glumdalclitch often carried me into the gardens of the court in my smaller box, and would sometimes take me out of it and hold me in her hand, or set me down to walk. I remember, before the dwarf left the Queen, he followed us one day into those gardens, and my nurse having set me down, he and I being close together, near some dwarf apple-trees, I must needs show my wit by a silly allusion between him and the trees, which happens to hold in their language as it doth in our. Whereupon, the malicious rogue watching his opportunity, when I was walking under one of them, shook it directly over my head, by which a dozen apples, each of them near as large as a Bristol barrel, came tumbling about my ears; one of them hit me on the back as I chanced to stoop, and knocked me down flat on my face, but I received no other hurt, and the dwarf was pardoned at my desire, because I had given the provocation.

Another day Glumdalclitch left me on a smooth grass-plot to divert myself while she walked at some distance with her governess. In the meantime there suddenly fell such a violent shower of hail, that I was immediately by the force of it struck to the ground: and when I was down, the hailstones gave me such cruel bangs all over the body, as if I had been pelted with tennis-balls; however I made a shift to creep on all four, and shelter myself by lying flat on my face on the lee-side of a border of lemon thyme, but so bruised from head to foot that I could not go abroad in ten days. Neither is this at all to be wondered at, because nature in that country observing the same proportion through all her operations, a hailstone is near eighteen hundred times as large as one in Europe, which I can assert upon experience, having been so curious to weigh and measure them.

But a more dangerous accident happened to me in the same garden, when my little nurse believing she had put me in a secure place, which I often entreated her to do, that I might enjoy my own thoughts, and having left my box at home to avoid the trouble of carrying it, went to another part of the garden with her governess and some ladies of her acquaintance. While she was absent and out of hearing, a small white spaniel belonging to one of the chief gardeners, having got by accident into the garden, happened to range near the place where I lay. The dog following the scent, came directly up, and taking me in his mouth, ran straight to his master, wagging his tail, and set me gently on the ground. By good fortune he had been so well taught, that I was carried between his teeth without the least hurt, or even tearing my clothes. But the poor gardener, who knew me well, and had a great kindness for me, was in a terrible fright. He gently took me up in both his hands, and asked me how I did; but I was so amazed and out of breath, that I could not speak a word. In a few minutes I came to myself, and he carried me safe to my little nurse, who by this time had returned to the place where she left me, and was in cruel agonies when I did not appear, nor answer when she called: she severely reprimanded the gardener on account of his dog. But the thing was hushed up, and never known at court; for the girl was afraid of the Queen's anger, and truly as to myself, I thought it would not be for my reputation that such a story should go about.

This accident absolutely determined Glumdalclitch never to trust me abroad for the future out of her sight. I had been long afraid of this resolution, and therefore concealed from her some little unlucky adventures that happened in those times when I was left by myself. Once a kite hovering over the garden made a swoop at me, and if I had not resolutely drawn my hanger, and run under a thick espalier, he would have certainly carried me away in his talons. Another time walking to the top of a fresh mole-hill, I fell to my neck in the hole through which that animal had cast up the earth, and coined some lie, not worth remembering, to excuse myself for spoiling my clothes. I likewise broke my right shin against the shell of a snail, which I happened to stumble over, as I was walking alone, and thinking on poor England.

I cannot tell whether I were more pleased or mortified, to observe in those solitary walks that the smaller birds did not appear to be at all afraid of me, but would hop about within a yard distance, looking for worms and other food with as much indifference and security as if no creature at all were near them. I remember a thrush had the confidence to snatch out of my hand with his bill a piece of cake that Glumdalclitch had just given me for my breakfast. When I attempted to catch any of these birds, they would boldly turn against me, endeavouring to pick my fingers, which I durst not venture within their reach; and then they would hop back unconcerned to hunt for worms or snails, as they did before. But one day I took a thick cudgel, and threw it with all my strength so luckily at a linnet that I knocked him down, and seizing him by the neck with both my hands, ran with him in triumph to my nurse. However, the bird, who had only been stunned, recovering himself, gave me so many boxes with his wings on both sides of my head and body, though I held him at arm's length, and was out of the reach of his claws, that I was twenty times thinking to let him go. But I was soon relieved by one of our servants, who wrung off the bird's neck, and I had him next day for dinner, by the Queen's command. This linnet, as near as I can remember, seemed to be somewhat larger than an English swan.

The Maids of Honour often invited Glumdalclitch to their apartments, and desired she would bring me along with her, on purpose to have the pleasure of seeing and touching me. They would often strip me naked from top to toe and lay me at full length in their bosoms; wherewith I was much disgusted; because, to say the truth, a very offensive smell came from their skins; which I do not mention or intend to the disadvantage of those excellent ladies, for whom I have all manner of respect: but I conceive that my sense was more acute in proportion to my littleness, and that those illustrious persons were no more disagreeable to their lovers, or to each other, than people of the same quality are with us in England. And, after all, I found their natural smell was much more supportable than when they used perfumes, under which I immediately swooned away. I cannot forget that an intimate friend of mine in Lilliput took the freedom in a warm day, when I had used a good deal of exercise, to complain of the strong smell about me, although I am as little faulty that way as most of my sex: but I suppose his faculty of smelling was as nice with regard to me, as mine was to that of his people. Upon this point, I cannot forbear doing justice to the Queen my mistress, and Glumdalclitch my nurse, whose persons were as sweet as those of any lady in England.

That which gave me most uneasiness among these Maids of Honour, when my nurse carried me to visit them, was to see them use me without any manner of ceremony, like a creature who had no sort of consequence. For they would strip themselves to the skin, and put on their smocks in my presence, while I was placed on their toilet directly before their naked bodies, which, I am sure, to me was very far from being a tempting sight, or from giving me any other emotions than those of horror and disgust. Their skins appeared so coarse and uneven, so variously coloured, when I saw them near, with a mole here and there as broad as a trencher, and hairs hanging from it thicker than packthreads, to say nothing further concerning the rest of their persons. Neither did they at all scruple, while I was by, to discharge what they had drunk, to the quantity of at least two hogsheads, in a vessel that held above three tuns. The handsomest among these Maids of Honour, a pleasant frolicsome girl of sixteen, would sometimes set me astride upon one of her nipples, with many other tricks, wherein the reader will excuse me for not being over particular. But I was so much displeased, that I entreated Glumdalclitch to contrive some excuse for not seeing that young lady any more.

One day a young gentleman, who was nephew to my nurse's governess, came and pressed them both to see an execution. It was of a man who had murdered one of that gentleman's intimate acquaintance. Glumdalclitch was prevailed on to be of the company, very much against her inclination, for she was naturally tender-hearted: and as for myself, although I abhorred such kind of spectacles, yet my curiosity tempted me to see something that I thought must be extraordinary. The malefactor was fixed in a chair upon a scaffold erected for the purpose, and his head cut off at a blow with a sword of about forty foot long. The veins and arteries spouted up such a prodigious quantity of blood, and so high in the air, that the great *jet d'eau* at Versailles was not equal for the time it lasted; and the head, when it fell on the scaffold floor, gave such a bounce, as made me start, although I were at least half an English mile distant.

The Queen, who often used to hear me talk of my sea-voyages, and took all occasions to divert me when I was melancholy, asked me whether I understood how to handle a sail or an oar, and whether a little exercise of rowing might not be convenient for my health. I answered that I understood both very well. For although my proper employment had been to be surgeon or doctor to the ship, yet often, upon a pinch, I was forced to work like a common mariner. But I could not see how this could be done in their country, where the smallest wherry was equal to a first-rate man-of-war among us, and such a boat as I could manage would never live in any of their rivers. Her Majesty said, if I would contrive a boat, her own joiner should make it, and she would provide a place for me to sail in. The fellow was an ingenious workman, and by my instructions in ten days finished a pleasure-boat with all its tackling, able conveniently to hold eight Europeans. When it was finished, the Queen was so delighted, that she ran with it in her lap to the King, who ordered it to be put in a cistern full of water, with me in it, by way of trial; where I could not manage my two sculls, or little oars, for want of room. But the Queen had before contrived another project. She ordered the joiner to make a wooden trough of three hundred foot long, fifty broad, and eight deep; which being well pitched to prevent leaking, was placed on the floor along the wall, in an outer room of the palace. It had a cock near the bottom to let out the water when it began to grow stale, and two servants could easily fill it in half an hour. Here I often used to row for my own diversion, as well as that of the Queen and her ladies, who thought themselves well entertained with my skill and agility. Sometimes I would put up my sail, and then my business was only to steer, while the ladies gave me a gale with their fans; and when they were weary, some of the pages would blow my sail forward with their breath, while I showed my art by steering starboard or larboard as I pleased. When I had done, Glumdalclitch always carried my boat into her closet, and hung it on a nail to dry.

In this exercise I once met an accident which had like to have cost me my life. For one of the pages having put my boat into the trough, the governess who attended Glumdalclitch very officiously lifted me up to place me in the boat, but I happened to slip through her fingers, and should have infallibly fallen down forty feet upon the floor, if by the luckiest chance in the world, I had not been stopped by a corking-pin that stuck in the good gentlewoman's stomacher; the head of the pin passed between my shirt and the waistband of my breeches, and thus I was held by the middle in the air till Glumdalclitch ran to my relief.

Another time, one of the servants, whose office it was to fill my trough every third day with fresh water, was so careless to let a huge frog (not perceiving it) slip out of his pail. The frog lay concealed till I was put into my

boat, but then seeing a resting-place, climbed up, and
made it lean so much on one side, that I was forced to
balance it with all my weight on the other, to prevent
overturning. When the frog was got in, it hopped at once
half the length of the boat, and then over my head, backwards and forwards, daubing my face and clothes with
its odious slime. The largeness of its features made it
appear the most deformed animal that can be conceived.
However, I desired Glumdalclitch to let me deal with it
alone. I banged it a good while with one of my sculls,
and at last forced it to leap out of the boat.

But the greatest danger I ever underwent in that kingdom was from a monkey, who belonged to one of the
clerks of the kitchen. Glumdalclitch had locked me up
in her closet, while she went somewhere upon business
or a visit. The weather being very warm, the closet window was left open, as well as the windows and the door
of my bigger box, in which I usually lived, because of
its largeness and conveniency. As I sat quietly meditating
at my table, I heard something bounce in at the closet
window, and skip about from one side to the other;
whereat, although I was much alarmed, yet I ventured
to look out, but stirred not from my seat; and then I
saw this frolicsome animal, frisking and leaping up and
down, till at last he came to my box, which he seemed
to view with great pleasure and curiosity, peeping in at
the door and every window. I retreated to the farther
corner of my room, or box, but the monkey looking in
at every side, put me into such a fright, that I wanted
presence of mind to conceal myself under the bed, as I
might easily have done. After some time spent in peeping, grinning, and chattering, he at last espied me, and
reaching one of his paws in at the door, as a cat does
when she plays with a mouse, although I often shifted
place to avoid him, he at length seized the lappet of my
coat (which being made of that country cloth, was very
thick and strong) and dragged me out. He took me up
in his right fore-foot, and held me as a nurse does a
child she is going to suckle, just as I have seen the same
sort of creature do with a kitten in Europe: and when I

offered to struggle, he squeezed me so hard, that I thought it more prudent to submit. I have good reason to believe that he took me for a young one of his own species, by his often stroking my face very gently with his other paw. In these diversions he was interrupted by a noise at the closet door, as if somebody were opening it; whereupon he suddenly leaped up to the window at which he had come in, and thence upon the leads and gutters, walking upon three legs, and holding me in the fourth, till he clambered up to a roof that was next to ours. I heard Glumdalclitch give a shriek at the moment he was carrying me out. The poor girl was almost distracted: that quarter of the palace was all in an uproar; the servants ran for ladders; the monkey was seen by hundreds in the court, sitting upon the ridge of a building, holding me like a baby in one of his forepaws, and feeding me with the other, by cramming into my mouth some victuals he had squeezed out of the bag on one side of his chaps, and patting me when I would not eat; whercat many of the rabble below could not forbear laughing; neither do I think they justly ought to be blamed, for without question the sight was ridiculous enough to every body but myself. Some of the people threw up stones, hoping to drive the monkey down; but this was strictly forbidden, or else very probably my brains had been dashcd out.

The ladders were now applied, and mounted by several men, which the monkey observing, and finding himself almost encompassed, not being able to make speed enough with his three legs, let me drop on a ridge tile, and made his escape. Here I sat for some time three hundred yards from the ground, expecting every moment to be blown down by the wind, or to fall by my own giddiness, and come tumbling over and over from the ridge to the eaves; but an honest lad, one of my nurse's footmen, climbed up, and putting me into his breeches pocket, brought me down safe.

I was almost choked with the filthy stuff the monkey had crammed down my throat: but my dear little nurse picked it out of my mouth with a small needle, and then

I fell a vomiting, which gave me great relief. Yet I was so weak and bruised in the sides with the squeezes given me by this odious animal, that I was forced to keep my bed a fortnight. The King, Queen, and all the court, sent every day to enquire after my health, and her Majesty made me several visits during my sickness. The monkey was killed, and an order made that no such animal should be kept about the palace.

When I attended the King after my recovery, to return him thanks for his favours, he was pleased to rally me a good deal upon this adventure. He asked me what my thoughts and speculations were while I lay in the monkey's paw, how I liked the victuals he gave me, his manner of feeding, and whether the fresh air on the roof had sharpened my stomach. He desired to know what I would have done upon such an occasion in my own country. I told his Majesty that in Europe we had no monkeys, except such as were brought for curiosities from other places, and so small that I could deal with a dozen of them together, if they presumed to attack me. And as for that monstrous animal with whom I was so lately engaged (it was indeed as large as an elephant), if my fears had suffered me to think so far as to make use of my hanger (looking fiercely and clapping my hand upon the hilt as I spoke) when he poked his paw into my chamber, perhaps I should have given him such a wound, as would have made him glad to withdraw it with more haste than he put it in. This I delivered in a firm tone, like a person who was jealous lest his courage should be called in question. However, my speech produced nothing else besides a loud laughter, which all the respect due to his Majesty from those about him could not make them contain. This made me reflect how vain an attempt it is for a man to endeavour doing himself honour among those who are out of all degree of equality or comparison with him. And yet I have seen the moral of my own behaviour very frequent in England since my return, where a little contemptible varlet, without the least title to birth, person, wit, or common sense, shall presume to look with importance, and put himself upon a foot with the greatest persons of the kingdom.

I was every day furnishing the court with some ridiculous story; and Glumdalclitch, although she loved me to excess, yet was arch enough to inform the Queen, whenever I committed any folly that she thought would be diverting to her Majesty. The girl, who had been out of order, was carried by her governess to take the air about an hour's distance, or thirty miles from town. They alighted out of the coach near a small foot-path in a field, and Glumdalclitch setting down my travelling box, I went out of it to walk. There was a cow-dung in the path, and I must needs try my activity by attempting to leap over it. I took a run, but unfortunately jumped short, and found myself just in the middle up to my knees. I waded through with some difficulty, and one of the footmen wiped me as clean as he could with his handkerchief; for I was filthily bemired, and my nurse confined me to my box till we returned home; where the Queen was soon informed of what had passed, and the footmen spread it about the court, so that all the mirth, for some days, was at my expense.

Chapter VI *Several contrivances of the Author to please the King and Queen. He shows his skill in music. The King inquires into the state of Europe, which the Author relates to him. The King's observations thereon.*

I USED TO attend the King's levee once or twice a week, and had often seen him under the barber's hand, which indeed was at first very terrible to behold; for the razor was almost twice as long as an ordinary scythe. His Majesty, according to the custom of the country, was only shaved twice a week. I once prevailed on the barber to give me some of the suds or lather, out of which I picked forty or fifty of the strongest stumps of hair. I then took a piece of fine wood, and cut it like the back of a comb, making several holes in it at equal distance with as small a needle as I could get from Glumdalclitch. I fixed in the stumps so artificially, scraping and sloping them with my knife toward the points, that I made a very tolerable comb; which was a seasonable supply, my own being so much broken in the teeth, that it was almost useless: neither did I know any artist in that country so nice and exact, as would undertake to make me another.

And this puts me in mind of an amusement wherein I spent many of my leisure hours. I desired the Queen's woman to save for me the combings of her Majesty's hair, whereof in time I got a good quantity, and consulting with my friend the cabinet-maker, who had received general orders to do little jobs for me, I directed him to make two chair-frames, no larger than those I had in my box, and then to bore little holes with a fine awl round those parts where I designed the backs and seats; through these holes I wove the strongest hairs I could pick out, just after the manner of cane-chairs in England. When they were finished, I made a present of them to her Majesty, who kept them in her cabinet, and used to show them for curiosities, as indeed they were the wonder of every one that beheld them. The Queen would have had me sit upon one of these chairs, but I absolutely refused to obey her, protesting I would rather die a thousand deaths than place a dishonourable part of my body on those precious hairs that once adorned her Majesty's head. Of these hairs (as I had always a mechanical genius) I likewise made a neat little purse about five foot long, with her Majesty's name deciphered in gold letters, which I gave to Glumdalclitch, by the Queen's consent. To say the truth, it was more for show than use, being not of strength to bear the weight of the larger coins, and therefore she kept nothing in it but some little toys that girls are fond of.

The King, who delighted in music, had frequent con-
certs at court, to which I was sometimes carried, and set
in my box on a table to hear them; but the noise was so
great, that I could hardly distinguish the tunes. I am
confident that all the drums and trumpets of a royal
army, beating and sounding together just at your ears,
could not equal it. My practice was to have my box removed from the places where the performers sat, as far
as I could, then to shut the doors and windows of it, and
draw the window curtains; after which I found their
music not disagreeable.

I had learned in my youth to play a little upon the
spinet. Glumdalclitch kept one in her chamber, and a
master attended twice a week to teach her: I call it a
spinet, because it somewhat resembled that instrument,
and was played upon in the same manner. A fancy came
into my head that I would entertain the King and Queen
with an English tune upon this instrument. But this appeared extremely difficult; for the spinet was near sixty
foot long, each key being almost a foot wide, so that,
with my arms extended, I could not reach to above five
keys, and to press them down required a good smart
stroke with my fist, which would be too great a labour,
and to no purpose. The method I contrived was this. I
prepared two round sticks about the bigness of common
cudgels; they were thicker at one end than the other,
and I covered the thicker ends with a piece of a mouse's
skin, that by rapping on them I might neither damage
the tops of the keys, nor interrupt the sound. Before the
spinet a bench was placed, about four foot below the
keys, and I was put upon the bench. I ran sideling upon
it that way and this, as fast as I could, banging the proper
keys with my two sticks, and made a shift to play a jig,
to the great satisfaction of both their Majesties: but it
was the most violent exercise I ever underwent, and yet
I could not strike above sixteen keys, nor, consequently,
play the bass and treble together, as other artists do;
which was a great disadvantage to my performance.

The King, who, as I before observed, was a prince of
excellent understanding, would frequently order that I

should be brought in my box, and set upon the table in his closet. He would then command me to bring one of my chairs out of the box, and sit down within three yards distance upon the top of the cabinet, which brought me almost to a level with his face. In this manner I had several conversations with him. I one day took the freedom to tell his Majesty, that the contempt he discovered towards Europe, and the rest of the world, did not seem answerable to those excellent qualities of the mind he was master of. That reason did not extend itself with the bulk of the body: on the contrary, we observed in our country that the tallest persons were usually least provided with it. That among other animals, bees and ants had the reputation of more industry, art and sagacity, than many of the larger kinds. And that, as inconsiderable as he took me to be, I hoped I might live to do his Majesty some signal service. The King heard me with attention, and began to conceive a much better opinion of me than he had ever before. He desired I would give him as exact an account of the government of England as I possibly could; because, as fond as princes commonly are of their own customs (for so he conjectured of other monarchs, by my former discourses), he should be glad to hear of any thing that might deserve imitation.

Imagine with thyself, courteous reader, how often I then wished for the tongue of Demosthenes or Cicero, that might have enabled me to celebrate the praise of my own dear native country in a style equal to its merits and felicity.

I began my discourse by informing his Majesty that our dominions consisted of two islands, which composed three mighty kingdoms under one sovereign, beside our plantations in America. I dwelt long upon the fertility of our soil, and the temperature of our climate. I then spoke at large upon the constitution of an English Parliament, partly made up of an illustrious body called the House of Peers, persons of the noblest blood, and the most ancient and ample patrimonies. I described that extraordinary care always taken of their education in arts and arms, to qualify them for being counsellors born to the king and kingdom, to have a share in the legislature, to be members of the highest Court of Judicature, from whence there could be no appeal, and to be champions always ready for the defence of their prince and country, by their valour, conduct, and fidelity. That these were the ornament and bulwark of the kingdom, worthy followers of their most renowned ancestors, whose honour had been the reward of their virtue, from which their posterity were never once known to degenerate. To these were joined several holy persons, as part of that assembly, under the title of Bishops, whose peculiar business it is to take care of religion, and of those who instruct the people therein. These were searched and sought out through the whole nation, by the prince and his wisest counsellors, among such of the priesthood as were most deservedly distinguished by the sanctity of their lives, and the depth of their erudition; who were indeed the spiritual fathers of the clergy and the people.

That the other part of the Parliament consisted of an assembly called the House of Commons, who were all principal gentlemen, freely picked and culled out by the people themselves, for their great abilities and love of their country, to represent the wisdom of the whole nation. And these two bodies make up the most august assembly in Europe, to whom, in conjunction with the prince, the whole legislature is committed.

I then descended to the Courts of Justice, over which the Judges, those venerable sages and interpreters of the law, presided, for determining the disputed rights and properties of men, as well as for the punishment of vice, and protection of innocence. I mentioned the prudent management of our treasury; the valour and achievements of our forces by sea and land. I computed the number of our people, by reckoning how many millions there might be of each religious sect, or political party among us. I did not omit even our sports and pastimes, or any other particular which I thought might redound to the honour of my country. And I finished all with a brief historical account of affairs and events in England for about an hundred years past.

This conversation was not ended under five audiences, each of several hours, and the King heard the whole with great attention, frequently taking notes of what I spoke, as well as memorandums of several questions he intended to ask me.

When I had put an end to these long discourses, his Majesty in a sixth audience, consulting his notes, proposed many doubts, queries, and objections, upon every article. He asked what methods were used to cultivate the minds and bodies of our young nobility, and in what kind of business they commonly spent the first and teachable part of their lives. What course was taken to supply that assembly when any noble family became extinct. What qualifications were necessary in those who were to be created new lords. Whether the humour of the prince, a sum of money to a court lady, or a prime minister, or a design of strengthening a party opposite to the public interest, ever happened to be motives in those advancements. What share of knowledge these lords had in the laws of their country, and how they came by it, so as to enable them to decide the properties of their fellow-subjects in the last resort. Whether they were always so free from avarice, partialities, or want, that a bribe, or some other sinister view, could have no place among them. Whether those holy lords I spoke of were always promoted to that rank upon account of their knowledge in religious matters, and the sanctity of their lives, had never been compliers with the times while they were common priests, or slavish prostitute chaplains to some nobleman, whose opinions they continued servilely to follow after they were admitted into that assembly.

He then desired to know what arts were practised in electing those whom I called commoners: whether a stranger with a string purse might not influence the vulgar voters to choose him before their own landlord, or the most considerable gentleman in the neighbourhood. How it came to pass, that people were so violently bent upon getting into this assembly, which I allowed to be a great trouble and expense, often to the ruin of their families, without any salary or pension: because this ap-

peared such an exalted strain of virtue and public spirit,
that his Majesty seemed to doubt it might possibly not
always be sincere: and he desired to know whether such
zealous gentlemen could have any views of refunding
themselves for the charges and trouble they were at, by
sacrificing the public good to the designs of a weak and
vicious prince in conjunction with a corrupted ministry.
He multiplied his questions, and sifted me thoroughly
upon every part of this head, proposing numberless enquiries and objections, which I think it not prudent or
convenient to repeat.

Upon what I said in relation to our Courts of Justice,
his Majesty desired to be satisfied in several points: and
this I was the better able to do, having been formerly
almost ruined by a long suit in chancery, which was decreed for me with costs. He asked, what time was usually
spent in determining between right and wrong, and what
degree of expense. Whether advocates and orators had
liberty to plead in causes manifestly known to be unjust,
vexatious, or oppressive. Whether party in religion or
politics were observed to be of any weight in the scale
of justice. Whether those pleading orators were persons
educated in the general knowledge of equity, or only in
provincial, national, and other local customs. Whether
they or their judges had any part in penning those laws
which they assumed the liberty of interpreting and gloss-
ing upon at their pleasure. Whether they had ever
at different times pleaded for and against the same
cause, and cited precedents to prove contrary opinions. Whether they were a rich or a poor corporation.
Whether they received any pecuniary reward for pleading or delivering their opinions. And particularly
whether they were ever admitted as members in the
lower senate.

He fell next upon the management of our treasury;
and said he thought my memory had failed me, because
I computed our taxes at about five or six millions a year,
and when I came to mention the issues, he found they
sometimes amounted to more than double; for the notes
he had taken were very particular in this point, because

he hoped, as he told me, that the knowledge of our conduct might be useful to him, and he could not be deceived in his calculations. But, if what I told him were true, he was still at a loss how a kingdom could run out of its estate like a private person. He asked me, who were our creditors; and where we should find money to pay them. He wondered to hear me talk of such charge-able and extensive wars; that certainly we must be a quarrelsome people, or live among very bad neighbours, and that our generals must needs be richer than our kings. He asked what business we had out of our own islands, unless upon the score of trade or treaty, or to defend the coasts with our fleet. Above all, he was amazed to hear me talk of a mercenary standing army in the midst of peace, and among a free people. He said, if we were governed by our own consent in the persons of our representatives, he could not imagine of whom we were afraid, or against whom we were to fight; and would hear my opinion, whether a private man's house might not better be defended by himself, his children, and family, than by half a dozen rascals picked up at a venture in the streets, for small wages, who might get a hundred times more by cutting their throats.

He laughed at my odd kind of arithmetic (as he was pleased to call it) in reckoning the numbers of our peo-ple by a computation drawn from the several sects among us in religion and politics. He said, he knew no reason, why those who entertain opinions prejudicial to the public, should be obliged to change, or should not be obliged to conceal them. And as it was tyranny in any government to require the first, so it was weakness not to enforce the second: for a man may be allowed to keep poisons in his closet, but not to vend them about for cordials.

He observed that among the diversions of our nobility and gentry I had mentioned gaming. He desired to know at what age this entertainment was usually taken up, and when it was laid down; how much of their time it em-ployed; whether it ever went so high as to affect their fortunes; whether mean vicious people, by their dexterity in that art, might not arrive at great riches, and sometimes keep our very nobles in dependence, as well as habituate them to vile companions, wholly take them from the improvement of their minds, and force them, by the losses they have received, to learn and practise that infamous dexterity upon others.

He was perfectly astonished with the historical account I gave him of our affairs during the last century, protesting it was only a heap of conspiracies, rebellions, murders, massacres, revolutions, banishments, the very worst effects that avarice, faction, hypocrisy, perfidiousness, cruelty, rage, madness, hatred, envy, lust, malice, or ambition could produce.

His Majesty in another audience was at the pains to recapitulate the sum of all I had spoken, compared the questions he made with the answers I had given, then taking me into his hands, and stroking me gently, delivered himself in these words, which I shall never forget nor the manner he spoke them in: My little friend Grildrig, you have made a most admirable panegyric upon your country; you have clearly proved that ignorance, idleness, and vice, may be sometimes the only ingredients for qualifying a legislator; that laws are best explained, interpreted, and applied by those whose interest and abilities lie in perverting, confounding, and eluding them. I observe among you some lines of an institution, which in its original might have been tolerable, but these half erased, and the rest wholly blurred and blotted by corruptions. It doth not appear from all you have said, how any one virtue is required towards the procurement of any one station among you; much less that men are ennobled on account of their virtue, that priests are advanced for their piety or learning, soldiers for their conduct or valour, judges for their integrity, senators for the love of their country, or counsellors for their wisdom. As for yourself (continued the King) who have spent the greatest part of your life in travelling, I am well disposed to hope you may hitherto have escaped many vices of your country. But by what I have gathered from your own relation, and the answers I have with much pains wringed and extorted from you, I cannot but conclude the bulk of your natives to be the most pernicious race of little odious vermin that nature ever suffered to crawl upon the surface of the earth.

Chapter VII *The Author's love of his country. He makes a proposal of much advantage to the King, which is rejected. The King's great ignorance in politics. The learning of that country very imperfect and confined. Their laws, and military affairs, and parties in the State.*

NOTHING BUT an extreme love of truth could have hindered me from concealing this part of my story. It was in vain to discover my resentments, which were always turned into ridicule; and I was forced to rest with patience while my noble and most beloved country was so injuriously treated. I am heartily sorry as any of my readers can possibly be, that such an occasion was given: but this prince happened to be so curious and inquisitive upon every particular, that it could not consist either with gratitude or good manners to refuse giving him what satisfaction I was able. Yet thus much I may be allowed to say in my own vindication, that I artfully eluded many of his questions, and gave to every point a more favourable turn by many degrees than the strictness of truth would allow. For I have always borne that laudable partiality to my own country, which Dionysius Halicarnassensis with so much justice recommends to an historian. I would hide the frailties and deformities of my political mother, and place her virtues and beauties in the most advantageous light. This was my sincere endeavour in those many discourses I had with that mighty monarch, although it unfortunately failed of success.

But great allowances should be given to a King who lives wholly secluded from the rest of the world, and must therefore be altogether unacquainted with the manners and customs that most prevail in other nations; the want of which knowledge will ever produce many prejudices, and a certain narrowness of thinking, from which we and the politer countries of Europe are wholly exempted. And it would be hard indeed, if so remote a prince's notions of virtue and vice were to be offered as a standard for all mankind.

To confirm what I have now said, and further, to show the miserable effect of a confined education, I shall here insert a passage which will hardly obtain belief. In hopes to ingratiate myself farther into his Majesty's favour, I told him of an invention discovered between three and four hundred years ago, to make a certain powder, into an heap of which the smallest spark of fire falling, would kindle the whole in a moment, although it were as big as a mountain, and make it all fly up in the air together, with a noise and agitation greater than thunder. That a proper quantity of this powder rammed into an hollow tube of brass or iron, according to its bigness, would drive a ball of iron or lead with such violence and speed, as nothing was able to sustain its force. That the largest balls thus discharged, would not only destroy whole ranks of an army at once, but batter the strongest walls to the ground, sink down ships, with a thousand men in each, to the bottom of the sea; and, when linked together by a chain, would cut through masts and rigging, divide hundreds of bodies in the middle, and lay all waste before them. That we often put this powder into large hollow balls of iron, and discharged them by an engine into some city we were besieging, which would rip up the pavements, tear the house to pieces, burst and throw splinters on every sides, dashing out the brains of all who came near. That I know the ingredients very well, which were cheap, and common; I understood the manner of compounding them, and could direct his workmen how to make those tubes of a size proportionable to all other things in his Majesty's kingdom, and the largest need not be above an hundred foot long; twenty or thirty of which tubes, charged with the proper quantity of powder and balls, would batter down the walls of the strongest town in his dominions in a few hours, or destroy the whole metropolis, if ever it should pretend to dispute his absolute commands. This I humbly offered to his Majesty, as a small tribute of acknowledgment in return of so many marks that I had received of his royal favour and protection.

The King was struck with horror at the description I had given of those terrible engines, and the proposal I had made. He was amazed how so impotent and grovelling an insect as I (these were his expressions) would entertain such inhuman ideas, and in so familiar a manner as to appear wholly unmoved at all the scenes of blood and desolation, which I had painted as the common effects of those destructive machines, whereof he said some evil genius, enemy to mankind, must have been the first contriver. As for himself, he protested that although few things delighted him so much as new discoveries in art or in nature, yet he would rather lose half his kingdom than be privy to such a secret, which he commanded me, as I valued my life, never to mention any more.

A strange effect of narrow principles and short views! that a prince possessed of every quality which procures veneration, love, and esteem; of strong parts, great wisdom, and profound learning, endued with admirable talents for government, and almost adored by his subjects, should from a nice unnecessary scruple, whereof in Europe we can have no conception, let slip an opportunity put into his hands, that would have made him absolute master of the lives, the liberties, and the fortunes of his people. Neither do I say this with the least intention to detract from the many virtues of that excellent King, whose character I am sensible will on his account be very much lessened in the opinion of an English reader: but I take this defect among them to have risen from their ignorance, they not having hitherto reduced politics into a science, as the more acute wits of Europe have

done. For I remember very well, in a discourse one day
with the King, when I happened to say there were several thousand books among us written upon the art of
government, it gave him (directly contrary to my intention) a very mean opinion of our understandings. He
professed both to abominate and despise all mystery,
refinement, and intrigue, either in a prince or a minister.
He could not tell what I meant by secrets of state, where
an enemy or some rival nation were not in the case. He
confined the knowledge of governing within very narrow
bounds; to common sense and reason, to justice and lenity, to the speedy determination of civil and criminal
causes; with some other obvious topics, which are not
worth considering. And he gave it for his opinion, that
whoever could make two ears of corn or two blades of
grass to grow upon a spot of ground where only one
grew before, would deserve better of mankind, and do
more essential service to his country than the whole race
of politicians put together.

The learning of this people is very defective, consisting
only in morality, history, poetry, and mathematics,
wherein they must be allowed to excel. But the last of
these is wholly applied to what may be useful in life, to
the improvement of agriculture, and all mechanical arts;
so that among us it would be little esteemed. And as to
ideas, entities, abstractions, and transcendentals, I could
never drive the least conception into their heads.

No law of that country must exceed in words the number of letters in their alphabet, which consists only in
two and twenty. But indeed few of them extend even to
that length. They are expressed in the most plain and
simple terms, wherein those people are not mercurial
enough to discover above one interpretation; and to
write a comment upon any law is a capital crime. As to
the decision of civil causes, or proceedings against criminals, their precedents are so few, that they have little
reason to boast of any extraordinary skill in either.

They have had the art of printing, as well as the Chinese, time out of mind. But their libraries are not very
large; for that of the King's, which is reckoned the big-

gest, doth not amount to above a thousand volumes, placed in a gallery of twelve hundred foot long, from whence I had liberty to borrow what books I pleased. The Queen's joiner had contrived in one of Glumdalclitch's rooms a kind of wooden machine five and twenty foot high, formed like a standing ladder; the steps were each fifty foot long. It was indeed a moveable pair of stairs, the lowest end placed at ten foot distance from the wall of the chamber. The book I had a mind to read was put up leaning against the wall. I first mounted to the upper step of the ladder, and turning my face towards the book, began at the top of the page, and so walking to the right and left about eight or ten paces, according to the length of the lines, till I had gotten a little below the level of my eyes, and then descending gradually till I came to the bottom; after which I mounted again, and began the other page in the same manner, and so turned over the leaf, which I could easily do with both my hands, for it was as thick and stiff as a pasteboard, and in the largest folios not above eighteen or twenty foot long.

Their style is clear, masculine, and smooth, but not florid, for they avoid nothing more than multiplying unnecessary words, or using various expressions. I have perused many of their books, especially those in history and morality. Among the rest, I was much diverted with a little old treatise, which always lay in Glumdalclitch's bedchamber, and belonged to her governess, a grave elderly gentlewoman, who dealt in writings of morality and devotion. The book treats of the weakness of human kind, and is in little esteem, except among the women and the vulgar. However, I was curious to see what an author of that country could say upon such a subject. This writer went through all the usual topics of European moralists, showing how diminutive, contemptible, and helpless an animal was man in his own nature; how unable to defend himself from the inclemencies of the air, or the fury of wild beasts; how much he was excelled by one creature in strength, by another in speed, by a third in foresight, by a fourth in industry. He added, that

nature was degenerated in these latter declining ages of
the world, and could now produce only small abortive
births in comparison of those in ancient times. He said,
it was very reasonable to think, not only that the species
of men were originally much larger, but also, that there
must have been giants in former ages, which, as it is
asserted by history and tradition, so it hath been confirmed by huge bones and skulls casually dug up in several parts of the kingdom, far exceeding the common
dwindled race of man in our days. He argued, that the
very laws of nature absolutely required we should have
been made in the beginning, of a size more large and
robust, not so liable to destruction from every little accident of a tile falling from a house, or a stone cast from
the hand of a boy, or of being drowned in a little brook.
From this way of reasoning the author drew several
moral applications useful in the conduct of life, but needless here to repeat. For my own part, I could not avoid
reflecting how universally this talent was spread, of
drawing lectures in morality, or indeed rather matter of
discontent and repining, from the quarrels we raise with
nature. And I believe, upon a strict enquiry, those quarrels might be shown as ill grounded among us as they
are among that people.

As to their military affairs, they boast that the King's
army consists of an hundred and seventy-six thousand
foot, and thirty-two thousand horse: if that may be called
an army which is made up of tradesmen in the several
cities, and farmers in the country, whose commanders
are only the nobility and gentry, without pay or reward.
They are indeed perfect enough in their exercises, and
under very good discipline, wherein I saw no great merit;
for how should it be otherwise, where every farmer is
under the command of his own landlord, and every citi-
zen under that of the principal men in his own city, chosen after the manner of Venice by ballot?

I have often seen the militia of Lorbrulgrud drawn out
to exercise in a great field near the city of twenty miles
square. They were in all not above twenty-five thousand
foot, and six thousand horse; but it was impossible for

me to compute their number, considering the space of ground they took up. A cavalier mounted on a large steed might be about an hundred foot high. I have seen this whole body of horse, upon a word of command, draw their swords at once, and brandish them in the air. Imagination can figure nothing so grand, so surprising, and so astonishing. It looked as if ten thousand flashes of lightning were darting at the same time from every quarter of the sky.

I was curious to know how this prince, to whose dominions there is no access from any other country, came to think of armies, or to teach his people the practice of military discipline. But I was soon informed, both by conversation and reading their histories. For in the course of many ages they have been troubled with the same disease to which the whole race of mankind is subject; the nobility often contending for power, the people for liberty, and the King for absolute dominion. All which, however happily tempered by the laws of the kingdom, have been sometimes violated by each of the three parties, and have once or more occasioned civil wars, the last whereof was happily put an end to by this prince's grandfather by a general composition; and the militia, then settled with common consent, hath been ever since kept in the strictest duty.

∞

Chapter VIII *The King and Queen make a progress to the frontiers. The Author attends them. The manner in which he leaves the country very particularly related. He returns to England.*

I HAD ALWAYS a strong impulse that I should some time recover my liberty, though it was impossible to conjecture by what means, or to form any project with the least hope of succeeding. The ship in which I sailed was the first ever known to be driven within sight of that coast, and the King had given strict orders, that if at any time another appeared, it should be taken ashore, and with all its crew and passengers brought in a tumbril to Lorbrulgrud. He was strongly bent to get me a woman of my own size, by whom I might propagate the breed: but I think I should rather have died than undergone the disgrace of leaving a posterity to be kept in cages like tame canary birds, and perhaps, in time, sold about the kingdom to persons of quality for curiosities. I was, indeed, treated with much kindness; I was the favourite of a great King and Queen, and the delight of the whole court, but it was upon such a foot as ill became the dignity of human kind. I could never forget those domestic pledges I had left behind me. I wanted to be among people with whom I could converse upon even terms, and walk about the streets and fields without fear of being trod to death like a frog or a young puppy. But my deliverance came sooner than I expected, and in a manner not very common; the whole story and circumstances of which I shall faithfully relate.

I had now been two years in this country; and about the beginning of the third, Glumdalclitch and I attended the King and Queen in a progress to the south coast of the kingdom. I was carried, as usual, in my travelling-box, which, as I have already described, was a very convenient closet of twelve foot wide. And I had ordered a hammock to be fixed by silken ropes from the four corners at the top, to break the jolts, when a servant carried me before him on horseback, as I sometimes desired, and would often sleep in my hammock while we were upon the road. On the roof of my closet, just over the middle of the hammock, I ordered the joiner to cut out a hole of a foot square, to give me air in hot weather as I slept, which hole I shut at pleasure with a board that drew backwards and forwards through a groove.

When we came to our journey's end, the King thought proper to pass a few days at a palace he hath near Flanflasnic, a city within eighteen English miles of the seaside. Glumdalclitch and I were much fatigued; I had gotten a small cold, but the poor girl was so ill as to be confined to her chamber. I longed to see the ocean, which must be the only scene of my escape, if ever it should happen. I pretended to be worse than I really was, and desired leave to take the fresh air of the sea, with a page whom I was very fond of, and who had sometimes been trusted with me. I shall never forget with what unwillingness Glumdalclitch consented, nor the strict charge she gave the page to be careful of me, bursting at the same time into a flood of tears, as if she had some foreboding of what was to happen. The boy took me out in my box about half an hour's walk from the palace, towards the rocks on the sea-shore. I ordered him to set me down, and lifting up one of my sashes, cast many a wistful melancholy look towards the sea. I found myself not very well, and told the page that I had a mind to take a nap in my hammock, which I hoped would do me good. I got in, and the boy shut the window close down to keep out the cold. I soon fell asleep, and all I can conjecture is, that while I slept, the page, thinking no danger could happen, went among the rocks to look for birds' eggs, having before observed him from my window searching about, and picking up one or two in the clefts. Be that as it will, I found myself suddenly awakened with a violent pull upon the ring which was fastened at the top of my box for the conveniency of carriage. I felt my box raised very high in the air, and then borne forward with prodigious speed. The first jolt had like to have shaken me out of my hammock, but afterwards the motion was easy enough. I called out several times as loud as I could raise my voice, but all to no purpose. I looked towards my windows, and could see nothing but the clouds and sky. I heard a noise just over my head like the clapping of wings, and then began to perceive the woful condition I was in; that some eagle had got the ring of my box in his beak, with an intent to let it fall on a rock like a tortoise in a shell, and then pick out my body, and devour it. For the sagacity and smell of this bird enable him to discover his quarry at a great distance, though better concealed than I could be within a two-inch board.

In a little time I observed the noise and flutter of wings to increase very fast, and my box was tossed up and down, like a sign-post in a windy day. I heard several bangs or buffets, as I thought, given to the eagle (for such I am certain it must have been that held the ring of my box in his beak), and then all on a sudden felt myself falling perpendicularly down for above a minute, but with such incredible swiftness that I almost lost my breath. My fall was stopped by a terrible squash that sounded louder to my ears than the cataract of Niagara; after which I was quite in the dark for another minute, and then my box began to rise so high that I could see light from the tops of my windows. I now perceived that I was fallen into the sea. My box, by the weight of my body, the goods that were in, and the broad plates of iron fixed for strength at the four corners of the top and bottom, floated about five foot deep in water. I did then, and do now suppose that the eagle which flew away with my box was pursued by two or three others, and forced to let me drop while he was defending himself against the rest, who hoped to share in the prey. The plates of iron fastened at the bottom of the box (for those were the strongest) preserved the balance while it fell, and hindered it from being broken on the surface of the water. Every joint of it was well grooved, and the door did not move on hinges, but up and down like a sash, which kept my closet so tight that very little water came in. I got with much difficulty out of my hammock, having first ventured to draw back the slip-board on the roof already mentioned, contrived on purpose to let in air, for want of which I found myself almost stifled.

How often did I then wish myself with my dear Glumdalclitch, from whom one single hour had so far divided me! And I may say with truth, that in the midst of my own misfortunes I could not forbear lamenting my poor nurse, the grief she would suffer for my loss, the displeasure of the Queen, and the ruin of her fortune. Perhaps many travellers have not been under greater difficulties and distress than I was at this juncture, expecting every moment to see my box dashed in pieces, or at least over-set by the first violent blast, or a rising wave. A breach in one single pane of glass would have been immediate death: nor could any thing have preserved the windows, but the strong lattice wires placed on the outside against accidents in travelling. I saw the water ooze in at several crannies, although the leaks were not considerable, and I endeavoured to stop them as well as I could. I was not able to lift up the roof of my closet, which otherwise I certainly should have done, and sat on the top of it, where I might at least preserve myself some hours longer than by being shut up, as I may call it, in the hold. Or, if I escaped these dangers for a day or two, what could I expect but a miserable death of cold and hunger! I was four hours under these circumstances, expecting and indeed wishing every moment to be my last.

I have already told the reader that there were two strong staples fixed upon that side of my box which had no window, and into which the servant who used to carry me on horseback would put a leathern belt, and buckle it about his waist. Being in this disconsolate state, I heard or at least thought I heard some kind of grating noise on that side of my box where the staples were fixed, and soon after I began to fancy that the box was pulled or towed along in the sea; for I now and then felt a sort of tugging, which made the waves rise near the tops of my windows, leaving me almost in the dark. This gave me some faint hopes of relief, although I was not able to imagine how it could be brought about. I ventured to unscrew one of my chairs, which were always fastened to the floor; and having made a hard shift to screw it down again directly under the slipping-board that I had lately opened, I mounted on the chair, and putting my mouth as near as I could to the hole, I called for help in a loud voice, and in all the languages I under-stood. I then fastened my handkerchief to a stick I usu-ally carried, and thrusting it up the hole, waved it several times in the air, that if any boat or ship were near, the seamen might conjecture some unhappy mortal to be shut up in the box.

I found no effect from all I could do, but plainly perceived my closet to be moved along; and in the space of an hour, or better, that side of the box where the staples were, and had no window, struck against something that was hard. I apprehended it to be a rock, and found myself tossed more than ever. I plainly heard a noise upon the cover of my closet, like that of a cable, and the grating of it as it passed through the ring. I then found myself hoisted up by degrees at least three foot higher than I was before. Whereupon I again thrust up my stick and handkerchief, calling for help till I was almost hoarse. In return to which, I heard a great shout repeated three times, giving me such transports of joy, as are not to be conceived but by those who feel them. I now heard a trampling over my head, and somebody calling through the hole with a loud voice in the English tongue: If there be any body below, let them speak. I answered, I was an Englishman, drawn by ill fortune into the greatest calamity that ever any creature underwent, and begged, by all that is moving, to be delivered out of the dungeon I was in. The voice replied, I was safe, for my box was fastened to their ship; and the carpenter should immediately come and saw an hole in the cover, large enough to pull me out. I answered, that was needless, and would take up too much time, for there was no more to be done, but let one of the crew put his finger into the ring, and take the box out of the sea into the ship, and so into the captain's cabin. Some of them upon hearing me talk so wildly thought I was mad; others laughed; for indeed it never came into my head that I was now got among people of my own stature and strength. The carpenter came, and in a few minutes sawed a passage about four foot square, then let down a small ladder, upon which I mounted, and from thence was taken into the ship in a very weak condition.

The sailors were all in amazement, and asked me a thousand questions, which I had no inclination to answer. I was equally confounded at the sight of so many

pigmies, for such I took them to be, after having so long
accustomed my eyes to the monstrous objects I had left.
But the Captain, Mr. Thomas Wilcocks, an honest worthy Shropshire man, observing I was ready to faint, took
me into his cabin, gave me a cordial to comfort me, and
made me turn in upon his own bed, advising me to take
a little rest, of which I had great need. Before I went to
sleep I gave him to understand that I had some valuable
furniture in my box, too good to be lost, a fine hammock,
an handsome field-bed, two chairs, a table, and a cabinet;
that my closet was hung on all sides, or rather quilted,
with silk and cotton; that if he would let one of the crew
bring my closet into his cabin, I would open it there
before him, and show him my goods. The Captain hearing me utter these absurdities, concluded I was raving:
however (I suppose to pacify me), he promised to give
order as I desired, and going upon deck sent some of
his men down into my closet, from whence (as I afterwards found) they drew up all my goods, and stripped
off the quilting; but the chairs, cabinet, and bedstead,
being screwed to the floor, were much damaged by the
ignorance of the seamen, who tore them up by force.
Then they knocked off some of the boards for the use
of the ship, and when they had got all they had a mind
for, let the hull drop into the sea, which by reason of
many breaches made in the bottom and sides, sunk to
rights. And indeed I was glad not to have been a specta-
tor of the havoc they made; because I am confident it
would have sensibly touched me, by bringing former passages into my mind, which I had rather forget.

I slept some hours, but perpetually disturbed with
dreams of the place I had left, and the dangers I had
escaped. However, upon waking I found myself much
recovered. It was now about eight o'clock at night, and
the Captain ordered supper immediately, thinking I had
already fasted too long. He entertained me with great
kindness, observing me not to look wildly, or talk incon-
sistently: and when we were left alone, desired I would
give him a relation of my travels, and by what accident
I came to be set adrift in that monstrous wooden chest.

He said, that about twelve o'clock at noon, as he was looking through his glass, he spied it at a distance, and thought it was a sail, which he had a mind to make, being not much out of his course, in hopes of buying some biscuit, his own beginning to fall short. That upon coming nearer, and finding his error, he sent out his long-boat to discover what I was; that his men came back in a fright, swearing they had seen a swimming house. That he laughed at their folly, and went himself in the boat, ordering his men to take a strong cable along with them. That the weather being calm, he rowed round me several times, observed my windows, and the wire lattices that defended them. That he discovered two staples upon one side, which was all of boards, without any passage for light. He then commanded his men to row up to that side, and fastening a cable to one of the staples, ordered them to tow my chest (as he called it) towards the ship. When it was there, he gave directions to fasten another cable to the ring fixed in the cover, and to raise up my chest with pulleys, which all the sailors were not able to do above two or three foot. He said they saw my stick and handkerchief thrust out of the hole, and concluded that some unhappy men must be shut up in the cavity. I asked whether he or the crew had seen any prodigious birds in the air about the time he first discovered me. To which he answered, that discoursing this matter with the sailors while I was asleep, one of them said he had observed three eagles flying towards the north, but remarked nothing of their being larger than the usual size, which I suppose must be imputed to the great height they were at; and he could not guess the reason of my question. I then asked the Captain how far he reckoned we might be from land; he said, by the best computation he could make, we were at least an hundred leagues. I assured him, that he must be mistaken by almost half, for I had not left the country from whence I came above two hours before I dropt into the sea. Whereupon he began again to think that my brain was disturbed, of which he gave me a hint, and advised me to go to bed in a cabin he had provided. I assured him I was well refreshed with his good entertainment and company, and as much in my senses as ever I was in my life. He then grew serious, and desired to ask me freely whether I were not troubled in mind by the consciousness of some enormous crime, for which I was punished at the command of some prince, by exposing me in that chest, as great criminals in other countries have been forced to sea in a leaky vessel without provisions; for although he should be sorry to have taken so ill a man into his ship, yet he would engage his word to set me safe on shore in the first port where we arrived. He added, that his suspicions were much increased by some very absurd speeches I had delivered at first to the sailors, and afterwards to himself, in relation to my closet or chest, as well as by my odd looks and behaviour while I was at supper.

I begged his patience to hear me tell my story, which I faithfully did from the last time I left England to the moment he first discovered me. And as truth always forceth its way into rational minds, so this honest worthy gentleman, who had some tincture of learning, and very good sense, was immediately convinced of my candour and veracity. But further to confirm all I had said, I entreated him to give order that my cabinet should be brought, of which I had the key in my pocket (for he had already informed me how the seamen disposed of my closet), I opened it in his presence and showed him the small collection of rarities I made in the country from whence I had been so strangely delivered. There was the comb I had contrived out of the stumps of the King's beard, and another of the same materials, but fixed into a paring of her Majesty's thumb-nail, which served for the back. There was a collection of needles and pins from a foot to half a yard long; four wasp-stings, like joiners' tacks; some combings of the Queen's hair; a gold ring which one day she made me a present of in a most obliging manner, taking it from her little finger, and throwing it over my head like a collar. I desired the Captain would please to accept this ring in return of his civilities, which he absolutely refused. I showed him a corn that I had cut off with my own hand, from a maid of honour's toe; it was about the bigness of a Kentish pippin, and grown so hard that when I returned to England, I got it hollowed into a cup, and set in silver. Lastly, I desired him to see the breeches I had then on, which were made of a mouse's skin.

I could force nothing on him but a footman's tooth, which I observed him to examine with great curiosity, and found he had a fancy for it. He received it with abundance of thanks, more than such a trifle could deserve. It was drawn by an unskilful surgeon, in a mistake, from one of Glumdalclitch's men, who was afflicted with the toothache, but it was as sound as any in his head. I got it cleaned, and put it into my cabinet. It was about a foot long, and four inches in diameter.

The Captain was very well satisfied with this plain relation I had given him, and said he hoped when we returned to England I would oblige the world by putting it on paper and making it public. My answer was that I thought we were already overstocked with books of travels; that nothing could now pass which was not extraordinary; wherein I doubted some authors less consulted truth than their own vanity, or interest, or the diversion of ignorant readers. That my story could contain little besides common events, without those ornamental descriptions of strange plants, trees, birds, and other animals, or of the barbarous customs and idolatry of savage people, with which most writers abound. However, I thanked him for his good opinion, and promised to take the matter into my thoughts.

He said he wondered at one thing very much, which was, to hear me speak so loud, asking me whether the King or Queen of that country were thick of hearing. I told him it was what I had been used to for above two years past, and that I admired as much at the voices of him and his men, who seemed to me only to whisper, and yet I could hear them well enough. But when I spoke in that country, it was like a man talking in the street to another looking out from the top of a steeple, unless when I was placed on a table, or held in any

person's hand. I told him, I had likewise observed another thing, that when I first got into the ship, and the
sailors stood all about me, I thought they were the most
little contemptible creatures I had ever beheld. For indeed while I was in that prince's country, I could never
endure to look in a glass after my eyes had been accustomed to such prodigious objects, because the comparison gave me so despicable a conceit of myself. The
Captain said that while we were at supper he observed
me to look at every thing with a sort of wonder, and
that I often seemed hardly able to contain my laughter,
which he knew not well how to take, but imputed it to
some disorder in my brain. I answered, it was very true;
and I wondered how I could forbear, when I saw his
dishes of the size of a silver three-pence, a leg of pork
hardly a mouthful, a cup not so big as a nut-shell; and
so I went on, describing the rest of his household-stuff
and provisions after the same manner. For, although the
Queen had ordered a little equipage of all things necessary for me while I was in her service, yet my ideas were
wholly taken up with what I saw on every side of me,
and I winked at my own littleness as people do at their
own faults. The Captain understood my raillery very
well, and merrily replied with the old English proverb,
that he doubted my eyes were bigger than my belly, for
he did not observe my stomach so good, although I had
fasted all day; and continuing in his mirth, protested he
would have gladly given an hundred pounds to have seen
my closet in the eagle's bill, and afterwards in its fall
from so great an height into the sea; which would certainly have been a most astonishing object, worthy to
have the description of it transmitted to future ages: and
the comparison of Phaeton was so obvious, that he could
not forbear applying it, although I did not much admire
the conceit.

The Captain, having been at Tonquin, was in his return to England driven north-eastward to the latitude of
44 degrees, and of longitude 143. But meeting a trade-
wind two days after I came on board him, we sailed
southward a long time, and coasting New Holland kept

our course west-south-west, and then south-south-west till we doubled the Cape of Good Hope. Our voyage was very prosperous, but I shall not trouble the reader with a journal of it. The Captain called in at one or two ports, and sent in his long-boat for provisions and fresh water, but I never went out of the ship till we came into the Downs, which was on the third day of June, 1706, about nine months after my escape. I offered to leave my goods in security for payment of my freight; but the Captain protested he would not receive one farthing. We took kind leave of each other, and I made him promise he would come to see me at my house in Redriff. I hired a horse and guide for five shillings, which I borrowed of the Captain.

As I was on the road, observing the littleness of the houses, the trees, the cattle, and the people, I began to think myself in Lilliput. I was afraid of trampling on every traveller I met, and often called aloud to have them stand out of the way, so that I had like to have gotten one or two broken heads for my impertinence.

When I came to my house, for which I was forced to enquire, one of the servants opening the door, I bent down to go in (like a goose under a gate) for fear of striking my head. My wife ran out to embrace me, but I stooped lower than her knees, thinking she could otherwise never be able to reach my mouth. My daughter kneeled to ask my blessing, but I could not see her till she arose, having been so long used to stand with my head and eyes erect to above sixty foot; and then I went to take her up with one hand, by the waist. I looked down upon the servants and one or two friends who were in the house, as if they had been pigmies, and I a giant. I told my wife, she had been too thrifty, for I found she had starved herself and her daughter to nothing. In short, I behaved myself so unaccountably, that they were all of the Captain's opinion when he first saw me, and concluded I had lost my wits. This I mention as an instance of the great power of habit and prejudice.

In a little time I and my family and friends came to a right understanding: but my wife protested I should never go to sea any more; although my evil destiny so ordered that she had not power to hinder me, as the reader may know hereafter. In the mean time I here conclude the second part of my unfortunate voyages.

PART III

A VOYAGE

TO LAPUTA, BALNIBARBI, LUGGNAGG,

GLUBBDUBDRIB & JAPAN.

Parts Unknown

LAND OF
St James Bay
Robbin I.
JESSO
Salmon
Sea of
Corea
C. Canal
Sandal
Corpus
Mura
Iedo
Shain
Chrico
Red Pt
Bosho Pt
Barnevelts
Absai I.
Ongeluckig I.
Bungo I.
South I.
Dimeris Straits
O I. Tanaxima
Sial
Glangu

Companys
Land
Stats I

Laputa
BALNIBARBI
Discovered, A.D. 1701
Lagado
Maldo-
nada
Glubbdubdrib

LUGGNAGG
Traldragdul
Clamegnig R.

I. Deserta
Urac
Timal

LUGGNAGG
and
BALNIBARBI,
with the Islands of
Laputa and Glubbdubdrib.

Chapter I *The Author sets out on his third voyage,
is taken by pirates. The malice of a Dutchman.
His arrival at an island. He is received into
Laputa.*

I HAD NOT been at home above ten days, when Captain
William Robinson, a Cornish man, Commander of the
Hope-well, a stout ship of three hundred tons, came to
my house. I had formerly been surgeon of another ship
where he was master, and a fourth part owner, in a voyage to the Levant; he had always treated me more like
a brother than an inferior officer, and hearing of my
arrival made me a visit, as I apprehended only out of
friendship, for nothing passed more than what is usual
after long absences. But repeating his visits often, expressing his joy to find me in good health, asking
whether I were now settled for life, adding that he intended a voyage to the East Indies in two months; at
last he plainly invited me, though with some apologies,
to be surgeon of the ship; that I should have another
surgeon under me besides our two mates; that my salary
should be double to the usual pay; and that having experienced my knowledge in sea-affairs to be at least equal
to his, he would enter into any engagement to follow
my advice, as much as if I had share in the command.

He said so many other obliging things, and I knew
him to be so honest a man, that I could not reject his
proposal; the thirst I had of seeing the world, notwithstanding my past misfortunes, continuing as violent as
ever. The only difficulty that remained was to persuade
my wife, whose consent, however, I at last obtained by
the prospect of advantage she proposed to her children.

We set out the 5th of August, 1706, and arrived at
Fort St. George the 11th of April, 1707. We stayed there

three weeks to refresh our crew, many of whom were sick. From thence we went to Tonquin, where the Captain resolved to continue some time, because many of the goods he intended to buy were not ready, nor could he expect to be dispatched in some months. Therefore in hopes to defray some of the charges he must be at, he bought a sloop, loaded it with several sorts of goods, wherewith the Tonquinese usually trade to the neighbouring islands, and putting fourteen men on board, whereof three were of the country, he appointed me master of the sloop, and gave me power to traffic for two months, while he transacted his affairs at Tonquin.

We had not sailed above three days, when a great storm arising, we were driven five days to the north-north-east, and then to the east; after which we had fair weather, but still with a pretty strong gale from the west. Upon the tenth day we were chased by two pirates, who soon overtook us; for my sloop was so deep loaden, that she sailed very slow, neither were we in a condition to defend ourselves.

We were boarded about the same time by both the pirates, who entered furiously at the head of their men, but finding us all prostrate upon our faces (for so I gave order) they pinioned us with strong ropes, and setting a guard upon us, went to search the sloop.

I observed among them a Dutchman, who seemed to be of some authority, though he was not commander of either ship. He knew us by our countenances to be Englishmen, and jabbering to us in his own language, swore we should be tied back to back, and thrown into the sea. I spoke Dutch tolerably well; I told him who we were, and begged him in consideration of our being Christians and Protestants, of neighbouring countries, in strict alliance, that he would move the Captains to take some pity on us. This inflamed his rage; he repeated his threatenings, and turning to his companions, spoke with great vehemence, in the Japanese language, as I suppose, often using the word *Christianos*.

The largest of the two pirate ships was commanded by a Japanese Captain, who spoke a little Dutch, but very imperfectly. He came up to me, and after several questions, which I answered in great humility, he said we should not die. I made the Captain a very low bow, and then turning to the Dutchman, said, I was sorry to find more mercy in a heathen, than in a brother Christian. But I had soon reason to repent those foolish words; for that malicious reprobate, having often endeavoured in vain to persuade both the Captains that I might be thrown into the sea (which they would not yield to after the promise made me, that I should not die), however prevailed so far as to have a punishment inflicted on me, worse in all human appearance than death itself. My men were sent by an equal division into both the pirate ships, and my sloop new manned. As to myself, it was determined that I should be set adrift in a small canoe, with paddles and a sail, and four days' provisions, which last the Japanese Captain was so kind to double out of his own stores, and would permit no man to search me. I got down into the canoe, while the Dutchman standing upon the deck, loaded me with all the curses and injurious terms his language could afford.

About an hour before we saw the pirates, I had taken an observation, and found we were in the latitude of 46 N. and of longitude 183. When I was at some distance from the pirates, I discovered by my pocket-glass several islands to the south-east. I set up my sail, the wind being fair, with a design to reach the nearest of those islands, which I made a shift to do in about three hours. It was all rocky; however I got many birds' eggs, and striking fire, I kindled some heath and dry sea-weed, by which I roasted my eggs. I ate no other supper, being resolved to spare my provisions as much as I could. I passed the night under the shelter of a rock, strowing some heath under me, and slept pretty well.

The next day I sailed to another island, and thence to a third and fourth, sometimes using my sail, and sometimes my paddles. But not to trouble the reader with a particular account of my distresses, let it suffice that on the fifth day I arrived at the last island in my sight, which lay south-south-east to the former.

This island was at a greater distance than I expected, and I did not reach it in less than five hours. I encompassed it almost round before I could find a convenient place to land in, which was a small creek about three times the wideness of my canoe. I found the island to be all rocky, only a little intermingled with tufts of grass and sweet smelling herbs. I took out my small provisions, and after having refreshed myself, I secured the remainder in a cave, whereof there were great numbers. I gathered plenty of eggs upon the rocks, and got a quantity of dry sea-weed and parched grass, which I designed to kindle the next day, and roast my eggs as well as I could. (For I had about me my flint, steel, match, and burning-glass.) I lay all night in the cave where I had lodged my provisions. My bed was the same dry grass and sea-weed which I intended for fuel. I slept very little, for the disquiets of my mind prevailed over my weariness, and kept me awake. I considered how impossible it was to preserve my life in so desolate a place, and how miserable my end must be. Yet I found myself so listless and desponding that I had not the heart to rise, and before I could get spirits enough to creep out of my cave the day was far advanced. I walked a while among the rocks; the sky was perfectly clear, and the sun was so hot that I was forced to turn my face from it: when all on a sudden it became obscured, as I thought, in a manner very different from what happens by the interposition of a cloud. I turned back, and perceived a vast opaque body between me and the sun, moving forwards toward the island: it seemed to be about two miles high, and hid the sun six or seven minutes, but I did not observe the air to be much colder, or the sky more darkened, than if I had stood under the shade of a mountain. As it approached nearer over the place where I was, it appeared to be a firm substance, the bottom flat, smooth, and shining very bright from the reflection of the sea below. I stood upon a height about two hundred yards from the shore, and saw this vast body descending almost to a parallel with me, at less than an English mile distance. I took out my pocket-perspective, and could plainly discover numbers of people moving up and down the sides of it, which appeared to be sloping, but what those people were doing, I was not able to distinguish.

The natural love of life gave me some inward motions of joy, and I was ready to entertain a hope that this adventure might some way or other help to deliver me from the desolate place and condition I was in. But at the same time the reader can hardly conceive my astonishment, to behold an island in the air, inhabited by men, who were able (as it should seem) to raise or sink, or put it into a progressive motion, as they pleased. But not being at that time in a disposition to philosophise upon this phenomenon, I rather chose to observe what course the island would take, because it seemed for a while to stand still. Yet soon after it advanced nearer, and I could see the sides of it, encompassed with several gradations of galleries, and stairs at certain intervals, to descend from one to the other. In the lowest gallery I beheld some people fishing with long angling rods, and others looking on. I waved my cap (for my hat was long since worn out) and my handkerchief towards the island; and upon its nearer approach, I called and shouted with the utmost strength of my voice; and then looking circumspectly, I beheld a crowd gather to that side which was most in my view. I found by their pointing towards me and to each other, that they plainly discovered me, although they made no return to my shouting. But I could see four or five men running in great haste up the stairs to the top of the island, who then disappeared. I happened rightly to conjecture, that these were sent for orders to some person in authority upon this occasion.

The number of people increased, and in less than half an hour the island was moved and raised in such a manner, that the lowest gallery appeared in a parallel of less than an hundred yards distance from the height where I stood. I then put myself into the most supplicating postures, and spoke in the humblest accent, but received no answer. Those who stood nearest over against me seemed to be persons of distinction, as I supposed by their habit. They conferred earnestly with each other,

looking often upon me. At length one of them called
out in a clear, polite, smooth dialect, not unlike in sound
to the Italian; and therefore I returned an answer in that
language, hoping at least that the cadence might be more
agreeable to his ears. Although neither of us understood
the other, yet my meaning was easily known, for the
people saw the distress I was in.

They made signs for me to come down from the rock,
and go towards the shore, which I accordingly did; and
the flying island being raised to a convenient height, the
verge directly over me, a chain was let down from the
lowest gallery, with a seat fastened to the bottom, to
which I fixed myself, and was drawn up by pulleys.

Chapter II *The humours and dispositions of the
    Laputians described. An account of their learn-
    ing. Of the King and his Court. The Author's
    reception there. The inhabitants subject to fear
    and disquietudes. An account of the women.*

AT MY ALIGHTING I was surrounded by a crowd of
people, but those who stood nearest seemed to be
of better quality. They beheld me with all the marks and
circumstances of wonder; neither indeed was I much in
their debt, having never till then seen a race of mortals
so singular in their shapes, habits, and countenances.
Their heads were all reclined either to the right or the
left; one of their eyes turned inward, and the other directly up to the zenith. Their outward garments were
adorned with the figures of suns, moons, and stars, interwoven with those of fiddles, flutes, harps, trumpets, gui-
tars, harpsichords, and many other instruments of music,
unknown to us in Europe. I observed here and there
many in the habit of servants, with a blown bladder fastened like a flail to the end of a short stick, which they

carried in their hands. In each bladder was a small quantity of dried pease, or little pebbles (as I was afterwards informed). With these bladders they now and then flapped the mouths and ears of those who stood near them, of which practice I could not then conceive the meaning; it seems the minds of these people are so taken up with intense speculations, that they neither can speak, nor attend to the discourses of others, without being roused by some external taction upon the organs of speech and hearing; for which reason those persons who are able to afford it always keep a flapper (the original is *climenole*) in their family, as one of their domestics, nor ever walk abroad or make visits without him. And the business of this officer is, when two or more persons are in company, gently to strike with his bladder the mouth of him who is to speak, and the right ear of him or them to whom the speaker addresseth himself. This flapper is likewise employed diligently to attend his master in his walks, and upon occasion to give him a soft flap on his eyes, because he is always so wrapped up in cogitation, that he is in manifest danger of falling down every precipice, and bouncing his head against every post, and in the streets, of justling others, or being justled himself into the kennel.

It was necessary to give the reader this information, without which he would be at the same loss with me, to understand the proceedings of these people, as they conducted me up the stairs, to the top of the island, and from thence to the royal palace. While we were ascending, they forgot several times what they were about, and left me to myself, till their memories were again roused by their flappers; for they appeared altogether unmoved by the sight of my foreign habit and countenance, and by the shouts of the vulgar, whose thoughts and minds were more disengaged.

At last we entered the palace, and proceeded into the chamber of presence, where I saw the King seated on his throne, attended on each side by persons of prime quality. Before the throne was a large table filled with

globes and spheres, and mathematical instruments of all
kinds. His Majesty took not the least notice of us, although our entrance was not without sufficient noise, by
the concourse of all persons belonging to the court. But
he was then deep in a problem, and we attended at least
an hour, before he could solve it. There stood by him
on each side a young page, with flaps in their hands, and

when they saw he was at leisure, one of them gently struck his mouth, and the other his right ear; at which he started like one awaked on the sudden, and looking towards me and the company I was in, recollected the occasion of our coming, whereof he had been informed before. He spoke some words, whereupon immediately a young man with a flap came up to my side, and flapped me gently on the right ear; but I made signs, as well as I could, that I had no occasion for such an instrument; which, as I afterwards found, gave his Majesty and the whole court a very mean opinion of my understanding. The King, as far as I could conjecture, asked me several questions, and I addressed myself to him in all the languages I had. When it was found that I could neither understand nor be understood, I was conducted by the King's order to an apartment in his palace (this prince being distinguished above all his predecessors for his hospitality to strangers), where two servants were appointed to attend me. My dinner was brought, and four persons of quality, whom I remembered to have seen very near the King's person, did me the honour to dine with me. We had two courses of three dishes each. In the first course there was a shoulder of mutton, cut into an equilateral triangle, a piece of beef into a rhomboides, and a pudding into a cycloid. The second course was two ducks, trussed up into the form of fiddles; sausages and puddings resembling flutes and hautboys, and a breast of veal in the shape of a harp. The servants cut our bread into cones, cylinders, parallelograms, and several other mathematical figures.

While we were at dinner, I made bold to ask the names of several things in their language; and those noble persons, by the assistance of their flappers, delighted to give me answers, hoping to raise my admiration of their great abilities, if I could be brought to converse with them. I was soon able to call for bread and drink, or whatever else I wanted.

After dinner my company withdrew, and a person was sent to me by the King's order, attended by a flapper. He brought with him pen, ink, and paper, and three or

four books, giving me to understand by signs, that he
was sent to teach me the language. We sat together four
hours, in which time I wrote down a great number of
words in columns, with the translations over against
them. I likewise made a shift to learn several short sentences. For my tutor would order one of my servants to
fetch something, to turn about, to make a bow, to sit,
or stand, or walk, and the like. Then I took down the
sentence in writing. He showed me also in one of his
books the figures of the sun, moon, and stars, the zodiac,
the tropics, and polar circles, together with the denominations of many figures of planes and solids. He gave
me the names and descriptions of all the musical instruments, and the general terms of art in playing on each
of them. After he had left me, I placed all my words
with their interpretations in alphabetical order. And thus
in a few days, by the help of a very faithful memory, I
got some insight into their language.

The word, which I interpret the *Flying* or *Floating
Island*, is in the original *Laputa*, whereof I could never
learn the true etymology. *Lap* in the old obsolete language signifieth *high*, and *untuh*, a *governor*, from which
they say by corruption was derived *Laputa*, from *Lapun-
tuh*. But I do not approve of this derivation, which seems
to be a little strained. I ventured to offer to the learned
among them a conjecture of my own, that *Laputa* was
quasi lap outed; *lap* signifying properly the dancing of
the sunbeams in the sea, and *outed*, a wing, which however I shall not obtrude, but submit to the judicious
reader.

Those to whom the King had entrusted me, observing
how ill I was clad, ordered a tailor to come next morning, and take my measure for a suit of clothes. This
operator did his office after a different manner from
those of his trade in Europe. He first took my altitude
by a quadrant, and then with a rule and compasses described the dimensions and outlines of my whole body,
all which he entered upon paper, and in six days brought
my clothes very ill made, and quite out of shape, by
happening to mistake a figure in the calculation. But my

comfort was, that I observed such accidents very frequent, and little regarded.

During my confinement for want of clothes, and by an indisposition that held me some days longer, I much enlarged my dictionary; and when I went next to court, was able to understand many things the King spoke, and to return him some kind of answers. His Majesty had given orders that the island should move north-east and by east, to the vertical point over Lagado, the metropolis of the whole kingdom below upon the firm earth. It was about ninety leagues distant, and our voyage lasted four days and an half. I was not in the least sensible of the progressive motion made in the air by the island. On the second morning about eleven o'clock, the King himself in person, attended by his nobility, courtiers, and officers, having prepared all their musical instruments, played on them for three hours without intermission, so that I was quite stunned with the noise; neither could I possibly guess the meaning, till my tutor informed me. He said that the people of their island had their ears adapted to hear the music of the spheres, which always played at certain periods, and the court was now prepared to bear their part in whatever instrument they most excelled.

In our journey towards Lagado, the capital city, his Majesty ordered that the island should stop over certain towns and villages, from whence he might receive the petitions of his subjects. And to this purpose several packthreads were let down with small weights at the bottom. On these packthreads the people strung their petitions, which mounted up directly like the scraps of paper fastened by school-boys at the end of the string that holds their kite. Sometimes we received wine and victuals from below, which were drawn up by pulleys.

The knowledge I had in mathematics gave me great assistance in acquiring their phraseology, which depended much upon that science and music; and in the latter I was not unskilled. Their ideas are perpetually conversant in lines and figures. If they would, for example, praise the beauty of a woman, or any other animal, they describe it by rhombs, circles, parallelograms, ellipses, and other geometrical terms, or by words of art drawn from music, needless here to repeat. I observed in the King's kitchen all sorts of mathematical and musical instruments, after the figures of which they cut up the joints that were served to his Majesty's table.

Their houses are very ill built, the walls bevil, without one right angle in any apartment, and this defect ariseth from the contempt they bear to practical geometry, which they despise as vulgar and mechanic, those instructions they give being too refined for the intellectuals of their workmen, which occasions perpetual mistakes. And although they are dexterous enough upon a piece of paper in the management of the rule, the pencil, and the divider, yet in the common actions and behaviour of life, I have not seen a more clumsy, awkward, and unhandy people, nor so slow and perplexed in their conceptions upon all other subjects, except those of mathematics and music. They are very bad reasoners, and vehemently given to opposition, unless when they happen to be of the right opinion, which is seldom their case. Imagination, fancy, and invention, they are wholly strangers to, nor have any words in their language by which those ideas can be expressed; the whole compass of their thoughts and mind being shut up within the two forementioned sciences.

Most of them, and especially those who deal in the astronomical part, have great faith in judicial astrology, although they are ashamed to own it publicly. But what I chiefly admired, and thought altogether unaccountable, was the strong disposition I observed in them towards news and politics, perpetually enquiring into public affairs, giving their judgments in matters of state, and passionately disputing every inch of a party opinion. I have indeed observed the same disposition among most of the mathematicians I have known in Europe, although I could never discover the least analogy between the two sciences; unless those people suppose, that because the smallest circle hath as many degrees as the largest, therefore the regulation and management of the world re-

quire no more abilities than the handling and turning of
a globe. But I rather take this quality to spring from a
very common infirmity of human nature, inclining us to
be more curious and conceited in matters where we have
least concern, and for which we are least adapted either
by study or nature.

These people are under continual disquietudes, never
enjoying a minute's peace of mind; and their disturbances proceed from causes which very little affect the
rest of mortals. Their apprehensions arise from several
changes they dread in the celestial bodies. For instance,
that the earth, by the continual approaches of the sun
towards it, must in course of time be absorbed or swallowed up. That the face of the sun will by degrees be
encrusted with its own effluvia, and give no more light
to the world. That the earth very narrowly escaped a
brush from the tail of the last comet, which would have
infallibly reduced it to ashes; and that the next, which
they have calculated for one and thirty years hence, will
probably destroy us. For if in its perihelion it should
approach within a certain degree of the sun (as by their
calculations they have reason to dread) it will conceive
a degree of heat ten thousand times more intense than
that of red-hot glowing iron; and in its absence from the
sun, carry a blazing tail ten hundred thousand and fourteen miles long; through which if the earth should pass
at the distance of one hundred thousand miles from the
nucleus or main body of the comet, it must in its passage
be set on fire, and reduced to ashes. That the sun daily
spending its rays without any nutriment to supply them,
will at last be wholly consumed and annihilated; which
must be attended with the destruction of this earth, and
of all the planets that receive their light from it.

They are so perpetually alarmed with the apprehensions of these and the like impending dangers, that they
can neither sleep quietly in their beds, nor have any
relish for the common pleasures or amusements of life.
When they meet an acquaintance in the morning, the
first question is about the sun's health, how he looked
at his setting and rising, and what hopes they have to

avoid the stroke of the approaching comet. This conversation they are apt to run into with the same temper that boys discover, in delighting to hear terrible stories of sprites and hobgoblins, which they greedily listen to, and dare not go to bed for fear.

The women of the island have abundance of vivacity: they contemn their husbands, and are exceedingly fond of strangers, whereof there is always a considerable number from the continent below, attending at court, either upon affairs of the several towns and corporations, or their own particular occasions, but are much despised, because they want the same endowments. Among these the ladies choose their gallants: but the vexation is, that they act with too much ease and security, for the husband is always so rapt in speculation, that the mistress and lover may proceed to the greatest familiarities before his face, if he be but provided with paper and implements, and without his flapper at his side.

The wives and daughters lament their confinement to the island, although I think it the most delicious spot of ground in the world; and although they live here in the greatest plenty and magnificence, and are allowed to do whatever they please, they long to see the world, and take the diversions of the metropolis, which they are not allowed to do without a particular licence from the King; and this is not easy to be obtained, because the people of quality have found by frequent experience how hard it is to persuade their women 'o return from below. I was told that a great court lady, who had several children, is married to the prime minister, the richest subject in the kingdom, a very graceful person, extremely fond of her, and lives in the finest palace of the island, went down to Lagado, on the pretence of health, there hid herself for several months, till the King sent a warrant to search for her, and she was found in an obscure eating-house all in rags, having pawned her clothes to maintain an old deformed footman, who beat her every day, and in whose company she was taken much against her will. And although her husband received her with all possible kindness, and without the least reproach, she soon after contrived to steal down again with all her jewels, to the same gallant, and hath not been heard of since.

This may perhaps pass with the reader rather for an European or English story, than for one of a country so remote. But he may please to consider, that the caprices of womankind are not limited by any climate or nation, and that they are much more uniform than can be easily imagined.

In about a month's time I had made a tolerable proficiency in their language, and was able to answer most of the King's questions, when I had the honour to attend him. His Majesty discovered not the least curiosity to enquire into the laws, government, history, religion, or manners of the countries where I had been, but confined his questions to the state of mathematics, and received the account I gave him with great contempt and indifference, though often roused by his flapper on each side.

Chapter III *A phenomenon solved by modern philosophy and astronomy. The Laputians' great improvements in the latter. The King's method of suppressing insurrections.*

I DESIRED LEAVE of this prince to see the curiosities of the island, which he was graciously pleased to grant, and ordered my tutor to attend me. I chiefly wanted to know to what cause in art or in nature it owed its several motions, whereof I will now give a philosophical account to the reader.

The Flying or Floating Island is exactly circular, its diameter 7837 yards, or about four miles and an half, and consequently contains ten thousand acres. It is three hundred yards thick. The bottom or under surface, which appears to those who view it from below, is one even

regular plate of adamant, shooting up to the height of
about two hundred yards. Above it lie the several minerals in their usual order, and over all is a coat of rich
mould, ten or twelve foot deep. The declivity of the
upper surface, from the circumference to the centre, is
the natural cause why all the dews and rains which fall
upon the island, are conveyed in small rivulets toward
the middle, where they are emptied into four large basins, each of about half a mile in circuit, and two hundred yards distant from the centre. From these basins
the water is continually exhaled by the sun in the day-
time, which effectually prevents their overflowing. Besides, as it is in the power of the monarch to raise the
island above the region of clouds and vapours, he can
prevent the falling of dews and rains whenever he
pleases. For the highest clouds cannot rise above two
miles, as naturalists agree, at least they were never
known to do so in that country.

At the centre of the island there is a chasm about fifty
yards in diameter, from whence the astronomers descend
into a large dome, which is therefore called *Flandona
Gagnole*, or the Astronomer's Cave, situated at the
depth of a hundred yards beneath the upper surface of
the adamant. In this cave are twenty lamps continually
burning, which from the reflection of the adamant cast
a strong light into every part. The place is stored with
great variety of sextants, quadrants, telescopes, astro-
labes, and other astronomical instruments. But the greatest curiosity, upon which the fate of the island depends,
is a loadstone of a prodigious size, in shape resembling
a weaver's shuttle. It is in length six yards, and in the
thickest part at least three yards over. This magnet is
sustained by a very strong axle of adamant passing
through its middle, upon which it plays, and is poised so
exactly that the weakest hand can turn it. It is hooped
round with an hollow cylinder of adamant, four foot
deep, as many thick, and twelve yards in diameter,
placed horizontally, and supported by eight adamantine
feet, each six yards high. In the middle of the concave
side there is a groove twelve inches deep, in which the

extremities of the axle are lodged, and turned round as there is occasion.

The stone cannot be moved from its place by any force, because the hoop and its feet are one continued piece with that body of adamant which constitutes the bottom of the island.

By means of this loadstone, the island is made to rise and fall, and move from one place to another. For with respect to that part of the earth over which the monarch presides, the stone is endued at one of its sides with an attractive power, and at the other with a repulsive. Upon placing the magnet erect with its attracting end towards the earth, the island descends; but when the repelling extremity points downwards, the island mounts directly upwards. When the position of the stone is oblique, the motion of the island is so too. For in this magnet the forces always act in lines parallel to its direction.

By this oblique motion the island is conveyed to different parts of the monarch's dominions. To explain the manner of its progress, let A B represent a line drawn cross the dominions of Balnibarbi, let the line c d represent the loadstone, of which let d be the repelling end, and c the attracting end, the island being over C; let the stone be placed in the position c d, with its repelling end downwards; then the island will be driven upwards obliquely towards D. When it is arrived at D, let the stone be turned upon its axle, till its attracting end points toward E, and then the island will be carried obliquely towards F; where if the stone be again turned upon its axle till it stands in the position E F, with its repelling point downwards, the island will rise obliquely towards F, where by directing the attracting end towards G, the island may be carried to G, and from G to H, by turning the stone, so as to make its repelling extremity point directly downwards. And thus by changing the situation of the stone as often as there is occasion, the island is made to rise and fall by turns in an oblique direction, and by those alternate risings and fallings (the obliquity being not considerable) is conveyed from one part of the dominions to the other.

The Country
of
BALNIBARBI,
with the floating Island of
Laputa.

But it must be observed that this island cannot move
beyond the extent of the dominions below nor can it
rise above the height of four miles. For which the astronomers (who have written large systems concerning the
stone) assign the following reason: that the magnetic vir-

tue does not extend beyond the distance of four miles, and that the mineral which acts upon the stone in the bowels of the earth, and in the sea about six leagues distant from the shore, is not diffused through the whole globe, but terminated with the limits of the King's dominions; and it was easy from the great advantage of such a superior situation, for a prince to bring under his obedience whatever country lay within the attraction of that magnet.

When the stone is put parallel to the plane of the horizon, the island standeth still; for in that case the extremities of it being at equal distance from the earth, act with equal force, the one in drawing downwards, the other in pushing upwards, and consequently no motion can ensue.

This loadstone is under the care of certain astronomers, who from time to time give it such positions as the monarch directs. They spend the greatest part of their lives in observing the celestial bodies, which they do by the assistance of glasses far excelling ours in goodness. For although their largest telescopes do not exceed three feet, they magnify much more than those of an hundred yards among us, and at the same time show the stars with greater clearness. This advantage hath enabled them to extend their discoveries much further than our astronomers in Europe; for they have made a catalogue of ten thousand fixed stars, whereas the largest of ours do not contain above one third part of that number. They have likewise discovered two lesser stars, or satellites, which revolve about Mars, whereof the innermost is distant from the centre of the primary planet exactly three of the diameters, and the outermost five; the former revolves in the space of ten hours, and the latter in twenty one and an half; so that the squares of their periodical times are very near in the same proportion with the cubes of their distance from the centre of Mars, which evidently shows them to be governed by the same law of gravitation, that influences the other heavenly bodies.

They have observed ninety-three different comets, and settled their periods with great exactness. If this be true (and they affirm it with great confidence), it is much to be wished that their observations were made public, whereby the theory of comets, which at present is very lame and defective, might be brought to the same perfection with other parts of astronomy.

The King would be the most absolute prince in the universe, if he could but prevail on a ministry to join with him; but these having their estates below on the continent, and considering that the office of a favourite hath a very uncertain tenure, would never consent to the enslaving their country.

If any town should engage in rebellion or mutiny, fall into violent factions, or refuse to pay the usual tribute, the King hath two methods of reducing them to obedience. The first and the mildest course is by keeping the island hovering over such a town, and the lands about it, whereby he can deprive them of the benefit of the sun and the rain, and consequently afflict the inhabitants with dearth and diseases. And if the crime deserve it, they are at the same time pelted from above with great stones, against which they have no defence but by creeping into cellars or caves, while the roofs of their houses are beaten to pieces. But if they still continue obstinate, or offer to raise insurrections, he proceeds to the last remedy, by letting the island drop directly upon their heads, which makes a universal destruction both of houses and men. However, this is an extremity to which the prince is seldom driven, neither indeed is he willing to put it in execution, nor dare his ministers advise him to an action, which as it would render them odious to the people, so it would be a great damage to their own estates, which lie all below, for the island is the King's demesne.

But there is still indeed a more weighty reason, why the kings of this country have been always averse from executing so terrible an action, unless upon the utmost necessity. For if the town intended to be destroyed should have in it any tall rocks, as it generally falls out in the larger cities, a situation probably chosen at first with a view to prevent such a catastrophe; or if it abound in high spires, or pillars of stone, a sudden fall might endanger the bottom or under surface of the island, which, although it consists, as I have said, of one entire adamant two hundred yards thick, might happen to crack by too great a shock, or burst by approaching too near the fires from the houses below, as the backs both of iron and stone will often do in our chimneys. Of all this the people are well apprised and understand how far to carry their obstinacy, where their liberty or property is concerned. And the King, when he is highest provoked, and most determined to press a city to rubbish, orders the island to descend with great gentleness, out of a pretence of tenderness to his people, but indeed for fear of breaking the adamantine bottom; in which case it is the opinion of all their philosophers that the loadstone could no longer hold it up, and the whole mass would fall to the ground.

About three years before my arrival among them, while the King was in his progress over his dominions, there happened an extraordinary accident which had like to have put a period to the fate of that monarchy, at least as it is now instituted. Lindalino, the second city in the kingdom, was the first his Majesty visited in his progress. Three days after his departure the inhabitants, who had often complained of great oppressions, shut the town gates, seized on the governor, and with incredible speed and labour erected four large towers, one at every corner of the city (which is an exact square), equal in height to a strong pointed rock that stands directly in the centre of the city. Upon the top of each tower, as well as upon the rock, they fixed a great loadstone, and in case their design should fail, they had provided a vast quantity of the most combustible fuel, hoping to burst therewith the adamantine bottom of the island, if the loadstone project should miscarry.

It was eight months before the King had perfect notice that the Lindalinians were in rebellion. He then commanded that the island should be wafted over the city.

The people were unanimous, and had laid in store of provisions, and a great river runs through the middle of the town. The King hovered over them several days to deprive them of the sun and the rain. He ordered many packthreads to be let down, yet not a person offered to send up a petition, but instead thereof very bold demands, the redress of all their grievances, great immunities, the choice of their own governor, and other the like exorbitances. Upon which his Majesty commanded all the inhabitants of the island to cast great stones from the lower gallery into the town; but the citizens had provided against this mischief by conveying their persons and effects into the four towers, and other strong buildings, and vaults underground.

The King being now determined to reduce this proud people, ordered that the island should descend gently within forty yards of the top of the towers and rock. This was accordingly done; but the officers employed in that work found the descent much speedier than usual, and by turning the loadstone could not without great difficulty keep it in a firm position, but found the island inclining to fall. They sent the King immediate intelligence of this astonishing event, and begged his Majesty's permission to raise the island higher; the King consented, a general council was called, and the officers of the loadstone ordered to attend. One of the oldest and expertest among them obtained leave to try an experiment. He took a strong line of an hundred yards, and the island being raised over the town above the attracting power they had felt, he fastened a piece of adamant to the end of his line, which had in it a mixture of iron mineral, of the same nature with that whereof the bottom or lower surface of the island is composed, and from the lower gallery let it down slowly towards the top of the towers. The adamant was not descended four yards, before the officer felt it drawn so strongly downwards that he could hardly pull it back. He then threw down several small pieces of adamant, and observed that they were all violently attracted by the top of the tower.

The same experiment was made on the other three towers, and on the rock with the same effect.

This incident broke entirely the King's measures, and (to dwell no longer on other circumstances) he was forced to give the town their own conditions.

I was assured by a great minister that if the island had descended so near the town as not to be able to raise itself, the citizens were determined to fix it for ever, to kill the King and all his servants, and entirely change the government.

By a fundamental law of this realm, neither the king, nor either of his two elder sons, are permitted to leave the island; nor the queen, till she is past child-bearing.

Chapter IV *The Author leaves Laputa; is conveyed to Balnibarbi, arrives at the metropolis. A description of the metropolis, and the country adjoining. The Author hospitably received by a great lord. His conversation with that lord.*

ALTHOUGH I cannot say that I was ill treated in this island, yet I must confess I thought myself too much neglected, not without some degree of contempt. For neither prince nor people appeared to be curious in any part of knowledge, except mathematics and music, wherein I was far their inferior, and upon that account very little regarded.

On the other side, after having seen all the curiosities of the island, I was very desirous to leave it, being heartily weary of those people. They were indeed excellent in two sciences for which I have great esteem, and wherein I am not unversed; but at the same time so abstracted and involved in speculation, that I never met with such disagreeable companions. I conversed only with women, tradesmen, flappers, and court-pages, dur-

ing two months of my abode there, by which at last I
rendered myself extremely contemptible; yet these were
the only people from whom I could ever receive a reasonable answer.

I had obtained by hard study a good degree of knowledge in their language; I was weary of being confined to
an island where I received so little countenance, and
resolved to leave it with the first opportunity.

There was a great lord at court, nearly related to the
King, and for that reason alone used with respect. He
was universally reckoned the most ignorant and stupid
person among them. He had performed many eminent
services for the crown, had great natural and acquired
parts, adorned with integrity and honour, but so ill an
ear for music, that his detractors reported he had been
often known to beat time in the wrong place; neither
could his tutors without extreme difficulty teach him to
demonstrate the most easy proposition in the mathematics. He was pleased to show me many marks of favour,
often did me the honour of a visit, desired to be informed in the affairs of Europe, the laws and customs,
the manners and learning of the several countries where
I had travelled. He listened to me with great attention,
and made very wise observations on all I spoke. He had
two flappers attending him for state, but never made use
of them except at court, and in visits of ceremony, and
would always command them to withdraw when we were
alone together.

I entreated this illustrious person to intercede in my
behalf with his Majesty for leave to depart, which he
accordingly did, as he was pleased to tell me, with regret:
for indeed he had made me several offers very advantageous, which however I refused with expressions of the
highest acknowledgment.

On the 16th day of February I took leave of his Majesty and the court. The King made me a present to the
value of about two hundred pounds English, and my
protector his kinsman as much more, together with a
letter of recommendation to a friend of his in Lagado,
the metropolis. The island being then hovering over a

mountain about two miles from it, I was let down from the lowest gallery, in the same manner as I had been taken up.

The continent, as far as it is subject to the monarch of the Flying Island, passes under the general name of *Balnibarbi*, and the metropolis, as I said before, is called *Lagado*. I felt some little satisfaction in finding myself on firm ground. I walked to the city without any concern, being clad like one of the natives, and sufficiently instructed to converse with them. I soon found out the person's house to whom I was recommended, presented my letter from his friend the grandee in the island, and was received with much kindness. This great lord, whose name was Munodi, ordered me an apartment in his own house, where I continued during my stay, and was entertained in a most hospitable manner.

The next morning after my arrival, he took me in his chariot to see the town, which is about half the bigness of London, but the houses very strangely built, and most of them out of repair. The people in the streets walked fast, looked wild, their eyes fixed, and were generally in rags. We passed through one of the town gates, and went about three miles into the country, where I saw many labourers working with several sorts of tools in the ground, but was not able to conjecture what they were about; neither did I observe any expectation either of corn or grass, although the soil appeared to be excellent. I could not forbear admiring at these odd appearances both in town and country, and I made bold to desire my conductor, that he would be pleased to explain to me what could be meant by so many busy heads, hands, and faces, both in the streets and the fields, because I did not discover any good effects they produced; but on the contrary, I never knew a soil so unhappily cultivated, houses so ill contrived and so ruinous, or a people whose countenances and habit expressed so much misery and want.

This Lord Munodi was a person of the first rank, and and had been some years Governor of Lagado, but by a cabal of ministers was discharged for insufficiency.

However, the King treated him with tenderness, as a well-meaning man, but of a low contemptible understanding.

When I gave that free censure of the country and its inhabitants, he made no further answer than by telling me that I had not been long enough among them to form a judgement, and that the different nations of the world had different customs, with other common topics to the same purpose. But when we returned to his palace, he asked me how I liked the building, what absurdities I observed, and what quarrel I had with the dress or looks of his domestics. This he might safely do, because every thing about him was magnificent, regular, and polite. I answered that his Excellency's prudence, quality, and fortune, had exempted him from those defects which folly and beggary had produced in others. He said if I would go with him to his country-house, about twenty miles distant, where his estate lay, there would be more leisure for this kind of conversation. I told his Excellency that I was entirely at his disposal, and accordingly we set out next morning.

During our journey he made me observe the several methods used by farmers in managing their lands, which to me were wholly unaccountable; for except in some very few places I could not discover one ear of corn or blade of grass. But in three hours travelling the scene was wholly altered; we came into a most beautiful country; farmers' houses at small distances, neatly built; the fields enclosed, containing vineyards, corn-grounds, and meadows. Neither do I remember to have seen a more delightful prospect. His Excellency observed my countenance to clear up; he told me with a sigh that there his estate began, and would continue the same till we should come to his house. That his countrymen ridiculed and despised him for managing his affairs no better, and for setting so ill an example to the kingdom, which however was followed by very few, such as were old, and willful, and weak like himself.

We came at length to the house, which was indeed a noble structure, built according to the best rules of ancient architecture. The fountains, gardens, walks, avenues, and groves were all disposed with exact judgement and taste. I gave due praises to every thing I saw, whereof his Excellency took not the least notice till after supper, when, there being no third companion, he told me with a very melancholy air that he doubted he must throw down his houses in town and country, to rebuild them after the present mode, destroy all his plantations, and cast others into such a form as modern usage required, and give the same directions to all his tenants, unless he would submit to incur the censure of pride, singularity, affection, ignorance, caprice, and perhaps increase his Majesty's displeasure.

That the admiration I appeared to be under would cease or diminish when he had informed me of some particulars, which probably I never heard of at court, the people there being too much taken up in their own speculations, to have regard to what passed here below.

The sum of his discourse was to this effect. That about forty years ago certain persons went up to Laputa, either upon business or diversion, and after five months continuance came back with a very little smattering in mathematics, but full of volatile spirits acquired in that airy region. That these persons upon their return began to dislike the management of every thing below, and fell into schemes of putting all arts, sciences, languages, and mechanics upon a new foot. To this end they procured a royal patent for erecting an Academy of Projectors in Lagado; and the humour prevailed so strongly among the people, that there is not a town of any consequence in the kingdom without such an academy. In these colleges the professors contrive new rules and methods of agriculture and building, and new instruments and tools for all trades and manufactures, whereby, as they undertake, one man shall do the work of ten; a palace may be built in a week, of materials so durable as to last for ever without repairing. All the fruits of the earth shall come to maturity at whatever season we think fit to choose, and increase an hundred fold more than they do at present, with innumerable other happy proposals. The only inconvenience is, that none of these projects are yet brought to perfection, and in the mean time, the whole country lies miserably waste, the houses in ruins, and the people without food or clothes. By all which, instead of being discouraged, they are fifty times more violently bent upon prosecuting their schemes, driven

equally on by hope and despair; that as for himself, being
not of an enterprising spirit, he was content to go on in
the old forms, to live in the houses his ancestors had built,
and act as they did in every part of life without innovation.
That some few other persons of quality and gentry had
done the same, but were looked on with an eye of contempt and ill-will, as enemies to art, ignorant, and ill com-
monwealth's-men, preferring their own ease and sloth
before the general improvement of their country.

His Lordship added that he would not by any further
particulars prevent the pleasure I should certainly take
in viewing the grand Academy, whither he was resolved
I should go. He only desired me to observe a ruined
building upon the side of a mountain about three miles
distant, of which he gave me this account. That he had
a very convenient mill within half a mile of his house,
turned by a current from a large river, and sufficient for
his own family as well as a great number of his tenants.
That about seven years ago a club of those projectors
came to him with proposals to destroy this mill, and
build another on the side of that mountain, on the long
ridge whereof a long canal must be cut for a repository
of water, to be conveyed up by pipes and engines to
supply the mill; because the wind and air upon a height
agitated the water, and thereby made it fitter for motion;
and because the water descending down a declivity
would turn the mill with half the current of a river whose
course is more upon a level. He said, that being then
not very well with the court, and pressed by many of his
friends, he complied with the proposal; and after employing an hundred men for two years, the work miscarried, the projectors went off, laying the blame entirely
upon him, railing at him ever since, and putting others
upon the same experiment, with equal assurance of success, as well as equal disappointment.

In a few days we came back to town, and his Excellency, considering the bad character he had in the Academy, would not go with me himself, but recommended
me to a friend of his to bear me company thither. My
lord was pleased to represent me as a great admirer of

projects, and a person of much curiosity and easy belief;
which indeed was not without truth, for I had myself
been a sort of projector in my younger days.

∞

Chapter V *The Author permitted to see the Grand
       Academy of Lagado. The Academy largely
       described. The Arts wherein the professors
       employ themselves.*

THIS ACADEMY is not an entire single building, but a
continuation of several houses on both sides of a
street, which growing waste was purchased and applied
to that use.

I was received very kindly by the Warden, and went
for many days to the Academy. Every room hath in it
one or more projectors, and I believe I could not be in
fewer than five hundred rooms.

The first man I saw was of a meagre aspect, with sooty
hands and face, his hair and beard long, ragged and
singed in several places. His clothes, shirt, and skin were
all of the same colour. He had been eight years upon a
project for extracting sun-beams out of cucumbers,
which were to be put into vials hermetically sealed, and
let out to warm the air in raw inclement summers. He
told me he did not doubt in eight years more he should
be able to supply the Governor's gardens with sunshine
at a reasonable rate; but he complained that his stock
was low, and entreated me to give him something as an
encouragement to ingenuity, especially since this had
been a very dear season for cucumbers. I made him a
small present, for my lord had furnished me with money
on purpose, because he knew their practice of begging
from all who go to see them.

I went into another chamber, but was ready to hasten
back, being almost overcome with a horrible stink. My

conductor pressed me forward, conjuring me in a whisper to give no offence, which would be highly resented, and therefore I durst not so much as stop my nose. The projector of this cell was the most ancient student of the Academy; his face and beard were of a pale yellow; his hands and clothes daubed over with filth. When I was presented to him, he gave me a close embrace (a compliment I could well have excused). His employment from his first coming into the Academy, was an operation to reduce human excrement to its original food, by separating the several parts, removing the tincture which it receives from the gall, making the odour exhale, and scumming off the saliva. He had a weekly allowance from the society, of a vessel filled with human ordure, about the bigness of a Bristol barrel.

I saw another at work to calcine ice into gunpowder, who likewise showed me a treatise he had written concerning the malleability of fire, which he intended to publish.

There was a most ingenious architect who had contrived a new method for building houses, by beginning at the roof, and working downwards to the foundation, which he justified to me by the like practice of those two prudent insects, the bee and the spider.

There was a man born blind, who had several apprentices in his own condition: their employment was to mix colours for painters, which their master taught them to distinguish by feeling and smelling. It was indeed my misfortune to find them at that time not very perfect in their lessons, and the professor himself happened to be generally mistaken: this artist is much encouraged and esteemed by the whole fraternity.

In another apartment I was highly pleased with a projector, who had found a device of ploughing the ground with hogs, to save the charges of ploughs, cattle, and labour. The method is this: in an acre of ground you bury, at six inches distance and eight deep, a quantity of acorns, dates, chestnuts, and other mast or vegetables whereof these animals are fondest; then you drive six hundred or more of them into the field, where in a few

CEB.
1894

days they will root up the whole ground in search of their food, and make it fit for sowing, at the same time manuring it with their dung. It is true, upon experiment they found the charge and trouble very great, and they had little or no crop. However, it is not doubted that this invention may be capable of great improvement.

I went into another room, where the walls and ceiling were all hung round with cobwebs, except a narrow passage for the artist to go in and out. At my entrance he called aloud to me not to disturb his webs. He lamented the fatal mistake the world had been so long in of using silk-worms, while we had such plenty of domestic insects, who infinitely excelled the former, because they understood how to weave as well as spin. And he proposed farther that by employing spiders the charge of dyeing silks should be wholly saved, whereof I was fully convinced when he showed me a vast number of flies most beautifully colored, wherewith he fed his spiders, assuring us that the webs would take a tincture from them; and as he had them of all hues, he hoped to fit everybody's fancy, as soon as he could find proper food for the flies, of certain gums, oils, and other glutinous matter to give a strength and consistence to the threads.

There was an astronomer who had undertaken to place a sun-dial upon the great weathercock on the town-house, by adjusting the annual and diurnal motions of the earth and sun, so as to answer and coincide with all accidental turnings by the wind.

I was complaining of a small fit of the colic, upon which my conductor led me into a room, where a great physician resided, who was famous for curing that disease by contrary operations from the same instrument. He had a large pair of bellows with a long slender muzzle of ivory. This he conveyed eight inches up the anus, and drawing in the wind, he affirmed he could make the guts as lank as a dried bladder. But when the disease was more stubborn and violent, he let in the muzzle while the bellows were full of wind, which he discharged into the body of the patient, then withdrew the instrument to replenish it, clapping his thumb strongly against the orifice of the fundament; and this being repeated three or four times, the adventitious wind would rush out, bringing the noxious along with it (like water put into a pump), and the patient recover. I saw him try both experiments upon a dog, but could not discern any effect from the former. After the latter, the animal was ready to burst, and made so violent a discharge, as was very offensive to me and my companions. The dog died

on the spot, and we left the doctor endeavouring to recover him by the same operation.

I visited many other apartments, but shall not trouble
my reader with all the curiosities I observed, being studious of brevity.

I had hitherto seen only one side of the Academy, the
other being appropriated to the advancers of speculative
learning, of whom I shall say something when I have
mentioned one illustrious person more, who is called
among them *the universal artist.* He told us he had been
thirty years employing his thoughts for the improvement
of human life. He had two large rooms full of wonderful
curiosities, and fifty men at work. Some were condensing
air into a dry tangible substance, by extracting the nitre,
and letting the aqueous or fluid particles percolate; others softening marble for pillows and pin-cushions; others
petrifying the hoofs of a living horse to preserve them
from foundering. The artist himself was at that time busy
upon two great designs; the first, to sow land with chaff,
wherein he affirmed the true seminal virtue to be contained, as he demonstrated by several experiments which
I was not skilful enough to comprehend. The other was,
by a certain composition of gums, minerals, and vegetables outwardly applied, to prevent the growth of wool
upon two young lambs; and he hoped in a reasonable
time to propagate the breed of naked sheep all over
the kingdom.

We crossed a walk to the other part of the Academy,
where, as I have already said, the projectors in speculative learning resided.

The first professor I saw was in a very large room,
with forty pupils about him. After salutation, observing
me to look earnestly upon a frame, which took up the
greatest part of both the length and breadth of the room,
he said perhaps I might wonder to see him employed in
a project for improving speculative knowledge by practical and mechanical operations. But the world would
soon be sensible of its usefulness, and he flattered himself that a more noble exalted thought never sprang in
any other man's head. Every one knew how laborious

the usual method is of attaining to arts and sciences; whereas by his contrivance the most ignorant person at a reasonable charge, and with a little bodily labour, may write books in philosophy, poetry, politics, law, mathematics, and theology, without the least assistance from genius or study. He then led me to the frame, about the sides whereof all his pupils stood in ranks. It was twenty foot square, placed in the middle of the room. The superficies was composed of several bits of wood, about the bigness of a die, but some larger than others. They were all linked together by slender wires. These bits of wood were covered on every square with paper pasted on them, and on these papers were written all the words of their language, in their several moods, tenses, and declensions, but without any order. The professor then desired me to observe, for he was going to set his engine at work. The pupils at his command took each of them hold of an iron handle, whereof there were forty fixed round the edges of the frame, and giving them a sudden turn, the whole disposition of the words was entirely changed. He then commanded six and thirty of the lads to read the several lines softly as they appeared upon the frame; and where they found three or four words together that might make part of a sentence, they dictated to the four remaining boys who were scribes. This work was repeated three or four times, and at every turn the engine was so contrived that the words shifted into new places, as the square bits of wood moved upside down.

Six hours a day the young students were employed in this labour, and the professor showed me several volumes in large folio already collected, of broken sentences, which he intended to piece together, and out of those rich materials to give the world a complete body of all arts and sciences; which however might be still improved, and much expedited, if the public would raise a fund for making and employing five hundred such frames in Lagado, and oblige the managers to contribute in common their several collections.

He assured me, that this invention had employed all his thoughts from his youth, that he had emptied the whole vocabulary into his frame, and made the strictest computation of the general proportion there is in books between the numbers of particles, nouns, and verbs, and other parts of speech.

I made my humblest acknowledgement to this illustrious person for his great communicativeness, and promised if ever I had the good fortune to return to my native country, that I would do him justice, as the sole inventor of this wonderful machine; the form and contrivance of which I desired leave to delineate upon paper. I told him, although it were the custom of our learned in Europe to steal inventions from each other, who had thereby at least this advantage, that it became a controversy which was the right owner, yet I would take such caution, that he should have the honour entire without a rival.

We next went to the school of languages, where three professors sat in consultation upon improving that of their own country.

The first project was to shorten discourse by cutting polysyllables into one, and leaving out verbs and participles, because in reality all things imaginable are but nouns.

The other project was a scheme for entirely abolishing all words whatsoever; and this was urged as a great advantage in point of health as well as brevity. For it is plain that every word we speak is in some degree a diminution of our lungs by corrosion, and consequently contributes to the shortening of our lives. An expedient was therefore offered, that since words are only names for *things*, it would be more convenient for all men to carry about them such things as were necessary to express the particular business they are to discourse on. And this invention would certainly have taken place, to the great ease as well as health of the subject, if the women, in conjunction with the vulgar and illiterate, had not threatened to raise a rebellion, unless they might be allowed the liberty to speak with their tongues, after the manner of their ancestors; such constant irreconcilable enemies to science are the common people. However, many of the most learned and wise adhere to the new scheme of expressing themselves by things, which hath only this inconvenience attending it, that if a man's business be very great, and of various kinds, he must be obliged in proportion to carry a greater bundle of things upon his back, unless he can afford one or two strong servants to attend him. I have often beheld two of those sages almost sinking under the weight of their packs, like pedlars among us; who, when they met in the streets, would lay down their loads, open their sacks, and hold conversation for an hour together; then put up their implements, help each other to resume their burthens, and take their leave.

But for short conversations a man may carry implements in his pockets and under his arms, enough to supply him, and in his house he cannot be at a loss. Therefore the room where company meet who practise this art, is full of all things ready at hand, requisite to furnish matter for this kind of artificial converse.

Another great advantage proposed by this invention was that it would serve as an universal language to be understood in all civilised nations, whose goods and utensils are generally of the same kind, or nearly resembling, so that their uses might easily be comprehended. And thus ambassadors would be qualified to treat with foreign princes or ministers of state, to whose tongues they were utter strangers.

I was at the mathematical school, where the master taught his pupils after a method scarce imaginable to us in Europe. The proposition and demonstration were fairly written on a thin wafer, with ink composed of a cephalic tincture. This the student was to swallow upon a fasting stomach, and for three days following eat nothing but bread and water. As the wafer digested, the tincture mounted to his brain, bearing the proposition along with it. But the success hath not hitherto been answerable, partly by some error in the *quantum* or composition, and partly by the perverseness of lads, to whom this bolus is so nauseous, that they generally steal aside, and discharge it upwards before it can operate; neither have they been yet persuaded to use so long an abstinence as the prescription requires.

Chapter VI *A further account of the Academy. The Author proposes some improvements, which are honourably received.*

IN THE SCHOOL of political projectors I was but ill entertained, the professors appearing in my judgement wholly out of their senses, which is a scene that never fails to make me melancholy. These unhappy people were proposing schemes for persuading monarchs to choose favourites upon the score of their wisdom, capacity, and virtue; of teaching ministers to consult the public good; of rewarding merit, great abilities, eminent services; of instructing princes to know their true interest by placing it on the same foundation with that of their people; of choosing for employments persons qualified to exercise them; with many other wild impossible chimæras, that never entered before into the heart of man to conceive, and confirmed in me the old observation, that there is nothing so extravagant and irrational which some philosophers have not maintained for truth.

But however I shall so far do justice to this part of the Academy, as to acknowledge that all of them were not so visionary. There was a most ingenious doctor who seemed to be perfectly versed in the whole nature and system of government. This illustrious person had very usefully employed his studies in finding out effectual remedies for all diseases and corruptions, to which the several kinds of public administration are subject by the vices or infirmities of those who govern, as well as by the licentiousness of those who are to obey. For instance, whereas all writers and reasoners have agreed, that there is a strict universal resemblance between the natural and the political body; can there be any thing more evident, than that the health of both must be preserved, and the diseases cured by the same prescriptions? It is allowed that senates and great councils are often troubled with redundant, ebullient, and other peccant humours, with many diseases of the head, and more of the heart; with strong convulsions, with grievous contractions of the nerves and sinews in both hands, but especially the right; with spleen, flatus, vertigoes, and deliriums; with scrofulous tumours full of foetid virulent matter; with sour frothy ructations, with canine appetites and crudeness of digestion, besides many others needless to mention. This doctor therefore proposed, that upon the meeting of a senate, certain physicians should attend at the three first days of their sitting, and at the close of each day's debate, feel the pulses of every senator; after which, having maturely considered, and consulted upon the nature of the several maladies, and the methods of cure, they should on the fourth day return to the senate house, attended by their apothecaries stored with proper medicines; and before the members sat, administer to each of them lenitives, aperitives, abstersives, corrosives, restringents, palliatives, laxatives, cephalalgics, icterics, apophlegmatics, acoustics, as their several cases required; and according as these medicines should operate, repeat, alter, or omit them at the next meeting.

This project could not be of any great expense to the public, and would, in my poor opinion, be of much use for the dispatch of business in those countries where senates have any share in the legislative power; beget unanimity, shorten debates, open a few mouths which are now closed, and close many more which are now open; curb the petulancy of the young, and correct the positiveness of the old; rouse the stupid, and damn the pert.

Again, because it is a general complaint, that the favourites of princes are troubled with short and weak memories, the same doctor proposed, that whoever attended a first minister, after having told his business with the utmost brevity and in the plainest words, should at his departure give the said minister a tweak by the nose, or a kick in the belly, or tread on his corns, or lug him thrice by both ears, or run a pin into his breech, or pinch his arm black and blue, to prevent forgetfulness; and at every levee day repeat the same operation, till the business were done or absolutely refused.

He likewise directed, that every senator in the great council of a nation, after he had delivered his opinion, and argued in the defence of it, should be obliged to give his vote directly contrary; because if that were done, the result would infallibly terminate in the good of the public.

When parties in a state are violent, he offered a wonderful contrivance to reconcile them. The method is this. You take a hundred leaders of each party, you dispose them into couples of such whose heads are nearest of a size; then let two nice operators saw off the occiput of each couple at the same time, in such a manner that the brain may be equally divided. Let the occiputs thus cut off be interchanged, applying each to the head of his opposite party-man. It seems indeed to be a work that requireth some exactness, but the professor assured us that if it were dexterously performed the cure would be infallible. For he argued thus: that the two half brains being left to debate the matter between themselves within the space of one skull, would soon come to a good understanding, and produce that moderation, as well as regularity of thinking, so much to be wished for in the heads of those who imagine they come into the world only to watch and govern its motion: and as to the difference of brains in quantity or quality among those who are directors in faction, the doctor assured us from his own knowledge that it was a perfect trifle.

I heard a very warm debate between two professors, about the most commodious and effectual ways and means of raising money without grieving the subject. The first affirmed the justest method would be to lay a certain tax upon vices and folly, and the sum fixed upon every man to be rated after the fairest manner by a jury of his neighbours. The second was of an opinion directly contrary, to tax those qualities of body and mind for which men chiefly value themselves, the rate to be more or less according to the degrees of excelling, the decision whereof should be left entirely to their own breast. The highest tax was upon men who are the greatest favourites of the other sex, and the assessments according to the number and natures of the favours they have received; for which they are allowed to be their own vouchers. Wit, valour, and politeness were likewise proposed to be largely taxed, and collected in the same manner, by every person's giving his own word for the quantum of what he possessed. But as to honour, justice, wisdom, and learning, they should not be taxed at all, because they are qualifications of so singular a kind, that no man will either allow them in his neighbour, or value them in himself.

The women were proposed to be taxed according to their beauty and skill in dressing, wherein they had the same privilege with the men, to be determined by their own judgment. But constancy, chastity, good sense, and good nature were not rated, because they would not bear the charge of collecting.

To keep senators in the interest of the crown, it was proposed that the members should raffle for employments, every man first taking an oath, and giving security that he would vote for the court, whether he won or no; after which the losers had in their turn the liberty of raffling upon the next vacancy. Thus hope and expectation would be kept alive, none would complain of broken promises, but impute their disappointments wholly to fortune, whose shoulders are broader and stronger than those of a ministry.

Another professor showed me a large paper of instructions for discovering plots and conspiracies against the government. He advised great statesmen to examine into the diet of all suspected persons; their times of eating; upon which side they lay in bed; with which hand they wiped their posteriors; to take a strict view of their excrements, and, from the colour, the odour, the taste, the

consistence, the crudeness or maturity of digestion, form
a judgement of their thoughts and designs. Because men
are never so serious, thoughtful, and intent, as when they
are at stool, which he found by frequent experiment; for
in such conjectures, when he used merely as a trial to
consider which was the best way of murdering the king,
his ordure would have a tincture of green, but quite
different when he thought only of raising an insurrection
or burning the metropolis.

The whole discourse was written with great acuteness,
containing many observations both curious and useful
for politicians, but as I conceived not altogether complete. This I ventured to tell the author, and offered if
he pleased to supply him with some additions. He received my proposition with more compliance than is
usual among writers, especially those of the projecting
species, professing he would be glad to receive farther
information.

I told him that in the kingdom of Tribnia, by the
natives called Langden, where I had sojourned some
time in my travels, the bulk of the people consist in
a manner wholly of discoverers, witnesses, informers,
accusers, prosecutors, evidences, swearers, together with
their several subservient and subaltern instruments, all
under the colours and conduct of ministers of state and
their deputies. The plots in that kingdom are usually the
workmanship of those persons who desire to raise their
own characters of profound politicians, to restore new
vigour to a crazy administration, to stifle or divert general discontents, to fill their pockets with forfeitures, and
raise or sink the opinion of public credit, as either shall
best answer their private advantage. It is first agreed
and settled among them, what suspected persons shall
be accused of a plot; then, effectual care is taken to
secure all their letters and papers, and put the criminals
in chains. These papers are delivered to a set of artists,
very dexterous in finding out the mysterious meanings
of words, syllables, and letters. For instance, they can
discover a close-stool to signify a privy council; a flock
of geese, a senate; a lame dog, an invader; a codshead,

a—; the plague, a standing army; a buzzard, a prime minister; the gout, a high priest; a gibbet, a secretary of state; a chamber-pot, a committee of grandees; a sieve, a court lady; a broom, a revolution; a mouse-trap, an employment; a bottomless pit, the treasury; a sink, the court; a cap and bells, a favourite; a broken reed, a court of justice; an empty tun, a general; a running sore, the administration.

When this method fails, they have two others more effectual, which the learned among them call acrostics and anagrams. First they can decipher all initial letters into political meanings. Thus, *N.* shall signify a plot; *B.* a regiment of horse; *L.* a fleet at sea; or secondly by transposing the letters of the alphabet in any suspected paper, they can discover the deepest designs of a discontented party. So for example if I should say in a letter to a friend, *Our brother* Tom *has just got the piles*, a skilful decipherer would discover that the same letters which compose that sentence may be analysed into the following words: *Resist, a plot is brought home; The tour.* And this is the anagrammatic method.

The professor made me great acknowledgements for communicating these observations, and promised to make honourable mention of me in his treatise.

I saw nothing in this country that could invite me to a longer continuance, and began to think of returning home to England.

Chapter VII *The Author leaves Lagado, arrives at Maldonada. No ship ready. He takes a short voyage to Glubbdubdrib. His reception by the Governor.*

THE CONTINENT of which this kingdom is a part extends itself, as I have reason to believe, eastward to that unknown tract of America, westward of California, and north of the Pacific Ocean, which is not above a hundred and fifty miles from Lagado, where there is a good port and much commerce with the great island of Luggnagg, situated to the north-west about 29 degrees north latitude, and 140 longitude. This island of Luggnagg stands south-eastwards of Japan, about an hundred leagues distant. There is a strict alliance between the Japanese Emperor and the King of Luggnagg, which affords frequent opportunities of sailing from one island to the other. I determined therefore to direct my course this way, in order to my return to Europe. I hired two mules with a guide to show me the way, and carry my small baggage. I took leave of my noble protector, who had shown me so much favour and made me a generous present at my departure.

My journey was without any accident or adventure worth relating. When I arrived at the port of Maldonada (for so it is called) there was no ship in the harbour bound for Luggnagg, nor likely to be in some time. The town is about as large as Portsmouth. I soon fell into some acquaintance, and was very hospitably received. A gentleman of distinction said to me that since the ships bound for Luggnagg could not be ready in less than a month, it might be no disagreeable amusement for me to take a trip to the little island of Glubbdubdrib, about five leagues off to the south-west. He offered himself and a friend to accompany me, and that I should be provided with a small convenient barque for the voyage.

Glubbdubdrib, as nearly as I can interpret the word, signifies the Island of *Sorcerers* or *Magicians*. It is about one third as large as the Isle of Wight, and extremely fruitful: it is governed by the head of a certain tribe, who are all magicians. This tribe marries only among each other, and the eldest in succession is Prince or Governor. He hath a noble palace, and a park of about three thousand acres, surrounded by a wall of hewn stone twenty foot high. In this park are several small enclosures for cattle, corn, and gardening.

The Governor and his family are served and attended by domestics of a kind somewhat unusual. By his skill in necromancy, he hath a power of calling whom he pleaseth from the dead, and commanding their service for twenty-four hours, but no longer; nor can he call the same persons up again in less than three months, except upon very extraordinary occasions.

When we arrived at the island, which was about eleven in the morning, one of the gentlemen who accompanied me, went to the Governor, and desired admittance for a stranger, who came on purpose to have the honour of attending on his Highness. This was immediately granted, and we all three entered the gate of the palace between two rows of guards, armed and dressed after a very antic manner, and something in their countenances that made my flesh creep with a horror I cannot express. We passed through several apartments, between servants of the same sort, ranked on each side as before, till we came to the chamber of presence, where after three profound obeisances, and a few general questions, we were permitted to sit on three stools near the lowest step of his Highness's throne. He understood the language of Balnibarbi, although it were different from that of his island. He desired me to give him some account of my travels; and to let me see that I should be treated without ceremony, he dismissed all his attendants with a turn of his finger, at which to my great astonishment

they vanished in an instant, like visions in a dream, when
we awake on a sudden. I could not recover myself in
some time, till the Governor assured me that I should
receive no hurt; and observing my two companions to
be under no concern, who had been often entertained
in the same manner, I began to take courage, and related
to his Highness a short history of my several adventures,
yet not without some hesitation, and frequently looking
behind me to the place where I had seen those domestic
spectres. I had the honour to dine with the Governor,
where a new set of ghosts served up the meat, and
waited at table. I now observed myself to be less terrified
than I had been in the morning. I stayed till sunset,
but humbly desired his Highness to excuse me for not
accepting his invitation of lodging in the palace. My two
friends and I lay at a private house in the town adjoining, which is the capital of this little island; and the next
morning we returned to pay our duty to the Governor,
as he was pleased to command us.

After this manner we continued in the island for ten
days, most part of every day with the Governor, and at
night in our lodging. I soon grew so familiarized to the
sight of spirits, that after the third or fourth time they
gave me no emotion at all; or if I had any apprehensions
left, my curiosity prevailed over them. For his Highness
the Governor ordered me to call up whatever persons I
would choose to name, and in whatever numbers among
all the dead from the beginning of the world to the present time, and command them to answer any questions I
should think fit to ask; with this condition, that my questions must be confined within the compass of the times
they lived in. And one thing I might depend upon, that
they would certainly tell me truth, for lying was a talent
of no use in the lower world.

I made my humble acknowledgements to his Highness
for so great a favour. We were in a chamber from
whence there was a fair prospect into the park. And
because my first inclination was to be entertained with
scenes of pomp and magnificence, I desired to see Alexander the Great, at the head of his army just after the

battle of Arbela; which upon a motion of the Governor's finger immediately appeared in a large field under the window where we stood. Alexander was called up into the room: it was with great difficulty that I understood his Greek, and had but little of my own. He assured me upon his honour that he was not poisoned, but died of a fever by excessive drinking.

Next I saw Hannibal passing the Alps, who told me he had not a drop of vinegar in his camp.

I saw Cæsar and Pompey at the head of their troops, just ready to engage. I saw the former in his last great triumph. I desired that the senate of Rome might appear before me in one large chamber, and an assembly of somewhat a latter age in counterview in another. The first seemed to be an assembly of heroes and demigods; the other a knot of pedlars, pickpockets, highway-men, and bullies.

The Governor at my request gave the sign for Cæsar and Brutus to advance towards us. I was struck with a profound veneration at the sight of Brutus, and could easily discover the most consummate virtue, the greatest intrepidity and firmness of mind, the truest love of his country, and general benevolence for mankind in every lineament of his countenance. I observed with much pleasure that these two persons were in good intelligence with each other, and Cæsar freely confessed to me that the greatest actions of his own life were not equal by many degrees to the glory of taking it away. I had the honour to have much conversation with Brutus; and was told, that his ancestor Junius, Socrates, Epaminondas, Cato the younger, Sir Thomas More, and himself were perpetually together: a sextumvirate to which all the ages of the world cannot add a seventh.

It would be tedious to trouble the reader with relating what vast number of illustrious persons were called up, to gratify that insatiable desire I had to see the world in every period of antiquity placed before me. I chiefly fed my eyes with beholding the destroyers of tyrants and usurpers, and the restorers of liberty to oppressed and injured nations. But it is impossible to express the satis-

faction I received in my own mind, after such a manner
as to make it a suitable entertainment to the reader.

Chapter VIII *A further account of Glubbdubdrib.
Ancient and modern history corrected.*

HAVING A DESIRE to see those ancients who were
most renowned for wit and learning, I set apart one
day on purpose. I proposed that Homer and Aristotle
might appear at the head of all their commentators; but
these were so numerous that some hundreds were forced
to attend in the court and outward rooms of the palace.
I knew and could distinguish those two heroes at first
sight, not only from the crowd but from each other.
Homer was the taller and comelier person of the two,
walked very erect for one of his age, and his eyes were
the most quick and piercing I ever beheld. Aristotle
stooped much, and made use of a staff. His visage was
meagre, his hair lank and thin, and his voice hollow. I
soon discovered that both of them were perfect strangers
to the rest of the company, and had never seen or heard
of them before. And I had a whisper from a ghost, who
shall be nameless, that these commentators always kept
in the most distant quarters from their principals in the
lower world, through a consciousness of shame and guilt,
because they had so horribly misrepresented the meaning of those authors to posterity. I introduced Didymus
and Eustathius to Homer, and prevailed on him to treat
them better than perhaps they deserved; for he soon
found they wanted a genius to enter into the spirit of a
poet. But Aristotle was out of all patience with the account I gave him of Scotus and Ramus, as I presented
them to him; and he asked them whether the rest of the
tribe were as great dunces as themselves.

I then desired the Governor to call up Descartes and Gassendi, with whom I prevailed to explain their systems to Aristotle. This great philosopher freely acknowledged his own mistakes in natural philosophy, because he proceeded in many things upon conjecture, as all men must do; and he found, that Gassendi, who had made the doctrine of Epicurus as palatable as he could, and the *vortices* of Descartes, were equally exploded. He predicted the same fate to *attraction*, whereof the present learned are such zealous asserters. He said that new systems of nature were but new fashions, which would vary in every age; and even those who pretend to demonstrate them from mathematical principles, would flourish but a short period of time, and be out of vogue when that was determined.

I spent five days in conversing with many others of the ancient learned. I saw most of the first Roman emperors. I prevailed on the Governor to call up Eliogabalus's cooks to dress us a dinner, but they could not show us much of their skill, for want of materials. A helot of Agesilaus made us a dish of Spartan broth, but I was not able to get down a second spoonful.

The two gentlemen who conducted me to the island were pressed by their private affairs to return in three days, which I employed in seeing some of the modern dead, who had made the greatest figure for two or three hundred years past in our own and other countries of Europe; and having been always a great admirer of old illustrious families, I desired the Governor would call up a dozen or two of kings with their ancestors in order for eight or nine generations. But my disappointment was grievous and unexpected. For instead of a long train with royal diadems, I saw in one family two fiddlers, three spruce courtiers, and an Italian prelate. In another, a barber, an abbot, and two cardinals. I have too great a veneration for crowned heads to dwell any longer on so nice a subject. But as to counts, marquesses, dukes, earls, and the like, I was not so scrupulous. And I confess it was not without some pleasure that I found myself able to trace the particular features, by which certain families are distinguished, up to their originals. I could plainly discover from whence one family derives a long chin, why a second hath abounded with knaves for two generations, and fools for two more; why a third happened to be crack-brained, and a fourth to be sharpers. Whence it came what Polydore Virgil says of a certain great house, *Nec vir fortis, nec femina casta.* How cruelty, falsehood, and cowardice grew to be characteristics by which certain families are distinguished as much as by their coat of arms. Who first brought the pox into a noble house, which hath lineally descended in scrofulous tumours to their posterity. Neither could I wonder at all this, when I saw such an interruption of lineages by pages, lackeys, valets, coachmen, gamesters, captains and pickpockets.

I was chiefly disgusted with modern history. For having strictly examined all the persons of greatest name in the courts of princes for an hundred years past, I found how the world had been misled by prostitute writers, to ascribe the greatest exploits in war to cowards, the wisest counsel to fools, sincerity to flatterers, Roman virtue to betrayers of their country, piety to atheists, chastity to sodomites, truth to informers. How many innocent and excellent persons had been condemned to death or banishment, by the practising of great ministers upon the corruption of judges, and the malice of factions. How many villains had been exalted to the highest places of trust, power, dignity, and profit: how great a share in the motions and events of courts, councils, and senates might be challenged by bawds, whores, pimps, parasites, and buffoons. How low an opinion I had of human wisdom and integrity, when I was truly informed of the springs and motives of great enterprises and revolutions in the world, and of the contemptible accidents to which they owed their success.

Here I discovered the roguery and ignorance of those who pretend to write *anecdotes*, or secret history, who send so many kings to their graves with a cup of poison; will repeat the discourse between a prince and chief minister, where no witness was by; unlock the thoughts and

cabinets of ambassadors and secretaries of state and
have the perpetual misfortune to be mistaken. Here I
discovered the secret causes of many great events that
have surprised the world, how a whore can govern the
back-stairs, the back-stairs a council, and the council a
senate. A general confessed in my presence, that he got
a victory purely by the force of cowardice and ill conduct; and an admiral, that for want of proper intelligence, he beat the enemy to whom he intended to betray
the fleet. Three kings protested to me, that in their
whole reigns they never did once prefer any person of
merit, unless by mistake or treachery of some minister
in whom they confided; neither would they do it if they
were to live again; and they showed with great strength
of reason that the royal throne could not be supported
without corruption, because that positive, confident, restive temper, which virtue infused into man, was a perpetual clog to public business.

I had the curiosity to enquire in a particular manner,
by what method great numbers had procured to themselves high titles of honour, and prodigious estates; and I
confined my enquiry to a very modern period: however,
without grating upon present times, because I would be
sure to give no offence even to foreigners (for I hope
the reader need not be told that I do not in the least
intend my own country in what I say upon this occasion),
a great number of persons concerned were called up,
and upon a very slight examination, discovered such a
scene of infamy, that I cannot reflect upon it without
some seriousness. Perjury, oppression, subornation, fraud,
panderism, and the like infirmities, were amongst the
most excusable arts they had to mention, and for these
I gave, as it was reasonable, great allowance. But when
some confessed they owed their greatness and wealth to
sodomy or incest, others to the prostituting of their own
wives and daughters; others to the betraying of their
country or their prince; some of poisoning, more to the
perverting of justice in order to destroy the innocent; I
hope I may be pardoned if these discoveries inclined me
a little to abate of that profound veneration which I am

naturally apt to pay to persons of high rank, who ought to be treated with the utmost respect due to their sublime dignity, by us their inferiors.

I had often read of some great services done to princes and states, and desired to see the persons by whom those services were performed. Upon enquiry I was told that their names were to be found on no record, except a few of them whom history hath represented as the vilest rogues and traitors. As to the rest, I had never once heard of them. They all appeared with dejected looks, and in the meanest habit, most of them telling me they died in poverty and disgrace, and the rest on a scaffold or a gibbet.

Among the rest there was one person whose case appeared a little singular. He had a youth about eighteen years old standing by his side. He told me he had for many years been commander of a ship, and in the sea fight at Actium had the good fortune to break through the enemy's great line of battle, sink three of their capital ships, and take a fourth, which was the sole cause of Antony's flight, and of the victory that ensued; that the youth standing by him, his only son, was killed in the action. He added that upon the confidence of some merit, the war being at an end, he went to Rome, and solicited at the court of Augustus to be preferred to a greater ship, whose commander had been killed; but without any regard to his pretensions, it was given to a youth who had never seen the sea, the son of Libertina, who waited on one of the emperor's mistresses. Returning back to his own vessel, he was charged with neglect of duty, and the ship given to a favourite page of Publicola, the vice-admiral; whereupon he retired to a poor farm at a great distance from Rome, and there ended his life. I was so curious to know the truth of this story, that I desired Agrippa might be called, who was admiral in that fight. He appeared, and confirmed the whole account, but with much more advantage to the captain, whose modesty had extenuated or concealed a great part of his merit.

I was surprised to find corruption grown so high and so quick in that empire, by the force of luxury so lately introduced, which made me less wonder at many parallel cases in other countries, where vices of all kinds have reigned so much longer, and where the whole praise as well as pillage hath been engrossed by the chief commander, who perhaps had the least title to either.

As every person called up made exactly the same appearance he had done in the world, it gave me melancholy reflections to observe how much the race of human kind was degenerate among us, within these hundred years past. How the pox under all its consequences and denominations had altered every lineament of an English countenance, shortened the size of bodies, unbraced the nerves, relaxed the sinews and muscles, introduced a sallow complexion, and rendered the flesh loose and rancid.

I descended so low as to desire that some English yeomen of the old stamp might be summoned to appear, once so famous for the simplicity of their manners, diet and dress, for justice in their dealings, for their true spirit of liberty, for their valour and love of their country. Neither could I be wholly unmoved after comparing the living with the dead, when I considered how all these pure native virtues were prostituted for a piece of money by their grand-children, who in selling their votes, and managing at elections, have acquired every vice and corruption that can possibly be learned in a court.

Chapter IX *The Author returns to Maldonada. Sails to the kingdom of Luggnagg. The Author confined. He is sent for to court. The manner of his admittance. The King's great lenity to his subjects.*

THE DAY OF OUR DEPARTURE being come, I took leave of his Highness the Governor of Glubbdubdrib, and returned with my two companions to Maldonada, where after a fortnight's waiting, a ship was ready to sail for Luggnagg. The two gentlemen, and some others, were so generous and kind as to furnish me with provisions, and see me on board. I was a month in this voyage. We had one violent storm, and were under a necessity of steering westward to get into the trade wind, which holds for above sixty leagues. On the 21st of April, 1709, we sailed into the river of Clumegnig, which is a seaport town, at the south-east point of Luggnagg. We cast anchor within a league of the town, and made a signal for a pilot. Two of them came on board in less than half an hour, by whom we were guided between certain shoals and rocks, which are very dangerous in the passage, to a large basin, where a fleet may ride in safety within a cable's length of the town wall.

Some of our sailors, whether out of treachery or inadvertence, had informed the pilots that I was a stranger and a great traveller, whereof these gave notice to a custom-house officer, by whom I was examined very strictly upon my landing. This officer spoke to me in the language of Balnibarbi, which by the force of much commerce is generally understood in that town, especially by seamen, and those employed in the customs. I gave him a short account of some particulars, and made my story as plausible and consistent as I could; but I thought it necessary to disguise my country, and call myself an Hollander, because my intentions were for Japan, and I knew the Dutch were the only Europeans permitted to enter into that kingdom. I therefore told the officer, that having been shipwrecked on the coast of Balnibarbi, and cast on a rock, I was received up into Laputa, or the Flying Island (of which he had often heard), and was now endeavouring to get to Japan, from whence I might find a convenience of returning to my own country. The officer said I must be confined till he could receive orders from court, for which he would write immediately, and hoped to receive an answer in a fortnight. I was carried to a convenient lodging, with a sentry placed at the door; however I had the liberty of a large garden, and was treated with humanity enough, being maintained all the time at the King's charge. I was visited by several persons, chiefly out of curiosity, because it was reported that I came from countries very remote of which they had never heard.

I hired a young man who came in the same ship to be an interpreter; he was a native of Luggnagg, but had lived some years at Maldonada, and was a perfect master of both languages. By his assistance I was able to hold a conversation with those who came to visit me; but this consisted only of their questions, and my answers.

The dispatch came from court about the time we expected. It contained a warrant for conducting me and my retinue to Traldragdubh or Trildrogdrib, for it is pronounced both ways as near as I can remember, by a party of ten horse. All my retinue was that poor lad for an interpreter, whom I persuaded into my service, and at my humble request, we had each of us a mule to ride on. A messenger was dispatched half a day's journey before us, to give the King notice of my approach, and to desire that his Majesty would please to appoint a day and hour, when it would be his gracious pleasure that I might have the honour to *lick the dust before his footstool*. This is the court style, and I found it to be more than a matter of form. For upon my admittance two days after my arrival, I was commanded to crawl on my belly,

and lick the floor as I advanced; but on account of my
being a stranger, care was taken to have it made so clean
that the dust was not offensive. However, this was a
peculiar grace, not allowed to any but persons of the
highest rank, when they desire an admittance. Nay,
sometimes the floor is strewed with dust on purpose,
when the person to be admitted happens to have powerful enemies at court. And I have seen a great lord with
his mouth so crammed, that when he had crept to the
proper distance from the throne, he was not able to
speak a word. Neither is there any remedy, because it is
capital for those who receive an audience to spit or wipe
their mouths in his Majesty's presence. There is indeed
another custom, which I cannot altogether approve of.
When the King hath a mind to put any of his nobles to

death in a gentle indulgent manner, he commands to
have the floor strowed with a certain brown powder, of
a deadly composition, which being licked up infallibly
kills him in twenty-four hours. But in justice to this
prince's great clemency, and the care he hath of his subjects' lives (wherein it were much to be wished that the
monarchs of Europe would imitate him), it must be mentioned for his honour, that strict orders are given to have
the infected parts of the floor well washed after every
such execution; which if his domestics neglect, they are
in danger of incurring his royal displeasure. I myself
heard him give directions, that one of his pages should
be whipped, whose turn it was to give notice about wash-
ing the floor after an execution, but maliciously had
omitted it; by which neglect a young lord of great hopes
coming to an audience, was unfortunately poisoned, although the King at that time had no design against his
life. But this good prince was so gracious as to forgive
the poor page his whipping, upon promise that he would
do so no more, without special orders.

To return from this digression; when I had crept
within four yards of the throne, I raised myself gently
upon my knees, and then striking my forehead seven
times on the ground, I pronounced the following words,
as they had been taught me the night before, *Ickpling
gloffthrobb squutserumm blhiop mlashnalt zwin tnod-
balkguffh slhiophad gurdlubh asht.* This is the compliment established by the laws of the land for all persons
admitted to the King's presence. It may be rendered into
English thus: *May your Celestial Majesty outlive the sun,
eleven moons and a half.* To this the King returned some
answer, which although I could not understand, yet I
replied as I had been directed: *Fluft drin yalerick dwul-
dom prastrad mirpush,* which properly signifies, *My
tongue is in the mouth of my friend,* and by this expression was meant that I desired leave to bring my interpreter; whereupon the young man already mentioned
was accordingly introduced, by whose intervention I
answered as many questions as his Majesty could put in
above an hour. I spoke in the Balnibarbian tongue, and

my interpreter delivered my meaning in that of Lugg-nagg.

The King was much delighted with my company, and ordered his *Bliffmarklub*, or High Chamberlain, to appoint a lodging in the court for me and my interpreter, with a daily allowance for my table, and a large purse of gold for my common expenses.

I stayed three months in this country out of perfect obedience to his Majesty, who was pleased highly to favour me, and made me very honourable offers. But I thought it more consistent with prudence and justice to pass the remainder of my days with my wife and family.

Chapter X *The Luggnaggians commended. A particular description of the Struldbrugs, with many conversations between the Author and some eminent persons upon that subject.*

THE LUGGNAGGIANS are a polite and generous people, and although they are not without some share of that pride which is peculiar to all Eastern countries, yet they show themselves courteous to strangers, especially such who are countenanced by the court. I had many acquaintance among persons of the best fashion, and being always attended by my interpreter, the conversation we had was not disagreeable.

One day in much good company I was asked by a person of quality, whether I had seen any of their *Struldbrugs*, or *Immortals*. I said I had not, and desired he would explain to me what he meant by such an appellation applied to a mortal creature. He told me, that sometimes, though very rarely, a child happened to be born in a family with a red circular spot in the forehead, directly over the left eyebrow, which was an infallible mark that it should never die. The spot, as he described it, was about the compass of a silver threepence, but in the course of time grew larger, and changed its colour; for at twelve years old it became green, so continued till five and twenty, then turned to a deep blue; at five and forty it grew coal black, and as large as an English shilling, but never admitted any further alteration. He said these births were so rare, that he did not believe there could be above eleven hundred *struldbrugs* of both sexes in the whole kingdom, of which he computed about fifty in the metropolis, and among the rest a young girl born about three years ago. That these productions were not peculiar to any family, but a mere effect of chance; and the children of the *struldbrugs* themselves were equally mortal with the rest of the people.

I freely own myself to have been struck with inexpressible delight upon hearing this account, and the person who gave it me happening to understand the Balnibarbian language, which I spoke very well, I could not forbear breaking out into expressions perhaps a little too extravagant. I cried out as in a rapture: Happy nation where every child hath at least a chance for being immortal! Happy people who enjoy so many living examples of ancient virtue, and have masters ready to instruct them in the wisdom of all former ages! but, happiest beyond all comparison are those excellent *struldbrugs,* who being born exempt from that universal calamity of human nature, have their minds free and disengaged, without the weight and depression of spirits caused by the continual apprehension of death. I discovered my admiration that I had not observed any of these illustrious persons at court; the black spot on the forehead being so remarkable a distinction, that I could not have easily overlooked it; and it was impossible that his Majesty, a most judicious prince, should not provide himself with a good number of such wise and able counsellors. Yet perhaps the virtue of those reverend sages was too strict for the corrupt and libertine manners of a court. And we often find by experience that young men are too opinionative and volatile to be guided by the sober dictates of their seniors. However, since the King

was pleased to allow me access to his royal person, I
was resolved upon the very first occasion to deliver my
opinion to him on this matter freely and at large, by the
help of my interpreter; and whether he would please to
take my advice or no, yet in one thing I was determined,
that his Majesty having frequently offered me an establishment in this country, I would with great thankfulness
accept the favour, and pass my life here in the conversation of those superior beings the *struldbrugs*, if they
would please to admit me.

The gentleman to whom I addressed my discourse,
because (as I have already observed) he spoke the language of Balnibarbi, said to me with a sort of a smile,
which usually ariseth from pity to the ignorant, that he
was glad of any occasion to keep me among them, and
desired my permission to explain to the company what
I had spoke. He did so, and they talked together for
some time in their own language, whereof I understood
not a syllable, neither could I observe by their counte
nances what impression my discourse had made on them.
After a short silence, the same person told me that his
friends and mine (so he thought fit to express himself)
were very much pleased with the judicious remarks I
had made on the great happiness and advantages of immortal life; and they were desirous to know in a particular manner, what scheme of living I should have formed
to myself, if it had fallen to my lot to have been born
a *struldbrug*.

I answered, it was easy to be eloquent on so copious
and delightful a subject, especially to me who have been
often apt to amuse myself with visions of what I should
do if I were a king, a general, or a great lord; and upon
this very case I had frequently run over the whole system
how I should employ myself and pass the time if I were
sure to live for ever.

That if it had been my good fortune to come into the
world a *struldbrug*, as soon as I could discover my own
happiness by understanding the difference between life
and death, I would first resolve by all arts and methods
whatsoever to procure myself riches. In the pursuit of

which by thrift and management, I might reasonably expect, in about two hundred years to be the wealthiest man in the kingdom. In the second place, I would from my earliest youth apply myself to the study of arts and sciences, by which I should arrive in time to excel all others in learning. Lastly, I would carefully record every action and event of consequence that happened in the public, impartially draw the characters of the several successions of princes and great ministers of state, with my own observations on every point. I would exactly set down the several changes in customs, language, fashions of dress, diet and diversions. By all which acquirements, I should be a living treasury of knowledge and wisdom, and certainly become the oracle of the nation.

I would never marry after threescore, but live in an hospitable manner, yet still on the saving side. I would entertain myself in forming and directing the minds of hopeful young men, by convincing them from my own remembrance, experience and observation, fortified by numerous examples, of the usefulness of virtue in public and private life. But my choice and constant companions should be a set of my own immortal brotherhood, among whom I would elect a dozen from the most ancient down to my own contemporaries. Where any of these wanted fortunes, I would provide them with convenient lodges round my own estate, and have some of them always at my table, only mingling a few of the most valuable among you mortals, whom length of time would harden me to lose with little or no reluctance, and treat your posterity after the same manner; just as a man diverts himself with the annual succession of pinks and tulips in his garden, without regretting the loss of those which withered the preceding year.

These *struldbrugs* and I would mutually communicate our observations and memorials through the course of time, remark the several gradations by which corruption steals into the world, and oppose it in every step, by giving perpetual warning and instruction to mankind; which, added to the strong influence of our own exam-

ple, would probably prevent that continual degeneracy
of human nature so justly complained of in all ages.

Add to all this the pleasure of seeing the various revolutions of states and empires, the changes in the lower
and upper world, ancient cities in ruins, and obscure villages become the seats of kings. Famous rivers lessening
into shallow brooks, the ocean leaving one coast dry,
and overwhelming another; the discovery of many countries yet unknown. Barbarity overrunning the politest nations, and the most barbarous become civilized. I should
then see the discovery of the longitude, the perpetual
motion, the universal medicine, and many other great
inventions brought to the utmost perfection.

What wonderful discoveries should we make in astronomy, by outliving and confirming our own predictions,
by observing the progress and returns of comets, with
the changes of motion in the sun, moon, and stars.

I enlarged upon many other topics, which the natural
desire of endless life and sublunary happiness could easily furnish me with. When I had ended, and the sum of
my discourse had been interpreted as before, to the rest
of the company, there was a good deal of talk among
them in the language of the country, not without some
laughter at my expense. At last the same gentleman who
had been my interpreter said he was desired by the rest
to set me right in a few mistakes, which I had fallen into
through the common imbecility of human nature, and
upon that allowance was less answerable for them. That
this breed of *struldbrugs* was peculiar to their country,
for there were no such people either in Balnibarbi or
Japan, where he had the honour to be ambassador from
his Majesty, and found the natives in both those kingdoms very hard to believe that the fact was possible; and
it appeared from my astonishment when he first mentioned the matter to me, that I received it as a thing
wholly new, and scarcely to be credited. That in the two
kingdoms above mentioned, where during his residence
he had conversed very much, he observed long life to
be the universal desire and wish of mankind. That whoever had one foot in the grave was sure to hold back

the other as strongly as he could. That the oldest had still hopes of living one day longer, and looked on death as the greatest evil, from which nature always prompted him to retreat; only in this island of Luggnagg the appetite for living was not so eager, from the continual example of the *struldbrugs* before their eyes.

That the system of living contrived by me was unreasonable and unjust, because it supposed a perpetuity of youth, health, and vigour, which no man could be so foolish to hope, however extravagant he may be in his wishes. That the question therefore was not whether a man would choose to be always in the prime of youth, attended with prosperity and health, but how he would pass a perpetual life under all the usual disadvantages which old age brings along with it. For although few men will avow their desires of being immortal upon such hard conditions, yet in the two kingdoms before mentioned of Balnibarbi and Japan, he observed that every man desired to put off death for some time longer, let it approach ever so late; and he rarely heard of any man who died willingly, except he were incited by the extremity of grief or torture. And he appealed to me whether in those countries I had travelled as well as my own, I had not observed the same general disposition.

After this preface he gave me a particular account of the *struldbrugs* among them. He said they commonly acted like mortals, till about thirty years old, after which by degrees they grew melancholy and dejected, increasing in both till they came to fourscore. This he learned from their own confession; for otherwise there not being above two or three of that species born in an age, they were too few to form a general observation by. When they came to fourscore years, which is reckoned the extremity of living in this country, they had not only all the follies and infirmities of other old men, but many more which arose from the dreadful prospect of never dying. They were not only opinionative, peevish, covetous, morose, vain, talkative, but uncapable of friendship, and dead to all natural affection, which never descended below their grandchildren. Envy and impotent desires are their prevailing passions. But those objects against which their envy seems principally directed, are the vices of the younger sort, and the deaths of the old. By reflecting on the former, they find themselves cut off from all possibility of pleasure; and whenever they see a funeral, they lament and repine that others have gone to a harbour of rest, to which they themselves never can hope to arrive. They have no remembrance of anything but what they learned and observed in their youth and middle age, and even that is very imperfect. And for the truth or particulars of any fact, it is safer to depend on common traditions than upon their best recollections. The least miserable among them appear to be those who turn to dotage, and entirely lose their memories; these meet with more pity and assistance, because they want many bad qualities which abound in others.

If a *struldbrug* happen to marry one of his own kind, the marriage is dissolved of course by the courtesy of the kingdom, as soon as the younger of the two comes to be fourscore. For the law thinks it a reasonable indulgence, that those who are condemned without any fault of their own to a perpetual continuance in the world, should not have their misery doubled by the load of a wife.

As soon as they have completed the term of eighty years, they are looked on as dead in law; their heirs immediately succeed to their estates, only a small pittance is reserved for their support, and the poor ones are maintained at the public charge. After that period they are held incapable of any employment of trust or profit, they cannot purchase lands or take leases, neither are they allowed to be witnesses in any cause, either civil or criminal, not even for the decision of meers and bounds.

At ninety they lose their teeth and hair, they have at that age no distinction of taste, but eat and drink whatever they can get, without relish or appetite. The diseases they were subject to still continue without increasing or diminishing. In talking they forget the common appellation of things, and the names of persons, even of those who are their nearest friends and relations. For the same reason they never can amuse themselves with reading, because their memory will not serve to carry them from the beginning of a sentence to the end; and by this defect they are deprived of the only entertainment whereof they might otherwise be capable.

The language of this country being always upon the flux, the *struldbrugs* of one age do not understand those of another, neither are they able after two hundred years to hold any conversation (farther than by a few general words) with their neighbours the mortals; and thus they lie under the disadvantage of living like foreigners in their own country.

This was the account given me of the *struldbrugs*, as near as I can remember. I afterwards saw five or six of different ages, the youngest not above two hundred years old, who were brought to me at several times by some of my friends; but although they were told that I was a great traveller, and had seen all the world, they had not the least curiosity to ask me a question; only desired I would give them *slumskudask*, or a token of remembrance, which is a modest way of begging, to avoid the law that strictly forbids it, because they are provided for by the public, although indeed with a very scanty allowance.

They are despised and hated by all sorts of people; when one of them is born, it is reckoned ominous, and their birth is recorded very particularly; so that you may know their age by consulting the registry, which however hath not been kept above a thousand years past, or at least hath not been destroyed by time or public disturbances. But the usual way of computing how old they are, is by asking them what kings or great persons they can remember, and then consulting history, for infallibly the last prince in their mind did not begin his reign after they were fourscore years old.

They were the most mortifying sight I ever beheld, and the women more horrible than the men. Besides the usual deformities in extreme old age, they acquired an additional ghastliness in proportion to their number of years, which is not to be described; and among half a dozen, I soon distinguished which was the eldest, although there was not above a century or two between them.

C.E.Brock
July 1894

The reader will easily believe, that from what I had
heard and seen, my keen appetite for perpetuity of life
was much abated. I grew heartily ashamed of the pleasing visions I had formed, and thought no tyrant could
invent a death into which I would not run with pleasure
from such a life. The King heard of all that had passed
between me and my friends upon this occasion, and rallied me very pleasantly, wishing I would send a couple
of *struldbrugs* to my own country, to arm our people
against the fear of death; but this it seems is forbidden
by the fundamental laws of the kingdom, or else I should
have been well content with the trouble and expense of
transporting them.

I could not but agree that the laws of this kingdom,
relating to the *struldbrugs*, were founded upon the
strongest reasons, and such as any other country would
be under the necessity of enacting in the like circumstances. Otherwise, as avarice is the necessary conse-
quent of old age, those immortals would in time become
proprietors of the whole nation, and engross the civil
power, which, for want of abilities to manage, must end
in the ruin of the public.

Chapter XI *The Author leaves Luggnagg, and sails
to Japan. From thence he returns in a Dutch
ship to Amsterdam, and from Amsterdam to
England.*

I THOUGHT THIS ACCOUNT of the *struldbrugs* might be
some entertainment to the reader, because it seems
to be a little out of the common way, at least I do not
remember to have met the like in any book of travels
that hath come to my hands; and if I am deceived, my
excuse must be, that it is necessary for travellers, who
describe the same country, very often to agree in dwell-

ing on the same particulars, without deserving the censure of having borrowed or transcribed from those who wrote before them.

There is indeed a perpetual commerce between this kingdom and the great empire of Japan, and it is very probable that the Japanese authors may have given some account of the *struldbrugs*; but my stay in Japan was so short, and I was so entirely a stranger to that language, that I was not qualified to make any enquiries. But I hope the Dutch upon this notice will be curious and able enough to supply my defects.

His Majesty having often pressed me to accept some employment in his court, and finding me absolutely determined to return to my native country, was pleased to give me his licence to depart, and honoured me with a letter of recommendation under his own hand to the Emperor of Japan. He likewise presented me with four hundred forty-four large pieces of gold (this nation delighting in even numbers), and a red diamond which I sold in England for eleven hundred pounds.

On the 6th day of May, 1709, I took a solemn leave of his Majesty and all my friends. This prince was so gracious as to order a guard to conduct me to Glanguenstald, which is a royal port to the south-west part of the island. In six days I found a vessel ready to carry me to Japan, and spent fifteen days in the voyage. We landed at a small port-town called Xamoschi, situated on the south-east part of Japan; the town lies on the western point, where there is a narrow strait, leading northward into a long arm of the sea, upon the north-west part of which, Yedo the metropolis stands. At landing, I showed the custom-house officers my letter from the King of Luggnagg to his Imperial Majesty. They knew the seal perfectly well; it was as broad as the palm of my hand. The impression was, *a King lifting up a lame beggar from the earth*. The magistrates of the town hearing of my letter, received me as a public minister. They provided me with carriages and servants, and bore my charges to Yedo, where I was admitted to an audience, and delivered my letter, which was opened with great ceremony, and explained to the Emperor by an interpreter, who then gave me notice by his Majesty's order, that I should signify my request, and, whatever it were, it should be granted for the sake of his royal brother of Luggnagg. This interpreter was a person employed to transact affairs with the Hollanders; he soon conjectured by my countenance that I was an European, and therefore repeated his Majesty's commands in Low Dutch, which he spoke perfectly well. I answered (as I had before determined) that I was a Dutch merchant, shipwrecked in a very remote country, from whence I travelled by sea and land to Luggnagg, and then took shipping for Japan, where I knew my countrymen often traded, and with some of these I hoped to get an opportunity of returning into Europe: I therefore most humbly entreated his royal favour, to give order that I should be conducted in safety to Nangasac. To this I added another petition, that for the sake of my patron the King of Luggnagg, his Majesty would condescend to excuse my performing the ceremony imposed on my countrymen, of trampling upon the crucifix, because I had been thrown into his kingdom by my misfortunes, without any intention of trading. When this latter petition was interpreted to the Emperor, he seemed a little surprised, and said he believed I was the first of my countrymen who ever made any scruple in this point, and that he began to doubt whether I was a real Hollander or no, but rather suspected I must be a Christian. However, for the reasons I had offered, but chiefly to gratify the King of Luggnagg by an uncommon mark of his favour, he would comply with the singularity of my humour; but the affair must be managed with dexterity, and his officers should be commanded to let me pass as it were by forgetfulness. For he assured me, that if the secret should be discovered by my countrymen the Dutch, they would cut my throat in the voyage. I returned my thanks by the interpreter for so unusual a favour, and some troops being at that time on their march to Nangasac, the commanding officer had orders to convey me safe thither, with particular instructions about the business of the crucifix.

On the 9th day of June, 1709, I arrived at Nangasac, after a very long and troublesome journey. I soon fell into the company of some Dutch sailors belonging to the *Amboyna*, of Amsterdam, a stout ship of 450 tons. I had lived long in Holland, pursuing my studies at Leyden, and I spoke Dutch well. The seamen soon knew from whence I came last: they were curious to enquire into my voyages and course of life. I made up a story as short and probable as I could, but concealed the greatest part. I knew many persons in Holland; I was able to invent names for my parents, whom I pretended to be obscure people in the province of Gelderland. I would have given the captain (one Theodorus Vangrult) what he pleased to ask for my voyage to Holland; but understanding I was a surgeon, he was contented to take half the usual rate, on condition that I would serve him in the way of my calling. Before we took shipping, I was often asked by some of the crew whether I had performed the ceremony above-mentioned. I evaded the question by general answers, that I had satisfied the Emperor and court in all particulars. However, a malicious rogue of a skipper went to an officer, and pointing to me, told him I had not yet trampled on the crucifix: but the other, who had received instructions to let me pass, gave the rascal twenty strokes on the shoulders with a bamboo, after which I was no more troubled with such questions.

Nothing happened worth mentioning in this voyage. We sailed with a fair wind to the Cape of Good Hope, where we stayed only to take in fresh water. On the 10th of April we arrived safe at Amsterdam, having lost only three men by sickness in the voyage, and a fourth who fell from the foremast into the sea, not far from the coast of Guinea. From Amsterdam I soon after set sail for England in a small vessel belonging to that city.

On the 16th of April, 1710, we put in at the Downs. I landed the next morning, and saw once more my native country after an absence of five years and six months complete. I went straight to Redriff, where I arrived the same day at two in the afternoon, and found my wife and family in good health.

PART IV

A Voyage

TO

THE COUNTRY OF THE HOUYHNHNMS.

Edels Land

Lewins Land

Nuyts Land

I St Francoi

I St Pieter

HOUYHNHNMS
LAND
Discovered A.D 1711

Sweers I

I Maelsuyker
De Wiis I

HOUYHNHNMS
LAND

Chapter I *The Author sets out as Captain of a ship. His men conspire against him, confine him a long time to his cabin, set him on shore in an unknown land. He travels up in the country. The Yahoos, a strange sort of animal, described. The Author meets two Houyhnhnms.*

I CONTINUED AT HOME with my wife and children about five months in a very happy condition, if I could have learned the lesson of knowing when I was well. I left my poor wife big with child, and accepted an advantageous offer made me to be Captain of the *Adventure*, a stout merchantman of 350 tons: for I understood navigation well, and being grown weary of a surgeon's employment at sea, which however I could exercise upon occasion, I took a skilful young man of that calling, one Robert Purefoy, into my ship. We set sail from Portsmouth upon the seventh day of August, 1710; on the fourteenth we met with Captain Pocock of Bristol, at Teneriffe, who was going to the bay of Campechy, to cut logwood. On the sixteenth he was parted from us by a storm; I heard since my return that his ship foundered, and none escaped but one cabin boy. He was an honest man, and a good sailor, but a little too positive in his own opinions, which was the cause of his destruction, as it hath been of several others. For if he had followed my advice, he might have been safe at home with his family at this time, as well as myself.

I had several men died in my ship of calentures, so that I was forced to get recruits out of Barbadoes, and the Leeward Islands, where I touched by the direction of the merchants who employed me, which I had soon too much cause to repent: for I found afterwards that most of them had been buccaneers. I had fifty hands on

board, and my orders were that I should trade with the
Indians in the South Sea, and make what discoveries I
could. These rogues whom I had picked up debauched
my other men, and they all formed a conspiracy to seize
the ship and secure me; which they did one morning,
rushing into my cabin, and binding me hand and foot,
threatening to throw me overboard, if I offered to stir.
I told them I was their prisoner and would submit. This
they made me swear to do, and then they unbound me,
only fastening one of my legs with a chain near my bed,
and placed a sentry at my door with his piece charged,
who was commanded to shoot me dead, if I attempted
my liberty. They sent me down victuals and drink, and
took the government of the ship to themselves. Their
design was to turn pirates, and plunder the Spaniards,
which they could not do, till they got more men. But
first they resolved to sell the goods in the ship, and then
go to Madagascar for recruits, several among them having died since my confinement. They sailed many weeks,
and traded with the Indians, but I knew not what course
they took, being kept a close prisoner in my cabin, and
expecting nothing less than to be murdered, as they
often threatened me.

Upon the ninth day of May, 1711, one James Welch
came down to my cabin; and said he had orders from
the Captain to set me ashore. I expostulated with him
but in vain; neither would he so much as tell me who
their new Captain was. They forced me into the long-
boat, letting me put on my best suit of clothes, which
were as good as new, and a small bundle of linen, but
no arms except my hanger; and they were so civil as not
to search my pockets, into which I conveyed what money
I had, with some other little necessaries. They rowed
about a league, and then set me down on a strand. I
desired them to tell me what country it was. They all
swore they knew no more than myself, but said that the
Captain (as they called him) was resolved, after they had
sold the lading, to get rid of me in the first place where
they could discover land. They pushed off immediately,

advising me to make haste, for fear of being overtaken
by the tide, and so bade me farewell.

In this desolate condition I advanced forward, and
soon got upon firm ground, where I sat down on a bank
to rest myself, and consider what I had best to do. When
I was a little refreshed I went up into the country, resolving to deliver myself to the first savages I should meet,
and purchase my life from them by some bracelets, glass
rings, and other toys which sailors usually provide themselves with in those voyages, and whereof I had some
about me. The land was divided by long rows of trees,
not regularly planted, but naturally growing; there was
great plenty of grass, and several fields of oats. I walked
very circumspectly for fear of being surprised, or suddenly shot with an arrow from behind or on either side.
I fell into a beaten road, where I saw many tracks of
human feet, and some of cows, but most of horses. At
last I beheld several animals in a field, and one or two
of the same kind sitting in trees. Their shape was very
singular and deformed, which a little discomposed me,
so that I lay down behind a thicket to observe them
better. Some of them coming forward near the place
where I lay, gave me an opportunity of distinctly mark-
ing their form. Their heads and breasts were covered
with a thick hair, some frizzled and others lank; they
had beards like goats, and a long ridge of hair down
their backs and the fore-parts of their legs and feet, but
the rest of their bodies were bare, so that I might see their
skins, which were of a brown buff colour. They had no
tails, nor any hair at all on their buttocks, except about
the anus; which, I presume, nature had placed there to
defend them as they sat on the ground; for this posture
they used, as well as lying down, and often stood on
their hind feet. They climbed high trees, as nimbly as a
squirrel, for they had strong extended claws before and
behind, terminating in sharp points, and hooked. They
would often spring and bound and leap with prodigious
agility. The females were not so large as the males; they
had long lank hair on their heads, but none on their
faces, nor any thing more than a sort of down on the

rest of their bodies, except about the anus, and pudenda. Their dugs hung between their fore-feet, and often reached almost to the ground as they walked. The hair of both sexes was of several colours, brown, red, black, and yellow. Upon the whole, I never beheld in all my travels so disagreeable an animal, nor one against which I naturally conceived so strong an antipathy. So that thinking I had seen enough, full of contempt and aversion, I got up and pursued the beaten road, hoping it might direct me to the cabin of some Indian. I had not got far when I met one of these creatures full in my way, and coming up directly to me. The ugly monster, when he saw me, distorted several ways every feature of his visage, and stared as at an object he had never seen before; then approaching nearer, lifted up his fore-paw, whether out of curiosity or mischief, I could not tell. But I drew my hanger, and gave him a good blow with the flat side of it, for I durst not strike him with the edge, fearing the inhabitants might be provoked against me, if they should come to know that I had killed or maimed any of their cattle. When the beast felt the smart, he drew back, and roared so loud that a herd of at least forty came flocking about me from the next field, howling and making odious faces; but I ran to the body of a tree, and leaning my back against it, kept them off by waving my hanger. Several of this cursed brood getting hold of the branches behind, leapt up into the tree, from whence they began to discharge their excrements on my head; however, I escaped pretty well, by sticking close to the stem of the tree, but was almost stifled with the filth, which fell about me on every side.

In the midst of this distress, I observed them all to run away on a sudden as fast as they could, at which I ventured to leave the tree, and pursue the road, wondering what it was that could put them into this fright. But looking on my left hand, I saw a horse walking softly in the field; which my persecutors having sooner discovered, was the cause of their flight. The horse started a little when he came near me, but soon recovering himself, looked full in my face with manifest tokens of wonder; he viewed my hands and feet, walking round me several times. I would have pursued my journey, but he placed himself directly in the way, yet looking with a very mild aspect, never offering the least violence. We stood gazing at each other for some time; at last I took the boldness to reach my hand towards his neck, with a design to stroke it, using the common style and whistle of jockeys when they are going to handle a strange horse. But this animal seeming to receive my civilities with disdain, shook his head, and bent his brows, softly raising up his right forefoot to remove my hand. Then he neighed three or four times, but in so different a cadence, that I almost began to think he was speaking to himself in some language of his own.

While he and I were thus employed, another horse came up; who applying himself to the first in a very formal manner, they gently struck each other's right hoof before, neighing several times by turns, and varying the sound, which seemed to be almost articulate. They went some paces off, as if it were to confer together, walking side by side, backward and forward, like persons deliberating upon some affair of weight, but often turning their eyes towards me, as it were to watch that I might not escape. I was amazed to see such actions and behaviour in brute beasts, and concluded with myself, that if the inhabitants of this country were endued with a proportionable degree of reason, they must needs be the wisest people upon earth. This thought gave me so much comfort, that I resolved to go forward until I could discover some house or village, or meet with any of the natives, leaving the two horses to discourse together as they pleased. But the first, who was a dapple gray, observing me to steal off, neighed after me in so expressive a tone, that I fancied myself to understand what he meant; whereupon I turned back, and came near him, to expect his farther commands, but concealing my fear as much as I could, for I began to be in some pain, how this adventure might terminate; and the reader will easily believe I did not much like my present situation.

The two horses came up close to me, looking with great earnestness upon my face and hands. The gray steed rubbed my hat all round with his right fore-hoof, and discomposed it so much that I was forced to adjust it better, by taking it off, and settling it again; whereat both he and his companion (who was a brown bay) appeared to be much surprised; the latter felt the lappet of my coat, and finding it to hang loose about me, they both looked with new signs of wonder. He stroked my right hand, seeming to admire the softness and colour; but he squeezed it so hard between his hoof and his pastern, that I was forced to roar; after which they both touched me with all possible tenderness. They were under great perplexity about my shoes and stockings, which they felt very often, neighing to each other, and

using various gestures, not unlike those of a philosopher,
when he would attempt to solve some new and difficult phenomenon.

Upon the whole, the behaviour of these animals was
so orderly and rational, so acute and judicious, that I at

last concluded they must needs be magicians, who had thus metamorphosed themselves upon some design, and seeing a stranger in the way, were resolved to divert themselves with him; or perhaps were really amazed at the sight of a man so very different in habit, feature, and complexion from those who might probably live in so remote a climate. Upon the strength of this reasoning, I ventured to address them in the following manner: Gentlemen, if you be conjurers, as I have good cause to believe, you can understand any language; therefore I make bold to let your worships know that I am a poor distressed Englishman, driven by his misfortunes upon your coast, and I entreat one of you, to let me ride upon his back, as if he were a real horse, to some house or village where I can be relieved. In return of which favour I will make you a present of this knife and bracelet (taking them out of my pocket). The two creatures stood silent while I spoke, seeming to listen with great attention; and when I had ended, they neighed frequently towards each other, as if they were engaged in serious conversation. I plainly observed, that their language expressed the passions very well, and the words might with little pains be resolved into an alphabet more easily than the Chinese.

I could frequently distinguish the word *Yahoo,* which was repeated by each of them several times; and although it was impossible for me to conjecture what it meant, yet while the two horses were busy in conversation, I endeavoured to practise this word upon my tongue; and as soon as they were silent, I boldly pronounced *Yahoo* in a loud voice, imitating, at the same time, as near as I could, the neighing of a horse; at which they were both visibly surprised, and the gray repeated the same word twice, as if he meant to teach me the right accent, wherein I spoke after him as well as I could, and found myself perceivably to improve every time, though very far from any degree of perfection. Then the bay tried me with a second word, much harder to be pronounced; but reducing it to the English orthography, may be spelt thus, *Houyhnhnm.* I did not succeed in this so well as the former, but after two or three farther trials, I had better fortune; and they both appeared amazed at my capacity.

After some further discourse, which I then conjectured might relate to me, the two friends took their leaves, with the same compliment of striking each other's hoof; and the gray made me signs that I should walk before him, wherein I thought it prudent to comply, till I could find a better director. When I offered to slacken my pace, he would cry *Hhuun, Hhuun*; I guessed his meaning, and gave him to understand as well as I could, that I was weary, and not able to walk faster; upon which he would stand a while to let me rest.

Chapter II *The Author conducted by a Houyhnhnm to his house. The house described. The Author's reception. The food of the Houyhnhnms. The Author in distress for want of meat, is at last relieved. His manner of feeding in this country.*

HAVING TRAVELLED about three miles, we came to a long kind of building, made of timber stuck in the ground, and wattled across; the roof was low, and covered with straw. I now began to be a little comforted, and took out some toys, which travellers usually carry for presents to the savage Indians of America and other parts, in hopes the people of the house would be thereby encouraged to receive me kindly. The horse made me a sign to go in first; it was a large room with a smooth clay floor, and a rack and manger extending the whole length on one side. There were three nags, and two mares, not eating, but some of them sitting down upon their hams, which I very much wondered at; but wondered more to see the rest employed in domestic business. These seemed but ordinary cattle; however, this confirmed my first opinion, that a people who could so far civilize brute animals, must needs excel in wisdom all the nations of the world. The gray came in just after, and thereby prevented any ill treatment which the others might have given me. He neighed to them several times in a style of authority, and received answers.

Beyond this room there were three others, reaching the length of the house, to which you passed through three doors, opposite to each other, in the manner of a vista; we went through the second room towards the third; here the gray walked in first, beckoning me to attend: I waited in the second room, and got ready my presents for the master and mistress of the house: they were two knives, three bracelets of false pearl, a small looking-glass, and a bead necklace. The horse neighed three or four times, and I waited to hear some answers in a human voice, but I heard no other returns than in the same dialect, only one or two a little shriller than his. I began to think that this house must belong to some person of great note among them, because there appeared so much ceremony before I could gain admittance. But, that a man of quality should be served all by horses, was beyond my comprehension. I feared my brain was disturbed by my sufferings and misfortunes: I roused myself, and looked about me in the room where I was left alone; this was furnished like the first, only after a more elegant manner. I rubbed my eyes often, but the same objects still occurred. I pinched my arms and sides to awake myself, hoping I might be in a dream. I then absolutely concluded, that all these appearances could be nothing else but necromancy and magic. But I had no time to pursue these reflections; for the gray horse came to the door, and made me a sign to follow him into the third room, where I saw a very comely mare, together with a colt and foal, sitting on their haunches, upon mats of straw, not unartfully made, and perfectly neat and clean.

The mare soon after my entrance, rose from her mat, and coming up close, after having nicely observed my hands and face, gave me a most contemptuous look; then turning to the horse, I heard the word *Yahoo* often repeated betwixt them; the meaning of which word I could not then comprehend, although it were the first I had learned to pronounce; but I was soon better informed, to my everlasting mortification: for the horse beckoning to me with his head, and repeating the word *Hhuun, Hhuun*, as he did upon the road, which I understood was to attend him, led me out into a kind of court, where was another building at some distance from the house. Here we entered, and I saw three of these detestable creatures, whom I first met after my landing, feeding upon roots, and the flesh of some animals, which I afterwards found to be that of asses and dogs, and now and then a cow dead by accident or disease. They were all tied by the neck with strong withes, fastened to a beam; they held their food between the claws of their fore-feet, and tore it with their teeth.

The master horse ordered a sorrel nag, one of his servants, to untie the largest of these animals, and take him into the yard. The beast and I were brought close together, and our countenances diligently compared, both by master and servant, who thereupon repeated several times the word *Yahoo*. My horror and astonishment are not to be described, when I observed in this abominable animal a perfect human figure: the face of it indeed was flat and broad, the nose depressed, the lips large, and the mouth wide. But these differences are common to all savage nations, where the lineaments of the countenance are distorted by the natives suffering their infants to lie grovelling on the earth, or by carrying them on their backs, nuzzling with their face against the mother's shoulders. The fore-feet of the Yahoo differed from my hands in nothing else but the length of the nails, the coarseness and brownness of the palms, and the hairiness on the backs. There was the same resemblance between our feet, with the same differences, which I knew very well, though the horses did not, because of my shoes and stockings; the same in every part of our bodies, except as to hairiness and colour, which I have already described.

The great difficulty that seemed to stick with the two horses, was to see the rest of my body so very different from that of a Yahoo, for which I was obliged to my clothes, whereof they had no conception. The sorrel nag offered me a root, which he held (after their manner, as we shall describe in its proper place) between his hoof and pastern; I took it in my hand, and having smelt it, returned it to him again as civilly as I could. He brought out of the Yahoo's kennel a piece of ass's flesh, but it smelt so offensively that I turned from it with loathing: he then threw it to the Yahoo, by whom it was greedily devoured. He afterwards showed me a wisp of hay, and a fetlock full of oats; but I shook my head, to signify that neither of these were food for me. And indeed, I now apprehended that I must absolutely starve, if I did not get to some of my own species; for as to those filthy Yahoos, although there were few greater lovers of mankind, at that time, than myself, yet I confess I never saw any sensitive being so detestable on all accounts; and the more I came near them, the more hateful they grew, while I stayed in that country. This the master horse observed by my behaviour, and therefore sent the Yahoo back to his kennel. He then put his fore-hoof to his mouth, at which I was much surprised, although he did it with ease, and with a motion that appeared perfectly natural, and made other signs to know what I would eat; but I could not return him such an answer as he was able to apprehend; and if he had understood me, I did not see how it was possible to contrive any way for finding myself nourishment. While we were thus engaged, I observed a cow passing by, whereupon I pointed to her, and expressed a desire to let me go and milk her. This had its effect; for he led me back into the house, and ordered a mare-servant to open a room, where a good store of milk lay in earthen and wooden vessels, after a very orderly and cleanly manner. She gave me a large bowl full, of which I drank very heartily, and found myself well refreshed.

About noon I saw coming towards the house a kind of vehicle, drawn like a sledge by four Yahoos. There was in it an old steed, who seemed to be of quality; he alighted with his hind-feet forward, having by accident got a hurt in his left fore-foot. He came to dine with our horse, who received him with great civility. They dined in the best room, and had oats boiled in milk for the second course, which the old horse ate warm, but the rest cold. Their mangers were placed circular in the middle of the room, and divided into several partitions, round which they sat on their haunches upon bosses of straw. In the middle was a large rack with angles answering to every partition of the manger; so that each horse and mare ate their own hay, and their own mash of oats and milk, with much decency and regularity. The behaviour of the young colt and foal appeared very modest, and that of the master and mistress extremely cheerful and complaisant to their guest. The gray ordered me to stand by him, and much discourse passed between him and his friend concerning me, as I found by the stranger's often looking on me, and the frequent repetition of the word *Yahoo*.

I happened to wear my gloves, which the master gray observing, seemed perplexed, discovering signs of wonder what I had done to my fore-feet; he put his hoof three or four times to them, as if he would signify that I should reduce them to their former shape, which I presently did, pulling off both my gloves, and putting them into my pocket. This occasioned farther talk, and I saw the company was pleased with my behaviour, whereof I soon found the good effects. I was ordered to speak the few words I understood, and while they were at dinner the master taught me the names for oats, milk, fire, water, and some others; which I could readily pronounce after him, having from my youth a great facility in learning languages.

When dinner was done the master horse took me aside, and by signs and words made me understand the concern that he was in, that I had nothing to eat. Oats in their tongue are called *hlunnh*. This word I pronounced two or three times; for although I had refused them at first, yet upon second thoughts I considered that I could contrive to make of them a kind of bread, which might be sufficient with milk to keep me alive, till I could make my escape to some other country and to creatures of my own species. The horse immediately ordered a white mare-servant of his family to bring me a good quantity of oats in a sort of wooden tray. These I heated before the fire as well as I could, and rubbed them till the husks came off, which I made a shift to winnow from the grain; I ground and beat them between two stones, then took water, and made them into a paste or cake, which I toasted at the fire, and ate warm with milk. It was at first a very insipid diet, though common enough in many parts of Europe, but grew tolerable by time; and having been often reduced to hard fare in my life, this was not the first experiment I had made how easily nature is satisfied. And I cannot but observe, that I never had one hour's sickness while I stayed in this island. 'Tis true, I sometimes made a shift to catch a rabbit or bird by springes made of Yahoos' hairs, and I often gathered wholesome herbs, which I boiled, or ate as salads with my bread, and now and then, for a rarity, I made a little butter, and drank the whey. I was at first at a great loss for salt; but custom soon reconciled the want of it; and I am confident that the frequent use of salt among us is an effect of luxury, and was first introduced only as a provocative to drink; except where it is necessary for preserving of flesh in long voyages, or in places remote from great markets. For we observe no animal to be fond of it but man: and as to myself, when I left this country, it was a great while before I could endure the taste of it in anything that I ate.

This is enough to say upon the subject of my diet, wherewith other travellers fill their books, as if the readers were personally concerned whether we fared well or ill. However, it was necessary to mention this matter, lest the world should think it impossible that I could find sustenance for three years in such a country, and among such inhabitants.

When it grew towards evening, the master horse ordered a place for me to lodge in; it was but six yards from the house, and separated from the stable of the

Yahoos. Here I got some straw, and covering myself with my own clothes, slept very sound. But I was in a short time better accommodated, as the reader shall know hereafter, when I come to treat more particularly about my way of living.

∞

Chapter III *The Author studious to learn the language; the Houyhnhnm his master assists in teaching him. The language described. Several Houyhnhnms of quality come out of curiosity to see the Author. He gives his master a short account of his voyage.*

MY PRINCIPAL endeavour was to learn the language, which my master (for so I shall henceforth call him), and his children, and every servant of his house, were desirous to teach me. For they looked upon it as a prodigy that a brute animal should discover such marks of a rational creature. I pointed to every thing and enquired the name of it, which I wrote down in my journal-book when I was alone, and corrected my bad accent by desiring those of the family to pronounce it often. In this employment, a sorrel nag, one of the under servants, was ready to assist me.

In speaking they pronounce through the nose and throat, and their language approaches nearest to the High Dutch or German of any I know in Europe; but is much more graceful and significant. The Emperor Charles V made almost the same observation, when he said that if he were to speak to his horse it should be in High Dutch.

The curiosity and impatience of my master were so great, that he spent many hours of his leisure to instruct me. He was convinced (as he afterwards told me) that I must be a Yahoo, but my teachableness, civility, and

cleanliness, astonished him; which were qualities altogether so opposite to those animals. He was most perplexed about my clothes, reasoning sometimes with
himself whether they were a part of my body; for I never
pulled them off till the family were asleep, and got them
on before they waked in the morning. My master was
eager to learn from whence I came, how I acquired those
appearances of reason which I discovered in all my actions, and to know my story from my own mouth, which
he hoped he should soon do by the great proficiency I
made in learning and pronouncing their words and sentences. To help my memory, I formed all I learned into
the English alphabet, and writ the words down with the
translations. This last after some time I ventured to do
in my master's presence. It cost me much trouble to
explain to him what I was doing; for the inhabitants have
not the least idea of books or literature.

In about ten weeks time I was able to understand
most of his questions, and in three months could give
him some tolerable answers. He was extremely curious
to know from what part of the country I came, and how
I was taught to imitate a rational creature; because the
Yahoos (whom he saw I exactly resembled in my head,
hands, and face, that were only visible), with some appearance of cunning, and the strongest disposition to
mischief, were observed to be the most unteachable of
all brutes. I answered that I came over the sea from a
far place, with many others of my own kind, in a great
hollow vessel made of the bodies of trees. That my companions forced me to land on this coast, and then left
me to shift for myself. It was with some difficulty, and
by the help of many signs, that I brought him to understand me. He replied, that I must needs be mistaken, or
that I *said the thing which was not.* (For they have no
word in their language to express lying or falsehood.)
He knew it was impossible that there could be a country
beyond the sea, or that a parcel of brutes could move a
wooden vessel whither they pleased upon water. He was
sure no Houyhnhnm alive could make such a vessel, nor
would trust Yahoos to manage it.

The word *Houyhnhnm*, in their tongue, signifies a *horse*, and in its etymology, *the perfection of nature*. I told my master, that I was at a loss for expression, but would improve as fast as I could; and hoped in a short time I should be able to tell him wonders: he was pleased to direct his own mare, his colt and foal, and the servants of the family, to take all opportunities of instructing me, and every day for two or three hours he was at the same pains himself. Several horses and mares of quality in the neighbourhood came often to our house upon the report spread of a wonderful Yahoo, that could speak like a Houyhnhnm, and seemed in his words and actions to discover some glimmerings of reason. These delighted to converse with me: they put many questions, and received such answers as I was able to return. By all these advantages I made so great a progress that in five months from my arrival I understood whatever was spoke, and could express myself tolerably well.

The Houyhnhnms who came to visit my master out of a design of seeing and talking with me, could hardly believe me to be a right Yahoo, because my body had a different covering from others of my kind. They were astonished to observe me without the usual hair or skin, except on my head, face, and hands; but I discovered that secret to my master, upon an accident which happened about a fortnight before.

I have already told the reader, that every night when the family were gone to bed it was my custom to strip and cover myself with my clothes. It happened one morning early that my master sent for me by the sorrel nag, who was his valet; when he came I was fast asleep, my clothes fallen off on one side, and my shirt above my waist. I awaked at the noise he made, and observed him to deliver his message in some disorder; after which he went to my master, and in a great fright gave him a very confused account of what he had seen. This I presently discovered; for going as soon as I was dressed to pay my attendance upon his Honour, he asked me the meaning of what his servant had reported, that I was not the same thing when I slept as I appeared to be at other times; that his valet assured him, some part of me was white, some yellow, at least not so white, and some brown.

I had hitherto concealed the secret of my dress, in order to distinguish myself as much as possible from that cursed race of Yahoos; but now I found it in vain to do so any longer. Besides, I considered that my clothes and shoes would soon wear out, which already were in a declining condition, and must be supplied by some contrivance from the hides of Yahoos or other brutes; whereby the whole secret would be known. I therefore told my master that in the country from whence I came those of my kind always covered their bodies with the hairs of certain animals prepared by art, as well for decency as to avoid the inclemencies of air, both hot and

cold; of which, as to my own person, I would give him
immediate conviction, if he pleased to command me;
only desiring his excuse, if I did not expose those parts
that nature taught us to conceal. He said my discourse
was all very strange, but especially the last part; for he
could not understand why nature should teach us to conceal what nature had given. That neither himself nor
family were ashamed of any parts of their bodies; but
however I might do as I pleased. Whereupon I first un-
buttoned my coat and pulled it off. I did the same with
my waistcoat; I drew off my shoes, stockings and
breeches. I let my shirt down to my waist, and drew up
the bottom, fastening it like a girdle about my middle
to hide my nakedness.

My master observed the whole performance with great
signs of curiosity and admiration. He took up all my
clothes in his pastern, one piece after another, and examined them diligently; he then stroked my body very gently and looked round me several times, after which he
said it was plain I must be a perfect Yahoo; but that I
differed very much from the rest of my species, in the
softness and whiteness and smoothness of my skin, my
want of hair in several parts of my body, the shape and
shortness of my claws behind and before, and my affectation of walking continually on my two hinder feet. He
desired to see no more, and gave me leave to put on
my clothes again, for I was shuddering with cold.

I expressed my uneasiness at his giving me so often
the appellation of Yahoo, an odious animal for which I
had so utter a hatred and contempt. I begged he would
forbear applying that word to me, and take the same
order in his family, and among his friends whom he suffered to see me. I requested likewise that the secret of
my having a false covering to my body might be known
to none but himself, at least as long as my present clothing should last; for as to what the sorrel nag his valet had
observed, his Honour might command him to conceal it.

All this my master very graciously consented to, and
thus the secret was kept till my clothes began to wear
out, which I was forced to supply by several contrivances

that shall hereafter be mentioned. In the meantime he desired I would go on with my utmost diligence to learn their language, because he was more astonished at my capacity for speech and reason than at the figure of my body, whether it were covered or no; adding that he waited with some impatience to hear the wonders which I promised to tell him.

From thenceforward he doubled the pains he had been at to instruct me; he brought me into all company, and made them treat me with civility, because, as he told them privately, this would put me into good humour and make me more diverting.

Every day when I waited on him, beside the trouble he was at in teaching, he would ask me several questions concerning myself, which I answered as well as I could; and by these means he had already received some general ideas, though very imperfect. It would be tedious to relate the several steps by which I advanced to a more regular conversation: but the first account I gave of myself in any order and length, was to this purpose:

That I came from a very far country, as I already had attempted to tell him, with about fifty more of my own species; that we travelled upon the seas, in a great hollow vessel made of wood, and larger than his Honour's house. I described the ship to him in the best terms I could, and explained by the help of my handkerchief displayed, how it was driven forward by the wind. That upon a quarrel among us, I was set on shore on this coast, where I walked forward without knowing whither, till he delivered me from the persecution of those execrable Yahoos. He asked me who made the ship, and how it was possible that the Houyhnhnms of my country would leave it to the management of brutes. My answer was that I durst proceed no further in my relation, unless he would give me his word and honour that he would not be offended, and then I would tell him the wonders I had so often promised. He agreed; and I went on by assuring him that the ship was made by creatures like myself, who in all the countries I had travelled, as well as in my own, were the only governing, rational animals;

and that upon my arrival hither I was as much astonished to see the Houyhnhnms act like rational beings, as
he or his friends could be in finding some marks of reason in a creature he was pleased to call a Yahoo, to
which I owned my resemblance in every part, but could
not account for their degenerate and brutal nature. I
said farther that if good fortune ever restored me to my
native country, to relate my travels hither, as I resolved
to do, every body would believe that I *said the thing
which was not*; that I invented the story out of my own
head; and with all possible respect to himself, his family
and friends, and under his promise of not being offended, our countrymen would hardly think it probable,
that a Houyhnhnm should be the presiding creature of
a nation, and a Yahoo the brute.

Chapter IV *The Houyhnhnms' notion of truth and
          falsehood. The Author's discourse disap-
          proved by his master. The Author gives a
          more particular account of himself, and the
          accidents of his voyage.*

MY MASTER heard me with great appearances of uneasiness in his countenance, because *doubting*, or
not believing, are so little known in this country, that
the inhabitants cannot tell how to behave themselves
under such circumstances. And I remember in frequent
discourses with my master concerning the nature of man-
hood in other parts of the world, having occasion to talk
of *lying* and *false representation*, it was with much difficulty that he comprehended what I meant, although he
had otherwise a most acute judgement. For he argued
thus: that the use of speech was to make us understand
one another, and to receive information of facts; now if
any one *said the thing which was not*, these ends were

defeated; because I cannot properly be said to understand him; and I am so far from receiving information, that he leaves me worse than in ignorance, for I am led to believe a thing black when it is white, and short when it is long. And these were all the notions he had concerning that faculty of *lying*, so perfectly well understood among human creatures.

To return from this digression; when I asserted that the Yahoos were the only governing animals in my country, which my master said was altogether past his conception, he desired to know whether we had Houyhnhnms among us, and what was their employment. I told him we had great numbers, that in summer they grazed in the fields, and in winter were kept in houses, with hay and oats, where Yahoo servants were employed to rub their skins smooth, comb their manes, pick their feet, serve them with food, and make their beds. I understand you well, said my master, it is now very plain, from all you have spoken, that whatever share of reason the Yahoos pretend to, the Houyhnhnms are your masters; I heartily wish our Yahoos would be so tractable. I begged his Honour would please to excuse me from proceeding any farther, because I was very certain that the account he expected from me would be highly displeasing. But he insisted in commanding me to let him know the best and the worst: I told him he should be obeyed. I owned that the Houyhnhnms among us, whom we called horses, were the most generous and comely animals we had, that they excelled in strength and swiftness; and when they belonged to persons of quality, employed in travelling, racing, or drawing chariots, they were treated with much kindness and care, till they fell into diseases or became foundered in the feet; and then they were sold, and used to all kind of drudgery till they died; after which their skins were stripped and sold for what they were worth, and their bodies left to be devoured by dogs and birds of prey. But the common race of horses had not so good fortune, being kept by farmers and carriers, and other mean people, who put them to great labour, and fed them worse. I described, as well as I could, our way of riding, the shape and use of a bridle, a saddle, a spur, and a whip, of harness and wheels. I added that we fastened plates of a certain hard substance called iron at the bottom of their feet, to preserve their hoofs from being broken by the stony ways on which we often travelled.

My master, after some expressions of great indignation, wondered how we dared to venture upon a Houyhnhnm's back, for he was sure that the weakest servant in his house would be able to shake off the strongest Yahoo, or by lying down and rolling on his back squeeze the brute to death. I answered that our horses were trained up from three or four years old to the several uses we intended them for; that if any of them proved intolerably vicious, they were employed for carriages; that they were severely beaten while they were young, for any mischievous tricks; that the males, designed for common use of riding or draught, were generally castrated about two years after their birth, to take down their spirits and make them more tame and gentle; that they were indeed sensible of rewards and punishments; but his Honour would please to consider, that they had not the least tincture of reason any more than the Yahoos in this country.

It put me to the pains of many circumlocutions to give my master a right idea of what I spoke; for their language doth not abound in variety of words, because their wants and passions are fewer than among us. But it is impossible to represent his noble resentment at our savage treatment of the Houyhnhnm race, particularly after I had explained the manner and use of castrating horses among us, to hinder them from propagating their kind, and to render them more servile. He said if it were possible there could be any country where Yahoos alone were endued with reason, they certainly must be the governing animal, because reason will in time always prevail against brutal strength. But considering the frame of our bodies, and especially of mine, he thought no creature of equal bulk was so ill contrived, for employing that reason in the common offices of life; whereupon he desired to know whether those among whom I lived resembled me or the Yahoos of his country. I assured him, that I was as well shaped as most of my age; but the younger and the females were much more soft and tender, and the skins of the latter generally as white as milk. He said I differed indeed from other Yahoos, being much more cleanly, and not altogether so deformed, but in point of real advantage he thought I differed for the worse. That my nails were of no use either to my fore or hinder-feet; as to my fore-feet, he could not properly call them by that name, for he never observed me to walk upon them; that they were too soft to bear the ground; that I generally went with them uncovered, neither was the covering I sometimes wore on them of the same shape or so strong as that on my feet behind. That I could not walk with any security, for if either of my hinder-feet slipped, I must inevitably fall. He then began to find fault with other parts of my body, the flatness of my face, the prominence of my nose, my eyes placed directly in front, so that I could not look on either side without turning my head; that I was not able to feed myself without lifting one of my fore-feet to my mouth; and therefore nature had placed those joints to answer that necessity. He knew not what could be the use of those several clefts and divisions in my feet behind; that these were too soft to bear the hardness and sharpness of stones without a covering made from the skin of some other brute; that my whole body wanted a fence against heat and cold, which I was forced to put on and off every day with tediousness and trouble. And lastly that he observed every animal in this country naturally to abhor the Yahoos, whom the weaker avoided and the stronger drove from them. So that supposing us to have the gift of reason, he could not see how it were possible to cure that natural antipathy which every creature discovered against us; nor consequently, how we could tame and render them serviceable. However, he would (as he said), debate the matter no farther, because he was more desirous to know my own story, the country where I was born, and the several actions and events of my life before I came hither.

I assured him how extremely desirous I was that he should be satisfied on every point; but I doubted much whether it would be possible for me to explain myself on several subjects whereof his Honour could have no conception, because I saw nothing in his country to which I could resemble them. That however I would do my best, and strive to express myself by similitudes, humbly desiring his assistance when I wanted proper words; which he was pleased to promise me.

I said my birth was of honest parents in an island called England, which was remote from this country, as many days' journey as the strongest of his Honour's servants could travel in the annual course of the sun. That I was bred a surgeon, whose trade it is to cure wounds and hurts in the body, got by accident or violence; that my country was governed by a female man, whom we called a Queen. That I left it to get riches, whereby I might maintain myself and family when I should return. That in my last voyage I was Commander of the ship, and had about fifty Yahoos under me, many of which died at sea, and I was forced to supply them by others picked out from several nations. That our ship was twice in danger of being sunk; the first time by a great storm, and the second, by striking against a rock. Here my master interposed, by asking me how I could persuade strangers out of different countries to venture with me, after the losses I had sustained, and the hazards I had run. I said they were fellows of desperate fortunes, forced to fly from the places of their birth, on account of their poverty or their crimes. Some were undone by lawsuits; others spent all they had in drinking, whoring, and gaming; others fled for treason; many for murder, theft, poisoning, robbery, perjury, forgery, coining false money, for committing rapes or sodomy, for flying from their colours, or deserting to the enemy, and most of them had broken prison; none of these durst return to their native countries for fear of being hanged, or of starving in a jail; and therefore were under the necessity of seeking a livelihood in other places.

During this discourse my master was pleased to interrupt me several times; I had made use of many circumlocutions in describing to him the nature of the several crimes, for which most of our crew had been forced to fly their country. This labour took up several days' conversation before he was able to comprehend me. He was wholly at a loss to know what could be the use or necessity of practising those vices. To clear up which I endeavoured to give some ideas of the desire of power and riches, of the terrible effects of lust, intemperance, malice and envy. All this I was forced to define and describe by putting of cases, and making of suppositions. After which, like one whose imagination was struck with something never seen or heard of before, he would lift up his eyes with amazement and indignation. Power, government, war, law, punishment, and a thousand other things had no terms wherein that language could express them, which made the difficulty almost insuperable to give my master any conception of what I meant. But being of an excellent understanding, much improved by contemplation and converse, he at last arrived at a competent knowledge of what human nature in our parts of the world is capable to perform, and desired I would give him some particular account of that land which we call Europe, but especially of my own country.

Chapter V *The Author, at his master's command, informs him of the state of England. The causes of war among the princes of Europe. The Author begins to explain the English constitution.*

THE READER may please to observe, that the following extract of many conversations I had with my master, contains a summary of the most material points which were discoursed at several times for above two years; his Honour often desiring fuller satisfaction as I farther improved in the Houyhnhnm tongue. I laid before him, as well as I could, the whole state of Europe; I discoursed of trade and manufactures, of arts and sciences; and the answers I gave to all the questions he made, as they arose upon several subjects, were a fund of conversation not to be exhausted. But I shall here only set down the substance of what passed between us concerning my own country, reducing it into order as well as I can, without any regard to time or other circumstances, while I strictly adhere to truth. My only concern is that I shall hardly be able to do justice to my master's arguments and expressions, which must needs suffer by my want of capacity, as well as by a translation into our barbarous English.

In obedience therefore to his Honour's commands, I related to him the Revolution under the Prince of Orange; the long war with France entered into by the said prince, and renewed by his successor the present Queen, wherein the greatest powers of Christendom were engaged, and which still continued: I computed at his request that about a million of Yahoos might have been killed in the whole progress of it, and perhaps a hundred or more cities taken, and thrice as many ships burnt or sunk.

He asked me what were the usual causes or motives that made one country go to war with another. I answered they were innumerable, but I should only mention a few of the chief. Sometimes the ambition of princes, who never think they have land or people enough to govern; sometimes the corruption of ministers, who engage their master in a war in order to stifle or divert the clamour of the subjects against their evil administration. Difference in opinions hath cost many millions of lives: for instance, whether flesh be bread, or bread be flesh; whether the juice of a certain berry be blood or wine; whether whistling be a vice or a virtue; whether it be better to kiss a post, or throw it into the fire; what is the best colour for a coat, whether black, white, red, or gray; and whether it should be long or short, narrow or wide, dirty or clean; with many more. Neither are any wars so furious and bloody, or of so long continuance, as those occasioned by difference in opinion, especially if it be in things indifferent.

Sometimes the quarrel between two princes is to decide which of them shall dispossess a third of his dominions, where neither of them pretend to any right. Sometimes one prince quarrelleth with another, for fear the other should quarrel with him. Sometimes a war is entered upon, because the enemy is too strong, and sometimes because he is too weak. Sometimes our neighbours want the things which we have, or have the things which we want; and we both fight, till they take ours or give us theirs. It is a very justifiable cause of a war to invade a country after the people have been wasted by famine, destroyed by pestilence, or embroiled by factions among themselves. It is justifiable to enter into war against our nearest ally, when one of his towns lies convenient for us, or a territory of land, that would render our dominions round and complete. If a prince sends forces into a nation where the people are poor and ignorant, he may lawfully put half of them to death, and make slaves of the rest, in order to civilize and reduce them from their barbarous way of living. It is a very kingly, honourable, and frequent practice, when one prince desires the assistance of another to secure him against an invasion, that the assistant, when he hath driven out the invader, should seize on the dominions himself, and kill, imprison or banish the prince he came to relieve. Alliance by blood or marriage is a frequent cause of war between princes; and the nearer the kindred is, the greater is their disposition to quarrel: poor nations are hungry, and rich nations are proud; and pride and hunger will ever be at variance. For these reasons, the trade of a soldier is held the most honourable of all others; because a soldier is a Yahoo hired to kill in cold blood as many of his own species, who have never offended him, as possibly he can.

There is likewise a kind of beggarly princes in Europe, not able to make war by themselves, who hire out their troops to richer nations, for so much a day to each man; of which they keep three fourths to themselves, and it is the best part of their maintenance; such are those in Germany and other northern parts of Europe.

What you have told me (said my master) upon the subject of war, does indeed discover most admirably the effects of that reason you pretend to: however, it is happy that the shame is greater than the danger; and that nature hath left you utterly uncapable of doing much mischief.

For your mouths lying flat with your faces, you can hardly bite each other to any purpose, unless by consent. Then as to the claws upon your feet before and behind, they are so short and tender, that one of our Yahoos would drive a dozen of yours before him. And therefore in recounting the numbers of those who have been killed in battle, I cannot but think that you have *said the thing which is not.*

I could not forbear shaking my head and smiling a little at his ignorance. And being no stranger to the art of war, I gave him a description of cannons, culverins, muskets, carabines, pistols, bullets, powder, swords, bayonets, battles, sieges, retreats, attacks, undermines,

countermines, bombardments, sea fights; ships sunk with
a thousand men, twenty thousand killed on each side;
dying groans, limbs flying in the air, smoke, noise, confusion, trampling to death under horses' feet; flight, pursuit, victory; fields strewed with carcases left for food to
dogs, and wolves, and birds of prey; plundering, stripping, ravishing, burning, and destroying. And to set forth
the valour of my own dear countrymen, I assured him
that I had seen them blow up a hundred enemies at once
in a siege, and as many in a ship, and beheld the dead
bodies come down in pieces from the clouds, to the great
diversion of the spectators.

I was going on to more particulars, when my master
commanded me silence. He said whoever understood the
nature of Yahoos might easily believe it possible for so
vile an animal to be capable of every action I had
named, if their strength and cunning equalled their malice. But as my discourse had increased his abhorrence
of the whole species, so he found it gave him a disturbance in his mind, to which he was wholly a stranger
before. He thought his ears being used to such abominable words, might by degrees admit them with less detestation. That although he hated the Yahoos of this
country, yet he no more blamed them for their odious
qualities, than he did a *gnnayh* (a bird of prey) for its
cruelty, or a sharp stone for cutting his hoof. But when
a creature pretending to reason could be capable of such
enormities, he dreaded lest the corruption of that faculty
might be worse than brutality itself. He seemed therefore confident, that instead of reason, we were only possessed of some quality fitted to increase our natural
vices; as the reflection from a troubled stream returns
the image of an ill-shapen body, not only larger, but
more distorted.

He added, that he had heard too much upon the subject of war, both in this and some former discourses.
There was another point which a little perplexed him at
present. I had informed him, that some of our crew left
their country on account of being ruined by *Law*; that I
had already explained the meaning of the word; but he

was at a loss how it should come to pass, that the law which was intended for every man's preservation, should be any man's ruin. Therefore he desired to be farther satisfied what I meant by law, and the dispensers thereof, according to the present practice in my own country; because he thought nature and reason were sufficient guides for a reasonable animal, as we pretended to be, in showing us what we ought to do, and what to avoid.

CEB.
1894

I assured his Honour that law was a science wherein I had not much conversed, further than by employing advocates, in vain, upon some injustices that had been done me: however, I would give him all the satisfaction I was able.

I said there was a society of men among us, bred up from their youth in the art of proving by words multiplied for the purpose, that white is black, and black is white, according as they are paid. To this society all the rest of the people are slaves. For example, if my neighbour hath a mind to my cow, he hires a lawyer to prove that he ought to have my cow from me. I must then hire another to defend my right, it being against all rules of law that any man should be allowed to speak for himself. Now in this case I who am the right owner lie under two great disadvantages. First, my lawyer, being practised almost from his cradle in defending falsehood, is quite out of his element when he would be an advocate for justice, which as an office unnatural, he always attempts with ill-will. The second disadvantage is that my lawyer must proceed with great caution, or else he will be reprimanded by the judges, and abhorred by his brethren, as one that would lessen the practise of the law. And therefore I have but two methods to preserve my cow. The first is to gain over my adversary's lawyer with a double fee, who will then betray his client by insinuating that he hath justice on his side. The second way is for my lawyer to make my cause appear as unjust as he can, by allowing the cow to belong to my adversary: and this, if it be skilfully done, will certainly bespeak the favour of the bench.

Now, your Honour is to know that these judges are persons appointed to decide all controversies of property, as well as for the trial of criminals, and picked out from the most dexterous lawyers, who are grown old or lazy, and having been biassed all their lives against truth and equity, are under such a fatal necessity of favouring fraud, perjury, and oppression, that I have known several of them refuse a large bribe from the side where justice lay, rather than injure the faculty, by doing anything unbecoming their nature or their office.

It is a maxim among these lawyers, that whatever hath been done before may legally be done again: and therefore they take special care to record all the decisions formerly made against common justice and the general reason of mankind. These, under the name of *precedents*, they produce as authorities, to justify the most iniquitous opinions; and the judges never fail of directing accordingly.

In pleading they studiously avoid entering into the merits of the cause, but are loud, violent, and tedious in dwelling upon all circumstances which are not to the purpose. For instance, in the case already mentioned, they never desire to know what claim or title my adversary hath to my cow; but whether the said cow were red or black, her horns long or short, whether the field I graze her in be round or square, whether she was milked at home or abroad, what diseases she is subject to, and the like; after which they consult precedents, adjourn the case from time to time, and in ten, twenty, or thirty years, come to an issue.

It is likewise to be observed, that this society hath a peculiar cant and jargon of their own, that no other mortal can understand, and wherein all their laws are written, which they take special care to multiply; whereby they have wholly confounded the very essence of truth and falsehood, of right and wrong; so that it will take thirty years to decide whether the field left me by my ancestors for six generations belongs to me, or to a stranger three hundred miles off.

In the trial of persons accused for crimes against the state the method is much more short and commendable: the judge first sends to sound the disposition of those in power, after which he can easily hang or save the criminal, strictly preserving all due forms of law.

Here my master interposing, said it was a pity that creatures endowed with such prodigious abilities of mind as these lawyers, by the description I gave of them, must certainly be, were not rather encouraged to be instructors of others in wisdom and knowledge. In answer to which I assured his Honour that in all points out of their own trade, they were the most ignorant and stupid generation among us, the most despicable in common conversation, avowed enemies to all knowledge and learning, and equally disposed to pervert the general reason of mankind in every other subject of discourse, as in that of their own profession.

Chapter VI *A continuation of the state of England under Queen Anne. The character of a first minister in the courts of Europe.*

MY MASTER was yet wholly at a loss to understand what motives could incite this race of lawyers to perplex, disquiet, and weary themselves, and engage in a confederacy of injustice, merely for the sake of injuring their fellow-animals; neither could he comprehend what I meant in saying they did it for hire. Whereupon I was at much pains to describe to him the use of money, the materials it was made of, and the value of the metals; that when a Yahoo had got a great store of this precious substance, he was able to purchase whatever he had a mind to; the finest clothing, the noblest houses, great tracts of land, the most costly meats and drinks, and have his choice of the most beautiful females. Therefore since money alone was able to perform all these feats, our Yahoos thought they could never have enough of it to spend or save, as they found themselves inclined from their natural bent either to profusion or avarice. That the rich man enjoyed the fruit of the poor man's labour, and the latter were a thousand to one in proportion to the former. That the bulk of our people were forced to live miserably, by labouring every day for small wages to make a few live plentifully. I enlarged myself much on these and many other particulars to the same purpose; but his Honour was still to seek; for he went upon a supposition that all animals had a title to their share in the productions of the earth, and especially those who presided over the rest. Therefore he desired I would let him know what these costly meats were, and how any of us happened to want them. Whereupon I enumerated as many sorts as came into my head, with the various

methods of dressing them, which could not be done without sending vessels by sea to every part of the world, as
well for liquors to drink, as for sauces, and innumerable
other conveniences. I assured him that this whole globe
of earth must be at least three times gone round, before
one of our better female Yahoos could get her breakfast
or a cup to put it in. He said that must needs be a
miserable country which cannot furnish food for its own
inhabitants. But what he chiefly wondered at, was how
such vast tracts of ground as I described should be
wholly without fresh water, and the people put to the
necessity of sending over the sea for drink. I replied that
England (the dear place of my nativity) was computed
to produce three times the quantity of food, more than
its inhabitants are able to consume, as well as liquors
extracted from grain, or pressed out of the fruit of certain trees, which made excellent drink, and the same
proportion in every other convenience of life. But, in
order to feed the luxury and intemperance of the males,
and the vanity of the females, we sent away the greatest
part of our necessary things to other countries, from
whence in return we brought the materials of diseases,
folly, and vice, to spend among ourselves. Hence it follows of necessity that vast numbers of our people are
compelled to seek their livelihood by begging, robbing,
stealing, cheating, pimping, forswearing, flattering, sub-
orning, forging, gaming, lying, fawning, hectoring, voting,
scribbling, star-gazing, poisoning, whoring, canting, libel-
ling, freethinking, and the like occupations: every one
of which terms, I was at much pains to make him
understand.

That wine was not imported among us from foreign
countries, to supply the want of water or other drinks,
but because it was a sort of liquid which made us merry
by putting us out of our senses, diverted all melancholy
thoughts, begat wild extravagant imaginations in the
brain, raised our hopes, and banished our fears, sus-
pended every office of reason for a time, and deprived
us of the use of our limbs, till we fell into a profound
sleep; although it must be confessed, that we always

awakened sick and dispirited and that the use of this liquor filled us with diseases, which made our lives uncomfortable and short.

But beside all this, the bulk of our people supported themselves by furnishing the necessities or conveniences of life to the rich, and to each other. For instance, when I am at home and dressed as I ought to be, I carry on my body the workmanship of an hundred tradesmen; the building and furniture of my house employ as many more, and five times the number to adorn my wife.

I was going on to tell him of another sort of people, who get their livelihood by attending the sick, having upon some occasions informed his Honour that many of my crew had died of diseases. But here it was with the utmost difficulty that I brought him to apprehend what I meant. He could easily conceive that a Houyhnhnm grew weak and heavy a few days before his death, or by some accident might hurt a limb. But that nature, who works all things to perfection, should suffer any pains to breed in our bodies, he thought impossible, and desired to know the reason of so unaccountable an evil. I told him we fed on a thousand things which operated contrary to each other; that we ate when we were not hungry, and drank without the provocation of thirst; that we sat whole nights drinking strong liquors without eating a bit, which disposed us to sloth, inflamed our bodies, and precipitated or prevented digestion. That prostitute female *Yahoos* acquired a certain malady, which bred rottenness in the bones of those who fell into their embraces; that this and many other diseases were propagated from father to son, so that great numbers come into the world with complicated maladies upon them; that it would be endless to give him a catalogue of all diseases incident to human bodies; for they could not be fewer than five or six hundred, spread over every limb and joint; in short, every part, external and intestine, having diseases appropriated to them. To remedy which there was a sort of people bred up among us, in the profession or pretence of curing the sick. And because I had some skill in the faculty, I would in gratitude to his Honour let him know the whole mystery and method by which they proceed.

Their fundamental is that all diseases arise from repletion, from whence they conclude that a great evacuation of the body is necessary, either through the natural passage or upwards at the mouth. Their next business is from herbs, minerals, gums, oils, shells, salts, juices, seaweed, excrements, barks of trees, serpents, toads, frogs, spiders, dead men's flesh and bones, birds, beasts and fishes, to form a composition for smell and taste the

most abominable, nauseous and detestable they can possibly contrive, which the stomach immediately rejects
with loathing; and this they call a vomit; or else from
the same store-house, with some other poisonous additions, they command us to take in at the orifice above
or below (just as the physician then happens to be disposed) a medicine equally annoying and disgustful to the
bowels; which relaxing the belly, drives down all before
it, and this they call a purge or a clyster. For nature
(as the physicians allege) having intended the superior
anterior orifice only for the intromission of solids and
liquids, and the inferior posterior for ejection, these artists ingeniously considering that in all diseases nature is
forced out of her seat, therefore to replace her in it the
body must be treated in a manner directly contrary, by
interchanging the use of each orifice, forcing solids and
liquids in at the anus, and making evacuation at the
mouth.

But besides real diseases we are subject to many that
are only imaginary, for which the physicans have invented imaginary cures; these have their several names,
and so have the drugs that are proper for them, and
with these our female Yahoos are always infested.

One great excellency in this tribe is their skill at prog-
nostics, wherein they seldom fail; their predictions in real
diseases, when they rise to any degree of malignity, generally portending death, which is always in their power,
when recovery is not; and therefore, upon any unexpected signs of amendment, after they have pronounced
their sentence, rather than be accused as false prophets,
they know how to approve their sagacity to the world
by a seasonable dose.

They are likewise of special use to husbands and wives
who are grown weary of their mates, to eldest sons, to
great ministers of state, and often to princes.

I had formerly upon occasion discoursed with my master upon the nature of government in general, and particularly of our own excellent constitution, deservedly
the wonder and envy of the whole world. But having
here accidentally mentioned a minister of state, he com-

manded me some time after to inform him what species
of Yahoo I particularly meant by that appellation.

I told him that a First or Chief Minister of State, who
was the person I intended to describe, was a creature
wholly exempt from joy and grief, love and hatred, pity
and anger; at least made use of no other passions but a
violent desire of wealth, power, and titles; that he applies
his words to all uses, except to the indication of his mind;
that he never tells a truth but with an intent that you
should take it for a lie; nor a lie but with a design that
you should take it for a truth; that those he speaks worst
of behind their backs are in the surest way of prefer-
ment; and whenever he begins to praise you to others
or to yourself, you are from that day forlorn. The worst
mark you can receive is a promise, especially when it is
confirmed with an oath; after which every wise man re-
tires, and gives over all hopes.

There are three methods by which a man may rise to
be chief minister: the first is by knowing how with prudence to dispose of a wife, a daughter, or a sister: the
second, by betraying or undermining his predecessor:
and the third is by a furious zeal in public assemblies
against the corruptions of the court. But a wise prince
would rather choose to employ those who practise the
last of these methods; because such zealots prove always
the most obsequious and subservient to the will and passions of their master. That these ministers having all employments at their disposal, preserve themselves in
power by bribing the majority of a senate or great council; and at last, by an expedient called an Act of Indem-
nity (whereof I described the nature to him) they secure
themselves from after-reckonings, and retire from the
public, laden with the spoils of the nation.

The palace of a chief minister, is a seminary to breed
up others in his own trade: the pages, lackeys, and por-
ter, by imitating their master, become ministers of state
in their several districts, and learn to excel in the three
principal ingredients, of insolence, lying, and bribery.
Accordingly they have a subaltern court paid to them
by persons of the best rank, and sometimes by the force

of dexterity and impudence arrive through several gradations to be successors to their lord.

He is usually governed by a decayed wench or favourite footman, who are the tunnels through which all graces are conveyed, and may properly be called, in the last resort, the governors of the kingdom.

One day in discourse my master, having heard me mention the nobility of my country, was pleased to make me a compliment which I could not pretend to deserve: that he was sure I must have been born of some noble family, because I far exceeded in shape, colour, and cleanliness, all the Yahoos of his nation, although I seemed to fail in strength and agility, which must be imputed to my different way of living from those other brutes; and besides I was not only endowed with the faculty of speech, but likewise with some rudiments of reason, to a degree that with all his acquaintance I passed for a prodigy.

He made me observe, that among the Houyhnhnms, the white, the sorrel, and the iron-grey, were not so exactly shaped as the bay, the dapple-grey, and the black; nor born with equal talents of the mind, or a capacity to improve them; and therefore continued always in the condition of servants, without ever aspiring to match out of their own race, which in that country would be reckoned monstrous and unnatural.

I made his Honour my most humble acknowledgements for the good opinion he was pleased to conceive of me; but assured him at the same time that my birth was of the lower sort, having been born of plain honest parents, who were just able to give me a tolerable education; that nobility among us was altogether a different thing from the idea he had of it; that our young noblemen are bred from their childhood in idleness and luxury; that as soon as years will permit, they consume their vigour and contract odious diseases among lewd females; and when their fortunes are almost ruined, they marry some woman of mean birth, disagreeable person, and unsound constitution, merely for the sake of money, whom they hate and despise. That the productions of such marriages are generally scrofulous, rickety, or deformed children; by which means the family seldom continues above three generations, unless the wife takes care to provide a healthy father among her neighbours or domestics, in order to improve and continue the breed. That a weak diseased body, a meagre countenance, and sallow complexion, are the true marks of noble blood; and a healthy robust appearance is so disgraceful in a man of quality, that the world concludes his real father to have been a groom or a coachman. The imperfections of his mind run parallel with those of his body, being a composition of spleen, dullness, ignorance, caprice, sensuality and pride.

Without the consent of this illustrious body no law can be enacted, repealed, or altered; and these have the decision of all our possessions without appeal.

∞

Chapter VII *The Author's great love of his native country. His master's observations upon the constitution and administration of England, as described by the Author, with parallel cases and comparisons. His master's observations upon human nature.*

THE READER may be disposed to wonder how I could prevail on myself to give so free a representation of my own species, among a race of mortals who were already too apt to conceive the vilest opinion of human kind, from that entire congruity betwixt me and their Yahoos. But I must freely confess that the many virtues of those excellent quadrupeds placed in opposite view to human corruptions, had so far opened my eyes and enlarged my understanding, that I began to view the actions and passions of man in a very different light, and to think the honour of my own kind not worth managing; which, besides, it was impossible for me to do before a person of so acute a judgement as my master, who daily convinced me of a thousand faults in myself, whereof I had not the least perception before, and which among us would never be numbered even among human infirmities. I had likewise learned from his example an utter detestation of all falsehood or disguise, and truth appeared so amiable to me, that I determined upon sacrificing every thing to it.

Let me deal so candidly with the reader as to confess that there was yet a much stronger motive for the freedom I took in my representation of things. I had not been a year in this country before I contracted such a love and veneration for the inhabitants, that I entered on a firm resolution never to return to human kind, but to pass the rest of my life among these admirable Houyhnhnms in the contemplation and practice of every virtue; where I could have no example or incitement to vice. But it was decreed by fortune, my perpetual enemy, that so great a felicity should not fall to my share. However, it is now some comfort to reflect that in what I said of my countrymen I extenuated their faults as much as I durst before so strict an examiner, and upon every article gave as favourable a turn as the matter would bear. For indeed who is there alive that will not be swayed by his bias and partiality to the place of his birth?

I have related the substance of several conversations I had with my master, during the greatest part of the time I had the honour to be in his service, but have indeed for brevity sake omitted much more than is here set down.

When I had answered all his questions, and his curiosity seemed to be fully satisfied, he sent for me one morning early, and commanding me to sit down at some distance (an honour which he had never before conferred upon me) he said he had been very seriously considering my whole story, as far as it related both to myself and my country; that he looked upon us as a sort of animals to whose share, by what accident he could not conjecture, some small pittance of reason had fallen, whereof we made no other use than by its assistance to aggravate our natural corruptions, and to acquire new ones which nature had not given us. That we disarmed ourselves of the few abilities she had bestowed, had been very successful in multiplying our original wants, and seemed to spend our whole lives in vain endeavours to supply them by our own inventions. That as to myself, it was manifest I had neither the strength nor agility of a common Yahoo, that I walked infirmly on my hinder feet, had found out a contrivance to make my claws of no use or defence, and to remove the hair from my chin, which was intended as a shelter from the sun and the weather. Lastly, that I could neither run with speed, nor climb trees like my brethren (as he called them) the Yahoos in this country.

That our institutions of government and law were plainly owing to our gross defects in reason, and by consequence, in virtue; because reason alone is sufficient to govern a rational creature; which was therefore a character we had no pretence to challenge, even from the account I had given of my own people; although he manifestly perceived that in order to favour them I had concealed many particulars, and often *said the thing which was not*.

He was the more confirmed in this opinion, because he observed that as I agreed in every feature of my body with other Yahoos, except where it was to my real disadvantage in point of strength, speed and activity, the shortness of my claws, and some other particulars where nature had no part; so from the representation I had given him of our lives, our manners, and our actions, he found as near a resemblance in the disposition of our minds. He said the Yahoos were known to hate one another more than they did any different species of animals; and the reason usually assigned was the odiousness of their own shapes, which all could see in the rest, but not in themselves. He had therefore begun to think it not unwise in us to cover our bodies, and by that invention conceal many of our own deformities from each other, which would else be hardly supportable. But he now found he had been mistaken, and that the dissensions of those brutes in his country were owing to the same cause with ours, as I had described them. For if (said he) you throw among five Yahoos as much food as would be sufficient for fifty, they will, instead of eating peaceably, fall together by the ears, each single one impatient to have all to itself; and therefore a servant was usually employed to stand by while they were feeding abroad, and those kept at home were tied at a distance from each other: that if a cow died of age or accident, before a Houyhnhnm could secure it for his own Yahoos, those in the neighbourhood would come in herds to seize it, and then would ensue such a battle as I had described, with terrible wounds made by their claws on both sides, although they seldom were able to kill one another, for want of such convenient instruments of death as we had invented. At other times the like battles have been fought between the Yahoos of several neighbourhoods without any visible cause; those of one district watching all opportunities to surprise the next before they are prepared. But if they find their project hath miscarried, they return home, and, for want of enemies, engage in what I call a civil war among themselves.

That in some fields of his country there are certain shining stones of several colours, whereof the Yahoos are violently fond, and when part of these stones is fixed in the earth, as it sometimes happeneth, they will dig with their claws for whole days to get them out, then carry them away, and hide them by heaps in their kennels; but still looking round with great caution, for fear their comrades should find out their treasure. My master said he could never discover the reason of this unnatural appetite, or how these stones could be of any use to a Yahoo; but now he believed it might proceed from the same principle of avarice which I had ascribed to mankind: that he had once, by way of experiment, privately removed a heap of these stones from the place where one of his Yahoos had buried it: whereupon the sordid animal missing his treasure, by his loud lamenting brought the whole herd to the place, there miserably howled, then fell to biting and tearing the rest, began to pine away, would neither eat nor sleep nor work, till he ordered a servant privately to convey the stones into the same hole and hide them as before; which when his Yahoo had found, he presently recovered his spirits and good humour, but took good care to remove them to a better hiding-place, and hath ever since been a very serviceable brute.

My master farther assured me, which I also observed myself, that in the fields where these shining stones abound, the fiercest and most frequent battles are fought, occasioned by perpetual inroads of the neighbouring Yahoos.

He said it was common when two Yahoos discovered such a stone in a field, and were contending which of them should be the proprietor, a third would take the advantage, and carry it away from them both; which my master would needs contend to have some kind of resemblance with our suits at law; wherein I thought it for our credit not to undeceive him; since the decision he mentioned was much more equitable than many decrees among us; because the plaintiff and defendant there lost nothing beside the stone they contended for, whereas our courts of equity would never have dismissed the cause while either of them had any thing left.

My master continuing his discourse, said there was nothing that rendered the Yahoos more odious than their undistinguishing appetite to devour every thing that came in their way, whether herbs, roots, berries, the corrupted flesh of animals, or all mingled together; and it was peculiar in their temper that they were fonder of what they could get by rapine or stealth at a greater distance than much better food provided for them at home. If their prey held out, they would eat till they were ready to burst, after which nature had pointed out to them a certain root that gave them a general evacuation.

There was also another kind of root very juicy, but somewhat rare and difficult to be found, which the Yahoos sought for with much eagerness, and would suck it with great delight; and it produced in them the same effects that wine hath upon us. It would make them sometimes hug, and sometimes tear one another; they would howl and grin, and chatter, and reel, and tumble, and then fall asleep in the dirt.

I did indeed observe that the Yahoos were the only animals in this country subject to any diseases; which, however, were much fewer than horses have among us, and contracted not by any ill-treatment they meet with, but by the nastiness and greediness of that sordid brute. Neither has their language any more than a general appellation for those maladies, which is borrowed from the name of the beast, and called *Hnea-Yahoo*, or the *Yahoo's evil*, and the cure prescribed is a mixture of their own dung and urine forcibly put down the Yahoo's throat. This I have since often known to have been taken with success, and do freely recommend it to my countrymen, for the public good, as an admirable specific against all diseases produced by repletion.

As to learning, government, arts, manufactures, and the like, my master confessed he could find little or no resemblance between the Yahoos of that country and those in ours. For he only meant to observe what parity there was in our natures. He had heard indeed some curious Houyhnhnms observe that in most herds there was a sort of ruling Yahoo (as among us there is generally some leading or principal stag in a park), who was always more deformed in body and mischievous in disposition than any of the rest. That this leader had usually a favourite as like himself as he could get, whose employment was to lick his master's feet and posteriors, and drive the female Yahoos to his kennel; for which he was now and then rewarded with a piece of ass's flesh. This favourite is hated by the whole herd, and therefore to protect himself, keeps always near the person of his leader. He usually continues in office till a worse can be found; but the very moment he is discarded, his successor, at the head of all the Yahoos in that district, young and old, male and female come in a body, and discharge

their excrements upon him from head to foot. But how
far this might be applicable to our courts and favourites,
and ministers of state, my master said I could best
determine.

I durst make no return to this malicious insinuation,
which debased human understanding below the sagacity
of a common hound, who has judgement enough to distinguish and follow the cry of the ablest dog in the pack,
without being ever mistaken.

My master told me there were some qualities remarkable in the Yahoos, which he had not observed me to
mention, or at least very slightly, in the accounts I had
given him of human kind. He said those animals, like
other brutes, had their females in common; but in this
they differed, that the she Yahoo would admit the male
while she was pregnant; and that the he's would quarrel
and fight with the females as fiercely as with each other.
Both which practices were such degrees of brutality, that
no other sensitive creature ever arrived at.

Another thing he wondered at in the Yahoos was their
strange disposition to nastiness and dirt, whereas there
appears to be a natural love of cleanliness in all other
animals. As to the former accusation, I was glad to let
it pass without any reply, because I had not a word to
offer upon it in defence of my species, which otherwise
I certainly had done from my own inclinations. But I
could have easily vindicated human kind from the impu-
tation of singularity upon the last article, if there had
been any swine in that country (as unluckily for me there
were not), which although it may be a sweeter quadru-
ped than a Yahoo, cannot I humbly conceive in justice
pretend to more cleanliness; and so his Honour himself
must have owned, if he had seen their filthy way of feeding, and their custom of wallowing and sleeping in the
mud.

My master likewise mentioned another quality which
his servants had discovered in several Yahoos, and to
him was wholly unaccountable. He said, a fancy would
sometimes take a Yahoo to retire into a corner, to lie
down and howl and groan, and spurn away all that came

near him, although he were young and fat, wanted neither food nor water; nor did the servants imagine what could possibly ail him. And the only remedy they found was to set him to hard work, after which he would infallibly come to himself. To this I was silent out of partiality to my own kind; yet here I could plainly discover the true seeds of spleen, which only seizeth on the lazy, the luxurious, and the rich; who, if they were forced to undergo the same regimen, I would undertake for the cure.

His Honour had further observed that a female Yahoo would often stand behind a bank or a bush, to gaze on the young males passing by, and then appear, and hide, using many antic gestures and grimaces, at which time it was observed that she had a most offensive smell; and when any of the males advanced, would slowly retire, looking often back, and with a counterfeit show of fear, run off into some convenient place where she knew the male would follow her.

At other times if a female stranger came among them, three or four of her own sex would get about her, and stare and chatter, and grin, and smell her all over; and then turn off with gestures that seemed to express contempt and disdain.

Perhaps my master might refine a little in these speculations, which he had drawn from what he observed himself, or had been told him by others; however, I could not reflect without some amazement, and much sorrow, that the rudiments of coquetry, censure, and scandal, should have place by instinct in womankind.

I expected every moment that my master would accuse the Yahoos of those unnatural appetites in both sexes, so common among us. But nature, it seems, hath not been so expert a school-mistress; and these politer pleasures are entirely the productions of art and reason, on our side of the globe.

Chapter VIII *The Author relates several particulars of the Yahoos. The great virtues of the Houyhnhnms. The education and exercises of their youth. Their general assembly.*

As I OUGHT to have understood human nature much better than I supposed it possible for my master to do, so it was easy to apply the character he gave of the Yahoos to myself and my countrymen; and I believed I could yet make farther discoveries from my own observation. I therefore often begged his favour to let me go among the herds of Yahoos in the neighbourhood, to which he always very graciously consented, being perfectly convinced that the hatred I bore those brutes would never suffer me to be corrupted by them; and his Honour ordered one of his servants, a strong sorrel nag, very honest and good-natured, to be my guard, without whose protection I durst not undertake such adventures. For I have already told the reader how much I was pestered by those odious animals upon my first arrival. And I afterwards failed very narrowly three or four times of falling into their clutches, when I happened to stray at any distance without my hanger. And I have reason to believe they had some imagination that I was of their own species, which I often assisted myself, by stripping up my sleeves, and showing my naked arms and breast in their sight, when my protector was with me. At which times they would approach as near as they durst, and imitate my actions after the manner of monkeys, but ever with great signs of hatred; as a tame jack-daw with cap and stockings is always persecuted by the wild ones, when he happens to be got among them.

They are prodigiously nimble from their infancy; however, I once caught a young male of three years old, and endeavoured by all marks of tenderness to make it quiet; but the little imp fell a squalling and scratching and biting with such violence that I was forced to let it go; and it was high time, for a whole troop of old ones came about us at the noise, but finding the cub was safe (for away it ran), and my sorrel nag being by, they durst not venture near us. I observed the young animal's flesh to smell very rank, and the stink was somewhat between a weasel and a fox, but much more disagreeable. I forgot another circumstance (and perhaps I might have the reader's pardon if it were wholly omitted), that while I held the odious vermin in my hands, it voided its filthy excrements of a yellow liquid substance, all over my clothes; but by good fortune there was a small brook hard by, where I washed myself as clean as I could;

although I durst not come into my master's presence, until I were sufficiently aired.

By what I could discover, the Yahoos appear to be the most unteachable of all animals, their capacities never reaching higher than to draw or carry burdens. Yet I am of opinion this defect ariseth chiefly from a perverse, restive disposition. For they are cunning, malicious, treacherous, and revengeful. They are strong and hardy, but of a cowardly spirit, and by consequence, insolent, abject, and cruel. It is observed that the red-haired of both sexes are more libidinous and mischievous than the rest, whom yet they much exceed in strength and activity.

The Houyhnhnms keep the Yahoos for present use in huts not far from the house; but the rest are sent abroad to certain fields, where they dig up roots, eat several kinds of herbs, and search about for carrion, or sometimes catch weasels and *luhimuhs* (a sort of wild rat), which they greedily devour. Nature hath taught them to dig deep holes with their nails on the side of a rising ground, wherein they lie by themselves; only the kennels of the females are larger, sufficient to hold two or three cubs.

They swim from their infancy like frogs, and are able to continue long under water, where they often take fish, which the females carry home to their young. And upon this occasion, I hope the reader will pardon my relating an odd adventure.

Being one day abroad with my protector the sorrel nag, and the weather exceeding hot, I entreated him to let me bathe in a river that was near. He consented, and I immediately stripped myself stark naked, and went down softly into the stream. It happened that a young female Yahoo, standing behind a bank, saw the whole proceeding, and inflamed by desire, as the nag and I conjectured, came running with all speed, and leaped into the water, within five yards of the place where I bathed. I was never in my life so terribly frighted; the nag was grazing at some distance, not suspecting any harm. She embraced me after a most fulsome manner; I roared as loud as I could, and the nag came galloping towards me, whereupon she quitted her grasp, with the utmost reluctancy, and leaped upon the opposite bank, where she stood gazing and howling all the time I was putting on my clothes.

This was a matter of diversion to my master and his family, as well as of mortification to myself. For now I could no longer deny that I was a real Yahoo in every limb and feature, since the females had a natural propensity to me, as one of their own species. Neither was the hair of this brute of a red colour (which might have been some excuse for an appetite a little irregular), but black as a sloe, and her countenance did not make an appearance altogether so hideous as the rest of the kind; for, I think, she could not be above eleven years old.

Having lived three years in this country, the reader I suppose will expect that I should, like other travellers, give him some account of the manners and customs of its inhabitants, which it was indeed my principal study to learn.

As these noble Houyhnhnms are endowed by nature with a general disposition to all virtues, and have no conceptions or ideas of what is evil in a rational creature, so their grand maxim is to cultivate reason, and to be wholly governed by it. Neither is reason among them a point problematical as with us, where men can argue with plausibility on both sides of the question; but strikes you with immediate conviction; as it must needs do where it is not mingled, obscured, or discoloured by passion and interest. I remember it was with extreme difficulty that I could bring my master to understand the meaning of the word *opinion*, or how a point could be disputable; because reason taught us to affirm or deny only where we are certain, and beyond our knowledge we cannot do either. So that controversies, wranglings, disputes, and positiveness in false or dubious propositions, are evils unknown among the Houyhnhnms. In the like manner when I used to explain to him our several systems of natural philosophy, he would laugh that a creature pretending to reason should value itself upon the knowledge of other people's conjectures, and in things where that knowledge, if it were certain, could be of no use. Wherein he agreed entirely with the sentiments of Socrates, as Plato delivers them, which I mention as the highest honour I can do that prince of philosophers. I have often since reflected what destruction such a doctrine would make in the libraries of Europe, and how many paths to fame would be then shut up in the learned world.

Friendship and benevolence are the two principal virtues among the Houyhnhnms, and these not confined to particular objects, but universal to the whole race. For a stranger from the remotest part is equally treated with the nearest neighbour, and wherever he goes looks upon himself as at home. They preserve decency and civility in the highest degrees, but are altogether ignorant of ceremony. They have no fondness for their colts or foals, but the care they take in educating them proceeds entirely from the dictates of reason. And I observed my master to show the same affection to his neighbour's issue that he had for his own. They will have it that nature teaches them to love the whole species, and it is reason only that maketh a distinction of persons, where there is a superior degree of virtue.

When the matron Houyhnhnms have produced one of each sex, they no longer accompany with their consorts, except they lose one of their issue by some casualty, which very seldom happens; but in such a case they meet again; or when the like accident befalls a person whose wife is past bearing, some other couple bestow him one of their own colts, and then go together again till the mother is pregnant. This caution is necessary to prevent the country from being overburthened with numbers. But the race of inferior Houyhnhnms bred up to be servants is not so strictly limited upon this article; these are allowed to produce three of each sex, to be domestics in the noble families.

In their marriages they are exactly careful to choose such colours as will not make any disagreeable mixture in the breed. Strength is chiefly valued in the male, and comeliness in the female; not upon the account of love, but to preserve the race from degenerating; for where a female happens to excel in strength, a consort is chosen with regard to comeliness. Courtship, love, presents, jointures, settlements, have no place in their thoughts, or terms whereby to express them in their language. The young couple meet and are joined, merely because it is the determination of their parents and friends: it is what they see done every day, and they look upon it as one of the necessary actions of a rational being. But the violation of marriage, or any other unchastity, was never heard of; and the married pair pass their lives with the same friendship and mutual benevolence that they bear to all others of the same species who come in their way; without jealousy, fondness, quarreling, or discontent.

In educating the youth of both sexes, their method is admirable, and highly deserves our imitation. These are not suffered to taste a grain of oats, except upon certain days, till eighteen years old; nor milk, but very rarely; and in summer they graze two hours in the morning, and as long in the evening, which their parents likewise observe; but the servants are not allowed above half that time, and a great part of their grass is brought home, which they eat at the most convenient hours, when they can be best spared from work.

Temperance, industry, exercise and cleanliness, are the lessons equally enjoined to the young ones of both sexes; and my master thought it monstrous in us to give the females a different kind of education from the males, except in some articles of domestic management; whereby, as he truly observed, one half of our natives were good for nothing but bringing children into the world; and to trust the care of our children to such useless animals, he said, was yet a greater instance of brutality.

But the Houyhnhnms train up their youth to strength, speed, and hardiness, by exercising them in running races up and down steep hills, and over hard stony grounds; and when they are all in a sweat, they are ordered to leap over head and ears into a pond or river. Four times a year the youth of a certain district meet to show their proficiency in running and leaping, and other feats of strength and agility; where the victor is rewarded with a song made in his or her praise. On this festival the servants drive a herd of Yahoos into the field, laden with hay and oats and milk, for a repast to the Houyhnhnms; after which these brutes are immediately driven back again, for fear of being noisome to the assembly.

Every fourth year, at the vernal equinox, there is a representative council of the whole nation, which meets in a plain about twenty miles from our house, and continues about five or six days. Here they enquire into the state and condition of the several districts; whether they abound or be deficient in hay or oats, or cows or Yahoos. And wherever there is any want (which is but seldom) it is immediately supplied by unanimous consent and contribution. Here likewise the regulation of children is settled: as for instance, if a Houyhnhnm hath two males, he changeth one of them with another that hath two females; and when a child hath been lost by any casualty, where the mother is past breeding, it is determined what family in the district shall breed another to supply the loss.

∞

Chapter IX *A grand debate at the general assembly of the Houyhnhnms, and how it was determined. The learning of the Houyhnhnms. Their buildings. Their manner of burials. The defectiveness of their language.*

ONE OF these grand assemblies was held in my time, about three months before my departure, whither my master went as the representative of our district. In this council was resumed their old debate, and indeed, the only debate which ever happened in that country;

whereof my master after his return gave me a very particular account.

The question to be debated was whether the Yahoos should be exterminated from the face of the earth. One of the members for the affirmative offered several arguments of great strength and weight, alleging that as the Yahoos were the most filthy, noisome, and deformed animals which nature ever produced, so they were the most restive and indocible, mischievous and malicious: they would privately suck the teats of the Houyhnhnms' cows, kill and devour their cats, trample down their oats and grass, if they were not continually watched, and commit a thousand other extravagancies. He took notice of a general tradition, that Yahoos had not been always in that country; but that many ages ago two of these brutes appeared together upon a mountain, whether produced by the heat of the sun upon corrupted mud and slime, or from the ooze and froth of the sea, was never known. That these Yahoos engendered, and their brood in a short time grew so numerous as to overrun and infest the whole nation. That the Houyhnhnms to get rid of this evil, made a general hunting, and at last enclosed the whole herd; and destroying the elder, every Houyhnhnm kept two young ones in a kennel, and brought them to such a degree of tameness, as an animal so savage by nature can be capable of acquiring; using them for draught and carriage. That there seemed to be much truth in this tradition, and that those creatures could not be *Ylnhniamshy* (or *aborigines* of the land), because of the violent hatred the Houyhnhnms, as well as all other animals, bore them; which although their evil disposition sufficiently deserved, could never have arrived at so high a degree, if they had been aborigines, or else they would have long since been rooted out. That the inhabitants taking a fancy to use the service of the Yahoos, had very imprudently neglected to cultivate the breed of asses, which were a comely animal, easily kept, more tame and orderly, without any offensive smell, strong enough for labour, although they yield to the other in agility of

body; and if their braying be no agreeable sound, it is
far preferable to the horrible howlings of the Yahoos.

Several others declared their sentiments to the same
purpose, when my master proposed an expedient to the
assembly, whereof he had indeed borrowed the hint
from me. He approved of the tradition mentioned by
the honourable member who spoke before, and affirmed
that the two Yahoos said to be first seen among them
had been driven thither over the sea; that coming to land
and being forsaken by their companions they retired to
the mountains, and degenerating by degrees, became in
process of time, much more savage than those of their
own species in the country from whence these two originals came. The reason of his assertion was that he had
now in his possession a certain wonderful Yahoo (meaning myself), which most of them had heard of, and many
of them had seen. He then related to them how he first
found me; that my body was all covered with an artificial
composure of the skins and hairs of other animals; that
I spoke in a language of my own, and had thoroughly
learned theirs; that I had related to him the accidents
which brought me thither; that when he saw me without
my covering I was an exact Yahoo in every part, only
of a white colour, less hairy, and with shorter claws. He
added how I had endeavoured to persuade him that in
my own and other countries the Yahoos acted as the
governing, rational animal, and held the Houyhnhnms in
servitude; that he observed in me all the qualities of a
Yahoo, only a little more civilized by some tincture of
reason, which however was in a degree as far inferior to
the Houyhnhnm race as the Yahoos of their country
were to me; that among other things I mentioned a custom we had of castrating Houyhnhnms when they were
young, in order to render them tame; that the operation
was easy and safe; that it was no shame to learn wisdom
from brutes, as industry is taught by the ant, and building by the swallow. (For so I translate the word *lyhannh*,
although it be a much larger fowl.) That this invention
might be practised upon the younger Yahoos here,
which, besides rendering them tractable and fitter for

use, would in an age put an end to the whole species without destroying life. That in the mean time the Houyhnhnms should be exhorted to cultivate the breed of asses, which, as they are in all respects more valuable brutes, so they have this advantage, to be fit for service at five years old, which the others are not till twelve.

This was all my master thought fit to tell me at that time of what passed in the grand council. But he was pleased to conceal one particular, which related personally to myself, whereof I soon felt the unhappy effect, as the reader will know in its proper place, and from whence I date all the succeeding misfortunes of my life.

The Houyhnhnms have no letters, and consequently their knowledge is all traditional. But there happening few events of any moment among a people so well united, naturally disposed to every virtue, wholly governed by reason, and cut off from all commerce with other nations, the historical part is easily preserved without burthening their memories. I have already observed that they are subject to no diseases, and therefore can have no need of physicians. However, they have excellent medicines composed of herbs, to cure accidental bruises and cuts in the pastern or frog of the foot by sharp stones, as well as other maims and hurts in the several parts of the body.

They calculate the year by the revolution of the sun and the moon, but use no subdivisions into weeks. They are well enough acquainted with the motions of those two luminaries, and understand the nature of eclipses; and this is the utmost progress of their astronomy.

In poetry they must be allowed to excel all other mortals; wherein the justness of their similes, and the minuteness, as well as exactness of their descriptions, are indeed inimitable. Their verses abound very much in both of these, and usually contain either some exalted notions of friendship and benevolence, or the praises of those who were victors in races and other bodily exercises. Their buildings, although very rude and simple, are not inconvenient, but well contrived to defend them from all injuries of cold and heat. They have a kind of tree, which at forty years old loosens in the root, and falls with the first storm: they grow very straight, and being pointed like stakes with a sharp stone (for the Houyhnhnms know not the use of iron), they stick them erect in the ground about ten inches asunder, and then weave in oat-straw, or sometimes wattles betwixt them. The roof is made after the same manner, and so are the doors.

The Houyhnhnms use the hollow part between the pastern and the hoof of their fore-feet as we do our hands, and this with greater dexterity than I could at first imagine. I have seen a white mare of our family thread a needle (which I lent her on purpose) with that joint. They milk their cows, reap their oats, and do all the work which requires hands, in the same manner. They have a kind of hard flints, which by grinding against other stones, they form into instruments, that serve instead of wedges, axes, and hammers. With tools made of these flints they likewise cut their hay and reap their oats, which there groweth naturally in several fields: the Yahoos draw home the sheaves in carriages, and the servants tread them in certain covered huts, to get out the grain, which is kept in stores. They make a rude kind of earthen and wooden vessels, and bake the former in the sun.

If they can avoid casualties, they die only of old age, and are buried in the obscurest places that can be found, their friends and relations expressing neither joy nor grief at their departure; nor does the dying person discover the least regret that he is leaving the world, any more than if he were upon returning home from a visit to one of his neighbours. I remember my master having once made an appointment with a friend and his family to come to his house upon some affair of importance, on the day fixed the mistress and her two children came very late; she made two excuses, first for her husband, who, as she said, happened that very morning to *shnuwnh*. The word is strongly expressive in their language, but not easily rendered into English; it signifies, *to retire to his first mother*. Her excuse for not coming sooner was that her husband dying late in the morning, she was a good while consulting her servants about a convenient place where his body should be laid; and I observed she behaved herself at our house as cheerfully as the rest, and she died about three months after.

They live generally to seventy or seventy-five years, very seldom to fourscore: some weeks before their death they feel a gradual decay, but without pain. During this time they are much visited by their friends, because they cannot go abroad with their usual ease and satisfaction. However, about ten days before their death, which they seldom fail in computing, they return the visits that have been made them by those who are nearest in the neighbourhood, being carried in a convenient sledge drawn by Yahoos; which vehicle they use, not only upon this occasion, but when they grow old, upon long journeys, or when they are lamed by any accident. And therefore when the dying Houyhnhnms return those visits, they take a solemn leave of their friends, as if they were going to some remote part of the country, where they designed to pass the rest of their lives.

I know not whether it may be worth observing that the Houyhnhnms have no word in their language to express any thing that is evil, except what they borrow from the deformities or ill qualities of the Yahoos. Thus they denote the folly of a servant, an omission of a child, a stone that cuts their feet, a continuance of foul or unseasonable weather, and the like, by adding to each the epithet of Yahoo. For instance, *Hhnm Yahoo, Whnaholm Yahoo, Ynlhmnd-wihlma Yahoo,* and an ill-contrived house *Ynholmhnm-rohlnw Yahoo.*

I could with great pleasure enlarge further upon the manners and virtues of this excellent people; but intending in a short time to publish a volume by itself expressly upon that subject, I refer the reader thither, and in the mean time, proceed to relate my own sad catastrophe.

Chapter X *The Author's economy, and happy life among the Houyhnhnms. His great improvement in virtue, by conversing with them. Their conversations. The Author has notice given him by his master that he must depart from the country. He falls into a swoon for grief, but submits. He contrives and finishes a canoe, by the help of a fellow-servant, and puts to sea at a venture.*

I HAD SETTLED my little economy to my own heart's content. My master had ordered a room to be made for me after their manner, about six yards from the house; the sides and floors of which I plastered with clay, and covered with rush-mats of my own contriving; I had beaten hemp, which there grows wild, and made of it a sort of ticking; this I filled with the feathers of several birds I had taken with springes made of Yahoos' hairs, and were excellent food. I had worked two chairs with my knife, the sorrel nag helping me in the grosser and more laborious part. When my clothes were worn to rags, I made myself others with the skins of rabbits, and of a certain beautiful animal about the same size, called *nnuhnoh*, the skin of which is covered with a fine down. Of these I likewise made very tolerable stockings. I soled my shoes with wood which I cut from a tree and fitted to the upper leather, and when this was worn out, I supplied it with the skins of Yahoos dried in the sun. I often got honey out of hollow trees, which I mingled with water, or ate with my bread. No man could more verify the truth of these two maxims, *That nature is very easily satisfied*; and *That necessity is the mother of invention.* I enjoyed perfect health of body, and tranquillity of mind; I did not feel the treachery or inconstancy of a friend, nor the injuries of a secret or open enemy. I had no occasion of bribing, flattering, or pimping to procure the favour of any great man or of his minion. I wanted no fence against fraud or oppression; here was neither physician to destroy my body, nor lawyer to ruin my fortune; no informer to watch my words and actions, or forge accusations against me for hire; here were no gibers, censurers, backbiters, pickpockets, highwaymen, housebreakers, attorneys, bawds, buffoons, gamesters, politicians, wits, splenetics, tedious talkers, controvertists, ravishers, murderers, robbers, virtuosos; no leaders or followers of party and faction; no encouragers to vice, by seducement or examples; no dungeon, axes, gibbets, whipping-posts, or pillories; no cheating shopkeepers or mechanics; no pride, vanity, or affectation; no fops, bullies, drunkards, strolling whores, or poxes; no ranting, lewd, expensive wives; no stupid, proud pedants; no importunate, overbearing, quarrelsome, noisy, roaring, empty, conceited, swearing companions; no scoundrels, raised from the dust for the sake of their vices, or nobility thrown into it on account of their virtues; no lords, fiddlers, judges, or dancing-masters.

I had the favour of being admitted to several Houyhnhnms, who came to visit or dine with my master; where his Honour graciously suffered me to wait in the room, and listen to their discourse. Both he and his company would often descend to ask me questions, and receive my answers. I had also sometimes the honour of attending my master in his visits to others. I never presumed to speak, except in answer to a question; and then I did it with inward regret, because it was a loss of so much time for improving myself; but I was infinitely delighted with the station of an humble auditor in such conversations, where nothing passed but what was useful, expressed in the fewest and most significant words; where the greatest decency was observed, without the least degree of ceremony; where no person spoke without being pleased himself, and pleasing his companions; where there was no interruption, tediousness, heat, or difference of sentiments. They have a notion that when people are met together, a short silence doth much improve conversation: this I found to be true; for during those little intermissions of talk, new ideas would arise in their thoughts, which very much enlivened the discourse. Their subjects are generally on friendship and benevolence, or order and economy; sometimes upon the visible operations of nature, or ancient traditions; upon the bounds and limits of virtue; upon the unerring rules of reason, or upon some determinations to be taken at the next great assembly; and often upon the various excellencies of poetry. I may add without vanity that my presence often gave them sufficient matter for discourse, because it afforded my master an occasion of letting his friends into the history of me and my country, upon which they were all pleased to descant in a manner not very advantageous to human kind; and for that reason I shall not repeat what they said: only I may be allowed to observe that his Honour, to my great admiration, appeared to understand the nature of Yahoos in all countries much better than myself. He went through all our vices and follies, and discovered many which I had never mentioned to him, by only supposing what qualities a Yahoo of their country, with a small proportion of reason, might be capable of exerting; and concluded, with too much probability, how vile as well as miserable such a creature must be.

I freely confess that all the little knowledge I have of any value was acquired by the lectures I received from my master, and from hearing the discourses of him and his friends; to which I should be prouder to listen than to dictate to the greatest and wisest assembly in Europe. I admired the strength, comeliness, and speed of the inhabitants; and such a constellation of virtues in such amiable persons produced in me the highest veneration. At first, indeed, I did not feel that natural awe which the Yahoos and all other animals bear towards them; but it grew upon me by degrees, much sooner than I imagined, and was mingled with a respectful love and gratitude, that they would condescend to distinguish me from the rest of my species.

When I thought of my family, my friends, my countrymen, or human race in general, I considered them as they really were, Yahoos in shape and disposition, perhaps a little more civilized, and qualified with the gift of speech, but making no other use of reason than to improve and multiply those vices whereof their brethren in this country had only the share that nature allotted them. When I happened to behold the reflection of my own form in a lake or fountain, I turned away my face in horror and detestation of myself, and could better endure the sight of a common Yahoo than of my own person. By conversing with the Houyhnhnms, and looking upon them with delight, I fell to imitate their gait and gesture, which is now grown into an habit, and my friends often tell me in a blunt way, that I trot like a horse; which, however, I take for a great compliment. Neither shall I disown that in speaking I am apt to fall into the voice and manner of the Houyhnhnms, and hear

myself ridiculed on that account without the least
mortification.

In the midst of all this happiness, and when I looked
upon myself to be fully settled for life, my master sent
for me one morning a little earlier than his usual hour.
I observed by his countenance that he was in some perplexity, and at a loss how to begin what he had to speak.
After a short silence he told me he did not know how I
would take what he was going to say; that in the last
general assembly, when the affair of the Yahoos was
entered upon, the representatives had taken offence at
his keeping a Yahoo (meaning myself) in his family
more like a Houyhnhnm than a brute animal. That he
was known frequently to converse with me, as if he
could receive some advantage or pleasure in my company; that such a practice was not agreeable to reason
or nature, nor a thing ever heard of before among them.
The assembly did therefore exhort him, either to employ
me like the rest of my species, or command me to swim
back to the place from whence I came. That the first of
these expedients was utterly rejected by all the Houyhnhnms who had ever seen me at his house or their
own: for they alleged that because I had some rudiments
of reason, added to the natural pravity of those animals,
it was to be feared I might be able to seduce them into
the woody and mountainous parts of the country, and
bring them in troops by night to destroy the Houyhnhnms' cattle, as being naturally of the ravenous kind,
and averse from labour.

My master added that he was daily pressed by the
Houyhnhnms of the neighbourhood to have the assembly's exhortation executed, which he could not put off
much longer. He doubted it would be impossible for me
to swim to another country, and therefore wished I
would contrive some sort of vehicle resembling those I
had described to him, that might carry me on the sea;
in which work I should have the assistance of his own
servants, as well as those of his neighbours. He concluded that for his own part he could have been content
to keep me in his service as long as I lived; because

he found I had cured myself of some bad habits and dispositions, by endeavoring, as far as my inferior nature was capable, to imitate the Houyhnhnms.

I should here observe to the reader, that a decree of the general assembly in this country is expressed by the word *hnhloayn*, which signifies an exhortation, as near as I can render it; for they have no conception how a rational creature can be compelled, but only advised or exhorted, because no person can disobey reason without giving up his claim to be a rational creature.

I was struck with the utmost grief and despair at my master's discourse, and being unable to support the agonies I was under, I fell into a swoon at his feet; when I came to myself he told me that he concluded I had been dead (for these people are subject to no such imbecilities of nature). I answered in a faint voice that death would have been too great an happiness; that although I could not blame the assembly's exhortation, or the urgency of his friends, yet, in my weak and corrupt judgement, I thought it might consist with reason to have been less rigorous. That I could not swim a league, and probably the nearest land to theirs might be distant above an hundred; that many materials, necessary for making a small vessel to carry me off, were wholly wanting in this country, which, however, I would attempt in obedience and gratitude to his Honour, although I concluded the thing to be impossible, and therefore looked on myself as already devoted to destruction. That the certain prospect of an unnatural death was the least of my evils; for supposing I should escape with life by some strange adventure, how could I think with temper of passing my days among Yahoos, and relapsing into my old corruptions, for want of examples to lead and keep me within the paths of virtue? That I knew too well upon what solid reasons all the determinations of the wise Houyhnhnms were founded, not to be shaken by arguments of mine, a miserable Yahoo; and therefore, after presenting him with my humble thanks for the offer of his servants' assistance in making a vessel, and desiring a reasonable time for so difficult a work, I told him I would endeavour to preserve a wretched being; and if ever I returned to England, was not without hopes of being useful to my own species by celebrating the praises of the renowned Houyhnhnms, and proposing their virtues to the imitation of mankind.

My master in a few words made me a very gracious reply, allowed me the space of two months to finish my boat; and ordered the sorrel nag, my fellow-servant (for so at this distance I may presume to call him) to follow my instructions, because I told my master that his help would be sufficient, and I knew he had a tenderness for me.

In his company my first business was to go to that part of the coast where my rebellious crew had ordered me to be set on shore. I got upon a height, and looking on every side into the sea, fancied I saw a small island towards the northeast: I took out my pocket-glass, and could then clearly distinguish it about five leagues off, as I computed; but it appeared to the sorrel nag to be only a blue cloud; for as he had no conception of any country beside his own, so he could not be as expert in distinguishing remote objects at sea as we who so much converse in that element.

After I had discovered this island, I considered no farther; but resolved it should, if possible, be the first place of my banishment, leaving the consequence to fortune.

I returned home, and consulting with the sorrel nag, we went into a copse at some distance, where I with my knife, and he with a sharp flint fastened very artificially after their manner to a wooden handle, cut down several oak wattles about the thickness of a walking-staff, and some larger pieces. But I shall not trouble the reader with a particular description of my own mechanics; let it suffice to say that in six weeks time, with the help of the sorrel nag, who performed the parts that required most labour, I finished a sort of Indian canoe, but much larger, covering it with the skins of Yahoos well stitched together, with hempen threads of my own making. My sail was likewise composed of the skins of the same animal; but I made use of the youngest I could get, the older being too tough and thick; and I likewise provided myself with four paddles. I laid in a stock of boiled flesh, of rabbits and fowls, and took with me two vessels, one filled with milk and the other with water.

I tried my canoe in a large pond near my master's house, and then corrected in it what was amiss; stopping all the chinks with Yahoos' tallow, till I found it staunch, and able to bear me and my freight. And when it was as complete as I could possibly make it, I had it drawn on a carriage very gently by Yahoos to the sea-side, under the conduct of the sorrel nag and another servant.

When all was ready, and the day came for my departure, I took leave of my master and lady and the whole family, my eyes flowing with tears, and my heart quite sunk with grief. But his Honour, out of curiosity, and perhaps (if I may speak it without vanity) partly out of kindness, was determined to see me in my canoe, and got several of his neighbouring friends to accompany him. I was forced to wait above an hour for the tide, and then observing the wind very fortunately bearing towards the island to which I intended to steer my course, I took a second leave of my master; but as I was going to prostrate myself to kiss his hoof, he did me the honour to raise it gently to my mouth. I am not ignorant how much I have been censured for mentioning this last particular. For my detractors are pleased to think it improbable that so illustrious a person should descend to give so great a mark of distinction to a creature so inferior as I. Neither have I forgot how apt some travellers are to boast of extraordinary favours they have received. But if these censurers were better acquainted with the noble and courteous disposition of the Houyhnhnms, they would soon change their opinion.

I paid my respects to the rest of the Houyhnhnms in his Honour's company; then getting into my canoe, I pushed off from shore.

Chapter XI *The Author's dangerous voyage. He ar-
rives at New Holland, hoping to settle there.
Is wounded with an arrow by one of the na-
tives. Is seized and carried by force into a
Portuguese ship. The great civilities of the
Captain. The Author arrives at England.*

I BEGAN THIS desperate voyage on February 15, 1714-5,
at 9 o'clock in the morning. The wind was very favourable; however, I made use at first only of my paddles; but considering I should soon be weary, and that
the wind might chop about, I ventured to set up my little
sail; and thus with the help of the tide I went at the rate
of a league and a half an hour, as near as I could guess.
My master and his friends continued on the shore till I
was almost out of sight; and I often heard the sorrel nag
(who always loved me) crying out, *Hnuy illa nyha majah
Yahoo,* Take care of thyself, gentle Yahoo.

My design was, if possible, to discover some small island uninhabited, yet sufficient by my labour to furnish
me with the necessaries of life, which I would have
thought a greater happiness than to be first minister in
the politest court of Europe; so horrible was the idea I
conceived of returning to live in the society and under
the government of Yahoos. For in such a solitude as I
desired I could at least enjoy my own thoughts, and reflect with delight on the virtues of those inimitable Houyhnhnms, without any opportunity of degenerating into
the vices and corruptions of my own species.

The reader may remember what I related when my crew
conspired against me and confined me to my cabin. How
I continued there several weeks without knowing what
course we took; and when I was put ashore in the long-
boat, how the sailors told me with oaths, whether true or

false, that they knew not in what part of the world we were. However, I did then believe us to be about ten degrees southward of the Cape of Good Hope, or about 45 degrees southern latitude, as I gathered from some general words I overheard among them, being I supposed to the south-east in their intended voyage to Madagascar. And although this were but little better than conjecture, yet I resolved to steer my course eastward, hoping to reach the south-west coast of New Holland, and perhaps some such island as I desired, lying westward of it. The wind was full west, and by six in the evening I computed I had gone eastward at least eighteen leagues, when I spied a very small island about half a league off, which I soon reached. It was nothing but a rock, with one creek, naturally arched by the force of tempests. Here I put in my canoe, and climbing up a part of the rock, I could plainly discover land to the east, extending from south to north. I lay all night in my canoe; and repeating my voyage early in the morning, I arrived in seven hours to the south-east point of New Holland. This confirmed me in the opinion I have long entertained, that the maps and charts place this country at least three degrees more to the east than it really is; which thought I communicated many years ago to my worthy friend Mr. Herman Moll, and gave him my reasons for it, although he hath rather chosen to follow other authors.

I saw no inhabitants in the place where I landed, and being unarmed, I was afraid of venturing far into the country. I found some shellfish on the shore, and ate them raw, not daring to kindle a fire, for fear of being discovered by the natives. I continued three days feeding on oysters and limpets, to save my own provisions; and I fortunately found a brook of excellent water which gave me great relief.

On the fourth day, venturing out early a little too far, I saw twenty or thirty natives upon a height, not above five hundred yards from me. They were stark naked, men, women, and children, round a fire, as I could discover by the smoke. One of them spied me, and gave notice to the rest; five of them advanced towards me, leaving the women and children at the fire. I made what haste I could to the shore, and getting into my canoe, shoved off: the savages observing me retreat, ran after me; and before I could get far enough into the sea, discharged an arrow, which wounded me deeply on the inside of my left knee (I shall carry the mark to my grave). I apprehended the arrow might be poisoned, and paddling out of the reach of their darts (being a calm day), I made a shift to suck the wound and dress it as well as I could.

I was at a loss what to do, for I durst not return to the same landing-place, but stood to the north, and was forced to paddle; for the wind, though very gentle, was against me, blowing north-west. As I was looking about for a secure landing-place, I saw a sail to the north-north-east, which appearing every minute more visible, I was in some doubt whether I should wait for them or no; but at last my detestation of the Yahoo race prevailed, and turning my canoe, I sailed and paddled together to the south, and got into the same creek from whence I set out in the morning, choosing rather to trust myself among these barbarians, than live with European Yahoos. I drew up my canoe as close as I could to the shore, and hid myself behind a stone by the little brook, which, as I have already said, was excellent water.

The ship came within half a league of this creek, and sent her long-boat with vessels to take in fresh water (for the place it seems was very well known), but I did not observe it till the boat was almost on shore, and it was too late to seek another hiding-place. The seamen at their landing observed my canoe, and rummaging it all over, easily conjectured that the owner could not be far off. Four of them well armed searched every cranny and lurkinghole, till at last they found me flat on my face behind the stone. They gazed awhile in admiration at my strange uncouth dress, my coat made of skins, my wooden-soled shoes and my furred stockings; from whence, however, they concluded I was not a native of the place, who all go naked. One of the seamen in Portuguese bid me rise, and asked who I was. I understood that language very well, and getting upon my feet, said

I was a poor Yahoo, banished from the Houyhnhnms, and desired they would please to let me depart. They admired to hear me answer them in their own tongue, and saw by my complexion I must be an European, but were at a loss to know what I meant by Yahoos and Houyhnhnms, and at the same time fell a laughing at my strange tone in speaking, which resembled the neighing of a horse. I trembled all the while betwixt fear and hatred: I again desired leave to depart, and was gently moving to my canoe; but they laid hold of me, desiring to know what country I was of, whence I came, with many other questions. I told them I was born in England from whence I came about five years ago, and then their country and ours were at peace. I therefore hoped they would not treat me as an enemy, since I meant them no harm, but was a poor Yahoo, seeking some desolate place where to pass the remainder of his unfortunate life.

When they began to talk, I thought I never heard or saw any thing so unnatural; for it appeared to me as monstrous as if a dog or cow should speak in England, or a Yahoo in Houyhnhnm-land. The honest Portuguese were equally amazed at my strange dress, and the odd manner of delivering my words, which however they understood very well. They spoke to me with great humanity, and said they were sure the Captain would carry me gratis to Lisbon, from whence I might return to my own country; that two of the seamen would go back to the ship, inform the Captain of what they had seen, and receive his orders; in the mean time, unless I would give my solemn oath not to fly, they would secure me by force. I thought it best to comply with their proposal. They were very curious to know my story, but I gave them very little satisfaction; and they all conjectured that my misfortunes had impaired my reason. In two hours the boat, which went loaden with vessels of water, returned with the Captain's command to fetch me on board. I fell on my knees to preserve my liberty; but all was in vain, the men having tied me with cords, heaved me into the boat, from whence I was taken into the ship, and from thence into the Captain's cabin.

His name was Pedro de Mendez; he was a very courteous and generous person; he entreated me to give some account of myself, and desired to know what I would eat or drink; said I should be used as well as himself, and spoke so many obliging things, that I wondered to find such civilities from a Yahoo. However, I remained silent and sullen; I was ready to faint at the very smell of him and his men. At last I desired something to eat out of my own canoe; but he ordered me a chicken and some exccllent wine, and then directed that I should be put to bed in a very clean cabin. I would not undress myself, but lay on the bed-clothes, and in half an hour stole out, when I thought the crew was at dinner, and getting to the side of the ship was going to leap into the sea, and swim for my life, rather than continue among Yahoos. But one of the seamen prevented me, and having informed the Captain, I was chained to my cabin.

After dinner Don Pedro came to me, and desired to know my reason for so desperate an attempt, assured me he only meant to do me all the service he was able, and spoke so very movingly, that at last I descended to treat him like an animal which had some little portion of reason. I gave him a very short relation of my voyage, of the conspiracy against me by my own men, of the country where they set me on shore, and of my three years residence there. All which he looked upon as if it were a dream or a vision; whereat I took great offence, for I had quite forgot the faculty of lying, so peculiar to Yahoos in all countries where they preside, and, consequently the disposition of suspecting truth in others of their own species. I asked him whether it were the custom in his country to *say the thing that was not.* I assured him I had almost forgot what he meant by falsehood, and if I had lived a thousand years in Houyhnhnm-land, I should never have heard a lie from the meanest servant, that I was altogether indifferent whether he believed me or no, but however, in return for his favours, I would give so much allowance to the corruption of his

nature as to answer any objection he would please to
make, and then he might easily discover the truth.

The Captain, a wise man, after many endeavours to
catch me tripping in some part of my story, at last began
to have a better opinion of my veracity, and the rather,
because he confessed he met with a Dutch skipper, who
pretended to have landed with five others of his crew
upon a certain island or continent south of New Holland,
where they went for fresh water, and observed a horse
driving before him several animals exactly resembling
those I described under the name of Yahoos, with some
other particulars, which the Captain said he had forgot;
because he then concluded them all to be lies. But he
added that since I professed so inviolable an attachment
to truth, I must give him my word of honour to bear
him company in this voyage, without attempting any
thing against my life, or else he would continue me a
prisoner till we arrived at Lisbon. I gave him the promise
he required, but at the same time protested that I would
suffer the greatest hardships rather than return to live
among Yahoos.

Our voyage passed without any considerable accident.
In gratitude to the Captain I sometimes sat with him at
his earnest request, and strove to conceal my antipathy
to human kind, although it often broke out, which he
suffered to pass without observation. But the greatest
part of the day I confined myself to my cabin, to avoid
seeing any of the crew. The Captain had often entreated
me to strip myself of my savage dress, and offered to
lend me the best suit of clothes he had. This I would
not be prevailed on to accept, abhorring to cover myself
with any thing that had been on the back of a Yahoo. I
only desired he would lend me two clean shirts, which
having been washed since he wore them, I believed
would not so much defile me. These I changed every
second day, and washed them myself.

We arrived at Lisbon, Nov. 5, 1715. At our landing
the Captain forced me to cover myself with his cloak, to
prevent the rabble from crowding about me. I was conveyed to his own house, and at my earnest request he

led me up to the highest room backwards. I conjured
him to conceal from all persons what I had told him of
the Houyhnhnms, because the least hint of such a story
would not only draw numbers of people to see me, but
probably put me in danger of being imprisoned, or burnt
by the Inquisition. The Captain persuaded me to accept
a suit of clothes newly made; but I would not suffer the
tailor to take my measure; however, Don Pedro being
almost of my size, they fitted me well enough. He accou-
tred me with other necessaries all new, which I aired for
twenty-four hours before I would use them.

The Captain had no wife, nor above three servants,
none of which were suffered to attend at meals, and his
whole deportment was so obliging, added to very good
human understanding, that I really began to tolerate his
company. He gained so far upon me that I ventured to
look out of the back window. By degrees I was brought
into another room, from whence I peeped into the street,
but drew my head back in a fright. In a week's time he
seduced me down to the door. I found my terror gradually lessened, but my hatred and contempt seemed to
increase. I was at last bold enough to walk the street in
his company, but kept my nose well stopped with rue,
or sometimes with tobacco.

In ten days Don Pedro, to whom I had given some
account of my domestic affairs, put it upon me as a matter of honour and conscience, that I ought to return to
my native country, and live at home with my wife and
children. He told me there was an English ship in the
port just ready to sail, and he would furnish me with
all things necessary. It would be tedious to repeat his
arguments, and my contradictions. He said it was altogether impossible to find such a solitary island as I had
desired to live in; but I might command in my own
house, and pass my time in a manner as recluse as I
pleased.

I complied at last, finding I could not do better. I
left Lisbon the 24th day of November, in an English
merchantman, but who was the master I never enquired.
Don Pedro accompanied me to the ship, and lent me

twenty pounds. He took kind leave of me, and embraced me at parting, which I bore as well as I could. During this last voyage I had no commerce with the master or any of his men; but pretending I was sick, kept close in my cabin. On the fifth of December, 1715, we cast anchor in the Downs about nine in the morning, and at three in the afternoon I got safe to my house at Rotherhith.

My wife and family received me with great surprise and joy, because they concluded me certainly dead; but I must freely confess the sight of them filled me only with hatred, disgust, and contempt, and the more by reflecting on the near alliance I had to them. For although since my unfortunate exile from the Houyhnhnm country, I had compelled myself to tolerate the sight of Yahoos, and to converse with Don Pedro de Mendez, yet my memory and imagination were perpetually filled with the virtues and ideas of those exalted Houyhnhnms. And when I began to consider that by copulating with one of the Yahoo species I had become a parent of more, it struck me with the utmost shame, confusion, and horror.

As soon as I entered the house, my wife took me in her arms and kissed me, at which, having not been used to the touch of that odious animal for so many years, I fell in a swoon for almost an hour. At the time I am writing it is five years since my last return to England: during the first year I could not endure my wife or children in my presence, the very smell of them was intolerable, much less could I suffer them to eat in the same room. To this hour they dare not presume to touch my bread, or drink out of the same cup, neither was I ever able to let one of them take me by the hand. The first money I laid out was to buy two young stone-horses, which I keep in a good stable, and next to them the groom is my greatest favourite; for I feel my spirits revived by the smell he contracts in the stable. My horses understand me tolerably well; I converse with them at least four hours every day. They are strangers to bridle or saddle; they live in great amity with me, and friendship to each other.

Chapter XII *The Author's veracity. His design in publishing this work. His censure of those travellers who swerve from the truth. The Author clears himself from any sinister ends in writing. An objection answered. The method of planting colonies. His native country commended. The right of the Crown to those countries described by the Author is justified. The difficulty of conquering them. The Author takes his last leave of the reader, proposeth his manner of living for the future, gives good advice, and concludes.*

THUS, GENTLE READER, I have given thee a faithful history of my travels for sixteen years and above seven months; wherein I have not been so studious of ornament as truth. I could perhaps like others have astonished thee with strange improbable tales; but I rather chose to relate plain matter of fact in the simplest manner and style; because my principal design was to inform, and not to amuse thee.

It is easy for us who travel into remote countries, which are seldom visited by Englishmen or other Europeans, to form descriptions of wonderful animals both at sea and land. Whereas a traveller's chief aim should be to make men wiser and better, and to improve their minds by the bad as well as good example of what they deliver concerning foreign places.

I could heartily wish a law was enacted, that every traveller, before he was permitted to publish his voyages, should be obliged to make oath before the Lord High Chancellor that all he intended to print was absolutely true to the best of his knowledge; for then the world would no longer be deceived as it usually is, while some writers, to make their works pass the better upon the public, impose the grossest falsities on the unwary reader. I have perused several books of travels with great delight in my younger days; but having since gone over most parts of the globe, and been able to contradict many fabulous accounts from my own observation, it hath given me a great disgust against this part of reading, and some indignation to see the credulity of mankind so impudently abused. Therefore since my acquaintance were pleased to think my poor endeavours might not be unacceptable to my country, I imposed on myself as a maxim, never to be swerved from, that I would *strictly adhere to truth*; neither indeed can I be ever under the least temptation to vary from it, while I retain in my mind the lectures and example of my noble master, and the other illustrious Houyhnhnms, of whom I had so long the honour to be an humble hearer.

—Nec si miserum Fortuna Sinonem
Finxit, vanum etiam mendacemque improba finget.

I know very well how little reputation is to be got by writings which require neither genius nor learning, nor indeed any other talent except a good memory or an exact journal. I know likewise that writers of travels, like diction-ary-makers, are sunk into oblivion by the weight and bulk of those who come after, and therefore lie uppermost. And it is highly probable that such travellers who shall hereafter visit the countries described in this work of mine, may, by detecting my errors (if there be any), and adding many new discoveries of their own, justle me out of vogue, and stand in my place, making the world forget that I was ever an author. This indeed would be too great a mortification if I wrote for fame: but, as my sole intention was the PUB-LIC GOOD, I cannot be altogether disappointed. For who can read of the virtues I have mentioned in the glorious Houyhnhnms, without being ashamed of his own vices, when he considers himself as the reasoning, governing ani-mal of his country? I shall say nothing of those remote nations where Yahoos preside; amongst which the least corrupted are the Brobdingnagians, whose wise maxims in morality and government it would be our happiness to observe. But I forbear descanting farther, and rather leave the judicious reader to his own remarks and applications.

I am not a little pleased that this work of mine can possibly meet with no censurers: for what objections can be made against a writer who relates only plain facts that happened in such distant countries, where we have not the least interest with respect either to trade or negotiations? I have carefully avoided every fault with which common writers of travels are often too justly charged. Besides, I meddle not the least with any party, but write without passion, prejudice, or ill-will against any man or number of men whatsoever. I write for the noblest end, to inform and instruct mankind, over whom I may, without breach of modesty, pretend to some superiority, from the advantages I received by conversing so long among the most accomplished Houyhnhnms. I write without any view towards profit or praise. I never suffer a word to pass that may look like reflection, or possibly give the least offence even to those who are most ready to take it. So that I hope I may with justice pronounce myself an author perfectly blameless, against whom the tribes of answerers, considerers, observers, reflecters, detecters, remarkers, will never be able to find matter for exercising their talents.

I confess it was whispered to me that I was bound in duty as a subject of England to have given in a memorial to a Secretary of State at my first coming over; because whatever lands are discovered by a subject belong to the Crown. But I doubt whether our conquests in the countries I treat of, would be as easy as those of Ferdinando Cortez over the naked Americans. The Lilliputians I think are hardly worth the charge of a fleet and army to reduce them; and I question whether it might be prudent or safe to attempt the Brobdingnagians; or whether an English army would be much at their ease with the Flying Island over their heads. The Houyhnhnms, indeed, appear not to be so well prepared for war, a science to which they are perfect strangers, and especially against missive weapons. However, supposing myself to be a minister of state, I could never give my advice for invading them. Their prudence, unanimity, unacquaintedness with fear, and their love of their country, would amply supply all defects in the military art. Imagine twenty thousand of them breaking into the midst of an European army, confounding the ranks, overturning the carriages, battering the warriors' faces into mummy by terrible yerks from their hinder hoofs. For they would well deserve the character given to Augustus: *Recalcitrat undique tutus.* But instead of proposals for conquering that magnanimous nation, I rather wish they were in a capacity or disposition to send a sufficient number of their inhabitants for civilizing Europe, by teaching us the first principles of honour, justice, truth, temperance, public spirit, fortitude, chastity, friendship, benevolence, and fidelity. The names of all which virtues are still retained among us in most languages, and are to be met with in modern as well as ancient authors; which I am able to assert from my own small reading.

But I had another reason which made me less forward to enlarge his Majesty's dominions by my discoveries. To say the truth, I had conceived a few scruples with relation to the distributive justice of princes upon those occasions. For instance, a crew of pirates are driven by a storm they know not whither, at length a boy discovers land from the topmast, they go on shore to rob and plunder, they see an harmless people, are entertained with kindness, they give the country a new name, they take formal possession of it for their King, they set up a rotten plank or a stone for a memorial, they murder two or three dozen of the natives, bring away a couple more by force for a sample, return home, and get their pardon. Here commences a new dominion acquired with a title by *divine right.* Ships are sent with the first opportunity, the natives driven out or destroyed, their princes tortured to discover their gold, a free licence given to all acts of inhumanity and lust, the earth reeking with the blood of its inhabitants: and this execrable crew of butchers employed in so pious an expedition, is a *mod-*

ern colony sent to convert and civilize an idolatrous and barbarous people.

But this description, I confess, doth by no means affect the British nation, who may be an example to the whole world for their wisdom, care, and justice in planting colonies; their liberal endowments for the advancement of religion and learning; their choice of devout and able pastors to propagate Christianity; their caution in stocking their provinces with people of sober lives and conversations from this the mother kingdom; their strict regard to the distribution of justice, in supplying the civil administration through all their colonies with officers of the greatest abilities, utter strangers to corruption; and to crown all, by sending the most vigilant and virtuous governors, who have no other views than the happiness of the people over whom they preside, and the honour of the King their master.

But, as those countries which I have described do not appear to have any desire of being conquered, and enslaved, murdered or driven out by colonies, nor abound either in gold, silver, sugar, or tobacco; I did humbly conceive they were by no means proper objects of our zeal, our valour, or our interest. However, if those whom it more concerns think fit to be of another opinion, I am ready to depose, when I shall be lawfully called, that no European did ever visit these countries before me. I mean, if the inhabitants ought to be believed; unless a dispute may arise about the two Yahoos, said to have been seen many ages ago in a mountain in Houyhnhnm-land, from when the opinion is, that the race of those brutes hath descended; and these, for anything I know, may have been English, which indeed I was apt to suspect from the lineaments of their posterity's countenances, although very much defaced. But, how far that will go to make out a title, I leave to the learned in colony-law.

But as to the formality of taking possession in my Sovereign's name, it never came once into my thoughts; and if it had, yet as my affairs then stood, I should perhaps in point of prudence and self-preservation have put it off to a better opportunity.

Having thus answered the only objection that can ever be raised against me as a traveller, I here take a final leave of all my courteous readers, and return to enjoy my own speculations in my little garden at Redriff, to apply those excellent lessons of virtue which I learned among the Houyhnhnms, to instruct the Yahoos of my own family as far as I shall find them docible animals; to behold my figure often in a glass, and thus if possible habituate myself by time to tolerate the sight of a human creature; to lament the brutality of Houyhnhnms in my own country, but always treat their persons with respect, for the sake of my noble master, his family, his friends, and the whole Houyhnhnm race, whom these of ours have the honour to resemble in all their lineaments, however their intellectuals came to degenerate.

I began last week to permit my wife to sit at dinner with me, at the farthest end of a long table, and to an-

swer (but with the utmost brevity) the few questions I
ask her. Yet the smell of a Yahoo continuing very offensive, I always keep my nose well stopped with rue, laven-
der, or tobacco leaves. And although it be hard for a
man late in life to remove old habits, I am not altogether
out of hopes in some time to suffer a neighbour Yahoo
in my company, without the apprehensions I am yet
under of his teeth or his claws.

My reconcilement to the Yahoo-kind in general might
not be so difficult, if they would be content with those
vices and follies only which nature hath entitled them to.
I am not in the least provoked at the sight of a lawyer, a
pickpocket, a colonel, a fool, a lord, a gamester, a politician, a whore-master, a physician, an evidence, a suborner,
an attorney, a traitor, or the like; this is all according to
the due course of things; but when I behold a lump of deformity and diseases both in body and mind, smitten with
pride, it immediately breaks all the measures of my patience; neither shall I be ever able to comprehend how
such an animal and such a vice could tally together. The
wise and virtuous Houyhnhnms, who abound in all excellencies that can adorn a rational creature, have no name
for this vice in their language, which hath no terms to express any thing that is evil, except those whereby they describe the detestable qualities of their Yahoos, among
which they were not able to distinguish this of pride, for
want of thoroughly understanding human nature, as it
showeth itself in other countries, where that animal presides. But I, who had more experience, could plainly observe some rudiments of it among the wild Yahoos.

But the Houyhnhnms, who live under the government
of reason, are no more proud of the good qualities they
possess, than I should be for not wanting a leg or an arm,
which no man in his wits would boast of, although he must
be miserable without them. I dwell the longer upon this
subject from the desire I have to make the society of an
English Yahoo by any means not insupportable; and
therefore I here entreat those who have any tincture of
this absurd vice, that they will not presume to come in
my sight.

SELECTED BIBLIOGRAPHY

Carnochan, W. B. *Lemuel Gulliver's Mirror for Man.* Berkeley: University of California Press, 1963.

Donoghue, Denis (ed.). *Jonathan Swift: A Critical Anthology.* Harmondsworth: Penguin, 1971.

Ehrenpreis, Irvin. *Swift: The Man, His Works, and the Age,* 3 vols. Cambridge: Harvard University Press, 1962–1983.

Lock, F. P. *The Politics of Gulliver's Travels.* Oxford: Clarendon Press, 1980.

Nokes, David. *Jonathan Swift, A Hypocrite Reversed: A Critical Biography.* London: Oxford University Press, 1985.

Quintana, Richard. *Swift: An Introduction.* London: Oxford University Press, 1955.

Rawson, C. J. *Gulliver and the Gentle Reader.* London: Routledge & Kegan Paul, 1973.

Tippett, Brian. *Gulliver's Travels.* London: Macmillan, 1989.

Traugott, John (ed.). *Discussions of Jonathan Swift.* Boston: D.C. Heath, 1962.

Tuveson, Ernest (ed.). *Swift: A Collection of Critical Essays.* Englewood Cliffs, N.J.: Prentice-Hall, 1964.

Zimmerman, Everett. *Swift's Narrative Satires: Author and Authority.* Ithaca: Cornell University Press, 1983.